THE PACK

THE MOON BLOOD SAGA

The Bite
The Hunt
The Pack

THE PACK

Z.W. TAYLOR

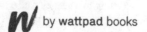

An imprint of Wattpad WEBTOON Book Group

Copyright © 2025 Z.W. Taylor

All rights reserved.

No portion of this publication may be reproduced or transmitted, in any form or by any means, without the express written permission of the copyright holders.

Published in Canada by Wattpad WEBTOON Book Group, a division of Wattpad WEBTOON Studios, Inc.

36 Wellington Street E., Suite 200, Toronto, ON M5E 1C7 Canada

www.wattpad.com

First W by Wattpad Books edition: July 2025

ISBN 978-1-99834-110-8 (Trade Paper original)
ISBN 978-1-99834-111-5 (eBook edition)

Names, characters, places, and incidents featured in this publication are either the product of the author's imagination or are used fictitiously. Any resemblance to actual persons (living or dead), events, institutions, or locales, without satiric intent, is coincidental.

Wattpad Books, W by Wattpad Books, Wattpad WEBTOON Book Group, and associated logos are trademarks and/or registered trademarks of Wattpad WEBTOON Studios, Inc. and/or its affiliates. Wattpad and associated logos are trademarks and/or registered trademarks of Wattpad Corp.

Library and Archives Canada Cataloguing in Publication information is available upon request.

Printed and bound in Canada

1 3 5 7 9 10 8 6 4 2

Cover design by Lesley Worrell
Image © Trevillion
Typesetting by Delaney Anderson

For mom, who never minded taking me to the bookstore or letting me stay up a little late to read.

"Reason says, 'The six directions are the boundary, and there is no way out'; Love says, 'There is a way, and I have many times traveled it.'"

—Rumi Translated by Arberry, *Mystical Poems of Rumi*

CHAPTER ONE

The scent of rogues hung in the air, a perfume of decay and rotten flesh. I drove a wooden stake into the ground; it was bright red, an alarm blaring a warning through the fog around us.

Remi hammered in another red stake close to a tree that was painted silver at the base. The silver paint marked the border of Thunderhead Pack territory. Across the clearing, not more than twenty feet from where we were staking the ground, bases of the trees were painted bright green, marking the Hemlock Pack's line within the Trapper's Forest.

My eyes lifted from the trees' green bases to the darkness waiting like an open mouth behind them. A small rabbit with jagged front teeth and mangy ears scuttled out of the woods. I let out a low snarl, shooing it back into the cursed forest from which it had come. In the back of my mind my beast started to pace, and the desire to chase caused my toes to curl into the cold dirt.

Over the past year at Thunderhead Pack we had been combing the woods with our small, secret rogue-hunting squad, and had only found whispers of scents to suggest rogues had been there. Nothing concrete. Nothing like a year ago when Remi and I had tracked a trail all the way to the Hemlock line before it disappeared.

We had not seen anything since then—no one had. There had been one sighting in late autumn at the ports close to Talia's pack. She'd tracked those rogues back stateside to Washington but the trail had dried up after that, then had completely died when the snow hit. Levi speculated that it was hard for anyone to move around in the unforgiving weather.

But when the snow melted, the Cache Pack, on the other side of the mountains, sounded the alarm: their trackers had found rogues on a human hiking trail that bordered their land. The trail was part of an area that was busy with tourists during summer season—and the warm embrace of May meant that swarms of humans would now be traveling to Alaska.

The thought of what could happen to people on the trail if they were to encounter rogue werewolves only brought back nightmares of the night I was first bitten. I thought I had long since outrun those night terrors, but some things felt too close to home out here, deep in the dark of the woods.

I drove another stake into the ground where the scent lingered. Only a foot away, it died. It was as though the smell was contained to a single area, just like Remi and I had found before. My beast nudged me on as my toes inched toward the darkness on the other side of the Hemlock Pack line.

"Mom will know if you go over there," Remi said from behind me.

Retracting my steps, I forced my beast to calm. "There's something out there."

Over my shoulder, I watched his lavender gaze cut past me and into the unknown. "I know," he agreed. "I wish Levi would just ask his fucking nephew if we could cross. It's not like we need to tear through their whole pack, just along the shared border."

Ethan. The pack second at Hemlock.

Levi had not told Hemlock Pack about the rogues we'd encountered, and the limitations that caused in our search grated at us on a daily basis. He had made a sincere effort to patch up the relationship with his extended family and improve his working affairs with Ethan, but there was still a long way to go. He was gradually drinking less on nights after he met with Ethan and his younger brother, Evan, on the pack line, but his nephews hadn't visited Thunderhead in all the time I'd been there—a part of me questioned whether they ever would.

"How nearby is your mom?" I asked.

"Close." He slammed another stake into the ground then wiped his hands on a pair of bicycle shorts that hugged his skin. The clothing—known as shifters—was magicked so it would shift with us.

I leaned against a tree and closed my eyes while the perfume of blood magic and decay blended together in my nostrils.

"This scent is maybe a week old." I kicked a small black porous stone away and watched it bounce among the tissue paper-thin leaves.

"You're too good at that," he observed.

I arched a brow. "At what?"

"Finding the blood magic."

My heart started to race. I couldn't tell him that most times it felt like traces of blood magic were trying to find me—whispering to me. Shifting my weight, I pointed to the grass, where the stalks were bent. "They slept here."

Remi knelt. "What the fuck were you all doing out here?" he uttered under his breath.

The sharp cracking of joints reshaping cut through the quiet, announcing the arrival of the Head Tracker, Bowie, Remi's mother. She shifted from her brown merle fur and into her skin; her long dark hair swayed behind her as she strode over to the stakes.

Wordlessly, she walked the perimeter we'd created, which wasn't more than ten feet across. She stopped at the stake I had stuck in the ground next to a silver-painted tree. Her nostrils flared before she backpedaled a few feet outside of the staked area and paused.

Her nostrils flared, and her eyes glowed in a violet storm that illuminated the new tattoos of tiny flowers under her right ear. "The scent is domed in?"

"It seems that way," I noted. "There's blood magic in the air. It's faint, but it's new. I can't say if it's only a few days or a week, but it's fresh."

Even in the late-afternoon dark I could see the corners of her mouth twitch into a tiny, proud smile. "Very good."

"Is this like last time?" I hadn't realized I had blurted out the question until it was hanging in the air around us.

"No," she answered quickly, before her eyes lifted back to the deep darkness of the forest that felt as if it was hungrily licking its lips while it watched us. Quietly, she added, "Although I find myself with déjà vu too often these days."

THE PACK

Remi inched closer to his mother. "What does that mean?"

Her smile turned bitter. "Hindsight is a cruel mistress."

Remi rocked back on his heels. "You know, Ma, we could just go over there?"

Bowie tilted her head with an amused smirk.

Remi persisted. "Hemlock never comes back here. They don't go into the woods. How would they know? There's something back there, I know it."

She chuckled under her breath. "You're right. Hemlock wolves are too afraid of the little rats scampering around here." With a snarl, she kicked at a squirrel that looked more like a skeleton venturing too close to her toes. "You know as well as I do that they are precious about their border, but there are some over there who do venture back into the woods. Not all of them are afraid of the darkness."

Remi held her gaze a beat before relenting with a sly smile. "Another day, then."

The tension in her shoulders left. "Maybe," she teased. She tapped her temple. "I'm updating our council. Leave the stakes and go home, get some rest. Very good work today."

Remi dipped his head in obedience. "Run fast," he whispered to her, with a soft smile.

"Like the wind," she replied, with a gentle smile of her own.

I grabbed my saddlebag off the ground and trotted after Remi. Darkness hugged around us with each silent step we took between the trees. We had just rounded a corner when a cool breath of air tickled my legs, and quiet started to slowly trickle around us.

I hadn't stopped hearing the whispers since they'd started last year, and I couldn't bring myself to tell Levi. With everything going on, I thought the voices in my head were the least of our concerns.

But more often than not, that thought was debated in moments like this. When the invasive silence made it so I could barely hear Remi walking next to me. Another cold breath blew past us that could have fooled me with its promises of snow.

I dug my toes into the ground as the beast in me pawed at the back of my mind. Something was starting to crackle in my veins when "Charlotte" was whispered from the darkness.

Remi stepped into my vision. "What is it?" he asked, his voice on edge as he bounced his glowing lavender gaze between me and the predatorial pitch-black in front of us.

Swallowing, I replied, "Nothing," and stepped around him. My beast snapped her jaws, anxious to leave this place.

Remi caught my shoulder. "Hey, you good?"

"I'm fine." I forced my reply then stepped away from his hold.

I heard him hum in disbelief, but he didn't press the matter.

Fur rolled over me as bones cracked quickly into place. My four paws hit the ground and I tore through the forest, desperately seeking the light that we found fading into the evening once we punched through the trees.

My beast yipped with relief over her shoulder at Remi, who followed us back to the familiar lawn that led to a quaint log home. A sign that read THE HEN HOUSE hung from a wooden post. Remi had carved the sign himself and placed it at the start of the footpath of smooth stones that Lander and Elliot had built for us in front of the house. A warm breeze stirred the beds of wildflowers. Before Gran had moved away, Andrea and I had promised her that we would continue to care for the garden.

THE PACK

Remi shifted first and jogged up the wooden porch steps. Andrea and I joked that he was practically another roommate, considering all the time he spent at our place. I shifted and let my toes sink into the grass; the stress slipped from my spine until the smell of copper danced around my nose. I rushed inside.

Andrea was inside at the kitchen sink, washing blood off her toned arms.

My heart skipped a beat. "What happened?"

Remi grabbed some ice from the freezer and wrapped it in a towel.

Turning the faucet off, Andrea replied, "I had a day. There was a fight on the northern Hemlock line."

Remi went to her and tried to dab her freshly split lip. She swatted his hand away then snatched the ice from him. He tossed his hands up in defeat and helped himself to the beer from the refrigerator. He uncapped one with a twist and handed it to Andrea.

"What do you mean 'a fight'?" I asked.

She tossed her long chestnut braid over her shoulder. "Ali got into it with their guards."

Remi's brows rose. "Ali?"

She took a long pull then turned to me with tired golden eyes. "I got a link earlier about a mountain lion sighting close to the northern border. I took one of the trackers with me to find it. We followed it all the way to the line, where we found Ali, some of our guards, and their guards in a full-out brawl.

"Our patrols called the cat in. Apparently, Ali caught the trail and followed it about half a mile into their border—"

"Aw, fuck," Remi groaned.

"And she didn't alert anyone over there?"

Andrea blew out a breath. "No, she told me later she forgot because she was trying to find the mountain lion."

I grimaced. "Poor Ali."

Remi blew out a long breath as he grabbed two more beers from the refrigerator. He uncapped one, and handed it to me before he settled down in a seat at our small breakfast table, nested alongside a wood-paneled wall. I arched a brow at him while he easily twisted the top off his, and took a long pull with a satisfied groan. Half the reason we had beer in the fridge was because he drank most of it.

Remi wiped a few drops off the corner of his mouth. "Fucking sucks. A fucking mountain lion? Come on . . ."

Levi had warned me that going that far into another pack's territory without asking for permission was a recipe for trouble, even if you had a good reason like Ali did.

"Yeah, and instead of stopping her and escorting her back, like they should have done, I guess they got into an argument. The next thing you know, I have a split fucking lip," Andrea grumbled.

I leaned my arms on the counter. "Where was Jake?" My teammate from the Hunt last year was second-in-command to the Head of Security at Hemlock, and usually found a way to run his patrol routes on our bordering pack line when I had mine scheduled so we could catch up. When everything was said and done, Jake truly had gone from being an ass to an angel.

"He got there when we did and helped me break it up," she explained.

Remi rubbed his temple. "Is Ali okay?"

Andrea shrugged. "She's fine but she's upset. She was trying to help. I can't believe they snapped like that. It's not like them . . . I don't know, something's going on over there."

"What do you mean?" Remi asked before taking another sip from his bottle.

"Jake pulled me aside and told me that they were tightening up the borders because of bears—"

Remi barked a laugh. "They don't lock things down like that for a bear. Send a squad in to handle it? Sure. But the whole border? That's bullshit."

"They are precious about the border," I noted. "Your mom said so earlier."

Andrea shrugged. "Jake said Ethan was wound up this morning. He wasn't sure why. Whatever it is, it has their guards worked up." She dabbed her lip with a hiss. It had started swelling and would probably show a bruise tomorrow. "So, did you find anything by that spot I told you guys about? I wasn't sure, there were some whiffs of a scent, but it seemed off."

Andrea had been inducted into the rogue squad early on, mostly because each time I came home after going out with Remi, she had this look in her eye like she was onto me. There was no lying to her. When she'd asked me about it, I was honest. I told her I couldn't say anything because I had promised Levi.

So her solution had been bringing it up to Levi one night at dinner, as casually as asking for the pepper. She offered to help, and swore an oath to him that she wouldn't tell anyone. And she didn't. Like Levi, to her a promise was sacred.

"It was like the first time we found it on the Hemlock border," I told her. "It was around an hour from where you showed me on the map. It looked like they'd been sleeping there. But it was so strange, it was like the scent was being trapped in that area. It completely died off within a foot of the perimeter."

"Blood magic?"

My heart picked up a slow, but trembling tempo. "Yes, fresh. A week maybe?"

"I can't believe you two can even smell it." She took the seat opposite Remi and turned sideways to face me. "It's always been silent to me."

"You have to get past being scared," I found myself admitting.

"And it was on the border?"

I nodded, meeting her golden gaze.

"My dad needs to know."

Her father, Billy, was the Head of Security at Hemlock. The man was also a phenomenal cook, had the best laugh, and had Andrea's name tattooed over his heart.

I blew out a breath. "You know we can't tell him. That's up to Levi and the rest of the pack council."

Remi's eyes went unfocused for a moment before he blinked back into the conversation. "Mom just confirmed that Hemlock is coming to the party tomorrow night. She said Levi wants to talk to them about the rogues."

"We already know Jake's coming, he asked for his favorite air mattress." I snickered.

"Sounds like Ethan and Evan could be too?" Remi added. "I don't think Billy is."

Andrea bit her lip. "He's not. He's got an elk hunt this weekend that he's jazzed about, but if Ethan is there, well, Dad trusts Ethan."

I bit the inside of my cheek. "Yeah, but a party isn't the best place to drop serious 'Hey, look, we found rogues and blood magic' news."

Andrea snorted in agreement. "Too bad Dad isn't coming, he's always the peacemaker." Which is exactly what he had tattooed on his knuckles.

I rested my cheek in my palm. "Well, what are the chances that this means we can finally go over there?"

Remi blew out a long breath. "Ethan has always been fair, and he's not a dumbass, but I don't know. Their pack lead, Thomas, he's a wild card from what Mom's said. We may get to go over there if we're lucky."

Andrea took another sip of her beer. "Whatever this shit on the border is, it's not bears, although we should all hope it is a rabid bear or something."

I cocked my head at her. "Why?"

"Because right now all actual sightings of rogues have been near major highways and tourist areas," she explained. "We have traces of them on our land but no sightings, and we're the only pack we know of that's found anything on their land. If Hemlock found something, it would mean this is a lot bigger problem than anyone thinks it is."

My beast pawed at me again. Anxiety had me tracing the scar on my leg, the skin twitching as I ran my fingers over it.

Andrea drummed her fingertips on the table. "Levi should have told them about the first time on the border."

I rubbed my temples with a groan. Levi had never told the leadership at Hemlock what Remi and I found last year, but he wouldn't have had much to tell them. The scent had faded after a day. When Remi and I went back to examine it the next morning, it was too faint to tell if it was from a rogue wolf or one of the foul animals from the forest—easily written off.

Levi wanted something more concrete to show them, something that couldn't be denied. But my gut told me Andrea was right it wasn't going to help build trust with anyone by keeping secrets from them.

"Do you think the scent will fade as fast?" I asked Remi.

He shrugged. "Last time it was out in the open. The wind could easily have been why it died so fast. This time it's confined to those trees. In theory, the trees should sustain it a little longer. But I don't know, that forest is fucked up."

"It is," I hummed.

Remi finished his beer and stood up with a long stretch. "I gotta head back, Mom wants me home for dinner."

Andrea arched a brow. "Bailing on us?"

He turned and gave Andrea a wide grin. "Just say the word, babe."

Andrea tossed a dishrag at him. "Get out of my house."

Our laughter followed him as he jogged out the door, leaving Andrea and me to the peace of the home we had worked so hard over the last year to make ours.

It had been a difficult change for me, not living with Levi, but Andrea and I often ended up over there for either breakfast or dinner, since we ruined half the things we tried to cook, and Levi made himself at home in our new house. He even brought in a recliner one day because he said we had "shitty seating." Only he used the recliner.

We had left our mark on this home. The walls and surfaces were decorated with pictures and mementos of the memories we had created—the peace we both had made for ourselves. My wolf and I were more than proud of the home we'd created, because it was *ours*, and we had done this for *ourselves*.

I walked over to the small table and took a seat across from her. She laid her hand out palm up for me. Smiling, I slapped mine into hers as she said, "My day was shit, how was yours?"

I snorted. "I hate that forest."

"Yet you are always going into it," she pointed out, releasing my hand to test the skin on her busted lip.

"It's what we do," I answered. "Do you think any of them know what's going on?"

"At Hemlock?"

I nodded.

"I don't know. I haven't heard anything from Dad. Jake would tell us. He tells us everything." Which was true. Jake took Team Shitheads very seriously, even after the Hunt. We had monthly video calls with Tia to stay in touch, and more often than not, Jake would come stay with us when Billy visited Andrea. "I'll feel better once my dad knows," she went on. "We're not dressing up tomorrow for the party, are we?"

I cringed. "God, no. But we can't look like swamp rats."

She waved me off. "We never do."

"That's debatable." I chuckled, because there had been plenty of mornings after too much wine with Bowie and Claire when it looked like we had crawled out of our graves.

She rolled her eyes. "We'll 'try.'"

"Fine."

"Fine." She snickered. "Do we have more ice cream in the freezer?"

"No, but we have cookies that Claire made."

A mischievous grin pulled her lips. She sprinted to the kitchen while I rushed to the sofa, then melted into it. Andrea flopped beside me and held out the plastic bag full of snickerdoodle cookies.

I took one. She took two. I practically inhaled mine, then took two more.

"We need to get the air mattress out for Jake."

She hummed in agreement. "He's just staying tomorrow night?"

I shrugged. "He said for the party, but you know him. He'll probably hang another day."

She snickered. "His fear of missing out is so endearing."

I turned to watch the wildflowers sway in the breeze outside the window. My beast paced in the back of my mind, both of us still thinking about the scent we had found earlier, deep in the dark of Trapper's Forest.

"What's wrong?" Andrea asked.

I rubbed my chest. It felt tight. It had felt this way all day.

"Nothing."

"I know when you're lying to me." She dipped her head, catching my gaze. "You've been on edge this whole week." She wasn't wrong. I had been feeling anxious the past few weeks. I figured venturing so much into the forest, where the whispers were, was the cause. "What did you hear in the forest?"

I couldn't look away from her. I felt like a kid caught with the extra Halloween candy they had hidden under their bed.

"Andrea—"

"Charlotte." She held a hand up. "You look at the darkness in there like you're expecting it to talk to you," she added, her voice growing a hair quieter. "There's moments when I think you're going to talk back."

"I didn't hear anything."

"Liar."

Sheepishly, I reached for another cookie. She pulled the bag away. My shoulders deflated. "I didn't hear anything," I repeated in a firmer voice.

She extended the bag back to me but didn't look relieved.

"Remember what I told you. If you hear your name being called by a voice in the forest, don't answer it. It's dangerous."

"What do you mean?" I asked too quickly.

She picked at the edge of a cookie. "When I was a kid, some of the older wolves at Hemlock would tell us stories about the forest. They always said cursed were the ones called by the forest, and damned were the ones who answered it. Dad always said it was the blood magic. Said it thrives on eating what's alive."

The cookies tasted like sand in my mouth. My beast whined in the back of my mind, but all I could do was force myself to swallow.

"Sounds like a terrible story for kids," I choked out.

Andrea shrugged. "Yeah, just be careful in there."

I held her golden gaze a moment then relented with a nod. "I will."

CHAPTER TWO

Three times in the middle of the night I woke sweating into my sheets. The first time, I had the urge to run, but to where, neither my beast nor I had any idea. The second time, it was a whisper of my name in the wind that yanked me from forest-filled dreams. The third time I woke, I realized that I'd rather be anywhere but my bed.

The dew on my toes settled the restlessness in my legs. The smell of coffee wound through the trees like a path that led all the way to the steps where Levi was sitting with a cup in his hand.

"I didn't finish the pot."

I breathed a tired smile. "On purpose?"

He snorted and walked inside the house that still felt like home—that would always be home.

THE PACK

I wiped the sweat off the back of my neck and jogged inside to find Derek, Levi's resident vampire roommate, strolling in my direction with an easy smile.

He pressed a kiss to my cheek. "Fresh biscuits and bacon are on the counter."

"Where are you off to?" I asked.

"Ah, Elliot and I are going to hunt then fornicate—brunch." He paused in the doorway with a smirk. "Care to join?"

"Jesus Christ," Levi grumbled from the kitchen.

I bit back a smile. "I'm good."

"We won't be back soon," he told me with a grin. In a blink, his vampire speed carried him with a zip out the door, across the yard, and out of sight, like he had never been there to begin with.

Levi's steps closed in behind me. He put a steaming cup of coffee and a plate of food on the table for me. "Sit."

Pulling out a chair, I sank into the seat. He picked up his latest book, a used paperback with pages so worn they looked like they would crumble between his calloused fingers.

His gaze lifted to mine, silver eyes pulsing a glow. "Long night."

"Couldn't sleep," I answered, taking a long sip from the mug.

He tilted his head with an inquisitive hum. A chill rushed across my skin as my chewing slowed—suddenly I was too aware of the bites I had taken. It felt like the whispers from last night were clinging to my skin for him to see.

"What?" I snapped unintentionally.

He slowly lifted a brow.

"Sorry." I finished the coffee in a desperate hope the caffeine would work faster. "It's probably the full moon—a moon-blood thing right? Didn't you say I'd always be a little more sensitive than other wolves?"

There was a hum in my veins I felt every day—moon blood is what Levi told me it was when I first shifted. He told me it was said that we were blessed by the Moon—had a little of her power in us. Some days it felt like nothing; but there were days when his own moon-blooded veins would sizzle to life and suck the air out of the room, it was in those moments that I knew it was very much a thing.

"I did," he answered, but I could tell he wasn't convinced. "You should run before the party. Work whatever bullshit this is out of your system."

"Right." I quickly agreed to his idea and the change of conversation. "I heard we're having visitors tonight?"

"Full moon, Charlie girl, and it's a party. We always like to invite our neighbors to our parties. We're party people," he retorted blandly, then casually sipped his coffee. His lips twitched as one side lifted in satisfaction, like he had an animal pinned in a corner. "Is that what you wanted to ask?"

I mustered whatever courage a half-drunk cup coffee could give. "Your nephews are coming."

"They are."

"I heard you were going to tell them about what we found—what we've been doing?"

"You've heard a lot."

I licked my lips. "I'm a good listener?"

He snorted a laugh. "Too good," he agreed, answering my question with an eye-roll. "Yes, we're going to talk to them. Tomorrow, though. Lander told me I couldn't be a buzzkill tonight."

"So, they're staying the night?"

He hummed in acknowledgment. "At David's."

My brows furrowed. I had figured that Levi would put them in an empty cabin or with Lander, not with the Thunderhead Head of Security. "That seems like a big deal?"

"It is and it isn't."

"Do you think they've seen anything?"

He tilted his head back and forth. "Hard to say. We haven't had any reports in the area from our other neighbors, but we all share the Trapper's Forest, and if Bowie's right, which she usually is, the signs are pointing west. To Hemlock."

"Will you call the witches to look at what we found?" I asked, because over time, he and Lander had deliberated if there was enough to have someone from our partner coven review.

"I want to see if the scent sticks around first," he noted. "If it dies again, that would be something of note to them."

"Remi did some gentle prying with trackers at Switchback the other day when he was running routes," I recounted. "They hadn't seen anything."

"Their pack lead isn't shy. Jackson would have said something to Lander or me if he thought they had something."

"Did you also invite them?" I asked.

"I did, but they have a weekend planting and prepping crops for the growth season so they can't get away. Shame," he hummed. "Jackson's a good wolf."

I leaned back in my seat and picked off the fatty parts of the bacon. "I can take them there—the Hemlock wolves. Back to the spot."

"Bowie's going to take them. They're not easy wolves."

"I think I can handle your nephews," I teased, slathering some jam on my biscuit.

"That's not what I meant." He leaned forward and rested his forearms on the table. "Do you remember me telling you about the rebels?"

"Yeah." My hands slowed their task. "Your father rescued Derek and Elliot from them when they were kidnapped, right?"

"That's right," he answered. "A lot of packs are not like ours, Charlotte. Some are, like Talia's. Others are more set in old ways. Stuck in the past. Many supported what the rebels were doing. The rebels hated the vampires, hated humans, and many did not look kindly on wolves who were not born." He dipped his head so his silver eyes locked with my gaze. My hands froze as a chill ran down my spine.

"Why?"

"Vampires and wolves have been warring since they were created," he explained. "The wolves looked down upon the vampires for drinking blood to live and the vampires looked at our kind like dogs—enslaved us for sport. The only thing that bonded us was the need to hide from humans—between the hunters, poachers, and religious zealots, we've always been at risk. The rebels hated the wolves who wanted to partner with the vampires to conceal us—they would have rather gone back to the days when wolves were able to hunt humans for fun."

"What?" My breath caught in my throat. The sound of my fork falling to the plate echoed around us.

Levi nodded while his words soaked painfully to my core. "The treaty was created because our kinds needed to work together. We had enough outside threats to deal with, we didn't need a war with each other too.

"My father was the pack lead when they were negotiating the treaty. Back then, there were plenty of packs who were not afraid to show their support for the rebels, who were the driving antitreaty party. At the time, Hemlock was run by Ethan and Evan's grandfather, Emmet. He and his buddy, the old pack lead at Switchback, Jeremiah Bones, both sided with the rebels and were very vocal about it—also not afraid to show their hate for packs that even associated with vampires."

"Are your nephews—"

"No," he quickly interjected. "Their father, Chris, Eve's brother, was a good man. He did not raise his sons by the ways of his father."

"What happened to Emmet?"

"Well, clearly their side lost when it came to the treaty." He snorted. "Should have known better than to test my father. Not many wolves were a match for him." He raised his coffee and finished his cup. "But more or less, Jeremiah and Emmet got into a lot of bad shit back then. The Regional Council had a mind to lock them up, but my father negotiated their freedom—if they agreed to the treaty they would not be imprisoned. They agreed to it, but I always thought it was a mistake because it meant they could still scheme and connect with old contacts. Over time that's what Emmet did. He and his mate were caught trying to have his own son killed, along with my father and me."

"What?" I gawked. "Why?!"

"Well," he answered tiredly, "Eve was technically engaged to Jeremiah Bones. Arranged mating. Obviously didn't work out that way."

My jaw dropped. "You're joking."

He stood. "Not in the least." He poured himself another cup then carried the pot over and topped mine off. "Chris challenged his father for pack lead in a death match and won. Emmet's mate ended up throwing herself on his pyre, as was tradition in the days of old."

He walked the coffeepot back to the kitchen with even steps that filled the quiet skirting around us.

"The wolves coming . . ." I found myself almost mumbling.

"They're not all like us."

I turned in my chair to see him leaning against the counter.

He went on. "I don't know who Ethan will bring, but we already had Ali in an altercation with them yesterday. Their pack is wound up from what we know. I need you to stay back. Do you understand?"

"All right." I relented, taking a shallow bite of my biscuit.

Levi watched me chew for a minute then crossed his arms over his chest. "You good?"

I thought of the whispers again, the smell of blood magic, and the stench of rogues. The biscuit suddenly tasted less like butter and apricot jam.

"Yeah."

"You sure?"

I should tell him. I should tell him about the whispers. I should tell him about how wound up I'd been the last few weeks. I should say something.

But something in me forced out, "Yes," instead of the answer that was screaming at me from the back of my mind.

Jake showed up promptly when he'd said he would, in the late afternoon with a saddlebag full of neatly folded clothes in hand. Together, he, Andrea, and I got his air mattress set up with a set of spare sheets before both of us found ourselves sitting with him. We caught him up on pack gossip and he proceeded to devour the rest of Claire's cookies. Andrea laughed and poked fun at him—I tried to join in, but my nerves were singing with anxiety.

I took Levi's advice and went on a run before the party. It was a good idea that brought me relief until Andrea's watchful gaze greeted me when I came home. My anxiety buzzed back to life. She and Jake left me to myself for the rest of the afternoon.

Dusk was settling in when we walked to the pack house while the moon lazily rose in the night, as if she was waking from an indulgent morning in bed.

Jake narrowed his watchful brown eyes at me. "You're not yourself."

I rubbed my clammy hands on my Thunderhead sweatshirt, which I wore over a pair of shifter shorts. "I'm fine. It's just the full."

"So she says," Andrea muttered under her breath. She looked like a model walking across the grass with her elegant long legs in cutoff jean shorts. She tossed her chestnut hair over her shoulder to look back at us. "At least we're not matching?"

My lips quirked into a tiny smile. "Party pooper."

She snorted and walked ahead. Jake waited a beat then nudged his shoulder with mine. "Seriously? You good?"

"Yeah." I bit the inside of the lip.

We were greeted with the sight of steady smoke from the bonfire behind the pack house; it curled into the sky and tangoed with the sound of laughter from the party, which sounded like it was almost in full swing.

"Is Levi already here?" Andrea asked over her shoulder.

"Yeah," I answered. "He came early with Lander and the vamps."

Someone with white-blond hair walked across the field in front of us. Silver eyes turned to me with something that started as a platonic glance before it heated into something else.

Liam lifted his hand to wave at us—at me.

I blew out a breath and waved back but I did not dare walk to him. Instead, my feet stood grounded. The desire in his eyes faded. He slowly lowered his hand before he continued his march to the party.

Jake let out a long whistle. "I thought that was over?"

I groaned. "It is."

Andrea snorted. "Correction—for Charlotte it is."

"Ah." Jake breathed. "Shit, it's been almost a year? Fucking waste of time, if you ask me."

"Hey!" I snapped.

Jake playfully shoved my shoulder. "Seems useless to spend your time on something that won't happen. You're pretty all right, too, I guess."

"Ass." I laughed.

"No, we're shitheads," he corrected. "Now, come on, I'm fucking hungry."

Andrea looped her arm with mine and pulled me forward. "Are your comrades here?" she asked Jake.

He snorted. "I'm not Ethan's or Evan's fucking keeper, but no," he answered. "They're not here yet."

With each step closer to the house, I felt something eat away at my resolve. Like moths chewing on an old garment. My legs ached to run again; instead, they stumbled after Andrea as we wound through the crowd and over to a set of coolers

THE PACK

where Bowie and Claire greeted us with fresh drinks extended our way.

"No one has ever looked more miserable to see one of my margaritas," Bowie teased, poking me in the ribs.

I swatted her hands away with a laugh. Claire tucked a loose strand of hair that had fallen out of my short ponytail. Her big brown eyes watched me a moment, a look of maternal concern flooding them.

"I'm fine," I assured her through the telepathic link that all children of the moon—vampires and wolves—could do.

Taking the margarita in hand, I quickly licked the salt off the rim then tipped it back and almost finished it. I prayed to the moon the tequila would mellow me out.

"Being hungover is not getting you out of tracking on the east border for caribou tomorrow," Bowie pointed out with a knowing smile.

Andrea snickered. "Are you kidding? She's been itching for a hunt for days."

I tugged at the collar of my sweatshirt. Sweat was beading on the back of my neck. A squeal ripped through the air. Two of the pack kids, Lyle and Penny, were chasing each other through the crowd. Claire shook her head at her youngest son, with his moppy brown hair and bright silver eyes.

"Bowie, did you bring that good tequila?" Jake's voice faded into the cacophony around me.

I felt my beast snap at me. My brows furrowed. I could feel her press closer—my nail beds itched as my claws begged to pierce through; my gums ached where my fangs waited to be released.

Andrea tilted her head to look at me. "Char?"

"I'm going to find Levi," was all I said before I darted away.

I could hear Andrea call my name, but her voice blended into the murmur around me that felt like suffocating reverberations across my skin. My beast howled in the back of my mind as a heavy hum in my veins picked up—my moon blood was sparking to life.

I needed air.

There were too many people. Too many scents. Too many sounds.

"Levi, where are you?" I frantically sent through our link.

I rubbed my chest as my lungs clenched. The hair on the back of my neck started to stand. I blew out a breath and looked at the ground. "We just need to keep it together for a little longer," I told myself and my beast.

"What is it?" Levi replied.

"Something is wrong."

I pushed my way between more people. I was going home. He could meet me there.

"What do you mean?" he asked as someone knocked into my shoulder.

"Something is wrong with me!"

My fingers shook as the air felt thinner around me. A hand took mine and yanked me through the crowd. I should have stopped Liam, but my desperation won out. Fresh air brushed my skin as he marched me across the grass. He led me to the front of the pack house where we paused next to a lantern someone had hung on a stake in the ground.

His silver eyes pulsed with concern. "What's wrong?"

"I need to go home. I don't know, Liam. I—" I paused and gasped for air.

THE PACK

I didn't realize how much I had been sweating. I closed my fingers into fists and tried to fight my beast back. She was howling in the back of my mind. I tried to take a breath, but it felt like the fresh air was being sucked down a drain.

"What the hell is happening to me?" I heard myself whine.

I tipped my head up to look at the sky. I could see the moon, but she wasn't in her fullness—not yet.

Liam's arms steadied my wavering stance. "Hey, let's go run now? We can catch up with the pack later?"

I was opening my mouth to answer when a young man broke through the tree line and jogged a few steps onto the foot trail that snaked up to the pack house. A group of wolves followed him.

His wild, wind-blown copper hair hung past his ears like new flames coming to life, but his turquoise eyes were firm with a steady glow. He was lanky, around the size of Liam. He looked scrappy, like in a split second he could either hug you or sink his teeth into you.

"Evan's here," Liam noted as he lifted his hand to wave, but Evan only offered a jerky nod back.

Another man walked out from the tree line and onto the footpath: tall, with long legs like tree trunks and scars littering his fit torso. In the dark his hair looked black, but in the moonlight there was a deep auburn tint. A dark ruby that almost seemed unnatural. Almost as peculiar as his eyes. He had two different-colored eyes: one hazel with bright flakes of amber and sky blue; the other was turquoise, shining like a blazing gemstone in the night.

He ran a hand over a defined jaw covered in stubble that looked a few days old. I wanted to trace the lines of his soft lips;

in that same instant, I also wanted to chop my own fingers off for thinking it. He spoke over his shoulder to some of the wolves behind him, and then he laughed, deep and rich, like molten chocolate that made my mouth water.

Liam said something else, but I didn't hear it; I couldn't hear Levi calling my name as he ran to me. I couldn't hear him trying to link me because all I heard was my beast howling and howling in a tornado of delirious desperation.

I shoved around Liam and stumbled forward as a sweet summer breeze combed its delicate fingers through the grass, bringing with it a new scent. The breath was sucked out of my lungs. I fell to my knees and inhaled like it was the last breath I'd ever have because it smelled so damn good—tasted so mouth-wateringly delicious.

The anxiety that had been plaguing me flowed into something else. Something warm. Something electric. Something that made my body feel tight.

I tugged my hair while I tried to inhale fresh air, but all I found was a mouthful of the scent my beast was begging me to follow. Begging me to chase—to fucking crawl to if I had to.

"Shit," I wheezed.

Someone yanked me to stand. I blinked and looked at silver eyes and wished they were the dual-colored ones that were now tattooed in my memory. "Charlotte—Charlotte, look at me," Levi demanded.

Another breeze blew past me. "I can't breathe." I heaved then inhaled rapidly. "I can't fucking breathe."

Liam's brows furrowed as he looked back to the group of visitors, then he turned back to me with heavy dread hanging on his shoulders like an iron coat.

"Levi!" I coughed and clung to his arms, which struggled to keep me standing. "Levi, I can't breathe!"

"Charlie—" Levi started to say before he paused and turned slowly to look at the group across from us.

Something vibrated across the ground and rippled over the grass. A delicious chill ran across my skin and traced up my neck like the fingers of a lover before running across my lips, beckoning them to part.

"You gotta be fucking kidding me," Levi snapped.

I sensed motion on the footpath, coming toward us.

"Ethan!" Levi bellowed. "I don't care if she is your fucking true mate, you keep your ass over there!"

Looking up, I found Ethan's eyes—hazel and turquoise—that burned like they had the light of the sun in them. The beast in me yipped, howling in delight at what we saw. Something crackled off him—a spark—a flicker from a lighter licking the end of a fuse to a firework. It stole whatever breath was in my lungs, leaving me gasping in fitful coughs for fresh air.

An electric hum sizzled to life in my veins in return as my beast surged forward. Levi's hands loosened a fraction on my arms. Shouting picked up again. The grass waved in front of me and my beast cried inside me, but all I could do was hold his gaze with mine.

That is until he blinked. Because when he blinked, I ran.

CHAPTER THREE

My four paws pounded the ground in a mad stampede past the tree line. The sounds of shouts and voices nipped at the back of my legs. And I knew Ethan was following.

Levi was wrong. There was no way Ethan was my true mate. This had to be something else. It had to be.

I just needed some fresh fucking air and quiet so I could think.

Luckily for me, my beast wasn't throwing a fit. She understood my distress, and while I knew she wanted me to turn and run toward the thing that I was running from, I was grateful that she was giving me the space I needed.

Together, we wound around trees and curled around boulders to the tracker training grounds, where I felt like I could lose him. But to my surprise, he avoided all the traps that I purposely tried to lead him through and somehow managed to gain ground on me in a forest that was supposed to be a home for me, not a playground for him.

Gritting my teeth, I tried to pull out as many tricks as I could to lose him. I ran tighter curls around trees, kicked up dust to cloud his vision, and picked my feet up to lighten my touch on the ground so my steps sounded only like a breeze curling over the leaves. But even still, the sound of his paws slamming against the ground made it feel like they were only a hair behind mine.

I looked over my shoulder—a mistake. He used the break in my concentration to charge forward and swing around to my left in an attempt to cut me off.

Sliding out of his way, I sprinted toward a sturdy set of trees with thick armlike limbs. A light bulb went off. My beast and I readied ourselves as we approached our target.

Lunging into the air, I shifted to my skin and caught a branch with my clawed hand. My limbs moved on their own as I climbed higher, and higher, and higher, until I was hit in the face with cold air once I surfaced at the canopy.

I sucked in a long breath and let a blanket of soberness fall over my mind, stilling the franticness that was there before.

"What the hell is happening?" I croaked quietly into the wind.

Taking another deep breath, I tried to savor my moment of peace, but reality slowly set in when my beast pawed my mind with a thought—a statement—that could not be true.

"No," I snapped out loud, disagreeing with her. "There's no way I have a true mate. That's fucking insane. I'm losing it. That's what this is."

She snapped her jaws at me as the tree began to shake.

I sank into the trembling leaves and clutched the limbs around me. I dared not move. I looked desperately for a way out, but then his scent pierced the canopy, followed by an arm.

My body screamed to run, my beast was howling at me to stay, but I was frozen like a stalked deer as he emerged fully from the leaves.

The breeze danced around us as he slowly turned until his dual-colored eyes held mine in what had to be shock. For a moment, we both sat in a silent stupor. A moment that felt too long, because in that moment I felt like all the insecurities I had buried were close to clawing their way out.

Then a smile took over his mouth like a sunrise breaking over the mountains. Something warm wrapped around me as a hum murmured between as us. The wind picked up, strumming a song through the leaves that we swayed to with the branches.

"I'm Ethan," he said, in a voice that sounded closer to one reserved for early mornings between sheets where midnight promises were lazily fulfilled.

"Charlotte," I heard myself rasp, as if I had forgotten how to speak.

His eyes searched mine. "I'm not going to hurt you."

"Okay." I looked back down at the leaves covering me because I wasn't sure what would happen if I kept looking at him. "This can't be possible."

He breathed a tired smile like this exchange was something we had done a thousand times before. "Clearly, it is."

My mouth snapped closed while tendrils of heat danced across my stomach. My gaze yanked away from his and to the silver mountains that glistened in the distance.

"You know, I've never had to chase a woman up a tree before."

I snapped my head around to see eyes full of laughter looking back at me. I pushed my hair behind my ears and stood slightly from the cover of the leaves. "I've never been chased up a tree before."

He nodded with an amused smile. "I guess that's fair." His voice was easy and calm. Why was he so calm? Why was the back of my neck sweating again? "Do you want to climb down?" he asked.

"No." I laughed. He laughed with me, and the melodic sound rolling off him somehow relaxed my spine and quieted my nerves. I found myself telling him, "Okay," because we couldn't hide in this tree forever, no matter how much I wanted to.

He pushed some leaves away. "All right. It would be great if you didn't fall out of this."

I rolled my eyes. "It would be great if you didn't chase me up another."

Ethan chuckled then dipped below the canopy. As we got close to the ground, snarls and howls rose around us. Ethan's smile faded. A firm line sealed across his lips as his eyes pulsed with a brighter glow. Something snapped off him, like a whip demanding attention with a cold crack into the air.

I sucked in a breath.

"Let's move fast." It wasn't a request, and I didn't argue.

But chaos has a way of worming its way into any moment. When Ethan jumped down to the ground, he opened his arms to catch me. I was close to taking the leap when the skin on my neck twitched.

Liam barreled for us with Remi on his heels. In a blink, Liam lunged at Ethan, who easily tossed him away. But Liam got back up and charged again.

Lander and Levi tried to pull Ethan and Liam apart. Evan charged in red-faced and tried to shove between Levi and Ethan. More wolves slid in, the fighting fueled by angry shouts and the sound of snapping teeth.

The tree shook around me and a cold hand clasped my shoulder. Elliot had a weary smile on his face. "Come on, love, David is going to distract them."

We curled our way to the back of the tree, where Elliot helped me down so I could tear away from the mayhem. Instead of going home, I found myself heading up a set of hills that led to one of my favorite spots in the pack territory.

The glacier lookout point felt like a safe haven. I made my way past the old tree stump to sit close to the ledge of the cliff. A light mist started to fall from the sky and kissed my heated skin.

I wasn't sure how long I had been out there when I smelled her coming. Bowie breached the brush and quietly sat next to me.

"Of all times for you to find your true mate, it was right before I was going to have a perfectly good margarita."

She flicked her long ponytail behind her shoulder and leaned back on her forearms. The glacier groaned in front of us. Pieces of ice shone like diamonds under the moonlight.

"I want to talk to you, and I want you to listen."

My spine straightened. I turned to look at her.

"Whatever happens next, it's important for you to remember that this is your choice." Her purple eyes softened as they pulsed a steady glow. "One of my favorite things about you is how you care for others around you, but now, Charlotte, is the time for you to be selfish.

"I didn't know my true mate either when I met him. I was

on vacation. I wanted to get away and I had a friend studying abroad in Japan who invited me to visit her. I was there not even a week when I found my mate. We were oceans apart, didn't know a thing about each other, but one look at him and it was like coming home. It was hard. We fought as hard as we fucked back then."

"Bowie—"

"Shh, this is my story," she chided with a cheeky smile. "In our culture, like any culture, there's a normal way to do things. But that doesn't mean that's how you have to do them. Wolves will follow each other—one mate will follow the other to their pack. Usually when true mates meet, well, it's more of a dive-in-headfirst-and-mark-each-other-then-ask-questions-later type of thing—"

"Fantastic."

"But that doesn't mean that's what you have to do. That's not what I did. I wasn't giving up my life here and I wasn't tying my soul to anyone that quick. I was in line to be the Head Tracker.

"I love my mate, but he was not in line for anything," she added with a chuckle. "He followed me here. I told him he couldn't mark me until he could catch me."

"And how long did that take?" I teased.

"Longer than he would have liked and shorter than I care to admit." A rare blush bloomed on her cheeks. She licked her lips as her eyes grew wistful. "He's everything to me. He is my compass. He is worth it. What we have is worth it. And you? You have worked so hard, my sweet girl, to be happy. It's worth giving it a chance to be happy. The moon has given you a gift, there is nothing wrong with taking it."

"But Levi—"

"Is a grown man who will have to respect your choices,"

she pointed out. "I won't lie, he will struggle with this. Ethan's pack is Eve's old pack. Her brother, Chris, was Ethan's father. It's where she and Lucas died. It's where Ethan's family died too. With everything going on, Levi may be a challenge," she tactfully explained. "But that's not your concern. Leave that to Lander."

"Bowie—"

"Charlotte, Ethan is a good man. I have known him his whole life. If you need an excuse to be selfish and do something purely for you, I am giving it to you."

I let out a long breath. "I don't know what to do."

She bumped my shoulder. "No one says you have to. But you have around thirty minutes," she added as she stood.

"Thirty minutes for what?" I asked.

She walked to the edge of the trees and turned to me with a smirk on her lips. Into the brush she said, "Bring her back or he'll send me after you, and I don't want to go hunting tonight."

I could feel him approach. The skin on my back twitched as this thing between us danced around me like the mist that was falling from the sky. He released a sigh as he took a seat next to me. The two of us stared out over the glacier rumbling like soft thunder while moonlight danced over it.

"I'm sorry I scared you earlier," he offered.

I dug my fingers into the grass. "I thought I was having a panic attack," I answered honestly.

He nodded, watching me carefully. He looked around. "Hold on." He stood and trotted back to the bushes, disappearing for a few moments before returning with a bottle of vodka in his hands.

Sitting back down, he opened it and tilted it toward his nose. His nostrils flared. "Still good." He took a sip, then offered it to me.

"Where did this come from?" I took the bottle from him.

"I grew up chasing Lucas and my brother around our pack lands. We used to hide booze all over the place."

I looked at the liquid with a wince. "Is it even safe to drink?"

"I guess we'll find out."

His eyes never left mine except to watch my lips touch where his once were. I quickly took a long, grimacing sip, then handed it back to him.

"Am I supposed to shake your hand? How does this work?"

The hand holding the vodka paused halfway to his lips. He barked a laugh that kept going. He hunched over, the sound of it contagious, drawing a laugh from me.

He sat up and took a swig from the bottle then passed it to me. "You know, we wait our whole lives for this—it's like a fairy tale. My parents weren't even true mates. No one really tells you what to do when you find them." He paused, a deep laugh reverberating off him. "It really is awkward."

I took another cringe-worthy sip. "I thought I was losing it. I couldn't breathe."

"I thought I was about to pass out," he admitted. "I had been wound up all day. I even went on two runs before making the long-ass run over here only to almost pass out on the pack house lawn."

My lips twitched into a small smile. "I ran too. Didn't help."

He breathed a smile. "This isn't what humans do, right?" he asked, his face serious except for the little twitch at the corner of his lips.

It was my turn to laugh. His lips curled back in a smile as I passed the bottle to him. At this pace we'd finish it, and at the rate my heart was still pulsing, I needed it.

"No, it's not," I replied. "How did you know I was human before?"

His thumb swiped a drop escaping his lips. "You're the pack lead's charge, it's not really a secret."

"Right." It was my turn to reach for the bottle. The anxiety monsters were cackling in the back of my mind, which ran through all the details he could already know about me—all the details I would prefer he didn't know about me. "How much did they tell you?"

The kindness in his eyes was unsettling because it was so welcoming. So earnest and without an ulterior motive. "Just the basics—when you were bitten, Lander had to send out a report because of the rogues. Any news of rogues like that in the area has to be reported to the region."

"Oh." I wasn't going to pour my heart out just yet, but he deserved to at least have an understanding. Everyone had some baggage. I had a closet full of bones. "When I was bit, I was out here because I was running from someone. I was—" Taking another sip, I tried to muster some courage. "I was in a relationship I should have left a long time before I did."

He let me finish, watching me for a moment before gently taking the bottle from me. "What happened to him?"

"I don't want to know anymore," I found myself whispering, an admission that was more to myself than anything. "I'm sorry, this is—well, I'm sure not what you were expecting . . . This is happening, isn't it?"

He watched me a moment then asked, "Do you want this to happen?"

My voice caught because in my gut I felt that if I said no it really would be the end of it. Regardless of the moon, or fate, or whatever this pull was, I felt like if that's what I wanted, he would respect it.

But Bowie was right; I could not let my past control my future, and I would never forgive myself if I didn't try.

"I think so," I answered back before adding, "Yes."

He returned an easy smile to me. "Then we do this our way. We make our own choices," he added with a hardness that I didn't think he'd intended. His eyes briefly tipped to the moon in a look that seemed like spite. I wondered for a moment if he hated her as much as Levi did. "This is our choice."

"Even if you have to hike over here every day?" I asked with a slight tease to cover the uncontrollable tremble in my voice.

He nodded, no smile visible on his face before he said, "Yes."

"What would we normally do now?" I found myself asking.

"Usually, we'd take all our clothes off and make sweet love until the sun comes up."

My cheeks flushed. I felt more self-aware than ever of how my shifters stuck to my skin. His lips curled before a laugh broke his serious facade. I shook my head with a laugh and took the bottle from him.

The vodka burned down my throat. I coughed before shoving the liquor back to him. "I kinda hate normal things."

"Me too," he answered quietly.

"I don't know what to do. And you never even asked me out?" I found myself huffing.

He snickered. "Do you want to go hunt for deer tomorrow?"

"That's not romantic."

He playfully narrowed his gaze. "I can be romantic." Pausing a beat he said, "We can take it day by day? Maybe we should start by making sure you don't run up more trees?"

"Agreed," I replied with a firm nod.

He twisted the cap back on the bottle. A comfortable quiet settled between us. A hum rolled off him, soft, like a spring rain. Something about him, the more I focused, smelled pure—clean, like every piece of his scent was carefully stitched into a neat tapestry.

"You're moon-blooded."

He tilted his head and watched me, amused. "As are you. It's easy to smell on you."

"Claire—they told me I smell like the moon, and Levi a little now, I guess."

He hummed, contemplative. "Only just a little," he added.

"Is it supposed to mean something, that we both are? Is this like a moon's will thing?"

He shrugged. "I quit trying to figure out what her will was a long time ago, seeing she never seemed to care a whole lot about mine."

My eyes shifted away as silence filled the space between us again.

A pressure tapped on the outside of my mind. Ethan tapped on his temple, eyes heavy with hope as he watched me.

Blinking, I let the link shoot through my mind like a comet. But something else connected between us, like two magnets that were trying to pull us together over an electric line.

Swallowing, I tried to shake the overwhelming feeling away. "What are you planning on doing with that?"

His eyes danced with delight. "Send you sweet nothings, obviously." He stood and brushed his hands on his shifter shorts. "Come on, let's get you back before Levi sends Bowie after me."

I rolled my eyes and let him follow me back to my house.

THE PACK

Moving through the thick trees, we fell into a comfortable silence. I'd steal a glance at him and kept catching him doing the same. As we neared the house he pushed some branches out of our way.

"So no deer hunting, but what about breakfast?"

I felt my heart skip a beat. "I like breakfast."

"Yeah?" he asked with a gaze that I wanted to fall asleep looking at.

Shit, I was so fucked.

"Yeah, that sounds nice."

He watched me a moment before saying, "I mean, unless you had something else in mind?"

"No." I walked faster before the inner dialogue in my head could spew out of my lips.

He lifted a brow. "Really?"

I cut my eyes to his, which had turned serious until I saw the corner of his mouth pull back into an amused smile. Groaning inwardly, I marched away from his laughter. "You're not funny."

He jogged a few steps to catch up with me. "Sunshine, I'll have you know that I am."

Rolling my eyes, I broke through the trees onto the lawn of my home. "You know—"

"We have an audience," he murmured into my mind.

Dread rolled over me as I froze at the tree line.

"It's not too late to run," he said, and part of me wanted to see if he was actually serious.

When we approached the house, we found Levi waiting on the porch in his normal rocking chair, like it was another easy evening.

Andrea was in the doorway, shifting her weight back and

forth restlessly; Jake waited next to the Hen House sign with Evan, who had a split lip that was bleeding to match his scuffed knuckles. Jake yanked Evan to him and hissed something harsh under his breath. But Evan kept his blazing turquoise eyes set on Levi while his fingers twitched as if his claws were ready to come out to play.

Jake shoved Evan an inch back and shook his head. "I'm not stopping you again," he warned him.

Ethan blew out a long breath like he had seen this too many times before. Suddenly, all his playfulness was gone; his mouth set into a tight line that matched the ridged edges of his face, which looked dangerous in the moonlight.

"Evan?" Ethan's even tones sliced across the yard.

Evan jerked his gaze away from Levi to face his brother. His turquoise eyes looked like two lasers ready to burn the world down. "I'm fine." The shiner on his cheek said he wasn't.

Ethan's jaw ticked a hair. Slowly, he turned his head away from his brother to look directly at the person on my porch. Levi's eyes pulsed a glow as moon blood started to hum off him.

I tilted my head to look up at Ethan. *"I'll see you tomorrow?"*

The hardness in his eyes was replaced with something that made my breath catch. *"Breakfast."*

"I like pancakes."

He struggled to hide his smile. *"We'll see what I can whip up."* Stepping around me, he said, "Ev, we're going to David's."

"Are you fucking kidding me?" Evan spat.

Jake shoved Evan back one last time. "You're going to David's. As was planned," he griped. Then he strode to the house as he called over his shoulder, "And I'm staying on my nice fucking air mattress, as was planned."

Vicious cracks were quickly eating through Evan's control. Something crackled off him and hissed across the grass—the moon blood in his veins was angry. "We're not fucking staying."

"We are," Ethan stated in a calm, low warning like incoming thunder.

Evan's mouth snapped shut. He watched Ethan a moment, a searing silent conversation clearly being had, then he took off into the woods.

Ethan's shoulders did not relax. "I'll see you tomorrow," he told me, but his eyes were focused in a direct challenge to Levi. Then he looked back at me with a tiredness that I could feel in my bones. "In the morning?"

"The morning," I agreed.

He gave me one last parting glance then disappeared into the darkness, leaving me under the fullness of the moon that I had somehow forgotten was there.

"Should I follow them?" Jake asked Levi from the doorway.

"No, Remi is," Levi answered with an iciness that I hadn't experienced in a while.

"Fuck," I hissed under my breath.

The walk to the porch took longer than I remembered. Levi stood slowly once I reached the top step. He didn't look at me, but I could see his fingers twitching as if they were fighting to not clench into a fist. "When you're ready to talk about it, come home. I'm going to run with Lander," he said. He brushed by me and ran into the trees.

Andrea pulled me inside and shut the door. She grabbed my face and forced me to look at her molten golden eyes. "Hey," she said. "Are you okay?"

"Yeah, I'm—"

"Charlotte." Her eyes pulsed heavy with worry. Her beast was close to her skin. "Char, are you okay?"

I felt something wet fall down my cheeks and my hands started to shake. "I just—it's just—holy shit."

"It's a lot," she noted.

"Hey!" Jake said as he cracked open a beer. "At least we get to be like real neighbors now? I mean, that's pretty tight?"

"Fuck off, Jake," Andrea groaned. She marched to the freezer and pulled out our favorite In Case of Emergency ice cream.

"What?!" He strode over to me. "They'll be fine. Evan's just a hothead."

"I don't understand. I thought Lander said things were better between them and Levi?"

Jake gave me a tight smile. "They felt like he abandoned them for years, and he lost his entire world and his mind when he almost went rogue." He paused and shook his head. "They were just kids—we all were just kids. They wanted—needed—him to be there for them."

"He lost his mind," I pointed out. "Like you said."

Jake nodded slowly. "Seems like his mind is just fine now. Seems like it has been for a while. And he took you in . . ."

"Jake," Andrea warned him.

"What's that supposed to mean?" I swiveled my head to look between the two, who were clearly in a silent debate of their own. "Guys?"

Jake gave Andrea a long look. She shook her head. "It's their business, not ours."

Jake snorted. "Fuck 'em."

"Jake!"

He waved her off. "Team Shitheads." Turning back to me, he

opened his mouth a few times then finally said, "Look, everyone understood when Levi went crazy. They were kids, and it was hard, and they were hurt, but they *knew* why he had to be away from them. But then he got better, and he never called. And he kept getting better and never called. Then he took you in, as one of his own, and never called—"

Andrea dropped her head into her palms. "Jake."

He put an arm on my shoulder. "Look. Levi, Evan—neither of them are right. It's not your fault, but I do think it made the hurt worse. Knowing he was fine, and with you, but he never called on them."

Fucking hell, Levi, what kind of a mess did you get me into?

"It's their bullshit, let them sort it out." Jake shrugged.

"He's right, Charlotte," Andrea stated.

Jake dipped his head and stepped closer. "Besides, a lot of people would say you're blessed by the moon to have found your true mate."

"What do you think?" I found myself murmuring back.

Jake shrugged. "Maybe this time you are?"

CHAPTER FOUR

I waited until Andrea and Jake were long asleep before I snuck out of our house and ran in the direction of Levi's. He was sitting on the porch steps with a glass of whiskey in hand and the bottle next to him. Silver eyes cut to me and froze me in my tracks.

"Nice night."

"Fucking lovely night." He finished his drink. Carefully, I took a seat next to him while he refilled his glass. He offered it to me. I didn't refuse. "You really know how to fuck up a decent party."

I set the glass down between us. "Maybe I should have let you keep smoking?"

He was silent. Instead, he took the bottle and tipped it back.

THE PACK

My beast pressed closer and watched him. His skin looked too tight on his body, like he may snap into his fur at any moment.

"I didn't think I would have a true mate," I admitted to him. His brows furrowed as he turned to face me. "I was a human before, and... I don't know—after everything..."

"I never cease to be surprised when it comes to you," he answered.

My hand quickly found the glass and brought it up for another sip. "What do I do?"

"What do you mean?"

Carefully, I set the glass down next to me. "I mean, doesn't one wolf follow the other? Aren't I supposed to go with him?"

He scoffed a laugh. "You're not going anywhere."

My brow lifted as my beast snapped her teeth in the back of my mind. "Bowie said it was my choice."

"Did she?" he taunted. He snatched the glass back. "And what is your choice then, Charlotte?"

"That's not the point!" My words were fast, like a flickering tongue of fire.

Levi was not amused. His jaw ticked as he took a long sip, finishing the glass before slamming it between us. "Charlotte, it's not that simple—" He rubbed his face like he was praying this was all a dream. When he looked at me again, it wasn't anger in his eyes, but pain. A deep sadness I hadn't seen in his silver orbs for a long time.

"It's where they died. It's where Eve died—where Lucas died. Where our unborn child *died*." Leaning back he looked at the moon with a sneer on his lips. He shook his head and faced me again. "Three packs share the Trapper's Forest on their land: Hemlock, Switchback, and us—Thunderhead. That forest is a curse to all of us—there's something happening in those woods. We both know it."

I opened my mouth to speak but silence came out. Levi poured himself another glass.

"All signs point to Hemlock, and you're out of your mind if you think I'm going to let you just go there—"

Something snapped inside me and crackled through my veins. "I can handle myself."

"When it comes to hordes of rogues even the strongest wolves fall," he said, snarling. "Ethan's father and brother were strong men. My wife and son were the strongest people I knew, and they were slaughtered like fucking animals—a bear is one thing, but I won't make the same mistakes twice."

"It's not like last time," I quickly countered.

He breathed a bitter laugh. "Isn't it?"

"I mean, Levi," I argued, "we don't know if 'hordes' of rogues are what we're dealing with. We don't know what we're dealing with."

"Exactly," he said, his tone clipped.

I bit my lip before finally saying, "Levi, this is my decision."

"And this is mine, Charlotte." A cold current pulsed off him and seeped through my skin to my bones. My beast snapped her teeth again at the rattle that shook through us.

It would be my decision, but there was no talking to him tonight, and there was no convincing him when I didn't know what I was going to do either—I needed time to think. I needed a better plan.

But I also needed him; I knew I would always need Levi in my life.

"Why are they so angry with you?" I found myself asking.

Levi took the glass with him when he stood up. "Because, Charlie girl, I'm an asshole."

His steps carried him back into the house where the door slammed behind him, leaving me with the silence of the night around me and the full moon above me.

The next morning, Ethan was waiting at the front door of my house when I walked into the kitchen. Levi was already sitting at our small table with a cup of coffee in hand and a book in the other, while Jake snored away on his air mattress. Pausing, I looked at the door then back at Levi.

"How long as he been there?"

"No idea."

"So you just let him stand out there?"

"It's not going to kill him."

I rolled my eyes and frantically smoothed my hair while avoiding Levi's watchful eye. My beast was pacing in the back of my mind, pawing in delight as something warm blew across the pull between Ethan and me. Once I opened the door and let his scent flow in, it was like a summer breeze that curled around me.

His dual-colored eyes grew dark with a heaviness that had no room for platonic promises. His hair was wind tousled and held more of an amber tint in the sunlight that painted our porch and danced along the sleeves of his long-sleeve green Hemlock shirt, which somehow molded to his fit arms. I didn't dare look down at the gray sweatpants he was wearing. I was already perspiring enough as it was.

"Good morning," Levi called from behind me.

As I blinked, part of me wondered if I could melt into the floor.

"Hello," I practically stammered. My beast shook her head at me.

"Morning," he replied in an intimate tone that didn't shy away from the onlooker inside my home.

"Do, um, do you want some coffee?" He looked over his shoulder with a tired expression. I leaned around him to see Evan pacing at the bottom of the steps. "Does he want coffee?" Evan froze and his brows tightened. I bit my lip and offered him a small wave. "I'm Charlotte."

Evan tipped his head back in exasperation. "I know."

A snarl rolled off Ethan that made me gasp for air. Evan hissed through his teeth then jogged to the door and offered me a tight smile. "I'm Evan. It's nice to meet you. May I have some coffee?"

I nodded slowly. "Cups are above the pot. Creamer is in the refrigerator."

"Thanks." He made his way to the kitchen then stilled a few feet in front of Levi. The hair on his arms rose before he crossed them over his chest.

Levi held a hand up. "Evan, unfortunately for you I am in the mood, and your brother won't help you this time."

"Evan." Ethan sighed with a shake of his head. "Just grab a fucking cup of coffee."

Evan watched Ethan a moment before trudging to the coffeepot like he was serving some kind of life sentence. "Do you still want coffee?" I asked Ethan.

He leaned against the door frame. "Do we have to get it here?"

"No," Levi answered for him. He put his book down and tipped his chin at me. "Take him to the forest."

"What the fuck?" Evan hissed before he snapped his jaw closed and inspected Jake. Luckily, Jake could sleep through a bomb—he kept snoring soundly without a stir.

My beast and I cocked our heads as I held Levi's gaze. "I thought Bowie was going to."

"Change of plans." He leaned forward with a pulse in his silver eyes. "Show him what you found."

"I should go too," Evan quickly said.

"You're staying." Ethan's tone was unwavering.

Evan slammed the mug on the counter but one arc of Levi's brow froze him in place. "If we have too many people all at once it will pollute the scent. Your brother needs to see this first, then he can decide what he wants to do."

"And what am I going to do?" Evan countered.

Levi leaned back in his chair and picked his book up. "Breakfast won't kill you, Evan."

Evan's jaw ticked. "Ethan—"

"Do as he says, Ev," Ethan ordered.

I bit my lip. *"You're sure?"* I asked Levi.

Levi nodded. "Go."

"What if he asks about what we were doing? Before?"

Without missing a beat he said, *"Tell him."*

"But—"

"I won't make you lie to your mate," he answered simply. *"You're his mate. He'll listen to you."*

I bit back the curse that I wanted to hiss at Levi and forced myself to stay composed. "Give me a few minutes to change," I told Ethan.

Ethan was waiting in his own shifter shorts when I emerged outside, his clothes neatly folded and laid in the rocking chair on the porch. I forced my eyes forward while we jogged down the stairs and quietly made our way from the house and into the trees. His hand cautiously took mine and pulled me to a stop. "He said there's something in the Trapper's Forest. What is it?"

"I could explain but I think it's better if you see it for yourself."

"All right," he replied. His fingers loosened around my hand, but they didn't release it. The feeling of his skin on mine sent tingles up my arm that I wished I could ignore.

I had to get control of this.

He blew out a long breath then said, "First date in the Trapper's Forest?"

A laugh skittered out of me. "You're not getting out of pancakes. Did you want to stop for coffee?"

He shook his head with a tired smile. "Let's get in and get out. Lead the way."

My shift rolled over me as together we charged west. The whole time it was hard to focus, knowing he was next to me; my beast was mesmerized by the color of his fur, both of us unable to tell if it was auburn or black, even in the daylight. Scars littered his body, like ours, patches of fur missing in some places. He looked dangerous—alert—and yet still, there was something calm about him, something that had an odd way of calming my nerves.

When we reached the edge of the Trapper's Forest, I shifted back to my skin. The gloom that lay before us was already tightly wrapped around the sickly trees. It didn't help that it was overcast.

Moon blood crackled through my veins. I stepped ahead. "Walk where I do."

He didn't say anything. He quietly followed me into the dark between the trees where red eyes glowed through the shadowy thorn-filled brush. The farther we went, the more the air felt like the inside of a crypt. Cold and still with a staleness from being away from the outside world for too long. The hair on the back of my neck rose as my beast paced.

We wound around a bend that delivered us to the spot where the stakes still stood in the ground. A horned owl was perched on one of them. He twisted his head completely around to look at us with malicious scarlet eyes. A warning screech tore out of his brittle beak at us; I returned his greeting with a snarl of my own that had him quickly taking flight on frayed wings.

I nudged my chin toward the stakes. "Go see for yourself."

Ethan rubbed his jaw as he carefully approached the area, and the moment he stepped across the boundary of the stakes, he froze. The muscles in his back tensed so tightly they seemed to spasm. Fingers started to turn to claws, which he ran through his thick locks with a ragged breath. He could smell them—the rogues.

He walked around the area before shifting to his fur. I leaned against a tree and watched him pace the perimeter three times before he meticulously nosed through the space. He shifted back to his skin and, taking a knee in the grass, picked up some dirt and held it to his nose. With a hiss he threw it to the ground as if it burned him.

"There's blood magic in the air," I noted as I approached him. "It's faint but fresh. Maybe a week old?"

"How did you find this?" His voice was hard, distant.

Swallowing, I could feel the truth in my throat. The truth that I had to speak. Because tiny lies were the first cuts that frayed the fabric of anything good, and I wouldn't do that to him or to myself.

"Levi tasked a small group of us to case the forest. We've been at it for the past year."

"Why?"

I couldn't stop myself because something about this damn man made me want to tell him everything.

"Because there's something wrong with this forest. Levi knows it. Bowie knows it. And I feel it too. With all the rogue incidents, it makes sense."

Ethan pointed to the stakes. "It's contained to this area. How is that possible?"

"I don't know." With a shrug, I added, "Levi mentioned having a witch look at it."

He stood straight, taking me in carefully before his eyes pulsed a glimmer. "Have you seen this before?"

"Once," I answered truthfully. "A year ago. On the southern part of the border we share with you, but it wasn't the same. The scent died fast. Remi and I went back to look at it the next day. It had faded so much it was hard to tell if it was rogue or a dead animal rotting nearby."

"Why didn't you say anything?"

"Why did you tighten your borders over a 'bear'?" I countered with air quotations.

His brows lifted in amusement. As he tilted his head, the corner of his mouth twitched into a smirk. "A year is a long time to keep quiet."

"I think Levi wanted to wait until we had something real for you to see. Like I said, before, a year ago, it just vanished. I think he was worried you, or whoever you sent, wouldn't believe us."

He watched me a moment then brushed his hands on his shifter shorts, which hugged much too perfectly to his strong legs. I quickly cut my gaze ahead of me, across the border and into the woods, but it didn't stop the flush that I could feel blooming over my cheeks.

"This was all you found here?"

Leaves skirted my toes as icy air puffed past my feet. The trees started to rock like they were being moved by wind, but there was no wind—not this deep in the woods. My beast paced as we searched the darkness ahead of us—the darkness that always felt like it could find us.

"What is it?" He turned me to face him. His hands on my shoulders distracted me from the tendrils of cold nipping at my toes in a sinister tease.

Slowly, I nodded my head across the border. "There's something back there. I don't know how I know, I just do."

He cut his eyes to the forest then back to me. "The traps are bad back there."

"Then I suggest you don't fall into one."

The smirk on his full lips was too beautiful to hate. He hesitantly glanced back into the darkness. "You're sure you want to go in there?"

Nodding quickly, I answered with a firm "Yes."

He watched me a moment, then relented. "Twenty minutes, then we get out of here."

My feet practically skipped around him as my beast inched closer in delight. "Pancakes! You do owe me breakfast."

"Is that right?" His rich voice was like a velvet blanket.

I shook the shiver it sent over my skin away along with the laughter that was bubbling in me as I reached a tree with the base painted green. Closing my eyes, I inhaled deeply and soaked in the essence of the forest, trying to pick out anything that felt like a trace of something we could track.

"Charlotte," the whispers called, because of course they did. They always called this deep in the darkness.

My eyes snapped open. Ethan was carefully watching me, but I ignored his curious gaze and stepped across the border.

The frigid air danced around us and twirled the leaves as if it was creating a parade for our entrance. My beast snarled in the back of my mind because both of us knew this place had omens lurking around every corner.

Evergreen brush stood like people crammed shoulder to shoulder at a concert. Their branches scratched my arms as I shoved my way through them. After breaking through a wall of green, I heard it—the song of silver buzzing like a mosquito. Along the ground, lines of silver wire spread out from the base of the brush. My hand shot out and stopped Ethan from taking another step.

Pausing, I heard the faint sound of hushed voices in the distance. But it was different from the whispers. The whispers usually called for me; these voices sounded like a garbled group of people. It was like trying to eavesdrop on someone behind a thick closed door—certain sounds felt familiar but recognizing a full word was impossible.

"Do you hear that?"

Ethan arched a brow and shook his head. "No."

Of course he didn't. Of course I was the one with the voices in her head.

I blew out a breath and pointed to the ground—to a trip line that was tied between two bushes. "Walk exactly where I do."

THE PACK

I half expected him to say we had to turn back, but instead, he followed me in a delicate hopscotch over the lines that waited like knives ready to slice through our skin. The voices grew louder with each step I took; I had started out slow, but my beast was anxious—eager to see what was ahead, and as soon as the smell of fresh blood magic curled around me, I was too.

Ethan called for me, but I was sailing over the silver until I hit safe ground where my feet could run. "This way!" I called over my shoulder.

I kept shoving through the thicket until I hit a clearing. Sunlight poured through the opening of trees and illuminated something ruby red in the throngs of grass. The hushed voices danced around me and grew louder and louder the closer I got to the object in the center.

"Charlotte!" Ethan's hand latched around my arm and pulled me to face him. "Did you not hear me calling you?"

I realized how close we were. How I was a breath away from being painted onto his fit torso; how his hand had somehow found my waist—and how much I liked the way it felt. I did the thing I shouldn't and met his eyes. And when I did, I felt the pull between us almost crackle, as if it was electricity sparking to life.

"I was distracted," was all I could muster. "It smells like blood magic."

His eyes had trailed down to look at my lips. "It does," he agreed quietly, in a promise that trailed along my skin like I wished his fingers would.

I stepped out of his grip to look at the object in the grass. He knelt then carefully peeled back the tendrils of foliage to reveal a smooth, glassy stone; under the surface something dark and liquid red swirled like water being stirred in a glass.

"Fuck me." He swore under his breath.

He leaned back on his heels and turned to face me with a solemn expression. "You asked earlier why I tightened the borders."

"I did."

"I don't want to have secrets with you." It sounded like a plea. Like a part of his soul begging me not to break it.

In turn, I felt myself nod because the fractured parts of me could only hope that he didn't shatter what I had left to give. "I don't want to have secrets with you either."

He picked up the crimson stone. It glimmered in the rays of daylight. "The other day I found a cloud of blood magic, fresh blood magic, in a space just like this. Open to the sky. To the moon." His jaw clenched like he was fighting to keep from snapping his own teeth. "I had seen something like it before the attack. The forest wasn't forbidden back then, but Dad did not allow us to go in on our own. My older brother, Eli, and I never listened because we always thought we were bigger monsters than the ones in here."

He breathed a sad smile and shook his head. "Two weeks before the attack, in a clearing just like this, I found a stone exactly like this one. It was lying in the grass like a fresh egg. But when I brought Eli to see it, it was gone. Only the faint scent of blood magic remained, and Eli didn't think it warranted getting Dad riled up."

"Why didn't you take it with you? When you found it?"

"It reeked of blood magic. Dad always warned us about it—told us never to touch anything that smelled like it. I wish I would have anyway." He shook his head slowly while his eyes went distant, as if he was watching a memory play out on the shiny surface of the stone in front of us. "I always thought about that stone. Eli joked that I had gotten into the bad weed, but I knew what I saw."

"Do you know what it is?"

His wary gaze made my toes cringe in the grass. "Only because it became my obsession for a short time. It's called a Bloodstone. It's made with blood magic."

CHAPTER FIVE

The stone glowed in the middle of Levi's kitchen table next to the old map of Jake's that we had used during the Hunt. The crimson under the surface swirled like a sandstorm in the Sahara. All anyone could do was watch it swirl in silence—in horrifying awe.

The Thunderhead Pack council was waiting for us when we arrived at Levi's—the importance of our cargo warranted an emergency meeting. Ethan was quick to brief everyone on what the stone was, how we'd found it, and how he knew what it was. But after he finished, all anyone could do was stare at the red stone that swirled like a whirlpool on the table.

Remi shifted on his feet next to me. I caught him share a rare, anxious glance with his mother that sent my beast into a frenzy in the back of my mind. It didn't help that Lander looked like he had seen a ghost, or that Levi looked as if he wished he was seeing a ghost. Even David remained silent, somberly staring at the stone with his single green eye.

The stone was whispering. It hadn't stopped; I could hear its faint murmurs even after Ethan put it into his saddlebag so we could carry it back. But the sound reminded me more of trying to overhear a group of people talking, like I was a small child again, eavesdropping on my parents and their friends after dinner. It didn't call to me like the whispers in the woods, but still, I felt drawn to it. The urge to try to understand what was being said was driving my beast to incessantly pace.

I clenched my eyes shut and prayed I wasn't the only person who could hear this thing. That thought in itself scared me almost more than what the stone itself was.

Lander was the first to break the silence. "What do you think?" he asked David.

David let out a long whistle. "From what I've researched, it looks exactly like a Bloodstone, but I'll be damned if it is. Been outlawed for hundreds of years." He shrugged at Ethan. "Bit of a history buff."

He pointed back at the stone. "From what I read, the last time someone saw one, it was almost two hundred years ago, and it was quickly destroyed. They're bad news. Dark, dark magic."

David lifted his gaze to Levi, standing rigid next to Lander. "The vampires are old, Levi. They've seen a lot. They could help here."

"We'd have to involve Leo," Lander pointed out, referencing the head of the West Coast vampire coven, and, according to Levi, one of the first vampires ever created.

Levi didn't blink when he countered, "No, we wouldn't."

David's single green eye held Levi's. "Levi, if this is truly a Bloodstone, they need to know. This could be very bad."

The liquid swirled faster in the stone as the voices emanating from it picked up. My beast snapped her teeth. I wanted to bury the damn thing six feet under.

"I know." Levi relented.

Remi approached the table. He peered at the map then tapped a spot close to the notated Hemlock border. "That's where the rogue patch was." His finger trailed west until it was in the empty margins of the map. "If this map kept going and showed Hemlock, where you're saying you found it would be around here. Deep in pack territory. So, did the rogues drop it there?" I didn't think the room could get quieter, but his question seemed to suck the air out of it. "It didn't get there on its own."

Bowie nodded in agreement. "And Hemlock wolves don't go into the forest, it's forbidden."

David lifted an amused brow at the Thunderhead Head Tracker. "Of all people, you know that doesn't stop anyone."

She pulled out a chair for herself and sat down. "You have a point, but Ethan knows as well as I that his wolves stay out of that forest—fear will do that."

The moon blood in Ethan's veins sizzled and snapped like cold oil being poured into a hot pan. I sucked in my breath as something across the pull, the tether between us, heated a desire in me to flash my teeth at the room. I clenched my mouth shut.

Ethan shook his head at Bowie. "Generations of our kind were slaughtered there and the horde of rogues that killed our families hid there before they attacked—spilled our blood there. Can you blame them?"

Her eyes softened at his words. Lander stepped forward

and placed a hand on the back of her chair. "Remi's not wrong, though. It didn't just get there," he pointed out diplomatically.

"We need to up our guards," David stated. "But, Levi, we need information. We don't know what it is we're really dealing with."

"Do it," Levi agreed. "Ethan, have you told Thomas?"

Ethan crossed his arms over his chest. The hum pulsing off him wasn't stopping, and neither were the garbled voices coming from the stone. "Not yet."

Levi tilted his head and inspected him like he was trying to peer through a fogged window. "Well, it was on your land, Ethan. What's done with it is technically your call."

Ethan looked like he wished it wasn't his call. "I have to take it up with Thomas. You know that. It's his decision."

"That's not what I meant," Levi countered tightly. "We should talk."

Ethan scoffed a laugh. "We should."

Levi took in the rest of the room. "Clear out. David, handle the guards and lock that fucking thing up until Ethan decides what to do with it." He nodded at the stone in the center of the table.

"Consider it done," David told him. He tossed the stone back into the saddlebag. The voices quieted, almost silent. My wolf practically collapsed with relief.

"Come on, you two," Bowie told me and Remi. "You both have sheep duty this afternoon, and you're not getting out of it."

I shoved off the counter to follow her. Something tingled across the tether between Ethan and me. I looked over my shoulder to find his dual-colored eyes trained on me. *"I still owe you breakfast."*

My lips quirked into a tiny smile. *"You really need to learn to ask me out,*" I countered, before I jogged into the woods after Remi.

We ran together back to my cottage, where Andrea was pacing on the porch. Her shoulders relaxed when we came up the stairs. "I've had to stop him twice from running after you and Ethan."

"Who?" I asked.

"Evan," she groaned.

Remi snorted and jogged into the house, where Jake was chowing down on a cinnamon roll. Evan jumped from his seat and stormed over. "What did you find?"

I narrowed my gaze. "Ask your brother."

Remi snickered as he walked to the refrigerator and pulled out a jug of orange juice then started to pour it into glasses. I stepped around Evan's menacing frame and took a cup from Remi. Evan turned to face me; his turquoise eyes pulsed. "You found something related to the rogues, didn't you?"

"Ev, man, I am going to tell you this one last time." Jake wiped his mouth then put his napkin in his lap. "You're being a dick."

Evan tossed his hands out beside him. "Come on?!"

"Nah, I'm on her team," Jake countered, tapping his coffee mug to my glass of juice. He forked another cinnamon roll onto his plate. "We'll know when it's right for us to know."

"Fuck it." Evan snarled. He barreled out the door, and from the looks of it, Andrea was not going to try to stop him.

Jake looked longingly at his plate then handed it to Andrea. "Fuck me—keep this warm for me?"

Andrea nodded with a tired smile and put his plate in the microwave. Curses trailed from him as he sprinted out the door after Evan.

Remi sat in Jake's seat. His lips pulled into a catlike smile. "Why would he ask if something was related to the rogues if he didn't have suspicions himself?" He drummed his fingers on the tabletop. "Now we know they know."

Andrea furrowed her brows. "They're a hot topic in the region. It could be nothing."

Remi shook his head. "Evan's not wound up over nothing." Remi nudged his chin toward the door. "Whatever is going on, they're aware of something—Ethan, Evan, and Jake."

"But Jake tells us everything," Andrea countered.

Remi shook his head. "I don't think so, babe. Not when it comes to things like this. If they have information they are keeping secret, he's going to keep his mouth shut." He continued to drum his fingers. "Come to think of it, Keeley hasn't mentioned anything to me either. I've tried to pry—damn, I thought she didn't know a thing, but there's no way she wouldn't know. She's got her dad's nose."

"Who?" I asked.

"Keeley is a tracker over at Hemlock," Remi explained. "Cash was her dad. He was their old Head Tracker and one of Mom's best friends. He died in the attack." My chest twisted unexpectedly. There were too many graves at Hemlock. "She's a good wolf. She'll be good to know over there," he added.

Andrea leaned a hand against the counter. "So, what did you find?"

I could feel Remi's gaze on me. Could hear the whispers in my head. I ran my fingers through my hair. "It's called a Bloodstone. We found it on their land. Ethan let me cross the border."

"Already infiltrating, proud of ya," Remi chimed with a grin.

Andrea cast him a long look before she cut her molten gaze to me. "What the fuck is a Bloodstone?"

Carefully, I recounted what had happened that morning and what Ethan had said—what David had said to us at Levi's.

Andrea swore under her breath when I was done. "My dad has to know."

"I know," I agreed. "Maybe he already does? It seems maybe there's a lot more going on over at Hemlock..."

She bit her lip. "I feel like he would have said something—" The disappointment hanging off her made me want to console her. Give her the last of our favorite snacks to cheer her up.

Remi took a sip of his juice. "There's plenty Mom doesn't tell me," he offered. "But, hey, this is good news."

Both Andrea and I turned to him while he forked a giant cinnamon roll onto a plate. "Explain yourself," she retorted.

He licked some frosting off his fingers then snatched a napkin. "Ethan's already letting Charlotte go into the woods on his land—where we have been wanting to track for a year. I mean, it's our opportunity to snoop—"

"Whoa, whoa, whoa." I threw my hands up and shook my head. "Remi, I—"

"Charlotte." His tone was suddenly serious. "We both know there's something over there. You proved today there is. We have been looking for an in, and now we have one."

"I'm not—" I quickly shook my head because he wasn't wrong. There was something in those woods. Something I wanted to chase—something that I felt wanted me to chase it.

And I did finally find something tangible today. Something that we could all point a finger at. Something more than traces of blood magic and trails of scents.

But this thing with Ethan, whatever it turned out to be—I couldn't sabotage it.

"I'm not going to hide things from him," I told Remi. "Or go around him."

Remi shrugged. "Sounds like you won't have to." He took a bite from the cinnamon roll, devouring almost half of it. "So, you gonna let him mark you soon?"

"Remi!" Andrea hissed.

"What? Don't you want to see what's in is head?"

My brows furrowed. "What do you mean?"

"Mates can send images to each other," he explained. "Dad and Mom do it all the time. Sometimes they can pass through what they're seeing in real time. It's fucking trippy."

The blood drained from my face.

Andrea dropped her head in her palms. "Shouldn't you be doing anything else?!"

Remi waved her off. "Fine. I gotta go anyhow. Promised Mom I'd finish up the laundry before sheep duty." He snatched his cinnamon roll and paused next to me. "Hey, real talk, I'm happy for you. I hope you know that."

My heart twisted because over the last year Remi had become one of my closest friends. Leaving the pack would mean leaving all my friends.

I leaned my cheek in my palm. "Thanks, Rem."

He winked at Andrea then headed out the door, leaving us to the quiet of the house. She shook her head then turned back to face me. "You finally found some evidence."

"I don't know if it makes me feel better, though." I took an overly large bite of a cinnamon roll.

She chewed her lip as she leaned back in her seat. "Remi's right. Evan and Jake do know more than they're saying."

I knew she was thinking that if Hemlock guards were in the

loop, then her father, who was head of Hemlock security, also had inside information. "Maybe your dad didn't want to worry you?"

"Maybe?" Her fingers drummed on the table while I ate. She only stopped to swipe her finger across some frosting before she picked up the beat again.

I set my fork down when I finished. She laid her palm flat on the table. "If you want to move over there, I'll go with you."

My brows furrowed. "What?"

"Don't be an idiot. You'll need a friend over there at Ethan's pack. And you're stuck with me."

"Andrea, I—"

"It's what I want," she interjected.

"What's it like at Hemlock?"

"Not like here."

"What does that mean?"

She shrugged. "It's different. I guess you'll see eventually."

"Remi's not wrong either."

She shook her head at me. "Not all of his ideas are good ones, and besides, the forest is forbidden at Hemlock. You have to have special permission to enter."

I filed that away as a problem to solve later. We'd gone in today. If I did follow Ethan to Hemlock, we were going into that forest again. I was going to find whatever it was that was hiding in there.

"They're sensitive about these things," Andrea added. "A lot of people died there—brutally. Their pack council was completely erased—executed—I mean, Jesus, Jake's parents were."

I gasped. "What do you mean?"

"His dad was their Head of Security," she noted. "He was one of Dad's close friends."

Jake never spoke about the attack or his parents other than what he had shared with me during the Hunt—that they had been murdered during the attack. I never asked for more information. If he wanted to share, it was his business to do so.

"Your dad—how did he survive?"

She rubbed her face. "He was with me," she murmured. "He always made an annual trip to see me. It was a normal day. My ex-bondmate and I had plans to grill.

"I remember like it was yesterday. Dad was helping me make hamburger patties when he got a call. His hands had raw meat on them, so he used his elbow to answer the phone," she added with a light laugh. Her eyes grew misty as shivers covered her arms. "It was one of the guards—it sounded horrible. Dad realized the pack link had gone silent. He got in the car and drove back. He said when he could hear the pack again, it was . . ." She shook her head. "He was too late."

CHAPTER SIX

That afternoon Remi and I lay in the sun watching the sheep lazily graze until we were told to move them to another pasture. Then we both struggled to keep the herd of oversized cotton balls walking in generally the same direction. One of the lambs ended up wandering into the trees by the pasture; I jogged after it and quickly scooped it up before it could stray farther away.

The little rascal squirmed in my arms before settling and resting his head on my shoulder. Levi teased me that they weren't pets, but they were like little balls of bouncing cotton candy when they were this young—they were hard not to fawn over.

I carried the lamb over to the rest of the herd, which was already snacking on the crisp green grass. Setting him down,

I cooed, "Go to your mother." It shook itself with delight then scampered excitedly to the other lambkins.

A vibration danced along the tether between Ethan and me. I looked around and found him approaching the pasture. With each step he took our link shimmered like snowflakes frolicking, as carefree as the lambs in the field.

"I see Levi didn't kill you."

He breathed an easy smile. "I'm hard to kill."

I bit back a smile. "Well, you've only been here for a day. Plenty of time for Levi to work something out."

A warm chuckle shook his chest, a sound as comforting as the crackling of a fire in a fireplace. "Would you like some company watching these furballs?"

Playfully, I narrowed my gaze. "This is not a date."

He rolled his eyes. "No, it's not. But I'm willing to bet Remi would like a reprieve from this penance."

"He would!" Remi jumped up from his place on the soft grass and offered Ethan a mock salute. "Her Second, bless you," he said before taking off in the direction of the pack house.

I lifted a brow. "Do you even know how to make pancakes?"

He snorted a laugh and followed me up the green incline to a cushiony patch of grass. I collapsed into its feathery embrace and forced myself to keep from sneaking peeks at the man next to me—but Ethan didn't make it easy. He leaned back on his forearms so the sun could slide over his fit torso. My fingers twitched as heat flooded me with the need to slide my palm over where the sun touched.

"He's worried about you—Levi." Ethan's voice cut through the murmur of the sheep.

"I know." I knew what Levi talked to him about was their

business, but if I was involved, it made it my business; the inquisitive side of me was too curious to not tiptoe forward. "What will you do about the stone?"

"I have to bring it to Thomas first." A line I'd heard before, but here, with just me, it sounded like he was growing quickly tired of using it.

"That's not what I meant," I parried. "What do you want to do?"

There was a scar along the outside of his cheek that glimmered in the sunlight when he tilted his head, like he was carefully choosing what to say next. "Levi said I could trust you?"

Swallowing, I replied with a silent nod.

He leaned closer. "Thomas won't commission a search party without hard evidence. Our pack has been through a lot—Thunderhead too—but he's careful," he tactfully stated. "Of the pack. He doesn't want to stir up a panic, same as Levi. Up until now, we haven't found anything to warrant an official hunt."

I was quickly learning to read between his lines. "You've been searching too." The second I said it, he confirmed it with a tiny twitch in the corner of his mouth that lifted to a sly smile. "Remi thought Jake and Evan knew something—he wasn't wrong."

"No," Ethan breathed. "Levi's not wrong to be doing what he's doing. He's right to have you all hunt through the woods. There's something in there. I've known it. Evan's known it too. I asked Thomas over a year ago to let me take a small group to patrol, and he said no. To be fair, we didn't have any evidence aside from reports of odd sounds some guards heard at the edge of the line.

"The second time our wolves heard something out of place, he told me no again. The third time, I didn't ask. Evan convinced me. So, our small group goes in when we can, and up until today, we haven't found anything."

"What did they hear?" My heart raced in my chest. The sound of the whispers started to echo in the chambers of my memories and for once, I felt slight hope that I wasn't absolutely nuts.

"Snapping—more like popping. According to the wolves who heard it, it sounded like those fireworks that pop when you throw them on the ground."

I tamped down my disappointment. My beast nudged me tenderly in solidarity. "So, what now?"

"I take the stone to Thomas and ask for an official search—we'd keep it quiet from the rest of the pack, like you have here." He rubbed the scruff that was close to turning into a thin beard.

"Then we keep hunting?" I asked.

His lips parted in a smile. "What is this 'we' business?"

I looked away because the heat pulsing between us was going to make me sweat. "You can't expect me to do nothing."

"Our forest is forbidden to wolves outside of pack leadership. Only Thomas can grant you permission to enter it."

"Seems like I already have someone on the inside with him," I pointed out. "Besides, it's not my first rodeo in there."

He tilted his head as he watched me. "You don't mind the forest?"

I shrugged. "It doesn't matter. If it needs to be found in there, then in there we go."

"Levi warned me that you had a good nose."

I snorted a laugh.

He turned and lay back next to me, his eyes fluttering closed to the bright light. My mouth opened with another question but instead, I found myself studying him in the sunshine. He had a tiny scar on the bottom left corner of his lip that made me wonder how it would feel against my own.

"I can take a photo if you want."

"You know, maybe you should have been a comedian?"

His lips curled into a smile as his eyelids parted slightly. He watched me for a moment then pushed a stray strand of hair behind my ears. "Not me, Evan was the jokester of the family. Used to always have Mom laughing." He leaned back in the grass. "Lander, in the report he sent over when you were attacked by those rogues—it noted you had no known relatives..."

"Yeah," I answered. "Dad passed when I was really young. I barely remember him. And Mom," I said on the edge of a long breath that felt heavier than it should, "well, she was in a car accident when I was eighteen. I lived with my uncle for a bit until I went to college, but I've lost touch with him. I wouldn't even know how to find him."

"I'm sorry."

"It was a long time ago. But I think Mom would have tried to move up here if she'd known. She, I think, would have been pro-werewolf," I added with a laugh, which he joined me in.

"What was she like?" he asked.

"Quirky, but she had the best laugh. Wildly smart. She was an architect. She loved being a mom. I think half of what we did together was so she could enjoy it—pillow forts, movie days, ditching school for a fair."

"My mom was like that too," he offered with a half-smile. "At the pack—well, a lot of packs—they homeschool, but we usually do it together as a group. Our pack has a schoolhouse. Of course, as the pack lead's mate she would 'have an emergency' that she 'needed us for,' which meant she would take us home for a full movie day."

"Really?"

He nodded with a wistful smile. "She loved being a mom too."

"What about your dad?"

"He was like Aunt Eve. We always said his hair was actually on fire when he was mad," he added with a contagious laugh that spread to me.

I leaned back in the grass as sunlight kissed my face, oh-so-aware of his presence next to me, but I didn't care. My beast and I agreed that we liked this.

"Tomorrow?" he asked. I turned back to face him.

It was my turn to push his hair out of his eyes, and when I did, I realized what a mistake it was. Because the pull between us turned into something molten the moment he closed his eyes while my fingers ran through his silky strands.

I carefully pulled my hand back to my chest. He watched my fingers before reaching forward with his own, carefully grasping them until they were easily intertwined together.

I didn't pull away.

I didn't want to.

He watched our hands for a moment then lifted his gaze back to mine. "Tomorrow will you take me to the other site? Where you found the rogue scents the first time?"

"You really need to learn to ask me out."

His laughter was rich and deep and something that I could listen to on repeat. "How about coffee?"

"How did we scale down from breakfast to coffee?"

He smirked. "As you wish, sunshine."

"Oh my god." I groaned while he laughed next to me.

He laid his head back in the grass while I watched a few lambs playing in the field. He was quiet, but it was a quiet that I found comfort in. A comfort, I realized, that I could very easily get used to.

The next morning Ethan showed up at my house with two cups of coffee and a bag of muffins. It wasn't pancakes, but I still couldn't hide my delight when I saw the small purple flower he had tucked into the paper bag for me.

Together, we went back to the border where Remi and I had first found the scent of rogues a year ago. Nothing was there, of course, only rolling hills and green flags rippling in the wind. Ethan said nothing. He watched the flags wave in the breeze then ordered Evan to take the Bloodstone back to Hemlock that very day.

For the next few days Ethan would wait on my doorstep with breakfast in hand before following me and Remi into the Trapper's Forest. After a few days, I told him he could let himself in and wait in the kitchen. After a week, he would knock on my bedroom door then crack it enough to extend a to-go cup through the open space. After two more weeks, he worked his way to sitting on the edge of my bed with the cup in hand while he patiently waited for me to muster the strength to leave the covers.

He had only gone back to Hemlock twice to check on things; each time Evan returned stubbornly in tow. Each time, when Levi asked for an update about the Bloodstone, Ethan would report that Thomas was still "thinking over things."

It grated against Levi's resolve like acid eating through thin fabric. I didn't know what else Thomas wanted. Lander chalked it up to being thoughtful of the pack. Levi said he thought Thomas should shove his head up his ass a little farther.

Ethan told me to wait, a word that I felt like he knew too well, as he had also been waiting on me to decide what we would do—anyone could see that. Many wolves at Thunderhead also felt the need to tell me as much.

Today, however, was the first time, in most likely forever, that I was disappointed by the smell of coffee. Because the person peeking into my room to bring it to me was not the one I wanted.

Derek sauntered over with a saucy smile. "Expecting someone else?"

He set the mug on the bedside table while I rubbed the sleep out of my eyes. "Why would you say that?"

Derek smirked. "Darling, you know you're Elliot's and my adopted love child, right?"

I rolled my eyes and sat up. "Ethan's coming back from Hemlock today."

"So, you won't be sleeping over again?" He grinned.

"It's your fault for giving me too much wine." Last night I had told Andrea I was going to lie down for just a minute, and the next thing I knew, Elliot was tucking me in in my old room at Levi's.

Derek took my hand in his and pressed it to his mouth. "It's hard to think that not long ago I was cleaning up a bite on your leg."

My throat clenched. "Derek..."

His dark eyes were almost watery as they studied my face. "Do you like him? I mean *him*."

"I do," I answered. Because even without this pull, this soulmate thing, that was the honest truth.

He sighed. "I would be nowhere without Elliot. I know you know that."

"Derek—"

"I would be so lost without him," he said in a hushed voice that I wasn't sure he even wanted me to hear. He gave my hand another squeeze before leaving me in my room.

Derek and Elliot left me to my thoughts throughout the day while I helped them with the greenhouse at Levi's. We'd decided to expand it this year so Andrea and I could also plant there, since our little cottage didn't have an ideal space for one. After a long day of pulling weeds, we gathered again for a dinner that made Andrea feel "like a fat walrus."

I stayed after Andrea left and helped Elliot with the dishes. He dried his hands on a dish towel then tossed it next to the sink. "That was delightful, though the jalapeños were a bit spicy, eh?"

"You don't like spicy," I teased.

Derek rounded the counter and pressed his lips to Elliot's cheek. "We love spicy."

Elliot watched him for a second then laughed under his breath. I quickly washed the last plate and put it in the drying rack next to the sink, eager to avoid whatever silent intimate moment was occurring.

"What else do we need to do?" I asked.

Elliot looked around the kitchen, searching for anything we had forgotten to clean, as a buzz combed over my skin. I felt something crackle over the pull between Ethan and me.

"He's here," I whispered.

Derek rushed to the window and peeked between the horizontal blinds. "No, he's not, but—oh, there he is!"

Elliot and I darted to find a spot on either side of Derek.

Elliot dipped his head between the horizontal shades. "He grew up well, so he did."

"I know. It's not even fair," Derek muttered.

I felt my cheeks heat. Elliot leaned back with a smirk. "I think we could bounce a quarter off that arse."

Derek barked in laughter. I wanted to evaporate and fly to another place where it was quiet. I was starting to understand more and more why Levi liked his solitude.

But I couldn't resist looking too. I peered through the blinds with them and watched Ethan walk right up to the porch.

I heard Levi's bedroom door smack the wall. I jumped away and scurried to the kitchen. Levi stepped out of his room, rolling his eyes at the vampires.

"Ethan's here," I told him.

"I know," he said, right as a knock echoed through the house.

Levi opened the door. Ethan smiled, although it didn't reach his eyes. "Uncle."

"Ethan."

"We just finished dinner, but I can make you a plate?" Derek offered.

Ethan smiled politely and shook his head. "I came for Charlotte—I thought we could go on a quick run?" As he leaned around Levi, his gaze locked on mine. "Do you want to go?"

Elliot arched a brow. "*I hope for your sake, love, it's not quick at all,*" he said through our link.

My cheeks flamed. "Sure," I managed to say before I pulled off my sweatshirt and strode forward in my shifters.

I squeezed around Levi and tied my hair up while we silently slipped away into the night. Finally, when we were out of sight of my unwanted audience, I said, "Hey."

He turned to me with a breathy smile. "Hey, yourself."

A strange tension built around us as we walked through the trees. "How was home?"

He shrugged. "The same. Did you miss me too much while I was gone?"

Yes, I wanted to say, but I didn't understand why I did. We barely knew each other and already it felt wrong when he wasn't with me.

I bit back a smile. "Where are you taking me?"

He jogged forward. "You'll see."

We ran in our fur toward the cliff, darting around trees and stealing glances at each other. Soon we were climbing uphill where the trees thinned out, close to the glacier that bordered the land, though a different area than the cliff I was so fond of. The smell of burning sugar was heavy in the air, and a neon-blue glow in the distance pulsed into the night sky. He took us to a set of thick trees, close to the groaning and cracking ice that thundered as if it was right next to us.

We shifted to our skin. Ethan turned to me. "Through the trees."

"What is it?" I asked.

His hand reached for mine. "Come on and see for yourself."

I stared at his palm for a moment before taking it, letting his fingers weave through mine. The beast in me pulsed in contentment as a cool wave of static ran down my arms.

Together we walked ahead, into the trees where the smell of fresh caramel—of magic—grew heavy. Pausing behind the last line of trees, he held a finger to his lips then tapped his temple. A speck of pulsing neon blue floated past his cheek. It was tiny, like a single piece of glitter.

THE PACK

My eyes went wide. He smiled, then pushed a branch out of our way—clearing the path to the glacial valley ahead. I stepped forward then let him pull me to kneel in the grass.

My breath hitched as I took in the sight below.

The grassy hill curled down to the glacier, which was a bright cotton-candy blue with a milky hue. Hundreds of thousands of orbed lights like the one I had just seen sailed through the sky. All electric neon blue, all pulsing as they shot out of the hands of the group of people below.

They made a line along the edge of the ice, sending the magical blue spears dancing and twisting into the night sky. A few bubbles floated past us; one was the size of my fingernail, another the size of a golf ball, the last was about the size of a quarter and floated only an inch away from the tip of my nose. My breath hitched as I shrank away from it, but Ethan's arms steadied me in place.

"It won't hurt you," he murmured. He reached a hand out and carefully cupped an orb with his palm, like he would a lightning bug, then opened it for my inspection. The little orb flickered then floated back into the sky, leaving his hand unscathed. "See? It's safe."

I peered back down at the glacier. One woman had long white hair and wore long green skirts. As she twirled, magic spiraled out of her hands and curled around her, almost as if it wanted to partake in the dance that she was doing. In that moment I was sure that she was the most graceful thing I had ever seen, dancing on a piece of glacial ice that reflected the light of her magic like it was made of diamonds.

Ethan leaned back in the grass. "They're resetting part of the Thunderhead border. They're scheduled reset part of the Hemlock border too."

Blue sparks reflected in his eyes. The hazel eye almost looked purple in the light. "The illusion?"

He nodded. "Magic fades, so we need their help regularly. Usually they're here all night, probably won't be done until morning."

"It's beautiful."

He leaned forward and brushed some hair behind my ear. "They usually don't want us too close, but we can go down once they move farther up the line."

"We can go down there?!"

The woman I was watching stopped moving. She stepped off her icy platform in unison with the other people along the line, then walked about a hundred yards and stopped. She stepped back onto her platform of ice and started to dance again as magic spurted out of her hands and tangoed with her.

Ethan pulled me to stand. Something pulsed across the pull as a few blue sparks floated by. My skin heated with a flush, but I was too entranced by the magic around me to care.

Ethan led us closer to the glacier, closer to where the woman had been standing. The floating orbs sparkled around us.

I reached to catch one that glowed over my palm. A laugh escaped my lips. A giggle at the little lantern I now held.

"I forgot what it's like." His voice was hushed, yet the deep undertone of it sent delicious prickles over my arms.

My gaze lifted to meet his. He was watching me like I was a sunrise he had been waiting through a long night to see.

"What?" I murmured back.

"Seeing magic for the first time," he answered.

Blue dots swooped around us, tickling my legs and finding their way into my hair. Something sparked and crackled between us—something that tasted too good to be simply the moon's will.

He threaded his hands through my hair, pulling me to him so his lips could melt against mine. Magic sizzled around us as something ignited over the pull; my hands wrapped around his neck while his lips moved over mine like water. Stubble teased my skin while heat pooled in my core. He tasted better than the smell of sugar around us and felt like a dream I wanted to never wake from.

Bowie was right; I should try for this relationship. Truly try. The second he kissed me I knew that if I didn't, I would regret it forever. Because the second he kissed me, I knew I wasn't afraid to want him anymore.

He pulled away and leaned his forehead against mine. His ragged breath fanned over my lips. "We should get you back."

My lips brushed over his. "No, we shouldn't."

His eyes lifted to mine, desire reflected in the fierce glow from my own. "No, we shouldn't," he echoed, before kissing me again.

CHAPTER SEVEN

The fire crackled and released little embers into the night air, like summer's form of snowflakes. Heat bathed my bare arms and legs, which had grown cold in the unusually cool night breeze. An arm was wrapped around me, pulling me closer to the body I had been subtly snuggling against.

Ethan had stayed a few days into the weekend for the bonfire that Remi had organized. He was laughing with Remi while Remi and Ali recounted some story about how they had tried and failed to kill a mountain goat. Andrea dug another beer out of the cooler and tossed it to me before taking her seat next to Remi. Wordlessly, Ethan took the beer from me, twisted the top off, then handed it back.

I bit my lip as a flush ran over me. Andrea cocked a brow as her golden eyes darted to him before bouncing back to me. A soft smile formed on her mouth.

"You look good together."

"Andrea—"

"Stop it and just enjoy it," she chastised me as she opened her beer. She chugged down almost half of it then smiled while she wiped a few drops off her lips. *"Just don't let Liam see a mark on you. He looked like he was going to fucking combust earlier."*

"I thought he was leaving for Talia's this weekend?"

Because of the incident that first night when Liam plowed into Ethan at the tree, Lander thought a change of scenery would be good for Liam. He was supposed to be moving to Talia's for the summer. Claire thought the sea breeze would do him well.

"Tomorrow. I told Claire I'd go and help move him in." Andrea leaned forward on her forearms. *"I imagine we'll be moving soon too?"*

I tried to ignore her knowing gaze. "Andrea—"

"It's the busy season, Charlotte," she chided me. *"Summer moves fast and there's a lot to do before winter. You know that. His pack needs him. Commuting like this won't be sustainable."*

"My pack needs me too," I countered.

"Thunderhead can spare a tracker. Hemlock can't spare their second."

The one thing I hated more than her being right was the smug look on her face when she knew that I was about to agree with her; and the sooner I went over to Hemlock, the sooner I could track in that forest.

A sly smile slowly slid onto her mouth. *"Char, did you know I used to babysit Ethan and Evan when they were pups?"*

Evan groaned. "It was like two times."

"It was definitely more than two times," Ethan corrected him.

"You used to have the biggest crush on me, Ev," Andrea teased with a gleaming smile.

Remi grinned. "Hard not to when you have a hot babysitter."

"Piss off," she grumbled. "Besides, Evan was the cutest little kid."

"Andrea." Evan gave her a pleading look.

I rolled my eyes at him. "Play nice, Evan, or no friendship bracelets for you."

"Why the fuck would I want one?" he griped.

I shrugged. "Jake has one."

"He does not," he countered.

"Ask him," I retorted, with a broad smile.

"Loves it too," Andrea added. "Dad has some, too, that Penny made him."

Evan crushed his beer can as he stood. "I'm going to the pits."

Ethan watched his brother for a moment before giving him a tight nod. My eyes hung on his retreating form. I had tried to make small talk with the guy, tried to be friendly, but it was like trying to cuddle a porcupine.

I leaned closer to Ethan. "Is he okay?" I whispered into his ear.

His thumb drew circles on my shoulder as his face dipped close to my ear, hot breath dancing delightfully across my skin. "He'll be fine. Do you want to walk around?"

"Okay," I replied, turning my face slightly so we were only a breath away.

"Get a room!" Remi groaned. "Seriously, man, you're stealing my bestie."

Ethan laughed as we stood. "I'm sure she can make you a friendship bracelet too."

THE PACK

He pulled me away from the group and down a winding path that led between a few other bonfires. We waved to David at one. He was roasting marshmallows with Lyle and Penny, who proceeded to set hers on fire.

We walked a few more paces until we found a smaller fire that had been abandoned and sat on a fallen log in front of it, both of us quiet as the crackle filled the clear night. All the stars were heavy in the sky, like they were close enough to be plucked.

Ethan watched the fire snap in front of us then looked at me with hope in his eyes. "It's not a hard run, from Hemlock to Thunderhead." Something tightened in my core while my beast started to pace. "The views aren't so bad either."

There were days when I still felt too young to be an adult making adult decisions. I found that happening more often than not in this world—but the reality was I was a grown woman, with a beautiful thing handed to me. I needed to not be afraid of it.

"I'll go," I said. He blinked, almost as if he wasn't sure if he'd heard me. "To your pack. I'll go with you."

His mouth parted slightly as his eyes pulsed a glow. "You're sure?"

"Yes," I affirmed. "Things with me—I know this hasn't been 'normal.' I just—I didn't—well, this . . ." I tried to explain. My hands waved around us. "I thought I had a good handle on this life, and in a blink, it feels so new to me—it is still so new to me. I want to try, and—"

His lips were on mine, stealing my words before they could keep rambling out of my mouth. "This is ours. We do things our way. Yeah?"

"Okay," I agreed. Out of the corner of my eye, I could spot a few people at another nearby bonfire eyeing us. I shook away their gazes. "I feel like everyone is watching."

Fingers tugged my chin back to face him. "Good," he said, before he kissed me again.

The bond between us pulsed as something sizzled through me. My mouth grew more needy while my hands grew more sure. When his hands found my waist, something sparked across the pull, burning like a fuse until it pulsed with a steady need.

"This thing is something," I panted.

"I know." He laughed, breathless as well.

I pushed my hair behind my ears. "Is it always like this?"

He cocked his head with a teasing smile. "Ready to be rid of me?" I rolled my eyes as he pulled me closer to him with a laugh. "Apparently, as it gets stronger we can feel each other's emotions."

"What? No way."

"Really."

He took my hands as the fire stuttered in front of us. My heart raced again, but for a different reason. Having so much access to someone's mind, to their feelings, was a thought that made my inner anxiety lick its teeth.

Shaking away my nerves, I said, "I still need to tell Levi."

He blew out a long breath. "We can do it together."

I shook my head. "No. I need to do it alone. I'll do it tomorrow." I bit my lip and peered back up at him. "Still nothing from Thomas?"

His eyes pulsed with something that seemed more animal than human. "No." My beast shook her fur out, attentive to the conversation. "He was happy to hear another tracker would potentially be coming. We need more."

"He can't ignore the stone."

"He can ignore a lot," he muttered under his breath, an admission I wasn't sure he wanted me to hear. "It would be better to have the approval of the pack lead, but Thomas doesn't trust Levi. A lot of wolves don't, Charlotte."

"Because he's out of his mind?" I drawled. I had heard the rumors since day one. Ethan nodded. "You know he's not."

Ethan leaned back and looked at the fire. He still didn't trust Levi, that much was clear. Part of me couldn't blame him; not after what I knew had happened.

"Not about this he's not. But we have to be careful. If word gets around that two packs are searching the forest for traces of rogues, it could set the region into a panic—bring attention we don't need yet from the Regional Council. We don't want to be the pack that cried wolf, so to speak."

"We can keep it quiet."

He arched a brow. "You're going to be trouble, aren't you?"

"Not intentionally." I tried to tease him, but I also did not want him to think I would go behind his back.

His lips curled into an easy smile. "Andrea cornered me already. There's a house you guys can move into."

"Of course she did." I laughed. "Thank you."

"For what?"

"Letting her come too."

He shook his head. "You don't need to thank me for that. She's always welcome back."

"Well, still . . ."

He squeezed one of my thighs. "Do I get brownie points for that, then?"

I laughed before he covered my mouth with his again. For

a moment I allowed myself to forget about the rogues and the problems ahead. I let myself relish how good his hand felt in mine and how sweet his lips tasted in the summer night.

Levi was on his porch early the next morning. My beast began to pace when I stopped at the bottom the stairs.

"We need to talk."

This house was my home. This pack was my home. I didn't like the idea of leaving, but I also knew what I wanted.

Wordlessly, Levi jogged down the stairs and waved me forward. Together we silently slipped into the woods and ran northwest until we were at Hemlock's border, where the evergreens grew thick and fresh spruce smelled like it was a perpetual holiday season. Levi led us along the pack line until we approached a small stream nestled between a set of boulders. The stream wound around the boulders then trailed off west into the woods that I knew would eventually turn into the Trapper's Forest.

The Trapper's Forest covered the majority of our border with Hemlock—it covered the whole border with Switchback, but this was one of the few places we could access the border where it didn't touch.

Levi shifted to his skin, and I shifted right after him. He walked to a tree with silver painted on the base and pulled some sweatpants from the burrow. He pulled the pants on then walked to the stream.

"This is where I met Eve," he said, nudging his chin toward the boulders. "She was right there. Standing in the sunlight like a goddamn angel."

My throat clenched as the beast in me crawled forward. "Levi, what is this?"

"I know." He turned to face me with tired silver eyes. "Lander told me it was inevitable. You going with Ethan. He's right."

"And what about the other night?" The night he lost it on me and said the complete opposite.

Levi kicked the dirt. "Not my best moment."

I licked my lips as the speech I had prepared in my mind suddenly felt like chalk in my mouth. "I like him!" I blurted.

His brows rose high.

I inhaled a deep breath. "I like him," I said more calmly, but the minute I opened my mouth again it all spilled out. "A lot. It fucking scares me but I think what scares me more is not trying. And I mean, this is supposed to be like the greatest gift from fate or whoever the fuck is in charge? Well, after everything, I think I am well owed my gift, but I like him and it's what I want."

His nostrils flared. "He already came to talk to me about it."

My brows furrowed. "And?"

He shrugged. "I've been having a lot of bad moments lately."

"Levi . . ." I grumbled.

"I know you can take care of yourself," he admitted to me. "But Eve could too. My son could too."

"Levi, I—"

He held a hand up. "David talked sense into me. Claire threatened me. Hate to upset her," he muttered. "You're right. It's a gift, a fucking good one. And you're right, you should give it a chance."

Relief washed over me. I nodded slowly as the wheels in my mind turned. "The rogues? What about them?"

"Bowie and David can handle it here," he stated. "But over there, you need to follow Ethan's lead."

"He said Thomas is thinking things over."

He scoffed. "Thinking things over my ass. It doesn't matter what Thomas does, Ethan will do the right thing." He dipped his head to look at me. "Do you know where we are?"

"Yes," I answered. "The water leads into their pack. The Trapper's Forest isn't far from here."

"That's right." He pointed. "That stream there? It goes for a little while then meets up with a footpath. The footpath runs along the stream into their pack. The stream comes from the mountains, runs all the way here. Used to be your favorite swimming hole," he added with a tired smile. "It fills into a pond on their side before continuing to our pack. From that pond to where we are standing, it's a two-hour run. It's the shortest route between the two packs."

I tugged my hair. "A footpath through the Trapper's Forest?"

"Eve and I made it," he explained. "Well, I mostly made it so we could sneak across safely until she could stay here for good."

My beast perked up. "Why are you telling me this?"

"That pack is not like ours, Charlotte. You're going to have to be careful. Watch your hide. There are plenty of them who still abide by the old ways. Plenty who would not mind if the old ways came back. I'm sure some of those wolves would love to see Derek and Elliot chased out of the state or worse."

"But the treaty—"

"Doesn't say you have to be nice to everyone or welcome them into your home with open arms. Our affiliation with vampires is a big reason there was always tension between the packs. When Ethan's father, Chris, took over, that changed, but those feelings are not far gone. Things aren't always fair." He leaned back against a tree and asked, "Do you remember how I told you about Ethan's grandfather, Emmet? His brother was killed by vampires. Dad always thought that's what set him on a bad path."

I didn't say anything. Quietly, I waited for him to continue.

"It was a ways before the treaty. Things were bad with interspecies relations. Hemlock wanted the vampires executed for what they did, and they wanted to be the ones to do it. But those vampires were members of a large coven stateside. Killing them would have made things worse, from what Dad recalled." He shoved his hands into his pockets. "It was decided that the vampires be extradited back to their coven to be punished. They got house arrest for fifty years."

"How old was his brother?"

"A boy," Levi breathed. "They killed him and some other kids after an altercation at a festival in town, according to a surviving witness. Left them for dead in a shipping yard. The kid who survived hid until a nearby pack could come help."

"That's horrible."

"It is," Levi agreed. "Emmet's desire for revenge got him heavily involved with the rebels—the Pure Seven as they called themselves, a nod to the seven original wolves created by the moon.

"There's bad blood on both sides. Peace has been a path forged in nothing but blood and can easily be undone by it too. There's plenty that some people can't move past. Some things cut deep enough to make canyons that last generations."

"Ethan's fair," I noted.

Levi hummed with a nod. "His father was too. He was a good man, one of my closest friends. And he was smart. Christopher

Everette was not stupid." He stopped and shook his head in disbelief. "None of us were and look what happened."

I took a step forward and cocked my head. "Why are you telling me this?"

"Because you need to know what you're getting yourself into."

Narrowing my gaze, I asked, "What are you not telling me?"

He watched me for a moment then murmured, "It's not safe."

"Why?" I stepped closer, something pulsing harder in me. "What is over there, Levi?"

"I don't know." I could see that much and more in his eyes. "All I know is she died there. Lucas died there. Rogues come in, desecrate the place, then what? No one takes over? Nothing is stolen? The place wasn't pillaged, not like it would have been if that was the point." He closed his mouth. It was the most that I had ever heard him talk about his opinion on what happened. I wasn't sure whether to keep prodding or let it sit. "I don't know what you'll find there. Knowing you, it will be what I couldn't."

"I don't like this."

"I don't either," he agreed. "But you know how to take care of yourself now. The best I can do is prepare you as much as I can for what's to come. Now, you'll always have a safe way home."

I felt my eyes tear, then looked at the stream to keep from looking at Levi. "And you trust me to go with him?"

I heard him push off the tree. "I trust you to handle yourself." I turned to face him, and he added, "And I trust him to take care of you."

CHAPTER EIGHT

It smelled weird.

That was the first thing I noticed when Andrea and I arrived at the small cottage tucked into the steep, rocky hills that sloped up toward the silver mountains. The smell of dozens of wolves scattered along the winding cobblestone path in front of the house. It mixed in a dizzying dance with the flowers planted in the front flowerbeds.

It had only been a week since Levi showed me the footpath in the forest, and the days after had moved in a blur while Andrea and I scrambled to pack. But somehow, amid the chaos, Ethan had found time to prep the house for our arrival. He stocked it with some essentials: toilet paper, coffee, eggs, milk, bread, cheese, a frozen pizza, and a few bottles of wine. He'd even left a note on a bottle of wine that read *Drinks later?*

God, he was so perfect, and I was such a mess. What would he do when he peeled the layers back to see the ugly, the pain, the broken that would never dissipate? I shuddered to think of it but immediately scolded myself for it.

My past was gone. I didn't need Ethan to see the rotten bones of it.

I didn't want him to.

Standing in my new room, painted a soft green, I pulled a shirt out of my bag and pressed it to my nose. It still smelled like Derek—I had stolen it from him, but before I left, he'd told me to keep it. Laid across my bed was my bearskin blanket, made from the bear I had killed on the Hunt, and which still smelled of Levi.

My eyes filled with tears. This was my idea. My decision. But all of the sudden I felt so very desperate to see home again.

"Hey, Char!" I heard Andrea call from the kitchen. "Can you come here for a sec?"

"Coming!"

I brushed my eyes then pulled the rest of my shirts out of my suitcase. I set them aside to put away later, then realized there was something in the bottom—Jake's map of the part of the Trapper's Forest on Thunderhead Pack land, which he'd gotten from Billy for us to study for the Hunt. The one that had sat next to a Bloodstone on Levi's kitchen table only a few weeks ago.

I traced the drawings of cats that noted mountain lion territory in the eastern corner. I always thought they looked like strange cows.

My brow furrowed. I had no idea why Levi would pack it for me other than to maybe return it to Billy? But something in me told me that wasn't the case. The same gut feeling drove me to fold it up so I could shove it to the back of my underwear drawer.

"Char?!"

"Be right there!"

I jogged into our small kitchen, which sported a retro gas-burning stove juxtaposed with a microwave that had more buttons than a typewriter. Andrea was standing on a wooden chair, struggling to hang curtains over the large window in the breakfast nook. Quickly, I pulled another chair from the small, round table, and jumped up to help her.

"Rod in the hook," she ordered.

"Sounds kinky," I teased.

She snorted. Together, we secured the rod in its fastenings. I jumped down from my chair and pulled the curtains open; what greeted me was the sight of people staring back at me from the footpath. They were crowded together, whispering until they saw that I'd spotted them. Then they were silent in what I assumed was a conversation over a link.

Andrea beat her fist on the window and smiled at them with her fangs showing. They scattered about as fast as I could blink.

I put a hand on my hip. "We're never going to make friends this way."

"We have enough friends." She snickered before offering me a reassuring smile. "You're new—we're new. They're curious. It will wear off."

I sank into the chair. The wetness in my eyes had returned. "Right."

"You still good for dinner at Dad's before the full tonight?"

I nodded. Billy lived a few minutes up the footpath from us. While Andrea wasn't thrilled about having him practically in our backyard, he did have a grill.

"Good." She smiled. "He should be here soon to help with the rest of the boxes. I'm surprised he wasn't here when we showed up."

I snorted. "I'm sure you're going to be getting a lot of him."

"Him and Jake," she added with an eye-roll.

Kitty-corner across the way was a two-story log house where Ethan used to live with Evan and their sister, Evangeline. But as of recently, he'd moved to a house farther up the hills and deeper in the woods. Jake opted to move out of Billy's and take his place.

I tried not to assume it had anything to do with me, because we'd agreed to take things one day at a time. And I needed one day at time right now.

The skin on the back of my neck twitched as something pulsed across the bond like a fairy dancing along the surface of a pond. "Ethan's almost here."

"This mate-bond shit is starting to freak me out," she muttered.

"Makes two of us," I said on the edge of a long breath.

He waved to us through the window on his way to the door. I opened it before he could knock. His hair was damp from a shower, and the scent of his aftershave wrapped around me and made my mouth water. Heat slowly simmered in me before it turned to something molten when he greeted me with a quick kiss.

I had to get a hold of myself. I couldn't lose myself in this thing—this incessant lust.

"Ready to visit the pack house? I want to get you officially checked in," he explained.

I rocked back on my heels. "Ah, all the paperwork."

"Not that much," he replied. "We can do a tour after."

"With or without clothing?" Andrea called from behind me.

THE PACK

I shot her a glare over my shoulder. She shrugged with a devious smile as she drove a spoon into a jar of peanut butter.

"Right," I muttered. I snatched my old Thunderhead sweatshirt and pulled it on over my shifters. "We should get a move on it."

We fell in step together along the footpath. We hadn't even made it a few yards when the door to Evan's house flew open. A young woman with a cape of fiery red hair that matched the angry red on her cheeks charged forward. She stopped in front of Ethan and crossed her arms over her petite frame, her green eyes narrowed to slits. "Did we forget something?"

Ethan watched her a moment then tilted his head before asking, "Did you?" He waited a beat then said, "Charlotte, this is my sister, Evangeline."

I lifted my hand in a small wave. "It's nice to meet you."

"Hi," she griped, before stomping her foot. "Remi said that someone didn't put my name on the list for the Hunt next year. The list fills up fast!" Bowie wouldn't have more than six groups at a time in the forest for safety reasons.

Ethan kept his face neutral. "Evangeline, this isn't really the time."

"Oh really?! And when will you have the time, My Second?" she spat.

I felt my beast cock her head, her own mouth slightly dropping in shock.

Ethan lowered his head a hair. "We'll talk later."

She rolled her eyes. "I'm eighteen. I can make my own decisions. Besides, she got to go," she snipped.

The slam of the door reverberated across the lawn and through the cloud of dirt she had created when she stormed away. I took his hand and pulled him forward. The tension was not something I cared to marinate in any longer.

Ethan was quiet for a few moments before saying, "I'm sorry."

"That's not your fault." His sister was her own person. Responsible for her own behavior.

He rubbed the back of his neck. "I should have talked to you about it more," he admitted.

"About what?"

"Their feelings for Levi make things difficult."

"And that extends to me?"

"It shouldn't," he answered, dodging the real answer that in my gut I knew to be true, but I also had the feeling that now wasn't the time to keep digging.

Instead, I let myself fall into easy conversation with him while we made the long walk to the pack house. Ethan more than enjoyed his role as my tour guide, especially once the pack house came into view.

It was built lodge-style among the boulders and trees, as if it had grown from the mountains. As we approached I could feel a wind sweep past my cheeks. Ethan pulled me around the side of the building so I could see over the cliff that it was sitting on top of; the boulders deep in the ground kept the foundation stable on the rocky ledge that led to a small valley below. My eyes found a switch trail leading from the house before hair-pining back and forth down the cliff to picturesque green pastures, where a red barn was nestled among the lush grass.

"This is beautiful," I told him.

"It's hard to beat," he agreed, before he tugged me back to the front of the building.

Inside, natural light flowed through the abundance of

windows, as if the entire space was open to the outside. Ethan led me up a set of stairs and down a hall. We stopped at a door; he knocked a few times before opening it and ushering me into a large office.

A woman with long blond hair jumped from her chair in front of a large round window and rushed to us. Her delicate smile highlighted her sharp cheekbones.

"You made it," she said with a voice that reminded me of a songbird. Her hair swayed around her waist as her crystal-blue eyes assessed me. "Ethan, the moon has blessed you, she's so gorgeous."

"Hello," I greeted her with a tiny smile.

"Miranda, introduce yourself to the poor girl," a voice called from behind her. It was strained, gravelly, as if the speaker's throat was bone-dry.

"Oh, dear moon, look at me getting carried away. I'm Miranda. Thomas's mate." She pulled me into a brisk hug. "I'm so glad you're here."

"Charlotte, clearly," I replied, giving a small laugh as she stepped aside.

Ethan pulled me back to his side as a man approached. It took everything I had in me to not look away. To not gape.

I had heard rumors about Thomas. About how he was tortured during the attack. How he barely survived. How everyone thought he wouldn't be able to shift again.

I thought they were ghost stories, but the poor man in front of me had lived through real horrors. Angry burn scars covered the left side of his face and chewed through his skin along his smile line, leaving gaps, windows to his teeth. It looked as if fire had licked down the side of his neck all the way to his left forearm, intertwining with deep scars that he also sported on his right arm.

He reached forward with his right hand to shake mine. It was missing two fingers—his pointer and middle finger—but I didn't dare pull away from his grip when my hand was in his.

"The skin isn't growing back any time soon, girlie."

"Oh, I—"

"Thomas!" Miranda chastised him, while Ethan stood with a bored expression.

Thomas waved me off with a chuckle. "What? Miranda says I make up for being unbearably hideous with my obvious charm."

"Debatable," Miranda hummed.

Thomas laughed and scratched the back of his neck. He had on a bracelet of black matte beads and one of woven leather with a pearly luminescent stone. I wanted to look away from it, but I could not stop staring. My beast cocked her head while we focused in on what sounded like humming? It couldn't be humming—it had to be—

"So, Charlotte." Thomas's voice yanked me from my trance. "We got most of your paperwork filled out, just need you to sign a few things. Also, I would love to hear from you about that little stone you and Ethan found."

"I already reported what she said," Ethan evenly stated.

Thomas nodded, amused. "Yes, but she's right here, and there's nothing like a firsthand account, is there?"

Before Ethan could answer I offered Thomas a polite smile. "I don't mind. If you want, we can talk while I sign the paperwork?"

Thomas's mouth pulled into a slow smile like a skeletal accordion. "A multitasker. I love it." He waved me forward to his desk. "Take a seat."

THE PACK

I heard the door click shut. Miranda gestured us forward like she was showing us to our table at brunch. Ethan walked ahead and pulled a chair out for me. I sat while Thomas set a manila folder on the table.

Ethan stood next to my chair. His hand slid across the back and planted safely on my shoulder. "We were going to do a tour as well today."

Thomas flipped open the folder and slid a pack of papers over to me before dropping a pen in the middle of them. "Good day for it," he stated, pointing to a thick black line at the bottom of the page. "Just need your signature on the bottom of the page—normal stuff here. Transfer agreement that we'll send to the Regional Council, and then I have some copies of your identification and passport that I need you to initial—"

"What's in the agreement?"

Thomas paused, considering me.

I shrugged innocently. "When I was a human I worked for lawyers. Always good to read once and then over again."

He tapped his finger on the paper. With each tap it felt like he was losing patience over questions I hadn't even asked. "Very standard. All wolves moving from other packs sign one. Thunderhead has the same boilerplate."

Ethan's hand squeezed my shoulder. "I put it all together for you," he assured me. *"You're not signing your soul away."*

"Yes, well, I'd like to make sure of that myself," I answered, a little tighter than I'd intended.

I knew better than to just sign things. To agree to things. To smile while you handed the keys to your own cage over with each smooth stroke.

I picked the pages up and scanned them. Thomas lifted a

brow. Like he was an amused cat watching a mouse play in a trap he had set. "Like I said, standard. Says you're on a ninety-day probation period that will be waived once your mate marks you. A mark is your ticket into the pack, which I assume will be the case here?"

My anxiety flared. I forced a smile and finished reading. It was a lot of jargon, but it didn't make me feel as though I was signing my unborn firstborn child away.

"Don't assume too much," I jested, then laughed tightly to cover the strain in my voice. Swallowing, I picked up the pen. "You guys really need to make this electronic."

Thomas barked a laugh that would have made me jump in my seat if Ethan's hand hadn't been on my shoulder. Miranda swept around his desk and sat on the arm of Thomas's chair with a warm smile.

"I have been telling him that for years. Men," she said, like it was a joke I was in on.

"Right..."

I slid forward in my seat and began to sign. My pen scraping against the paper was the only sound that slithered around us.

Miranda propped her chin up on her first. "So, Charlotte, Ethan said you found the stone in an open area? On the border?"

I hummed in confirmation. "That's right. About ten minutes directly west of an area we had staked out on our land."

"What gave it away?" she asked. Thomas leaned back in his seat and crossed his arms over his chest.

My pen stilled a moment. "The blood magic. It was faint but I could smell it."

Thomas tilted his head to the side and inspected me with a gaze that made my skin shiver. "What do you mean?"

Ethan stood like a soldier at my side while his thumb rubbed circles on my shoulder.

Thomas was still staring at me. "Wasn't there blood magic at that rogue patch Ethan told us about? How did you not confuse it?"

"Confuse it?" I said with a forced sweetness in my voice that I had not had to use in a long time—another life ago, one that I'd thought I could leave behind. But in this moment I was grateful for the muscle memory of those survival instincts.

I signed the last page and pushed the folder back to him. "The scent, it was boxed in at Thunderhead, like something was containing it, but at the edge of the border it was almost like feeling a few raindrops before a storm. Finding the first few drops is the hardest because unlike water, smell isn't always as condensed, but it was there. Once I locked onto it, it was easier to find."

Miranda's brows were high on her forehead. She clasped her hands in excitement. "Thomas, we do need more trackers and she'll be perfect!"

He grunted in an agreement before he swiped a hand over his rigid jaw. "And the stone? Anything else around it?"

I shook my head and answered honestly. "No, but to be fair, I didn't have a chance to look."

"David is sure it's a Bloodstone," Ethan asserted. "If that's what we have—"

"It would cause a fucking panic," Thomas almost snarled. "David," he spat. "He has no idea—no one does until the witches confirm it."

Ethan was quiet. His fingers continued their movement on my shoulders, but his tender caresses did little to hide the tension growing in the room.

"It's too bad they couldn't look at it when they were in the area, resetting the borders."

Thomas drummed his fingers on the table. "Our borders were and should be a top priority. It would be inefficient to have deterred them."

"We could request an audience with the witches?" Ethan offered carefully.

Thomas leaned forward and rested his elbows on his desk. "We can wait for a consultation at the Regional Council meeting. Considering that we have not had anything threaten our borders, the item isn't pressing."

I tried not to move. Tried to not show any emotion. Tried to stay neutral, because in times of potential combustion neutral kept you safe—kept the bomb from exploding.

But Ethan didn't have my instincts, and pressed, "If it is a Bloodstone, we'll feel like we've lost time because we haven't looked—"

"We will have no problem making up whatever time we need," Thomas countered tightly. "Especially now that we have a new, talented tracker."

Something shot over the bond between Ethan and me—something hot that coiled like a cobra ready to strike. I bit down on my lip and tried to take my mind off the feeling reverberating through me as the realization sunk in—I could feel his emotions, although now was not the ideal time to realize it.

"Who could easily help a small team start to comb through the woods," Ethan stated, in a tone that was hot enough to ignite the fuse Thomas had laid out for him.

But nothing ignited. I was braced for an explosion of hateful words in a tone that would make the receiver feel as if it was

THE PACK

all their fault. Guilt was like gunpowder to those who laid such traps, but this ploy was something entirely different.

Thomas leaned forward with his palms on the table. "We will not waste pack resources on a warrantless hunt. We will not create a panic among our people—among this region. If those stones have truly not been seen for hundreds of years, what makes us think that all of the sudden our pack is the 'chosen' place for this one?" He paused to scoff. "For all we know this is an elaborate prank."

Ethan did not move while Thomas spoke. His beast did not even rise to the occasion. His thumb kept drawing circles on my shoulder while his face remained even.

But after Thomas spoke, Ethan took a step forward, and it was then that I felt a whisper of a hum pulse off him.

"For an elaborate prank, it sure does reek of fucking blood magic."

"Goddammit Ethan!" Thomas snapped. He stood to his full height. "This pack has been through enough! You of all people should know that. Unless we have a pending threat, which we don't, we need to focus on the council meeting and the growing season ahead of us."

Before Ethan could respond, Miranda stood from her seat. "Thomas," she cooed gently.

Thomas's shoulders slightly deflated before he sat back in his chair. He turned his gaze to me. "I think it's time for your tour. You can go."

Miranda gave Ethan's arm a gentle squeeze. "I would love to take her."

I darted my eyes to Ethan.

"I need to go for a run," he admitted to me.

Standing, I forced a smile when I turned to Miranda. "It's kind of you to offer."

She clapped her hands before extending one to me. I took it and let her pull me outside and into the hall. Ethan's heavy footsteps followed us, stopping only when he closed the office door.

He brushed his lips against my cheek. "I'll see you at home," he told me out loud before he asked, *"Are you sure you want to go?"*

"Are you?" I countered.

"Don't let her yap your ear off," he warned before he disappeared down the stairs, completely avoiding the question.

Miranda took my arm. "You have to forgive Thomas," she softly pleaded. "He cares so much for this pack—they both do. It's coming from a good place, although it's not a good impression for you, which is not acceptable. I'll speak to him, of course."

I opened my mouth and closed it again because I wasn't sure what to say. I wasn't even sure what the fuck just happened in that office.

"Passionate people working together are eventually going to butt heads—men," she groaned. "Practically like children. Let's get out of here and get some fresh air. Lots of ground to cover."

"Sure," was all I could reply.

Levi was right: I was going to have watch my hide here—and my tongue.

CHAPTER NINE

Miranda took me through the kitchen and to a larger hall with long wooden tables that had strong legs made like tree trunks. "Dining area," she said before she turned to me with an expression, like she was exhausted by whatever it was she was about to say. "I'm sorry again about earlier—"

I waved her off. "We're not always our best selves all the time—"

"I couldn't say it better," she answered with a relieved exhale. "I know his appearance can be jarring—"

"Miranda, it's not his fault."

"It still startles me, to be honest," she explained with a tight smile. "He survived. I thought I'd lost him. He locked our daughter and me in our cellar and..." Her eyes trailed to a distant place.

"You don't have to go into it," I assured her.

"You're kind," she observed breathily, as if this surprised her. "Thank you."

She pushed her long hair behind her ears, shaking a pair of large porcelain-colored oval earrings. My eyes snagged on them a moment while I gathered my words.

I wasn't sure what it was about the gems. There was a strange aura coming from them, almost a vibration that sounded almost like something was droning off them ...

I wasn't a big jewelry girl, but I couldn't stop looking at them.

"They're so pretty," I blurted. "Your earrings."

Her hands flew to them as her eyes grew pleased with the compliment. "Oh, you're sweet! Thomas got them for me as an anniversary present. They're magicked so I can shift with them on."

"Really?"

"Mm-hmm," she hummed before adding with a wink, "Come on, now."

She walked me outside the pack house and down a path on the side of the mountain. She was careful to show me where certain areas of the hairpin-curled trail would get slick during ice and rain and was eager to introduce me to the handful of wolves we passed along the way down.

As we neared the edge of the tree line, I could smell sheep in the distance. Miranda jogged a few paces ahead of me then turned like she was a museum tour guide. "You're going to die once we get to the valley. It's where we keep the sheep. Up on top of the ridge, there's not a lot of good areas for them to graze and the terrain can be quite tricky. It's safer and easier for us to herd them down here."

THE PACK

"Just sheep?" I asked.

"And goats too," she replied. "God, they're such pesky things sometimes, but our pack is known for our wool, dairy, and meat. We're some of the top producers in the area," she added with a proud smile. "Our trackers are important to the flock. They help keep the animals safe, herd them to new pastures, track down lost ones, the whole song and dance."

"Who's in charge of the livestock?"

"Thomas. I swear that man loves those damn animals more than me sometimes. There've been days he's tried to let them in the house!"

I laughed alongside her.

"Now, come look at this!" She took my hand and pulled me down the trail a few yards, to where it ended next to soft grass. She pointed up.

My gaze followed her hand to see the pack house resting proudly at the top of the cliff. "Wow," I breathed.

My beast shook her head. She was already dreading the climb back up.

"I know, it's just so gorgeous. We love to show it off." Miranda beamed then waved for me to follow her.

We passed a herd of sheep with a few wolves lazily on guard lying in the sun on the grass, and we neared a small barnlike structure painted a sun-bleached red.

As we approached, a younger woman walked out of the barn. Her long blond hair swayed behind her and icy blue eyes latched onto me. Her steps were sure as she came straight at us. Miranda waved. "Darling, say hello to Charlotte—Charlotte, this is my daughter, Amber."

"It's nice to meet you," I said.

Amber smiled at me, tight, like a rubber band being pulled past its limit. "Hope your move went well."

"It was fine, thanks."

Amber turned her blank gaze to Miranda. "I'm going to Piper's for dinner. I won't be home later."

"Give her a squeeze from me," Miranda replied before Amber strode off. Miranda watched Amber's form fade into the tree line. "Always on the go, that one," Miranda added with a light laugh that did little to cover the tension in her voice. "First they crawl, then they walk, then you're constantly trying to keep track of them."

She paused and turned to me with a crisp smile. "I'll tell her to stop by later. You two can have some girl time."

My beast cocked her head in the back of my mind. Swallowing, I nodded politely back to her.

"There she is!" Billy's voice was the lifesaver I hadn't realized I needed.

Andrea was her father's daughter. His tall stature always reminded me of an old redwood tree; his short chestnut hair was cut in a military style and tattoos covered his forearms, but his golden eyes were always warm and welcoming, like a cup of hot chocolate.

His forest-green T-shirt had HEMLOCK GUARD written on the front in bold lettering that stretched across his broad chest as he opened his arms for me. My feet moved on their own, carrying me into a bear hug, in which he quickly swung me around.

"My second-favorite girl." He laughed as he sat me down.

"Billy!" Miranda shook her finger at him. "And what does that make me?"

He winked at Miranda. "Let's not make this awkward." She

THE PACK

laughed while Billy guided me forward. "I see Penny made you a new bracelet?"

I laughed and held up my wrist next to his. The bracelet Penny had made me almost matched the one on his wrist that also looked new. Mine had all-black beads and a blue stone in the middle, while he had a single pearly one that glistened in the light.

I shook the beads on my wrist. "She made it for me as a going-away present."

"That's adorable," Miranda cooed.

Billy hummed in agreement. "Thought I lost this one, glad I found it." His hand squeezed my shoulder. "Sorry I wasn't there earlier, kiddo, had to help some guards clean up one of our watchtowers on the line—got washed out with the rains we had." He paused and looked at Miranda. "It's too close to the creek. I knew we should have put the new one farther down."

She shrugged. "We'll just rebuild. That's what we do."

"I can help you find another spot?" I offered.

Billy laughed and pulled me back to his side. "What do you mean *can*? You *are* helping me find another spot," he added with a warm smile. "Glad to have another tracker here. Although I am going to need to borrow Amber again tomorrow afternoon. She's always good at putting the rotations together for me, and we need to organize our hunts."

"Do you not have a Head Tracker?" Maybe a dumb question, but I'd always assumed they did.

Billy shook his head with a tired smile. "No one stepped up after Cash died in the attack, and the group we have now is talented but young. I'm good at herding cats, Charlotte. You know that." He chuckled.

He stepped around me and gestured to the structure in front of us. "And this is one of my pride and joys."

My brows furrowed. "The barn?"

His laughter followed us all the way inside. There was feed and supplies for livestock, along with what looked like every tool known to man. There was an office in a small room that looked like it had more papers stacked on the desk than office space.

Andrea had warned me he was a pack rat, but, Jesus, this was bad.

"You ever thought about cleaning this?"

He crossed his arms over his chest. "Now, Charlotte, I'm glad you volunteered."

"Wow, already?"

He grinned. "There's another room by the office." He pointed to a door propped open by a cinder block. "All the trackers meet there every morning before setting out for their assignment—unless we're on a hunt, of course. I know you just got here, but I would love to ramp you up quick. Normally we'd take it slow, but you did the Hunt. I know you know your stuff. We're going to need help over the summer, especially with the council meeting coming up."

"Oh, dear moon," Miranda agreed. "We really are."

"Honestly, I've been itching to get out and explore, so that sounds great."

"Atta girl." Billy beamed. "How does tomorrow morning sound?"

"Perfect," I chirped.

He nodded. "Stop by the pack house before. We always have breakfast for folks working the early shifts, and tomorrow is your lucky day, because I'm cooking."

THE PACK

I felt my stomach rumble at the thought. The man was an amazing cook. I could never admit it to Derek, who usually held all my culinary affection, but Billy made these cheesy potatoes once that I could have bathed in.

"You're going to make me fat," I teased.

He snorted. "And I'm also going to have you run it off. I've got to get going, though. We need to move that back-field herd with the creek washed out," he explained to Miranda before giving me a brisk hug. "See you tonight, kiddo."

Miranda and I walked together along the crunchy gravel path, the sounds of the lambs murmuring in the distance.

"I'm glad you're here," she told me, like she was admitting a big secret. "I need another hand. I know you're still settling in, but we have that council meeting at the end of summer and it's going to take all of us."

"It's a regional meeting of pack leads? Levi explained a little before I left."

"That's right," she replied with a nod. "Two days. There's the meeting, then a hunt and party the first night. It's a lot to plan and prep for, and of course I have Amber and Evangeline, but they are both so young and distracted by everything." She pushed some hair behind her ears. "It's a lot to ask—"

"I don't mind," I told her, knowing that I wasn't in a position to say no, although in my gut, I knew I would probably regret saying yes. "When is it again?"

"In two months." Which wasn't a lot of time at all. It would fly by.

"Well, like I said. I don't mind."

She gave my arm a gentle squeeze. "Thank the moon. So happy you're here. You'll run with us tonight?"

"Can I? I'm not pack."

"I talked to Thomas earlier and asked if you could come with us tonight."

"You didn't have to—"

"No, I wanted to. We're excited to have you and, well, you'll be one of us soon. It's important to me that you feel welcome and have the chance to meet everyone," she replied.

"That's kind," I told her.

She nudged my shoulder with hers. "I think you and I are going to get along just fine, Charlotte."

CHAPTER TEN

"Charlotte, are you not hungry?"

Billy eyed my plate suspiciously. I had already stuffed myself with his potatoes earlier, but with the full moon coming, I felt anxious. I needed to run. My beast had been dying to be let loose since we got here, and I needed to let her before she drove us both nuts.

"I'm so full—it was amazing."

Jake forked a piece of steak off my plate. "I'll help you out."

Andrea shook her head at him. "Aren't you a good friend?"

Jake snorted. "Obviously."

Billy leaned back in his seat, the frame creaking from his size. "You love my steaks."

"I know, but I loved those potatoes too much," I answered. His lips curled into a warm smile.

I took my plate and Andrea's empty one to the sink and washed them off. My beast pawed at my mind as goose bumps broke out over my skin—the bond pulsed to life.

"Looks like you have a gentleman caller," Billy announced, with a nod to the door.

When I opened the door, I let myself have two seconds to be selfish. To let the scent of him wrap around me.

"I don't think I'm ever going to be able to sneak up on you, am I?" he asked as something dangerously delicious danced in his eyes.

I shook my head slowly. "Probably not."

"Guess I'll have to figure out another way to surprise you then, sunshine," he replied, his voice carrying a rasp in it that suddenly made the sweatshirt I had been wearing all day seem too thin. He tucked a piece of hair behind my ear and leaned closer, close enough I could feel his breath dance across my lips. "Sorry I missed dinner. I was on the border."

"Is everything—"

"It's fine," he quickly answered. "It's not that."

"Stop making out!" Jake called from inside the house.

Ethan leaned away from me and nudged his chin to Billy. "Do you mind if I kidnap her?"

"Typically, I would," Billy said with a tone that I felt would later tell me that I had a curfew. "But perhaps tonight we can make an exception. Everything okay?"

Ethan nodded. "A few traps spooked the guards. Nothing more."

"That's a relief," Billy answered. "We'll be along shortly. Jake has to finish the dishes."

Jake just shrugged in return. "I fucking love dishes. Jokes on you, assholes."

THE PACK

Ethan chuckled and pulled me with him out of the house. We walked down the footpath that was lit by old metal lanterns hanging on hooks nailed into the trees. Anticipation seemed to buzz through the air as people moseyed out of their homes and toward the pack house in excitement.

"It really is beautiful here," I said.

Ethan smiled as the candlelight hugged his face and curled over his strong jawline. *"I'm sorry about earlier. Thomas can be . . . trying."*

"Is he always like that?"

Ethan shrugged. *"Depends on the day."*

With people like Thomas, it did depend. I remembered too well how it felt to dance on eggshells; I prayed that this wasn't the case here.

"You understand what it means, because he said no to my request for a search party?" His eyes cut to me quickly with a seriousness that made my beast bristle her fur. *"Our pack lead has said no, unless the witches give him a reason at the council meeting."*

Thomas wasn't *my* pack lead, but I didn't want to stir anything up. Still, the gravity of Ethan's words weighed on me. I knew what I had the urge to do—I wanted to go into that forest—but I also knew in my gut I would feel wrong if I was the one to put Ethan in a precarious position or bring trouble to him.

"It's your call." I found myself echoing Levi's words.

"We do need your nose." He relented. *"But we'll need to fly under the radar, for now at least."*

"All right, then," I agreed.

His lips pressed to the back of my hand. *"I'm sorry I didn't get to show you around."*

"Miranda was fine. It was a nice walk," I answered.

"I had more in mind than a walk..."

A blush bloomed across my cheeks as something crackled across the pull between us. I kept my eyes focused on the path ahead—and only the path ahead.

"Where will we run? Down to the valley?"

"No," he answered, as we approached the group of people surrounding the pack house. "We just moved the animals out there to open pastures, and no one has the energy to herd them back tonight. We'll probably stay along the mountain. I'll show you."

"Oh, you will?" I found myself teasing back.

He arched a brow at me. "Planning to run up a tree again?"

I shrugged. "There's a lot of really nice trees here."

Ethan tipped his head back and laughed. He pulled me closer to his side and I was glad, because plenty of eyes were on us as we entered the crowd.

A tall man strode toward us with a smile. His blond hair was tied up in a small bun that bounced with every step he took. Ethan lifted a hand to him. "You're not worn out from earlier?"

The tall man ran a hand over his long face. "Shit, man, I swear someone put a jet engine on some of those sheep."

Ethan laughed with him then turned to me. "Char, this is Trey, our—"

"Unofficial sheep recovery expert." Trey laughed.

Smiling, I said, "It's nice to meet you."

"Likewise," he answered. "My mate, Sam, is dying to meet you. I'm sure she'll find you and drag you to the house eventually."

Ethan snorted a laugh. "She is good at that," he agreed before adding, "Sam is our pack doctor."

"Lucky you," I told Trey.

THE PACK

"I'm definitely batting well over my average. But I better find her before we all take off. I'm sure I'll see you around, Charlotte!"

Trey darted off back to the pack house. Ethan squeezed my hand. "He and Sam are good people. She's a firecracker, but a good wolf."

Something started to pulse in me, slowly humming to life. My eyes rose to the sky to look for the thing that I knew would be there soon enough—calling me.

Scanning the crowd, I spotted Evangeline with Amber. I raised my hand to wave at Evangeline, but she quickly avoided my gaze. Amber looked over her shoulder, her blond hair flowing behind her like silk. Her crystal eyes landed on me, holding my gaze for a second before they ripped away.

"Hey!" A pair of hands latched around my waist and squeezed.

I squealed with a jump then turned to see Andrea laughing behind me.

"I hate you!" I laughed.

She leaned an arm on my shoulder. Evan came up next to us, eyes cautiously trailing to Andrea. She shook her head at him before pursing her full lips. "Evan, you going to let me chase you tonight?"

Evan's cheeks colored. Andrea laughed under her breath as he crossed his arms over his chest.

"Be nice," I chided her. "Where's Jake?"

"Coming, he was finishing my steak," she answered.

Evan brushed his hands through his copper locks as he came to stand next to me. "Hey."

"Hi," I replied. "Good day?"

"Best day." He snorted before he quickly shut his mouth.

He tipped his head down before lifting it slightly to look at me. "Move go okay?"

"Yeah. Ethan said you helped get the house ready?" He only gave me a slight nod in confirmation. "You didn't have to do that, but thank you. Andrea and I are learning to be domestic. We would have lived in boxes for weeks."

Evan snorted a small laugh that seemed to surprise even him.

"Feral, that's what we are, Char. Feral," Andrea teased.

Evan searched the crowd and quickly found Evangeline. He went silent, eyes to the ground before they cut to Ethan, who had a distant look on his face.

"We should get moving," Evan announced, his voice almost cold. His eyes started to pulse a glow as the moon started to peek through the clouds. The moon blood in his veins pulsed off him, a wave moving like a pendulum swinging back and forth. "Where are you two going?"

I closed my eyes as her rays shone down. The beast in me was pawing hard, ready to run. The hum in me pulsed a little more as adrenaline teased my tongue.

"There's that meadow on the other side of the Black Rock. You want to come with us?" Ethan asked.

When I opened my eyes the moon was coming out of the clouds. The hair on the back of my neck stood. My beast needed to run. And run soon.

"Yeah." Evan grunted as people around us started to take off. He nudged his chin at Andrea. "You?"

"You all are stuck with me," she said, her golden eyes glowing like sunbeams cutting through the darkness. "Lead the way, Ethan."

THE PACK

Ethan tugged me forward, turning to me as something crackled off him, a sizzle that made the bond between us feel like electricity running down a copper wire. My breath caught, and the beast in me howled. His eyes were glowing, the golden specks in the hazel-colored eye starting to look closer to fire against the specks of blue.

"Follow me," he said, and I did.

Nothing felt as good as being in the moonlight, in the night, chasing a feeling—a high that we knew would disappear when the moon did. Nothing felt as good as running next to him. My beast kept chasing the little puddles of moonlight cascading between the tree limbs. Andrea and I took turns nipping at Ethan's legs. He playfully nipped back but my beast was quick; she darted out of the way then began to really run, our stride stretching out to chase the moon.

My beast and I were curling around a bend in the forest trail when cool air combed over our fur. A hush set in. I realized then that we had been running aimlessly—we hadn't been following Ethan. We were practically drunk on the moonlight.

I realized then, that we were alone.

It was just me and my beast in the dark. In the woods. In the forest that I knew very well was not safe.

We had somehow found our way to the Trapper's Forest. A place that was absolutely forbidden at Hemlock.

My beast blew out a breath as little red eyes blinked open in the dark. Something cold blew through the trees, tickling my paws as if it was toying with me. Darkness closed in around us. The moonlight felt like it was vanishing. There was another breeze, another gentle breath of air that murmured, "Charlotte."

I bolted.

I had no idea where I was going, but I knew it was the hell out of there. But it didn't matter how fast I ran, the darkness felt like it was nipping at my heels. I ran and ran, chasing the rare beams of moonlight cutting through the thick trees like streetlights leading me home.

But the moonlight didn't lead me back to my cottage or the pack house.

It led me to a great white tree.

A white tree with thick white branches and snow-white leaves. A white tree that was completely stained with bloody palm prints all the way from the base to the top of the trunk.

I was so stunned by it that I didn't see the rocks ahead of me. My feet caught and lost traction. Falling face first, I tumbled until I landed on soft grass. My skin rippled back into place, cool air biting where I now sported some respectable skid marks on my cheek and shoulder.

I pushed myself to stand with a groan.

The tree was in the center of a clearing where moonlight poured down its branches and danced on top of the soft, green grass surrounding it. Smooth river rocks lined the perimeter, creating a perfect circle. I felt something brush past my hair as the trees outside the circle waved their branches.

"Charlotte."

My head snapped forward to the sound of the whisper that felt like it was being murmured by someone standing directly in front of me.

"What the fuck?" I breathed.

My beast snapped her jaw. Frustration set in as my heart continued to pound.

"Charlotte," the voice called again.

THE PACK

I squeezed my eyes shut and prayed it was all a dream. But when I opened my eyes, I was shocked to see that the tree was bleeding. My mouth parted in horror at the sight of the bloody palm prints dripping down the clean bark as if they were freshly placed. With careful steps, I walked forward as my inner inquisitiveness got the better of me.

"Charlotte," I heard again.

I could barely control myself at this point. Curious, I reached for the thing that felt like it was slowly drawing me in. The base of the tree was only a breath away.

"Charlotte!" I heard a voice cry.

A body knocked me to the side and tackled me to the ground before a pair of hands yanked me up to sit. "What the hell were you doing?!" Billy cried.

I blinked and looked back at the tree. It wasn't bleeding anymore. It wasn't moving.

"I don't—" I shook my head in disbelief. My beast snapped her jaw in frustration. "I don't know. I got lost..."

I felt Billy's hands easily lift me to my feet and hold me steady. "Charlotte, you're one of Thunderhead's best trackers and you're telling me you got lost?"

"I'm sorry," I wheezed while I tried to make sense of it. "Billy, I—what even is this place?"

He looked at me like he wasn't sure if I was about to lose it or not, and, to be fair, I wasn't sure if I was going to either. He stepped back and released my shoulders. "It's our oathing tree. Pack leads swear allegiance to the Moon. Only pack leads are allowed to touch it."

"What?" I panted, still struggling to catch my breath. "What do you mean 'allowed'?"

"It's sacred," he answered in a hushed voice. "A place to be revered."

I swallowed the panic-driven tears that were threatening to spill. Billy looked me over before blowing out a breath. "We'll pretend that you did not run through the Trapper's Forest—sounds like you got a little moon drunk, kiddo."

"I'm sorry," I repeated in a mild tone that my beast snapped her teeth at.

"Charlotte?!"

Ethan's voice sobered me up quickly as a shiver ran up my back. I saw his eyes glowing in the darkness first, turquoise and hazel that I walked toward without being asked. Ethan jogged to me and practically yanked me to his chest. "Did you not hear us calling you?"

I shook my head at him. "I'm sorry—I don't know."

"How did you get here?" Ethan pressed.

"I thought you were behind me," was all I could say, and that was the truth. "I don't know."

And I fucking hated that. In his eyes I could see disbelief forming, and I didn't blame him. I would think I was full of it too—but what was I going to say?

"I'm sorry," I said again. "Can we go?" I asked, my voice quieter this time because there was something about this place—this tree—that made me feel like I was being watched by more than just Billy.

Ethan nodded slowly then lifted his head to Billy. "What were you doing out here?"

"Some young wolves were joking that they wanted to run in the forest. You know how kids are," he answered with light laugh. "Figured I would advise them to take a different route tonight.

Glad I was out here, though. Sounds like she got moon drunk—happens to the best of us."

Ethan wrapped an arm around me. "Let's get you home."

Andrea had arrived in the clearing with a look I knew too well. I jerked my head away, almost desperate to avoid her scrutinizing gaze. I couldn't blame her. I would be doing the same thing if I was in her place.

I should have ignored the voices. I should have never walked over to that tree.

The skin of my shoulder twitched as a chill swept up behind me. Turning over my shoulder, I expected to see Billy still watching us, but he was gone. All that was left was the tree standing in the spotlight of the moon, bleeding tears of blood like it was weeping at my retreat.

Andrea closed the curtains after Ethan left. *"I know you didn't get lost."* I didn't say anything, and it didn't matter. When I met her golden gaze again, I knew I was not going to be able to tell her no. *"You're telling me. Now."*

She took my hand and pulled me into my room then sat me on the bed. I felt my eyes tear as she closed all the curtains.

The weight on the bed shifted in front of me. She tapped her temple.

"In case anyone nosy is listening outside." I wrapped my arms around my stomach. Andrea crossed her legs in front of her. She let out a long breath and laid her hand palm up in front of me. I slapped mine in hers and let our fingers intertwine. *"Tell me."*

"You're right," I admitted.

Andrea listened carefully as I recounted what I had experienced and seen. I spared no detail because with her, I knew she'd eventually find out. After I finished, she was quiet for a long time. A long time that made my beast pace at the same beat as my anxiety drumming to life.

"You don't know who they are?"

"No." I shook my head. *"I don't recognize anyone."*

"This . . . shit, this is bad, Charlotte."

Dread filled me. I wanted to convince myself it was nothing. That it was just the forest. But that felt as useful as someone trying to convince themselves that they weren't sick when they had a clear fever. Prolonging the truth didn't mean the illness was nonexistent. It was always there, festering quietly.

"People have heard and seen things in there—it's haunted as hell. Usually normal for that place. I hoped you were just experiencing the normal fucked-up-ness of the forest."

"I don't think this is that." The confession screamed to life over the sound of my whisper.

Her golden eyes held mine in in a hug of regret. She bit her lip then nodded in a silent concession.

"Blood magic, it's not just forbidden because of what you can do with it or how it's made. It also torments the person conjuring it. It's said that the witch who cast the blood magic can hear the blood they cursed call to them. That the sound of it torments them, drives them mad as punishment for what they did." She blew out a breath. *"After the attack, people were desperate to find the culprits. Some got desperate and rounded up quite a few witches they thought were involved and walked them into the forest to see if any of them started to go nuts from hearing the blood magic."*

"I—" My hands started to shake.

Andrea squeezed them and leveled her gaze with mine. "*I know you didn't do any blood magic. You can barely follow a brownie recipe.*"

"*How is it made again?*"

She shivered. "*I'm not an expert, but from what I know, you can do it with stored blood—so blood that someone gave you—or fresh blood. But the fresh blood is better, the blood of a wolf or a vampire is very valuable, and a moon-blooded wolf? That's almost priceless. In the past, before the treaty, the vampires, some of them, worked with factions' cloisters to acquire blood magic.*

"*I don't know why, but I remember hearing about the blood banks that were busted. They kidnapped a lot of people—a lot of their own and a lot of wolves. There was a case where they found a pair of moon-blooded children drained dry.*"

"*Jesus Christ,*" I hissed. "*But this isn't that. This can't be that. I never—*"

"*I know,*" she pressed. "*But this pack . . . even at Thunderhead, this would be dangerous information.*"

"*Do you think?*" I paused and shook my head. "*I have nothing to do with what's going on! There's no way anyone could think that.*"

Andrea bit the corner of her mouth. "*We didn't have issues of rogues for a long time, until you were bit. You're one of a few people who can smell blood magic in the forest, a shifted human who has had less training than the wolves who have tried—and the cases we have found on the pack lands, you were there . . . It would look so fucking bad.*" She dipped her head slightly. "*No one knows?*"

"*No, not even Levi.*"

Andrea ran a hand through her hair. "*We can't say anything.*

No one can know, not until we can figure it out. It's too dangerous. We don't need people here to go on a witch hunt."

"But Ethan . . . I don't want to hide things from him." But I also wasn't sure how he'd react. What he'd do with the information.

"Then you can't follow them again. We can't risk someone catching on. I know you don't want to hide things from him, but my two cents? We find out more before we bring it to him."

I had never seen her this nervous before—this anxious. I was opening my mouth to reply when the pieces came together. If people found out, she would be guilty by association.

I couldn't do that to her. I wouldn't ever put her in that position.

"What if I am going crazy?"

She squeezed my hand. *"Then I'll go crazy with you."*

CHAPTER ELEVEN

There was a subtle hum in the background from a dusty old box fan that was working overtime in an attempt to move the languid air in the room. All it did was shift the muggy summer air around so it could cling onto my skin.

I picked at the strap of the shifter top sticking to my skin. I wished I had worn a loose T-shirt. I shouldn't have come to the tracker meetup early. I shouldn't have made it easy to be the target of everyone's gazes they walked in. An easy, lone target for the vultures craving a rumor.

"She's not even a full wolf, she was a human..."

"Why would the moon do that to him?"

I forced my eyes forward and continued to study the giant map of the pack lands that I had already memorized at least twice over by now. The paper map spanned the entire back wall and had a layer of plexiglass secured over it; dozens of notes in various colors of dry-erase marker and sticky notes littered the clear glass and brought life to the flat map.

The hand that grasped my shoulder drew a sharp jerk from my body. Jake arched a brow as he came to stand in view. "You good?"

No, I wasn't fucking good. I felt like the new kid placed two grades above where they were supposed to be at a new school.

"Didn't sleep well," I lied. I had barely slept at all. My dreams had kept me up all night. Dreams where I would wake up lying in a pool of blood next to Lucas. The roots of the tree had wrapped around his legs and yanked him deep into the trunk then gobbled him up like a snack. His silver eyes were beaming wide in horror as he yelled and yelled for me to help, but there was nothing I could do.

"Right . . ." Jake slowly replied. He leaned against the wall next to me and crossed his thick arms over his chest. "Heard you got lost?" Always to the point.

My nostrils flared as a tense breath left me. "I guess I did."

"That forest is fucked up no matter what pack you're in," he said in a tone that was more comforting than I would have expected. "It's forbidden here, so be careful."

Jake waved to a girl standing on her own. She jerked her chin up in a nod. Her chocolate-brown hair was twisted in two buns on top of her head, olive-green eyes flicking to me quickly before she looked back at her nails as if she was bored.

"Keeley," Jake explained. "Grew up together."

"You can go over there," I told him. "Besides, what are you doing here, anyway? Shouldn't you be with the guards?"

He snorted. "We're short on trackers. Billy asked if I'd help with some routes. Besides, can't leave you on your own, nerd."

"I don't need a babysitter, ass wipe," I teased.

"We're on a fucking team, dork."

"Whatever you say, muffin," I added, with a cheeky smile.

Jake shook his head. "Moron."

"Shithead."

His lips pulled into a smile as the door swung open. Evangeline's red curls bounced around her like a hive of bees as she followed Amber and another girl with strawberry-blond hair piled in a messy bun on top of her head. Evangeline scanned the room before her eyes landed on mine. I lifted my hand in a small wave, which I then tried to hide by running it through my short locks when she immediately turned away from me with a scowl.

Amber looked over her shoulder. Her crystal-blue eyes combed over me like she was trying to understand how the moon had constructed me, her lips pulling into a tight smile that was quickly becoming familiar.

Jake nudged my shoulder with his. "Don't read into it."

Billy strode in with a clipboard tucked under his thick bicep. "Morning, all," he said briskly as he moved to the map. The room immediately quieted as he jotted notes on the poorly erased surface. "We've got a lot to do this week."

He capped the pen and turned back to face the group. "The next few weeks we need to prioritize prepping for hunts. This week, we'll be mapping game trails. I want to make sure nothing has shifted since last year. We also need to track the predators moving around the area—the bears are out of hibernation and mountain lions will be on the move. We need to make sure we have eyes on their migration patterns."

He rolled his shoulders back then pointed to the board where he had circled a few areas. He paired people off and sent them on their way. Jake had left with Keeley, and there were only a few people left when he got to my name on the board.

Billy turned to me with an easy smile. "Your job is to learn the area," he added, enunciating the last part a little too much for my liking. "Piper is going to take you on the mountain route and show you the ropes this week, so you don't get lost," he noted.

The beast in the back of my mind snapped. I pushed her back and forced a neutral expression on my face. "That would be great," I told him. "I'd hate to have you follow me around all the time."

He waved over the girl with strawberry-blond hair. Her brown eyes were as dark as night and felt like two beads bouncing from one direction to the other as she shifted her gaze from Billy to me.

She cracked her neck before extending her hand. "Piper."

I took her hand and quickly shook it. "Charlotte."

"Run hard," Billy told us before we ventured out of the barn.

The sun kissed her taupe skin as her lanky arms stretched over her head in a catlike stretch. She let her hair loose from the bun and shook out the strands, which fell like a waterfall around her shoulders.

I shifted my weight on my feet as quiet settled in around us. "How long is the route?"

She studied me like she was trying to find a way to burrow under my skin. "It's not bad."

"At least it's nice out," I offered.

"I prefer the rain," she griped, before jerking her head forward. "This way."

THE PACK

My beast huffed in the back of my mind. We just had to get through the day, and luckily we would be running most of it.

Piper shifted into her brindled fur and darted off. Quickly, I shifted and ran after her; she led us up the mountain. We were careful to stay on the side of the forest that was not the Trapper's Forest, and watchful of the jagged slopes that waited for us like the open mouth of a predator. A crisp breeze greeted me when we punched through the tree line on the bare hills at the base of the mountain. Ahead, the land fought its way toward the sky until it eventually peaked.

Trees painted green lined the road and a few tattered green flags swayed in the wind like tired soldiers holding their posts. I shifted to my skin and sucked in a breath of the thin air, which disappointed my lungs—getting used to the altitude was going to be a journey.

Snow still clung to the peaks at the top of the mountain. The beast in me paced as something uneasy moved in my stomach.

"What's up there?" I found myself asking.

Piper turned to look up the mountain. "Those mountains are cursed."

"Cursed?"

My gaze lowered to meet her cold eyes. A chill ran over my skin that could have convinced me it was about to snow. "Apparently, there's silver up there. Humans used to try to mine it—used to try to hunt us too. It's wolf land now, but hardly. Apparently, you can't link up there."

"Why is it cursed? The silver?"

She turned to look at the mountain. The sharp edges of her face blended in with the ridges that looked prone to avalanches and mudslides. "They spilled our blood all the way up those mountains. Used our fur to keep themselves warm. The silver they brought back laces that forest—they're like the vampires, only thought of us as dogs."

I closed my mouth before any fiery retort could escape, but Piper didn't seem to notice the internal war I was having. She marched along the trail that lined the trees.

I jogged to catch up with her. "How long do we stay on this path?"

"About two miles," she stated. "There are some hills that the caribou like to graze. They're usually there—have been every year. It's not a hard route."

"It is really beautiful," I admitted. The hills ahead looked almost like the ocean as they rolled along into the horizon in front of us. Thick grass adorned with pink flowers blanketed them; my beast and I had the urge to find a place in the sun to take a nap.

"Yeah." She breathed next to me as something seemed to melt over her cold facade. "Different from Thunderhead, I'm sure."

"It is," I agreed, before allowing the sound of the ground crunching under our feet to fill the silence between us.

"I guess Levi is well?"

My beast cocked her head in the back of my mind. "He is. Still cranky, but he's doing really good."

She hummed in response, something deep and throaty that sounded closer to an alligator warning off encroaching competition. "I can't believe he took in a human."

I didn't know if that was a jab or an inside thought that somehow made its way outside. Regardless, I couldn't stop myself from saying, "Me too," because it was true.

"They said he saved you?"

I lifted my brows and studied her a moment. "Yeah. Rogues found me. I thought I would die that night."

"I'm sure you thought that through the shift too?"

My beast snapped her teeth. I forced a tight smile. "I did."

She breathed a laugh. "You have some luck, then. Surviving like that, then scoring one of the most eligible wolves over like four packs."

My stomach twisted at her words. I trusted Ethan—I was trying to trust Ethan, and I knew that would grow because we barely knew each other... but four packs?

"Shouldn't we be looking for where the caribou graze?"

"I told you, they'll be up here soon," she answered. "He seems different with you."

"Who?"

"Ethan."

I cut my eyes to hers. Her lips twitched, fighting to a hide smile, like a fox with a secret behind its teeth. My beast shook out her fur as my better instincts took hold of me.

"What do you mean?"

She shrugged. "He has friends here, but I don't know if anyone knows the guy that well besides his brother. It looks like you two are getting on well?"

Watch your hide, Levi had told me.

"It's hard to describe," I answered, heeding Levi's words.

"It can't be that hard," she countered, a sweetness in her voice that turned sour to my ears.

It wasn't hard; she was right.

It wasn't hard to admit how many things I liked about him. It hadn't been that long, but already he was working his way toward being a permanent part of me, which terrified me because I had worked my ass off to stand on my own two feet. Forever was a really fucking long time to tie yourself to someone, and I couldn't lose myself again. I would never let that happen.

It wouldn't be hard to let the thoughts in my head spill out, but it was even easier to keep silent. The patience Piper showcased was an easy facade—a lure to a sharp hook that would yank my lips open and force all my secrets out. The prying game was one I had played and been played by one too many times before.

"You'd be surprised," I answered.

The trees trembled in the wind next to us. They looked like bones glued back together, skeletons serving as a warning. From the corner of my eye I could see tiny red eyes appearing in the darkness of the Trapper's Forest.

"I think we're all surprised you haven't marked each other yet."

The bait was laid out in front of me. Her eyes glittered in dark anticipation while she awaited my response. The wind rolled down the hills and snaked through her curls, which danced like serpents around her face.

My beast pawed at the back of my mind. "We like to keep people on their toes."

She cackled like a hyena. The sound startled the vermin watching us through the thicket of dark foliage that stood at my back.

Piper walked ahead of me and peered into the Trapper's Forest. Her breath caught and her eyes glowed, almost as if she was watching a lover approach.

The darkness through the trees thickened, like a roux turning a sickly black. Cold snaked across the ground and tried to latch to my toes like leeches. My beast snapped her teeth; I stepped back from the tree line—from the darkness trying to find me.

Piper turned slowly to face me. The shadows of the forest wrapped around her and sharpened the lines of her face. Her bony fingers flexed.

My beast was close to my skin. I closed my fists to hide the claws that were starting to pierce through. Part of me wondered if she was just trying to scare me—was I overreacting?

But then she smiled, slowly, like a gaudy theater curtain, and revealed a set of shiny white teeth and sharp fangs.

My toes dug into the ground. My eyes bounced from her to the forest ahead and I half wondered if I was safer taking my chances in there—if I was safe at all with her.

She tipped her head back and laughed, then stepped away from the trees and into sun that melted the shadows from her form.

Rolling her eyes, she said, "I like to keep people on their toes too," before continuing along the path.

My beast snapped her teeth again while I gawked ahead at Piper. She paused and looked over her shoulder at me. "Are you coming?"

There was no turning back for me. It was either into that forest or after my new, oh-so-pleasant tour guide, but I didn't want to stir more rumors about me. I could only imagine what I would hear if I decided to ditch her.

I blew out a sharp breath and headed up the path. We fell back in step together, and into the unfriendly quiet that we had started with, a cold quiet that became the background noise for the rest of our journey—a quiet I much preferred.

When we returned, Piper ticked off the area that was listed on the whiteboard then jetted out of the room without another word.

I didn't wait around to see if she would come back.

My beast tore at the ground as I headed home, where I planned to take the longest shower of my life followed by a stiff drink. I shifted to my skin when I neared the house. On our porch, Evangeline was sitting on the steps, back as stiff as a board and arms crossed tight over her chest.

My steps slowed. "Hello?"

Her green eyes snapped up to meet mine. I felt my beast stand up and pace as we watched the young wolf in front of us. Standing slowly, Evangeline walked with cautious steps until she was a few feet in front of me.

The skin on my arm twitched. Quickly, I glanced over my shoulder to see Amber across the way, watching from Evangeline's porch.

Fantastic.

"Are you all right?" I asked her.

She blew out a breath then laced her hands in front of her as if she was about to hold court. "I'm Evangeline. Ethan's sister."

Nodding slowly, I looked back at Amber to see her rolling her eyes before she pushed off the porch. Turning back to Evangeline, I said, "Right, um, we met earlier."

"Right," she muttered, scolding herself. "I just, well—"

Footsteps quickly closed in. "It's not like she's a walrus! She's your sister-in-law," Amber hissed. Evangeline wrapped her arms around her waist as Amber paused next to her.

"She doesn't have a mark yet," Evangeline grumbled.

I held my hands up. "I am right here, you know?"

Amber tossed her icy-blond hair over her shoulder. "Sorry," she tiredly replied. "We should have said something at the tracker meetup earlier. It's nice to meet you without my mother hovering."

Evangeline shifted her weight to one leg. "And I live across the street, if you need anything."

"Great." I needed a shower and a stiff drink—preferably at the same time. "Do you want to come in?"

Amber shook her head as her frigid eyes took me in. "Sorry, we have plans. Another time?"

"Sure."

She pulled Evangeline forward. Evangeline muttered a goodbye as she passed, leaving me standing on the lawn with my mouth agape. The front door to my house pushed open and Jake walked through, pulling a sweatshirt off.

"I don't understand your kind," he said.

"My kind?"

"Women."

"How did you get into my house?"

He nudged his chin to the flowerpot on the porch. "You need a better hiding place for the spare key," he answered, before dropping the tiny piece of metal into my waiting palm. "It's quieter here. Evan and Evangeline were arguing again. At each other's throats."

"Do they do that often?"

He shrugged. "Often enough. Won't matter when I get to take your room."

My hand landed on my hip. "The hell does that mean?"

"Well," he said, as if what he was about to say was intended for a child, "I mean you and Ethan are gonna move in together eventually."

"I just met him!" Jesus Christ, this was supposed to be our

choice, at our pace, yet it felt like everyone had already decided for us.

"Right, and now you're here. Halfway there. Embrace it."

I ran my fingers through my hair. "Did you want something to eat?"

"Oh right, no," he quickly answered. "We're going to Billy's for dinner."

"You couldn't link me this?"

He rolled his eyes and stepped to the side to let me walk into the house. "How was today?" he asked, shutting the door behind him.

I paused at the kitchen island. "Billy had me run with Piper along the mountain trail."

Jake turned to quickly face me. "What?" He studied my face a moment before asking, "What happened?"

"Nothing," I answered, which was the truth.

Jake moved to stand opposite me at the island. He dipped his head, eyes narrowing in disbelief. "Nothing?"

My fingers drummed on the counter. I had chalked the whole incident up to general mean-girl pettiness—a power trip that had been too juicy for Piper to refuse—and swore to myself that I would think nothing of it after my shower. Down the drain with the bullshit.

"Charlotte?"

He was too tense. The hair on the back of his neck was slightly lifted while the muscles on his arms twitched like his own skin was becoming too tight for him.

I cocked my head. "Should it be something?"

Jake snorted in irritation. "She's dan—" He closed his mouth and shook his head. "She's bad news."

THE PACK

I lifted a brow. "You were going to say *dangerous*." Jake leaned away from the island, like a retreat in defeat. "Weren't you?"

"She's bad news, Charlotte," he repeated.

"Yeah, I figured that much out on my own," I clipped. "I'm going to shower," I told him, then marched straight to the bathroom, where I took an extra-long time in the shower mostly to annoy Jake, who proceeded to complain about how he hated being late the whole way to Billy's.

Ethan watched him curiously as we approached Billy's. He pushed off the porch post he had been leaning against and strode forward while Jake grumbled his way into the house.

Ethan's fingers teased the collar of my Thunderhead sweatshirt. "Maybe time for a green one."

I swatted his hand away. "I like this one." I liked how it still smelled like home.

"You could learn to like a new one?" he asked as his hand somehow snaked around my waist.

Suddenly, the tension from the events of the day faded away as something electric pulsed along this pull between us. I shifted out of the embrace that I wanted to fall comfortably back into—when had it become so comfortable so fast? Why hadn't I noticed?

My beast snapped her jaws at me. I knew I was in my head, but I'd rather be in my head than mindlessly going with the motions that someone else was choreographing.

"How was your day?" I asked.

"Probably not as good as yours," he answered.

"That can't be true." I started to laugh, when a familiar scent hit my nose.

Billy walked outside with an apron tied over his worn khakis and faded blue tee. He wiped his hands on a dish towel and slung it over his shoulder.

"You're very stylish," I told him.

His lips crinkled into a smile. "Man of many talents, kiddo. I'm making my famous potato casserole, so I hope you're hungry. Dinner will be ready in about twenty, so we have time." His eyes pulsed a heavy golden glow that studied me before shifting back to Ethan. "You're sure?"

Ethan nodded firmly. "Yes."

Billy returned inside. Ethan held his hand out for me. "Come on. To the basement."

I studied his hand. "The basement?"

"We're going to be proactive."

My beast shook out her fur. I placed my hand in Ethan's and let him lead me inside, where it looked like a normal dinner party was about to occur—glasses were set out and plates were stacked neatly next to the oven. But down a tiny staircase was a cluttered basement.

Andrea was sitting on one of dozens of boxes crowding the small space, while Jake and Evan studied a map lying flat on a foldable plastic table in the center of the room. Billy had more maps hung up on the walls, with pushpins pressed into them along with sticky notes with writing that was barely legible in the dim lighting.

Andrea lifted her golden gaze meet mine. She swirled her drink in her hand. "You made it."

I released Ethan's hand and walked to Andrea. She pulled a box over then patted the top of it for me.

Billy tossed a few pens on the table. He uncapped a neon-green highlighter and started to draw. Rising to stand, I slowly wandered over to stand next to him.

"Silver highlighted areas are the places you and Remi have found things at Thunderhead," he explained. "Everything in lime green is where our trackers and guards have reported strange things. Red is where you found the stone."

"What kinds of things have they reported?" I asked.

"Nothing like what you found. It sounded at first like people were being spooked by the forest, but now I'm not so sure. The areas highlighted in orange I think are potentially places that are something, rather than our wolves getting scared," he elaborated, as he continued to mark the paper.

"Dad's a little OCD," Andrea teased. "Except in the basement."

Billy smiled at his daughter as he pointed a pen at her. "Because someone has not come to help me organize it."

"You're highlighting in green," I pointed out.

"No shit," Evan groused.

My beast wanted to snap her teeth but I stopped her, although from the delight in Evan's eyes it looked as if he wanted to see how sharp her fangs were. Like he was itching for a fight.

"Some trackers today reported that they heard snapping in the forest again," Billy explained. He capped the pen set it next to the others on the map. "*Popping* is actually the word they used for it."

"Did you go out there?" Ethan asked.

Billy shook his head. "No, too many of Thomas's spies out today."

Ethan hummed in understanding. Billy gestured to the map. "It's just been us," he told Andrea and me. "We're combing through parts of the forest that seem the most likely to have something, but our numbers are small and we don't have the approval of our pack lead like you did at Thunderhead."

"And he's got his little group of spies," Evan groused.

I lifted a brow. Ethan nodded to me with a look on his face that said I would know all about these spies soon enough.

"Some people in the pack are very loyal to him. Want the past to be the past. Want our pack to live in a bubble where outside threats don't exist," Ethan explained.

"Or they're worried you'll unseat him," Evan muttered under his breath. "Not everyone in the pack is kissing his ass."

Ethan shot him a warning look. Andrea slid forward on her box seat. "So, what do you suggest, then? It's forbidden as fuck, and we've got tattletales running amok."

"We could go at night?" I offered.

Andrea's golden eyes snapped to me like I was about to shut my own hand in a drawer. Evan scoffed. "Are you out of your mind? You want to go into that forest at night?"

Shrugging, I said, "It's always dark in there. Daylight doesn't seem to make a big difference."

"She's not wrong," Billy agreed. "But we have to tread very carefully. He's worked up about your conversation the other day, Ethan. You pushed too far. He's suspicious that you'll go behind his back.

"And he doesn't trust her yet. He's got his eyes on her," he added with a nod to me. "He requested I put her with Piper today. Thought they'd get along..."

"Seriously?" Evan seethed before casting a quick, troubled glance in my direction.

"I can't say no," Billy added with a tired exhale. "Neither of us can."

"I know," Ethan conceded.

Billy's thumb spun the pearl bead on his bracelet while he watched the scene. My eyes couldn't help but lock onto it.

THE PACK

"People are buzzing about you, kiddo, You're the newest we've had in a while, Levi's pup, and *his* true mate," he added with a nudge of his chin toward Ethan, drawing my focus away from his bracelet. "But Thomas gets paranoid. He's worried about looking foolish foremost and causing unnecessary panic. You have to stay out of those woods until things calm down. It's for your own good."

"But this is—I'm good at this," I countered. "I won't get caught."

"We can't risk it," Billy replied with an apologetic smile. "This is too important."

I bit my tongue because he wasn't wrong in that regard, but the last thing I wanted to do was track caribou and herd sheep. Not when that forest was a big part of the reason I agreed to move in the first place.

"We go at night and take turns," Ethan stated. "We can't all be gone at once or someone will notice. Jake, you and Andrea go tomorrow night. Moon's waning, it will be dark out and give you some good coverage. Ev and Billy, wait until the weekend. We need to make sure we don't hear chatter about anyone seeing Jake and Andrea running around first."

"What about us?" I asked.

"By the new moon we should be fine," he answered. "We'll go together. Anyone catching us out will think we're stealing off together."

"Right." I rocked back on my heels as my beast paced in the back of my mind.

"So, we have a plan." Evan paused and nodded in approval. "I like a plan."

Billy knocked on the table. "I do too."

CHAPTER TWELVE

A quiet murmur droned behind me. Billy was laughing with Evan while the others finished up the dishes from dinner. I had stepped out on the porch for some space.

The smell of Ethan's shampoo announced his presence before the sound of his footsteps did. The pull toward him was growing stronger every day—a constant warm pulse. Always there. Always present.

His arms snaked around my waist from behind and pulled me back into his chest. I bit my lip and let myself be selfish in this satisfying moment. "Want to walk home?" he asked.

"I don't feel like going home," I admitted quietly, so only he could hear.

His chin rested on my shoulder as his body bent to further

curl around mine. "Doesn't want to go home," he mused playfully. "We could go skinny-dipping?"

"We could shave our heads too?"

He chuckled against my shoulder, the heat of his breath like fingers reaching under the collar of my sweatshirt to caress my skin.

"Will you come somewhere with me?"

A group of five people came into view along the footpath outside Billy's house. I could make out a few words they whispered when they caught sight of us. Then they were silent. Their eyes glazed with a distant look, a sign of another linked conversation that I knew in my gut had to do with me.

"Sure," I answered. Anywhere else sounded better.

Together we walked down the path before shifting into our fur and darting into the trees. Ethan was quiet as he led me through the woods, as if he could sense that I needed space to be in my head. Part of me hoped he was taking me on a surprise journey to Levi's, where I could sit on the porch and steal Levi's whiskey while he complained to me about something Lander had gotten into.

I missed them. I missed my home. I didn't realize how deeply I had buried my roots there until I decided to rip them out.

We broke through the trees and Ethan led me up an incline until we were practically climbing on boulders. He shifted to his skin, eyes glowing like the stars in the sky, and held his hand out for me. "It's tricky footing here."

I shifted to my skin and took his hand.

After I almost busted my ass a few times, we made it to a level surface on top of the ridge.

"This is so beautiful." I stared in awe at the firmament above.

Ethan pulled two thick blankets out of a saddlebag he had carried.

"Boy Scout," I teased.

He threw the blankets down on the boulder, where we both settled down before quiet set in.

"Why doesn't he trust me?" I asked Ethan. "Thomas?"

"Because he doesn't trust me," he admitted. "I think he knows we're venturing into the forest, he just can't prove it. Hopefully, he'll find something new to fixate on."

"Hopefully. So," I breathed. "You, me, and the trees... and the traps? It's, like, adventure date night?"

He shook his head. "You have to be the only girl who wants to go in there."

"Bowie," I pointed out.

He snorted. "She doesn't count."

"Fair," I agreed, because the woman was a breed of her own. "I still don't understand why he was so angry the other day at his office. He saw the stone. He has to understand?"

"He's very sensitive to the pack," Ethan answered in a tone that felt too diplomatic for what should be a cozy moment. "Very mindful of how it would be received by them, and by the region."

I swallowed and nodded at him. "But people would understand, right?"

He turned on his side to face me. His eyes seemed far off before they pulsed a glow. "After the attack, they looked for the culprits for such a long time. Poked, prodded, and upturned everyone's lives—after what we had been through, it was like another knife in the wound. Like we had to relive it over and over again with no end in sight. Everyone was relieved when the region closed the case—we weren't allowed to have funerals until it was over, because the bodies were being held for examination. We had to make a morgue in one of the meat lockers."

My breath caught. Ethan rested his head in his palm and continued. "Thomas doesn't want to dig up graves, and we have a lot of graves here. Too many," he said, his voice heavier than usual, his expression haunted. "If we want to go digging up ghosts, we need a smoking gun. We can't connect the Bloodstones to the rogues, not directly. In fact, they're circumstantial at best. Thomas needs something the pack would have no choice but to accept if they were to find out before he made the search public. They're already wound up enough about the news of rogue sightings, and the minute there's panic, it will spread like a disease."

"What if he finds out what we're doing?"

He pushed some hair behind my ears. "Let me worry about that."

But a large part of me did worry about it; the part of me that had seen anger like that before.

"So, Piper..."

"Don't worry about her."

I tilted my head. "Jake gave me the impression that she was dangerous?"

"She probably would like to think she is."

It was hard to be frustrated when he was looking at me like this. When his hair was falling slightly in his face and the light of the night sky illuminated the stubble that rolled along his jawline. When his fingers were tracing delicate lines on my arm, leaving a trail that felt like small, heated kisses.

"Well," I said with a tiny smirk, "was she far off when she told me that you were apparently the most eligible bachelor in like four packs?"

A rare blush coated his cheeks. "Jesus," he groaned.

I laughed. "Oh, your sister stopped by today too."

His brows lifted. "Really?"

"Yeah, she was, well, she was waiting on my porch when I got home. Amber came with her."

"She literally cannot do anything on her own," he muttered before eventually relenting. "I may have encouraged her."

"Encouraged her?"

"I was hoping she'd—what happened exactly?"

"It was fine." I waved him off. "It was just really odd. Amber was nice enough but—it was fine." Pausing a beat, I asked, "Is there something I can do?"

"It's not about you," he said, as if he was trying to kill another rumor before it started.

The wind picked up around us. I glanced at the stars, at the waning moon as a chill set in. I curled my toes into his legs, which were covered by long shifters that I envied. We ran hot as wolves, but my bare feet still got cold in the bare wind.

My free hand found his, and our fingers intertwined. "So tell me about it? I know only what I know from Levi and some others at Thunderhead," I explained before dipping my head so he could see that I meant it when I said, "I want to understand."

He sighed in agreement before pulling me slightly closer to his warm body.

"When we were kids, Levi was the best. We loved going to Uncle Levi's, and we loved when Lucas would come here. We spent a lot of time together, our two families. Obviously, we're neighbors, and Aunt Eve was Dad's sister. Dad and Levi were best friends.

"He was the best. An asshole, but a funcle in his own right.

And he was always there. He always said if something happened we could follow a secret path to his place that he and Aunt Eve made."

Something in my throat went tight while the tether between us started to feel more like a sad song paired with a melancholy murmur.

Ethan's fingers kept playing with mine as his eyes grew distant. "Evangeline hadn't yet shifted when our parents died. She was barely eight. Evan had shifted only the year before. He was fifteen. Still a kid. I guess we all were," he added with a small smile.

"And then they were gone. They were lost to us, and he was too. Evangeline wanted to stay with Levi. She didn't understand why we couldn't go live with him—didn't fully comprehend what happens to a wolf when they lose their true mate. Evan and I were old enough to know, and tried to explain it to her, but she was just a kid who was upset and wanted her uncle. I did too."

He swallowed and turned his head to look up at the sky. "A few years went by and he was still alive. He hadn't followed Eve and Lucas to the moon, so I thought, fuck it. Maybe he's getting better. Maybe that's a thing and he's not totally lost. So I went to see him."

I knew part of how this story went. Part of me wanted to tell him to stop, that he didn't need to keep going, but the other part of me felt like right now he needed someone to listen. To really listen.

"He looked like one of them," he said so quietly I almost didn't hear him. "Like a rogue. Lander had warned me. I didn't listen. Levi looked at me like he didn't know who I was."

"Did he?"

He shook his head. "He came to for a moment and told me to leave and never come back."

I wondered if Levi even remembered telling Ethan that. Part of me wanted to think he didn't; the better part of me believed he did.

Ethan continued. "Billy thought we should give him time, but even when it sounded like he was getting better, I still didn't trust him enough to bring Evan and Lina around him."

"He wouldn't have hurt you."

"You didn't see him like that," he said, turning to look at me. "He wasn't himself. He didn't know me, and he's known me my whole life." I looked away because I felt something twist across the pull between us, something that kicked up the beat of the sad song humming away. "We assumed after that, that he was gone, like they were."

I closed my eyes to hide the tears that were building. I knew what was coming next. Knew what the linchpin of it all was.

"Then I came along."

"Then you came along," he echoed. "Evan and I thought he had lost it. He came into my office and told me Levi had taken in a human. I was more concerned about the rogues at the time, because I didn't think it was true. Evan and I called Lander on speakerphone so we could both hear him say the words out loud. When he did, I thought he'd lost his mind too." He let out a long breath. "Evan and I assumed Lander was going to intervene, or that you would die."

His arm curled around me, pulling me closer while his fingers played mindlessly with the ends of my hair.

"But you didn't die," he said, as if he was watching the last piece of snow melt on a new spring day. "And Levi was somehow doing better. Coming around more. Then we heard that you were living with him, that he was training you, teaching you how to be a wolf—doing the things he did with us as kids and getting you ready for the Hunt, which none of us could believe. He was lost to us, but he took you in and claimed you as one of his own."

Christ, Levi. How could no one have told me this before?

"Evan has a hard time separating his feelings toward Levi from you. Evangeline too."

"And you?" I asked, now needing to look at him.

"I always knew those were his choices, not yours. You just had the bad luck of somehow getting mixed up with him. You didn't know. Evan's coming around, Evangeline will too."

I felt his lips press to my forehead in a silent apology.

"It wasn't bad luck," I said.

"What wasn't?"

"Him and me—getting mixed up with him. It wasn't bad luck at all."

He watched me closely and his eyes pulsed with something more animal than human, a hum buzzing off him as if his beast wanted to hear this for himself.

He should know. If we were spilling truths here on this rock, it was only fair that I was good and honest.

I sat up and pulled my sweatshirt off. "Do you know how I got mixed up with those rogues?"

His hand rested on my knee. "You don't have to—"

"I want to," I said, my voice holding more determination in it than I expected. "Levi saved my life. Then he helped me save myself. He—my ex—I never thought I would leave him like I did. I knew I had to. But it's so much more complicated when you're in it. You can't just leave, you know? There's so many details to work out, so many things you never thought you would need or have to do or . . . He almost killed me one night. I locked myself in a bathroom—I left California the next morning. Two days later, I was in Alaska, totally lost in the woods, and then I was attacked.

"When I woke up, I thought I had snapped. I thought Levi and Derek were lunatics. I thought a lot of things," I said, my voice trailing off as I thought back to a time that felt oceans away. "I didn't want to go to the pack. Lander pressed Levi, but I was scared. I didn't have a lot of friends before, in my old life, and I wasn't ready to be thrown into the open where people would ask questions. Stare. The stares were the worst back then.

"Levi was with me for every full moon, sat with me during every panic attack—I would wake up all the time thinking Nate was there with his hands around my neck, and Levi was the one telling me I could breathe. Reminding me I was safe."

I could feel the dampness building in my lachrymose eyes. Could feel my throat start to tighten. I sucked in a breath and continued. "Levi's all I have, do you understand? My parents are gone too. I don't have siblings. I have Levi and Derek and Elliot and Lander—I have them. And I hate what happened to you all, so much . . ." My mouth closed as a tear slid down my cheek.

"Baby, don't cry," he murmured, wiping the wetness from my cheek.

"It's not for me to fix, but Levi is going to be in my life. I need him in my life. I'm not trying to be difficult—"

"Don't say that," he replied as he pushed my hair back. "You're anything but that. Levi, that's something I need to deal with in general. I can't control my siblings, but you don't need to choose between your family and us."

"I don't want you to either."

"I won't have to," he promised.

I smiled and wiped my eyes again. "So, do you bring all your girls here?"

"The ones from all four packs? Clearly," he replied, with a smirk.

I rolled my eyes as a warmth spread through me—starting from my core and running down to my toes, which curled in delight. Fingers brushed the edge of my cheek before lips skimmed down the column of my neck, stopping to press a searing kiss on my cool skin.

I couldn't control the sound that came out of my mouth. I couldn't control how quickly my lips found his because I was desperate to feel them again, to taste his tongue as it swept against mine. I couldn't control hands that explored the hard planes of his chest while my legs wrapped around him.

He grabbed my thigh and hitched it around his back before pinning one of my hands above me as his mouth trailed along my collarbone to the juncture of my neck. To the place that made this pull swirl like a spring tornado while dampness soaked the fabric between my legs.

Forever. That's what this was; it was forever.

You couldn't undo tying your soul with someone else's; and what happened to your soul after you did? Was it even yours at all anymore or was it something else entirely?

"Charlotte." His voice snapped my head out of its spiral. "We're not doing that until you ask me to."

I swallowed. "Okay."

"Okay," he echoed.

"Okay?"

He arched a brow. "Okay?"

"Well, what are you planning to do?"

He smiled slowly, fangs gleaming in the starlight. "What I have been thinking about since you walked out of the house in these tiny shorts," he said before he descended.

It took him two seconds to rip my shorts off and one second to bury his face into my center. I closed my eyes and saw stars as he licked me into bliss under the night sky.

CHAPTER THIRTEEN

"Well?"

"Well?"

"You're a pain in my ass even from a pack away."

I miss you too, I wanted to say, but something stilled my tongue. Ethan's words had sat with me all night, heavy on my chest until dawn. I didn't understand how to reconcile my experience of Levi with Ethan's and his siblings'. They say time heals all wounds, but time had failed spectacularly in this case. Time allowed infection to brew under deep wounds.

"I'm good," I told Levi *"No mark . . ."*

He grunted in response.

It wasn't a topic I'd meant to bring up, but I couldn't stop thinking about it. About how after I took Ethan into my mouth and watched him come apart, something in me wanted nothing more than to sink my fangs into his chest.

Forever was such a long time.

"Thomas is an interesting character," I told Levi, needing to immediately change the subject.

He was quiet over our link before he said, *"Thomas has never been a people person. Just be careful."*

"Why?"

"Tracker comes over and starts asking questions, could cause unwanted suspicion." His words were pointed, like little knives that could easily cut my self-assuredness. *"What's on the agenda for this morning?"*

"Andrea and I are trying to not poison each other."

He snorted. *"Good luck."*

I paused a beat but finally asked, *"Have you found anything?"*

"No," he answered, his voice tired, like he himself had been out searching for too many sleepless nights. *"Not a fucking thing."*

"Maybe that's a good thing?"

"Stay close to Ethan and be careful. Their forest is not as tamed as ours. That's what happens when you leave it alone for too long."

"Right."

"I miss you. Be careful." The parting words popped into my mind, but I did not utter them across the link; instead I held them to me as I downed the rest of my coffee. Andrea padded into the kitchen in an oversized T-shirt with dark, puffy circles under her eyes. She tried to brush her fingers through her frizzy hair, which looked like a rat had chewed on the ends.

I arched a brow as I picked up the light aroma of whiskey peppering her scent. "What happened to you?"

She grabbed her favorite mug, one covered with daisies, and

poured it full to the top with black coffee. In one gulp, she finished almost half of it. I felt my beast cock her head in the back of my mind.

"While you were out getting drilled, I got drunk."

I clenched my mug. "I wasn't getting drilled," I huffed, although Ethan would argue that's exactly what his fingers had been doing.

Andrea snorted as she went for a refill. She assessed me. "Probably right. You don't look chipper enough."

I rolled my eyes. "So, you and Jake are on tap tonight?"

"We are not moving away from this conversation, young lady."

"What conversation?"

Andrea walked over to the table and sat next to me. "About how you haven't let him dick you down six ways to next Sunday yet."

"Andrea!"

She cringed with a hiss. Her fingers rubbed her temple. "Gentle, I'm delicate right now."

"You did this to yourself," I grumbled into my coffee. "You're good to go with Jake tonight?"

"Yes, I don't need you to sub in for me," she drawled as she continued to comb out her hair with her fingers. "There's still too much attention on you."

"I'm not a zoo animal," I found myself saying in a voice that was too small for my liking. "I wish people would just move on."

"Once he marks you they should," she noted.

"Why's that?"

Andrea snorted. "Because that's what's normal. What true mates do. They'll know it's real."

I slammed my coffee on the table. Liquid burned my fingers as it sloshed over but I didn't care. I felt something like ice run through me as the beast in me shook out her fur.

"Are people saying it's not real?"

She stood with her coffee in hand. "It doesn't matter," she told me before retreating to her room. "Get dressed. We'll have to grab breakfast at the pack house. Dad hates tardiness."

Although I was beginning to hate being early for my tracker shifts, Andrea didn't mind; she offered to wait with me in the tracker room, which I think was more so she could finish the breakfast tacos we'd snagged along the way. But once again, as the tracker team filed in, I found myself painted by their stares and coated by whispers. It was hard to ignore the murmurs that were not at all well concealed as they wove their way around and around the crowd.

"She follows him around like a pup."

"I wonder if she'll go back to Levi's?"

"Where's her mark?"

Andrea nudged her chin at Evangeline, who was standing with Amber and Piper. *"She needs new friends."*

I tried to shift my attention, but it was hard to do when I could hear Piper stirring the pot, and both Evangeline and Amber laughing at whatever she'd said.

"You know what happens to silly pups who get lost in the woods?" Andrea said, loud enough so Piper would hear, and hear she did. The three girls stopped talking and slowly turned to see Andrea smiling at them with her fangs showing.

"Andrea," I warned.

She snorted. *"What? Being nice isn't helping either. Might as well be a petty bitch."*

THE PACK

I rolled my eyes as Billy strode toward us. He eyed Andrea, shaking his head as if he had made her breakfast on a hungover morning one too many times before.

"My pride and joy," he addressed his daughter. "To what do I owe the pleasure of finding you here?"

Andrea jabbed her thumb in my direction. "She can't go anywhere without me."

My mouth dropped while she laughed into her next bite. Billy shook his head at her. "I need you at a guard station today."

"I know." She swallowed the last bite of her taco then tossed the foil wrapper in the trash by the door. "Jake isn't here yet. I've got time to spare."

"And you chose to spend it with me?"

She shoved his chest with a smile. "You're getting soft, old man."

He snorted at her. "Charlotte, did you get enough to eat at the pack house?"

"Plenty," I answered, with a smile.

Billy winked and squeezed my shoulder. He walked to the front of the room and started to write on the plexiglass. Andrea nudged my shoulder with hers. "That's my cue," she murmured to me.

She slipped out of the room while Billy made a few more notes. He turned and faced the group, running a hand over his face as he scanned us. "We had some reports that caribou are grazing in new spots. I need you all to confirm that. Amber, you're taking the ridge route—"

"Billy," Amber whined. Her fingers twirled the end of one of her natural platinum pigtails as she shifted her weight to one foot. A series of actions that seemed rehearsed, like she was ticking off boxes on the how to get off the shit list. She pursed her lips as her crystal-blue eyes completed the checklist, growing wider with a silent plea. "That is the worst route. It's so high up and takes forever to get up there! I had like a thousand blisters last time!"

"Amber," Billy warned, although the tone lost its bite quickly as it wavered. "We need you—"

"I'll go." He swiveled back to look at me. I pointed to the map on the opposite wall, where a familiar route was written next to my name along with Piper's. "I know where you want Piper to take me. The majority of it runs along the pack line with Thunderhead. I know it well. However, that ridge route looks like it runs close to Switchback? I've run over there a little, but I wouldn't mind seeing more."

Amber watched me for a moment like I was a puzzle piece she didn't expect. She nudged Evangeline next to her, who only shrugged.

Billy capped his marker. "The guards can be prickly over there, kiddo."

"Which is why I don't want to run it. We had an issue last time," Amber stated as her eyes grew colder, like a winter night with promises of a storm.

"I've never had an issue," I countered as the beast in me kick-drummed devious remarks that I knew would stir the rumor-driven pot steaming up the room. I bit my tongue. I didn't need to make things worse for myself—or for Ethan. "And I'll get to know more of the pack."

Billy thought a moment before relenting with a tired sign. "You're right, it will be good for you to learn new routes. I'll need you to mark the routes you already know for me—I should have known you already know the Thunderhead border."

THE PACK

"I can do that," I agreed.

"Good, then you're with Keeley today," he told me, before he rattled off other assignments.

Keeley found me once we were dismissed. She had her dark hair tied up again in space buns; freckles littered her cheeks as her full olive-green eyes watched me carefully. "Jake told me a little about you, it's good to meet you."

"Same," I answered.

We were headed for the door when I felt a hand on my shoulder. Billy stepped closer to us. "You two be careful. You're running along the line of the Trapper's Forest. Any issues and you call me immediately."

"We will," Keeley answered for us.

He reached for my arm and pulled me a step closer to him. "Remember, it's forbidden."

My beast shook out her fur and tried to help me shake off the unease his words created. My mood soured further when Piper called, "See you later, Charlotte!" with a fangy smile from the edge of the barn. "Don't get lost!"

I bit my lip and kept walking. I wasn't walking into that trap, not so easily, at least. Keeley looked over her shoulder before sliding closer to me. "She's trouble."

"I know," I grumbled.

We shifted to our fur and made a quick pace west to the Switchback Pack line. The sun was out, high and bright in the sky without a cloud to threaten it. Shifting back to my skin, I closed my eyes and let sunshine cover my cheeks as the song of swaying grass around us played. Keeley reached out to run a hand over the tops of the wildflowers growing along the hills.

"It's so beautiful," I murmured.

"It is," she answered with a light smile. "Remi told me about you before you came. He said you were pretty good at this. He said you were a good time, too, after a couple of glasses of wine."

I snorted. "He's such a brat."

She giggled. "He is. How was working for Bowie?"

"She's the best." I couldn't contain how the smile on my face grew from talking about my old friends. "Her and Rem are both great."

Her lips pulled into a tight smile. "I haven't seen her in too long. I need to. She was excited that Ethan put my name in for the Hunt next year. She was my dad's best friend."

Remi had told me that she was Cash's daughter before I left. I couldn't help but think back to when Bowie had told me in the car on the way back from Talia's how she'd found Cash—hung from a tree with his feet cut off.

"I'm sorry."

She bit her lip before she curled to backpedal in front of me. "Don't worry about Piper or Amber, for all that it matters. You're new and they're bored. They'll find something new to chew on soon enough."

"I hope so," I muttered. "Hopefully they didn't stir up too much already?"

She shrugged. "Only that you lived with vampires."

I lifted a brow. "I did."

She looked stunned for a second before she fell back in step with me. "I've never met one."

"Really?"

She nodded. I had thought Jake was an outlier, never having interacted with vampires before meeting my friends, but now it seemed that at this pack, he was the norm.

"They're very kind," I told her. The absence of them in my day-to-day life was heavier than I'd expected. I gestured at the path in front of us. "How much longer do we have?"

"Not long. It's all uphill from here. Gets really steep," she explained with an excitement that spread to me. "The guards are fine, too, Amber just pissed a few off, so I think it's more of a her thing."

"I'm sure their pack lead loved that."

"Have you met him?"

"No," I answered, which seemed to surprise her. "Levi said Jackson keeps to himself."

Keeley whistled lowly. "Levi's right. The allusive Jackson Bones."

A giggle escaped from my lips. "He sounds like a pirate."

Keeley cackled next to me. "Oh my god, you're right! Although I did hear a rumor that Ethan knows him. Like actually talks face-to-face with the guy."

"But why would that be a big deal? I mean, I'm sure he has to?"

Keeley nibbled on her lip before she realized I was absolutely not following where she was going. "Right, I guess you haven't heard this rumor. Allegedly, Jackson killed his pack lead and took over the pack. A hostile takeover of sorts. Very much not within the bounds of how things are normally done. Packs around here . . . how do I say this?" she muttered to herself before she carefully explained. "Keep their distance. The pack lead was his father."

My mouth dropped. I recalled what Levi had said about Jeremiah Bones, but he never mentioned a coup. "Seriously?"

Keeley licked her lips. "It's hard to say. It was on the day of the attack. Jackson claims the rogues did it, and no one can really prove otherwise, but it always seemed off. And the rumors never died. I don't know? Who knows?"

"Why would he kill his father?"

"I don't know, and frankly, I don't know if I want to know."

I hummed in agreement and followed her along the route to Switchback. It was becoming my new favorite to run. The mountain terrain was a challenge I welcomed. The inclines were slick rocks that had little grip on them, making it easy to fall and slide across the smooth surface; and with the thinner air, I had to pace myself to adjust to the altitude.

My beast and I both were delighted to run with Keeley, who had caramel-colored fur with small black stripes wrapping around her legs. She maneuvered easily over the terrain, like water snaking through the dirt—challenging us in a way we delighted in.

We continued along the Switchback border through the Trapper's Forest on a path that Keeley told me was both safe and approved by Thomas. On that path, the sickly trees faded and the hills of the mountain instead owned the terrain. For as far as I could see to the west, the trees lining the border were painted black, like soldiers wearing leather boots into battle.

Keeley yipped at me over her shoulder.

My beast could practically taste the caribou by the time Keeley led us to a ledge, which overlooked where they were lazily eating grass along the banks of a stream that curled down the mountain.

Keeley laid her head on her paws. *"This was easier than I thought."*

I blew out a breath. *"Speak for yourself."*

THE PACK

She laughed across our link. *"You'll get used to the altitude. The forest hides a lot of the incline. Anyhow, I told Billy we found them. We don't have to rush back right away."*

Inwardly, I groaned in thanks. She studied me until her wolf turned back to the herd below. *"He talked a lot about you, you know?"*

"Who?"

"Ethan," she stated carefully. *"He's not one to talk a lot, but he's friends with Sam's mate, Trey."*

"I met Trey at the full run. Sam is the pack doctor, right?"

"Yeah," Keeley confirmed. *"She's my cousin. I live with her and Trey—he's like an older brother to me—anyhow, it was one of the nights Ethan came back while you were still at Thunderhead. Sam more or less dragged him to our house and got him drunk, like drunk drunk. A rare thing for him, but Sam was determined to get some details out of him."*

I found myself smiling inwardly.

"Anyhow, Sam finally got him to talk. I've . . . well, I've never seen him like that. It was sweet," she added wistfully.

"Like what?"

She huffed as she laid her head on her paws. *"Giddy. Like he could hardly believe it himself."*

Something danced over the pull to Ethan, reminding me that it was ever present. Always there.

"So what now?" I asked, ready to change the topic before I found myself gushing about him too.

"We shift back and get the maps out and make some notes. Then when we get back, we'll add them to the game maps."

"You know, I have my game tags. Ethan picked them up for me."

Keeley watched me a moment. *"The caribou are right there..."* she observed.

"Would Billy be okay with it?"

She snorted. *"I'm an act-first, forgiveness-later person."* Keeley nudged her nose toward the deer. *"Go on."*

"No, we're both going."

She licked her teeth then asked, *"Which one?"*

"Come on... the biggest one." If we were going to have to ask for forgiveness, we might as well get the whole hog. I fell quiet, searching until I found a large stag with practically more horns than there were trees around. *"Him?"*

"Him," she agreed. *"Heads or tails?"*

"Dealer's choice."

"Heads," she decided. *"Let's move."*

We shuffled backward then together quietly stalked through the brush until we were right upon the herd. Under the cover of some bushes we waited and waited until finally, Keeley made the first move.

It was an easy dance with her. She hurtled forward while I curled around the back. The deer around us had already begun to run in a panic, but our target didn't move quickly enough.

Because right after he dodged an attempt from Keeley to take his neck, I locked my jaw onto his back leg. His single pause gave her the chance she needed to find his jugular. Blood was still spilling on the ground from his body as we shifted back to our skin.

She wiped her mouth then beamed at me with a smile. "I have some knives in my bag. No tarp."

"What about a log? We could tie its feet together and carry it that way? Do you have rope?"

"Of course." She snorted while she patted her saddlebag. "And I have water, a flashlight, ChapStick, granola—" I arched a brow at her only to earn a cheeky shrug. "What? I'm prepared. Spare me."

I laughed then helped her make quick work of dressing the deer before hanging him on a fallen branch I'd found. We each took an end, carrying it on our shoulders as we marched back the way we had come.

Keeley paused as the forest grew darker around us. The Trapper's Forest was quiet next to us as we walked along the pack line back to the pack house. I hadn't noticed the silence earlier because we were moving fast to get to the herd, but now, with our slower pace, it felt like the forest was reaching its hand out to taunt us.

A cold chill swept along the forest floor. I willed my racing heart to calm so I could focus. My beast pressed forward, both of us letting the scent of the forest flood our senses until something familiar hit. "There's old blood magic close to here. A silent spot. We need to keep moving."

"Silent spots don't move," she urged in a rushed whisper, like it had been a rule she had known since she was a child.

"They do," I asserted.

She snapped her mouth shut and began to walk faster. We barely made a turn around a boulder when a sound snapped through the woods. Keeley and I froze. The hair on the back of my neck rose.

"Probably an animal?" she whispered.

I held a finger up to my lips. She sucked in a breath and tapped her temple as more cracks sounded through the forest, like a series of firecrackers going off nearby. Keeley's nails turned to claws and my own body began to hum.

"What the hell was that?!"

I scanned the hovering darkness in front of us. Closing my eyes, I tried to focus my nerves so I could think. When I did, the smell of blood magic hit me again. Although this time, it wasn't old.

My eyes flew open. Keeley was looking around nervously. She bounced on her toes like she was ready to drop the deer and bolt. *"Charlotte, it's so quiet."*

"I know," I told her calmly. *"It's blood magic. You're okay. All right?"*

She shook her head at me. *"How can you tell?"*

"You have to calm down enough to focus," I explained.

She closed her eyes while I stared into the darkness. My beast was yipping in the back of my mind to run. To chase what was out there. To find what needed to be found.

"Charlotte . . ." she hissed. *"Nothing good comes from this forest. It's forbidden. We shouldn't go in there,"* she pleaded, like she knew that I already had the instinct to charge in.

My toes curled into the dirt. There was something back there—I knew there was. I knew I should link Ethan or Billy, but a better half of me wanted to search on my own first—find it on my own without someone hovering. No one hovered when I was at Thunderhead . . .

But this pack wasn't Thunderhead, and Levi wasn't wrong, there was something about this end of the forest that felt more feral compared to our portion back home.

"Charlotte . . ." The whisper sounded like it was right next to me. I whipped around only to see darkness ahead.

"Charlotte," something whispered again, this time a little farther away.

THE PACK

Andrea's words from the other night screamed into my memory like an alarm. Cold fear ran through me. I carefully snuck a glance at Keeley, praying she didn't notice—that she didn't suspect.

Keeley was still looking around, unaware of the panic attack I was about to have next to her. I shifted the pole on my shoulder. "Let's get out of here."

"This place, it's fucked up," she whispered to me. "Dad was never afraid of it, and at the end of the day they hung him in it."

"I'm sorry, Keeley."

"The blood magic's been allowed to fester for too long," she said quietly, in a bitter voice that grated against my skin. "We should have caught the witches who did it. Should have made them listen to the sound of it until they lost their minds."

My breath caught. My beast was pacing in the back of my mind. I cast my eyes to my toes and suppressed a whimper. I could never let anyone here know about the whispers. Andrea was right.

"They should have burned this fucking forest down," Keeley snarled.

I blew out a shaky breath. "Yeah, they should have."

CHAPTER FOURTEEN

Billy emerged from the pack house with Thomas as we approached. He laughed under his breath at the sight of the deer. Thomas shook his head with what looked like a smile fighting to be seen.

"My First," Keeley said to Thomas, with a bow of her chin.

Billy crossed his arms across his chest. "Girls, wasn't this supposed to be a scouting mission?" he chided us in a serious tone that did not match the playfulness in his eyes.

Keeley shifted the branch so she could face him directly. Her brow lifted as she tilted her chin in an amused challenge. "I told her it was all right."

"You did?" he inquired, an oozy layer of suspicion in his voice.

"It was my idea," I quickly interjected.

Thomas arched a brow at me. I dipped my head slightly to him. "Her First..." I greeted quickly before offering Billy an apologetic smile. "Sorry."

Billy waved me off. "Thirty percent goes to the pack. I can help you get it home and butchered but then I need to jet to a meeting here shortly."

"I can handle it, Bill." Thomas slapped him on his shoulder. "You two don't need to carry that home. You had a long run." Gone from him was the anger and ice from our first meeting and now there was something too casual for comfort.

"You don't mind?" Billy asked.

"Not at all," he answered, with a kind smile that revealed a few sharp teeth through the stretched, frayed skin over his mouth. "Keeley, go on home. I'll help Charlotte get this to her place."

"If you come by later, I can give you your half," I told her.

"Sounds good." She wiped some sweat off her brow and handed her end of the branch to Thomas. "Thanks, My First. Honestly, you're right. Going to the barn would have killed me."

Thomas barked a laugh as he took over Keeley's burden. Grabbing the log, he flicked his wrist so the pearl stone of his bracelet wouldn't get caught on the bark. I shook my head and tried to ignore the soft hum that seemed to be coming from it. Hearing the whispers was enough for me today.

"You two would have most likely rolled down it with how tired you both look," Thomas chuffed.

"I'll leave you two to it," Billy told us before he marched back to the pack house.

Keeley waved goodbye, and Thomas and I set off back to my house with the deer between us.

"Well, how was it?" he said over his shoulder.

My beast was on alert, pacing in the back of my mind. It didn't help that we had walked almost halfway to the house in a thick silence. Part of me wished he would have lectured me about breaking the rules rather than leaving me to my own speculative thoughts.

"How was what, Her Fir—"

"Honestly, Charlotte, you're practically family." My beast cocked her head. "'Thomas' is fine. But not Tommy. An older wolf used to call me that as a kid, and I hated the son of a bitch."

"Right." I tried to keep my tone neutral. Tried to act like he didn't jar me. "Um, you mean the run?"

"Yeah? Haven't been able to get out there in a while. What did you think?"

"It was tough," I answered, which made him chuckle. "I'm not used to the altitude. But it's really pretty up there."

"Used to be where I would sneak off with Miranda," he added, with a sly grin back at me.

"Used to?" I tried to tease him.

His shoulders shook as he laughed harder. "We gotta keep things interesting, Charlotte. You'll understand soon enough."

We stepped onto the little path and made our way between the homes. Dusk had set in. A few wolves were going by each lantern and opening the glass panes to light the candles inside.

"It's so cool you guys have all these lanterns," I noted.

"Ah, yeah, been that way for a long time. Those lanterns are older some of the wolves here. We keep them lit year-round, especially in snowstorms. They can help people find their way home."

"They're very lovely."

"I thought about switching them to battery-powered ones, but Miranda threw a fit. She's got a thing for tradition." The deer was getting heavy on my shoulder, and I was focused on holding up my end while keeping up with his longer stride when he went on, "That route runs next to the Trapper's Forest. You didn't have any trouble, did you?"

"It was—" He glanced back at me briefly and I caught the look in his eyes. The kind of look a parent has when they know their child has done something wrong. "It was fine. It's a weird place," I added with a shrug.

"It is," he agreed. "And dangerous. Too many have died in there thinking they're bigger and badder than the magic that's festered there for generations. I don't let wolves go in unless I absolutely have to."

I had just opened my mouth to reply when something sizzled along the pull. Something that felt dangerous and drenched in dread. Leaning around Thomas, I could see Ethan waiting on my doorstep.

Thomas paused at my fence and lifted a hand to Ethan. Together, we set the deer down. "Little rule breaker over here!"

Ethan's lips pulled into a smile that didn't reach his eyes. He dipped his head as he approached us. "My First." He curled around the deer to me and pressed a quick kiss to my temple. "Well, it is a good deer," he pointed out to Thomas.

Thomas brushed his hands on his jeans. "It is. You did good today," he told me.

Ethan was silent, suddenly still next to me.

"Thanks, but I had help," I said, desperate for the interaction to be over.

"Well, either way, good work," he told me. "I think you're in good hands here," he added before bidding us goodbye and disappearing down the stone path.

I turned to Ethan. "Is everything okay?"

"Yeah," he breathed, but I didn't believe him.

I didn't believe him because his eyes kept darting behind me in the direction of where Thomas had gone. My beast pawed at me and inwardly I nodded at her. We were tucking this moment away for later—and we were certainly bringing it up.

Red circled the drain of the sink while I washed the blood off my arms. I heard the back door close as Ethan stole into the kitchen. The skin on my shoulders twitched as he neared; arms wrapped around my middle and pulled me to his firm chest as I switched the water off.

"How was the run? Other than bringing me the extra work of dressing a deer."

Swallowing, I turned to face him. "I smelled blood magic in the forest. It was fresh."

His frowned. "What do you mean 'in the forest'? Did you go into the Trapper's Forest?"

"No." A strange defensiveness filled my voice. "It was on the border near Switchback. It . . . there was a silent spot there and then I smelled it. Then we heard cracking—popping. It does sound like those fireworks you mentioned."

His jaw ticked a hair. "I'll tell Jake to make sure he and Andrea look into it tonight."

"Or we could go?"

He looked at the floor then back at me. "We talked about this. We agreed."

I did agree to play by the rules. I did promise him that I wouldn't go snooping without him; and I knew if it was me, I would be frustrated too. I should do better to heed his advice. To heed Andrea's. To stay away from the whispers. But another part of me needed to hunt. Needed to find the things that hid in the darkness of the woods.

"Thomas still has an eye on you. He asked me if something was wrong with the borders—he thought that's why Billy sent you out with Keeley."

"No, I volunteered," I told him. "Well, it was that or to be stuck with Piper again."

He hummed as understanding flooded his face.

"Why not just ask Billy himself?" I queried. "Seems weird?"

"I don't know, but he seemed worked up when he asked me about it. I told him to ask Billy, but he said he couldn't get a hold of him." He blew out a breath.

"He really needs to learn to relax," I grumbled.

Ethan rolled his eyes then pressed his nose into my hair. Another nugget, another nonanswer my beast and I were saving away for a better time to ask.

"The blood magic? It wasn't near anything?"

I shook my head against his chest. "Nothing notable, but I also didn't go looking for anything."

"Was there anything else?"

A chill ran through me. My legs felt frozen to the ground, like they were paralyzed in front of oncoming headlights. I blew out a breath and pressed myself closer to him. "No."

Until I knew what the hell the whispers were, I wasn't about to speak of them. They already took up too much real estate in my life and I wasn't about to create more chaos in his.

"We can mark where you found it on the map in Billy's basement. There's got to be a pattern," he muttered. He rubbed his jaw as his eyes drifted far away. "I had a feeling you were close to the forest." His raw voice was quiet, almost as if he was trying to keep the forest from hearing us even so far from it. "I felt off. Then my chest felt so damn tight, it was like I could feel the silence of that place around me. And I knew. I knew you were in a silent spot. I almost came after you, but then Keeley linked me to tell me you guys were carrying a deer back."

I rubbed my hand over my chest. "The pull, this is how it's supposed to work, right?"

"Supposedly," he answered, mirroring my worried expression. How much about this thing did either of us actually know?

"Earlier just now, I could feel it too—you—over the pull. You were tense when I walked up to the house with Thomas."

I could see from the way his jaw ticked that he was still worried.

"We really need to work on sending each other different emotions." The deviousness in his eyes made my stomach flutter, but I did not miss that he had deflected my question again.

I wormed out of his hold. My mind was too tired to keep prying for today.

"I need to shower. I want the deer guts off me." I headed for the bathroom.

"Seems like a big job," I heard him say before something fluttered over the pull. Something warm, that slowly oozed its way to my core. A heat that I knew he felt, too, because the sensation along the bond between us was emitted from him.

Feeling bold, I licked my lips and looked over my shoulder. "I felt that."

His eyes flashed with heat as something raw like wildfire twirled around my core. He closed the space between us in a few steps. My breath caught as a delicious rush cascaded over the bond and fingered up my spine. His mouth descended on mine, melting every thought in my brain away until all that consumed me was him—the feeling of his hands cupping my ass as he carried me to the bathroom, the way he said my name when he murmured it against my neck, and how illegally soft his lips were.

He yanked the curtain open while my hand clumsily twisted the faucet on. I pulled his shirt off as he stepped us under the warm stream of water. Steam filled the tiny bathroom as cool tiles kissed my back. His hands yanked my shifter top up, a sports bra that suddenly felt way too tight—too much like a barrier between us. What started as a feverish heat flooding the pool turned into pure electricity when his mouth latched around my nipple.

If I wasn't breathless and boneless after this was all said and done, it would have to be one of the greatest tragedies to ever happen.

I wasn't sure if I was ready for forever, but I was ready for now. Here. With him. And not because there was this thing, this pull between us, but because I wanted him. A want—a need—I saw reflected as he looked at me like I was the only thing that mattered in this world.

Then he blinked, breaking the moment as needy desperation took its place.

My frantic fingers fumbled as they tried to unbuckle his

belt while his hands roughly yanked my shifter shorts down just enough so one hand could find my center. The minute his fingers pressed inside me, he groaned against my neck. "Fuck, baby."

His fingers moved as his mouth captured mine again in a slow, languid, wet kiss. I rocked my hips against his hand ... and then something banged from inside the house.

"Can you two not wait?!" Andrea yelled.

We almost slipped on the wet tile from the startling sound of her voice. Ethan carefully set me down as we steadied ourselves on our feet.

"Go away!" I called back.

"Why the fuck is there a deer hanging in our backyard over the flowers I just planted?!"

"Because I put it there!" Ethan shouted back.

"You don't live here!" she screeched.

"Andrea!" I shrieked.

"Fuck, you two! I am having a beer!"

"Are you staying?!" I cried before gawking at Ethan.

"It's my house!"

Ethan blinked then deep laughter ripped through him. My own chest shook as it spread to me. He leaned his head on my shoulder then pulled my shorts back up. I pulled my top down. Water was still spraying us.

"Do you want to stay for dinner?" I asked. He looked at his soaking jeans then broke out in laughter again.

"Sure," he said, breathless, cheeks flushed.

I licked my lips then rose onto my toes to kiss him. He groaned into my mouth as his slick torso pressed against me.

"Oh my god, you two!" Andrea was insistent.

"He's staying for dinner!" I shouted.

Andrea was quiet a moment then finally said, "Well, if he's staying, he's cooking!"

Ethan nipped at my lips. "Do I get to eat you later at least?"

Grinning, I shoved him out of the shower. "Go, I actually do need to bathe."

He shook his head and snatched a towel from the counter. I didn't dare look at him when he pulled his jeans off; otherwise Andrea was likely going to burn the house down with me in it. When the door clicked closed behind him, I leaned back against the cool tiles, praying to calm the heat still pulsing over the pull between us.

CHAPTER FIFTEEN

I tapped my pen on the end of the desk Miranda had set up for me in her office. Out of the thirty-three packs invited, not even half of them had confirmed attendance to the event, which was not helpful as the summer days felt like they were quickly slipping away.

"We're still missing a lot of responses." I set my pen down and leaned back in my seat. "We only have twelve so far."

Miranda set her mason jar of water down. Her nose crinkled in a way that Thomas had noted as "cute" one time in a meeting when she was trying to discuss the agenda. That same meeting, I'd begun to regret my offer to help. Besides it being a ton of work, our group was less than enthusiastic. Ethan dozed through most of the first meeting, while Thomas did a crossword puzzle.

THE PACK

Evangeline took furious notes while Amber mostly picked her nails while subtly trying to steal glances at me—specifically, at my neck and my wrist.

The lack of Ethan's mark was starting to weigh on me, not just from the looks I kept receiving—which ranged from curious to skeptical to suspicious—but because the pull between us was getting stronger and I worried that it wasn't going to give me more time to do this my way. I was worried that the desire from it was going to steal my mind from me—from both of us.

"I'll get Thomas to follow up," Miranda grumbled. "He had one job and of course he's going to leave me to do it all."

"Well, you have me," I offered politely.

Her shoulders relaxed. "I know, and I am so very grateful. What are you and Ethan getting into tonight?"

The fucking forest, finally, after over a week and a half of waiting since the meeting in Billy's basement. The new moon could not have come soon enough.

Neither Jake nor Andrea had found anything when they'd set out, even after they went to the exact spot where I had smelled the blood magic with Keeley. Evan and Billy had been just as unsuccessful, which only fueled the fire of my determination. Remi would be out tonight too. Apparently, they had also smelled fresh blood magic at Thunderhead a few days ago, but he didn't know anything more to share with me.

"He's cooking me dinner," I answered.

Miranda beamed back at me. "Oh, you've already got him trained!"

It took everything in me to bite my tongue instead of releasing the tempting snarky response. "He's making steaks, or so he said."

She laughed and rocked back in her chair. "I remember when

Thomas wined and dined me—enjoy it!" She quickly looked at the analog clock on her desk. "Goodness, it's already after five. Get out of here and go have a good time!"

"You're sure?" I asked for good measure.

Her hand flew to her chest. "You're too kind, but, yes, please go let that man romance you!"

I quickly gathered my things and said my goodbyes before darting out of the pack house. The directions Ethan gave me were easy enough to follow. I ran in my fur down the lantern-lit path until it ended, then continued through the trees and up the hills. There were some lone lanterns hanging on the trees along the way, with candles that were close to burning out.

Ethan's house was a cozy A-frame tucked into the trees. Green shutters adorned the windows and there was a tidy log pile stacked next to it. A breeze ran across my fur almost like an eager greeting as I approached.

He stepped out of the house and ran a hand through his damp hair. I shifted to my skin and let my feet carry me straight to him, where his lips easily melted against mine.

He pulled away first and took my saddlebag from me. "We have a change of plans."

"Oh?"

He tossed my bag inside then picked up another from a spot by the door. "We need to go to Switchback. Tonight."

My beast started to pace while I fell in step with him. "What do you mean?" I asked, before I added through our link, *"We're supposed to go into the forest tonight, it's our night."*

"I know," he answered in a tone of regret. *"But Jackson said he found a Bloodstone. He wants us to look at it—he specifically asked if you would nose around where they found it."*

"Me?"

He nodded.

"Jackson? The Jackson Bones?"

"The Jackson Bones," he echoed.

I bit my tongue and tried to quell the frustration snapping inside of me. *"Context helps,"* I pressed patiently.

Without missing a beat, he admitted, *"We're friends. We've been friends for a long time. Since we were teenagers."*

"I wish you would have told me about this." Words that were my kind version of saying *Why didn't you tell me?*

"I should have." Regret flashed in his eyes.

We were not supposed to have secrets. I wanted to call him out but immediately stopped myself when I remembered the secrets I carried; the memory of the whispers was like cackling hyenas.

"And Thomas doesn't know?"

"No," he answered quickly. *"Jackson's father, Jeremiah, was one of Thomas's close friends. Thomas stopped being a Jackson fan after Jackson killed Jeremiah and still is very much not a Jackson fan."*

"So, he did kill his father."

He watched me a moment, weighing how I would react.

"Yes, and Jeremiah deserved it. Their pack lived in fear. He was an absolute monster. There was no rule of law with him, not with him and his cronies running things as they pleased." His jaw clenched. *"No one there will say it was anything but the rogues that day. The pack is incredibly loyal to Jackson."*

"I thought that there was supposed to be a challenge for pack lead?"

"Not when the pack lead is a murdering maniac." His jaw

ticked as his shoulders tensed. *"Jackson didn't care about the political fallout. He saved them."*

"So, I'm assuming we keep this quiet?"

"Charlotte." He stopped walking and faced me directly. *"You cannot tell anyone. Not Andrea. Not Levi."* His nostrils flared as he exhaled heavily.

I could tell by his tone that this knowledge wasn't just dangerous—it was deadly.

"I understand."

It was enough to satisfy him. My beast pressed closer to my skin while I tightened my ponytail. Something danced through my veins, sparking heat when Ethan pulled his sweatshirt off. He shoved it into the saddlebag with a satisfied smirk. *"We've got to get moving—it's a long run."* Then out loud he added, "Keep up."

Something crackled across the bond between us that made my mouth water. My beast rushed forward as we shifted to our fur and charged into the night with him.

He was not wrong about the time it would take to get there. Half the reason it took so long was because we had to double back over and over in order to confuse our scent from other Hemlock trackers. It was well past midnight when we arrived at the Switchback Pack line, where two guards with electric lanterns were leaning against a thick tree painted black at the base.

They both nodded to Ethan and murmured, "Her Second," as we shifted to our skin.

Ethan nodded back. "Where is he?" he asked. "He's supposed to meet—"

"Bro! Took you long enough!" someone ahead of us shouted.

THE PACK

Ethan lifted his hand in a tired wave at the two men approaching. One looked exhausted. He had bags under his eyes and his midnight hair was sticking out in every direction—unlike his counterpart, who practically bounced with every giddy step he took like a kid who had had way too much sugar.

I heard Ethan groan under his breath.

"Charlotte, this is Jackson."

Jackson grinned with a wide smile that I was sure broke plenty of hearts. He was an all-American panty-dropper with golden locks that hung around his ears, sleepy green eyes, and dimples that gave him an air of boyish innocence. But with the swagger of his walk and the puff of his chiseled chest, he was certainly anything but innocent.

"It's about time!" He walked right up to me and grabbed me by the shoulders then yanked me in for a hug. "Come on, bring it in. We're like family now."

"Jackson," Ethan groused.

He released me, and when he did, I found myself stumbling back to Ethan, who steadily pulled me to his side. Jackson held his arms out, and it was then that I realized how scarred his entire upper body was. Scars that looked like they had come from more than just sparring. Some were clean. Purposeful. I knew in my gut they were, because I had those too.

"Come on, man! What? I can't be excited to meet my best fucking friend's true mate?!"

Ethan pinched the bridge of his nose while the wiry man behind Jackson stepped around him with a meek wave. "Hey, I'm Caden. Nice to meet you," he told me before nodding to Ethan. "Her Second."

Jackson jabbed his thumb in Caden's direction. "Shit, sorry,

Charlotte. This is my second, Caden. My other best friend. But that's it. I don't have fucking time for more."

"Right." I glanced at Ethan, who looked like he was close to tackling his "best friend" to the ground.

"You wanted to show us something?" Ethan asked with a forced patience that seemed routine with Jackson.

Jackson pointed a mother-like finger at him. "Don't be cranky. Did you eat? You're a bitch when you don't eat."

Ethan rubbed his temple, actively avoiding Jackson's inquisitive gaze. Caden ran his hands through his hair before he slapped Jackson's shoulder. "Why don't we take them to the stone, then we can eat?"

Jackson cut his eyes to Caden before jerking a nod. "All right, fucking voice of reason. But we're out of those pizzas, you gotta get me more when you go into town, Ethan."

My mouth dropped. I tilted my head to Ethan. "You grocery shop for him?"

Jackson scoffed like he was almost offended. "Bro, did you not tell her about us?"

"I told her tonight!" Ethan hissed.

"Tonight?!" Jackson rolled his eyes. "What, don't you love me anymore?" he taunted with a wicked smile.

Ethan rolled his eyes. "The moon did not grant me enough patience—"

"Ethan said you wanted me to look at something." I rocked back on my heels. "A Bloodstone?"

The playfulness melted away from him. He glanced at Ethan then cut his green eyes to me. "Heard you have a good nose."

"It's pretty good," I answered while my beast shook her fur out, letting a hum pulse outward.

He snorted, amused. "My trackers are good, but they wanted a second opinion. Follow me. Watch your footing."

I didn't realize what he meant until I found myself walking up steep inclines and around tricky knife-edge turns around sharp corners of rock that punched through the ground. We edged down a corkscrewed path until I saw the sickly trees somehow standing tall among the harsh terrain.

Caden was grim next to me. "Trapper's Forest. Only something that fucked up would find a way to grow out here."

"Yeah," I breathed, and tried to ignore the fingers of anxiety tightening around my chest.

Ethan ran behind me as we made our way down the precarious path through the Trapper's Forest until we reached an opening in the trees. Moonlight poured through the clearing and glimmered off the surface of a smooth red stone.

Jackson said nothing and didn't stop me when I ran ahead. I could smell it already. A sickly sweetness that danced with the chilly breeze, tickling my sides as I neared the clearing. Soon I could hear the murmurs rolling over my skin like silk. There were so many voices coming from the stone—I tried to focus on one, but it was impossible to make out the words. It sounded like someone speaking underwater. I bit my lip. How to break through the surface?

"Charlotte?" I looked over my shoulder to see both Ethan and Jackson watching me curiously.

"Stay there," I bid them, before I crossed into the moonlight.

My breath caught in my throat at the sickly-sweet smell of blood magic thick in the circle. "Fuck me," I murmured. "It's fresh." I turned around to face Jackson. "Why did you want me?"

Jackson cocked his head at me. "Heard you're good at

sniffing out blood magic," he noted. "Ethan said you and Remi found those places yourselves on Thunderhead. I want whatever details you can find."

I inhaled again. "This is new—less than a week. Maybe a day?"

"Is it like what you saw before at Thunderhead?" Jackson asked. When I met his gaze, I knew then that this is why he wanted me here.

Nodding slowly, I answered. "Yes. The scent dies, just like it did at Thunderhead. The stone, it's just like how Ethan and I found the first one." Taking a few steps around the border, I inhaled again. "Pray the breeze blows this blood magic out of here before it starts moving on its own."

"It doesn't move," one of the guards said.

"It does," I corrected before I turned back to Jackson. "It's like the longer it has to sit, the wilder it gets."

Jackson breathed a satisfied smile. He nudged Ethan's shoulder with his own. "Hot and smart, good for you, man."

Ethan only shook his head with a bored expression.

I rolled my eyes. Taking a leap into the air, I shifted to my fur. My beast snapped her teeth in the night while I sat back and let her senses take over. She nosed through the ground that reeked of blood magic before we turned and trotted to the center of the circle, where the stone lay.

A whimper fell from her lips. The sound of the murmurs grated against her ears. I quickly shifted back to my skin and knelt in front of it.

"It's okay," I assured her, although she was not convinced. She snapped her teeth at me in warning when I reached for it, then howled when my fingertips were only a breath away.

THE PACK

When my fingers touched the surface of the swirling red stone, screaming ripped through the silence, as if dozens of people were being tortured right next to me.

The moment I ripped my hand away the screams stopped. Sucking in a breath, I gritted my teeth and reached for it again only to be greeted with a symphony of wailing echoing around me as the voices sang a liturgy of torment and agony.

I yanked my hand away and fell back into something firm. The cries stopped. Hands steadied me before helping me stand.

My beast was snarling now, pawing at the corners of my mind—angry at whatever this thing was. And, hell, I was too.

"Charlotte?"

I had forgotten I had an audience. I wondered if they'd heard the screams, but when I scanned their faces, I realized they hadn't. They were all cautiously watching me.

Ethan pulled me closer to him. *"I felt that. Whatever that was."*

Dread pooled in my stomach. I blew out a breath. "It's—it feels bad. Very bad," I told him. It wasn't exactly a lie, but fuck me, I wasn't ready to admit it to him. I wasn't ready to deal with it myself.

It had taken me long enough to accept that I was a fucking werewolf, that I could have a happy and normal life as a werewolf. Whatever this was, it felt like acid corroding away whatever hopeful image of my future I had.

I leaned around him in hopes of ignoring the scrutinizing gaze exuding from his dual-colored eyes, which I knew in this moment would see my mask quickly cracking.

"Have you looked around the area?"

Jackson shook his head. "Not yet, I told my guards here to stay with it until we could confirm—"

"That it was like what we found on the Thunderhead-Hemlock border," I answered for him. I scanned the darkness around us. "The rogues were camping at Thunderhead, we think. The stone we found was not a mile into the Hemlock side of the border."

Caden lifted his chin at the guards. "Get some trackers and go. Do a mile perimeter of the area. Tell no one."

The two guards dipped their heads and left their lanterns before disappearing into the darkness. I walked the boundary of the clearing and looked for anything out of place, but it was all normal-appearing forest floor.

"You should talk to Levi," I advised him. "Let Bowie come here and look at it. Levi can be . . . I know he's—"

Jackson held up a hand. "A good pack lead," he stated, enunciating every word. "A little unhinged," he added with a dark laugh, "but I like that about him."

A hand reached for my shoulder. Ethan stood next to me with the stone in hand. The sight of it made me want to throw up. Because if I'd had any hope that Ethan had heard what I heard—that there wasn't something wrong with me—it was crushed the moment I saw him holding it easily in his palm.

"Let's get inside," Ethan said before smiling darkly at Jackson with his fangs showing. "And, please, dear, feed us."

Jackson grinned back with all his teeth showing.

We followed him back to his pack house, where he took us to the basement, which housed the pack's library. Ethan handed the stone to Caden. "Lock it up," Jackson told Caden, who tucked it into a leather pouch, muting the hums. My shoulders relaxed; I could feel my beast start to settle in the back of my mind.

Jackson ran a hand over his face. "Was hoping to meet you

under better circumstances. You know, brunch, mimosas—something fun?"

Ethan pulled a chair out for me in front of a small table. Happily, I got off feet that were screaming from the laborious trip.

"*Fun* for her is what we just did," he snorted with a shake of his head before taking a seat next to me.

Jackson huffed, "Ha!" then quickly sobered. "This isn't good. Finding two stones on two separate pack lands. It's not a coincidence."

"It's not," Ethan agreed.

Jackson turned a chair backward and straddled it. He rested his chin on the back. "Ethan said the other place you found a scent of rogues was on a border to Hemlock. You never found one on the Switchback-Thunderhead border?"

"No," I told him. "Remi hasn't updated me on anything yet either."

"What will you tell him?" Jackson asked.

I opened my mouth and closed it, thinking back to how Levi had handled the stone Ethan and I had found. "It's on your land. I suppose that's your call."

He watched me a moment and nodded, pleased. "I'd like to talk to Levi myself. I'll call him in the morning."

Caden padded back into the room with a laptop under his arm. He sat down and opened it up. "I set up a system for this place—took a minute to catalog this hellhole."

I couldn't imagine trying to. The rows and rows of shelves seemed to go on like an ocean.

Caden's fingers pounded away on the keyboard. "Once they found the stone this afternoon, I started running searches. This library is one of the oldest in the region, if not in the country. There are only a few texts that mention a Bloodstone. Which is surprising considering the amount of inventory we have."

"Yeah, well, dear old Dad destroyed a lot." Jackson looked like the words tasted bitter in his mouth.

Ethan's hand covered my knee. He drew circles with his thumb while Caden kept typing.

"Are there any details you can think of?" Caden asked me. "Anything Levi told you? The more I have to reference, the more I may be able to index more texts of use."

I leaned back in my seat. "David—you should talk to David. He seemed to know a bit, he's into history," I explained. "According to him, these are illegal and were made illegal hundreds of years ago, I think. No one has heard of them, so the question is who is ballsy enough to make them and why are they here? We know they take blood magic to create . . . maybe start with the known cases of them? I would be curious how they appeared in the past and how they were used."

Caden chewed his bottom lip. "I'll reach out to David after Jackson talks to Levi. This helps."

Jackson knit his fingers together on the back of the chair. "So we know that Hemlock and now Switchback have found them. But what we don't know is if other packs have and they're just keeping quiet."

Ethan hummed in agreement. "What do you think the odds of that are?"

"I would normally say low, but we've got something that is supposed to be extinct in our area. Twice." He shrugged slowly. "We do have that council meeting coming up . . ." Ethan's brows rose in amusement. Jackson drummed his fingers against the back of the chair. "This issue crosses pack lines. Seems like a worthy topic to bring up."

Ethan seemed impressed. A sly smile pulled at the edge of his mouth. "It's on your land and it's your right to bring it up, Her First."

Jackson snorted a laugh. "It is, but if it's brought up to the council you know we'll need a better messenger than an usurper."

Ethan hummed. "Lander will know what to do."

"And you?" Jackson asked him with a pointed stare. "What about Thomas?"

Ethan barked a laugh. "You know I can't bring this to him."

I slid forward in my seat. "But Jackson could?" I suggested. "This is the second time, surely he can't ignore it."

Jackson propped his head on his hands with a grim smile. "It's amazing what some people will do when they don't want to admit they're wrong."

"This is bigger than being right," I countered.

"I know," Jackson easily agreed. "I'll let you know what Levi says," he told Ethan, then slapped him on the shoulder. "Come on, let's feed your girl since apparently you don't."

Jackson stood then his eyes went distant a moment and his nostrils flared. Something crackled off him—immediately, I recognized moon blood pulsing to life. He stormed away as fur pierced the skin of his arms.

Ethan hissed a curse under his breath. His body tensed like stone that could shatter at any minute. "His guards found a rogue camp. It sounds like the area you found at Thunderhead. The scent is trapped inside the area."

Nausea bubbled up; I met Ethan's heavy gaze and said, "I don't think I'm hungry anymore."

Jackson walked us back to the border. He was silent the whole way, but as we walked, I felt something knocking at the corner of my mind. I glanced at Jackson, who lifted a brow at me. I swallowed and let the link sizzle into my mind like a sparkler whirling around the air on a hot summer night.

"*Be good to him,*" Jackson said, his voice soft with a sincerity that set me off-kilter. "*I may be an obnoxious, amazingly good-looking man who is so jealous my friend bagged you, but he's been through it. We all have. He takes a lot on himself. Cares too much. I'm rambling . . . you get the idea.*"

"*I do,*" I murmured back before I found myself telling him, "*I think it's great he has someone like you. Everyone needs someone in their corner.*"

Smiling gently, he replied, "*I knew I would like you. You're good together. I told him you would be. I had a good feeling about it.*"

"Stop flirting with her." Ethan glanced between the two of us. "Leaving me out of the link already, Charlotte? How could you."

"Like I would try to steal my best friend's girl. Come on, man," Jackson replied with a mock pout.

I shoved Ethan's chest. "Don't worry, he wouldn't shut up about how pretty he is."

Ethan smiled as a rich laughter reverberated around us. Jackson bid us both goodbye before we disappeared into the forest.

By the time we arrived back at Ethan's house, gentle sunbeams of dawn were close to breaking through the night sky. My beast yipped and curled through the wildflowers up the hill to his home. Ethan's beast only shook his head in amusement, running ahead of us before Ethan changed into his skin, his fitted shifters hugging his muscular legs too well.

My skin rippled over me until cool dawn air brushed my legs.

Ethan set our packs down before heading for the kitchen. I followed him then lifted myself to sit on top of the counter. "How did you meet him? Jackson?"

He poured himself a glass of water then leaned against the island opposite me. "Eli trained as a guard. After he graduated the Hunt, I would keep him company when he worked shifts on the border. One day we started finding notes on the trees—they were from Jackson. We thought they were fake at first, but eventually we agreed to meet him. He didn't want Eli or me to say anything about what was going on at Switchback. I never told anyone either."

"What was going on over there?" I asked gently.

"His dad was a sadist. He had a group of followers who thought he walked on water, big enough to keep people in line, according to Jackson. I think Dad and Levi always suspected but they never had proof."

He tipped the glass back and chugged the liquid down. "His father was obsessed with having boys and preserving his line," he explained while he refilled his glass. "He had a harem of women he was constantly trying to impregnate. He would always kill the babies born female. Somehow one of the women managed to convince him to keep Jackson's sister, Jane, alive."

Horror rolled over me. "What?"

He nodded slowly. "I didn't know Jackson then, but I know

our trackers found remains—children's bones—in the Trapper's Forest close to their border. Dad went over with Thomas, and Jackson's father refused to talk to Dad. He agreed to talk with Thomas, but Thomas came back with a black eye and a broken nose after their meeting. He was lucky."

"They were babies . . ."

"Yeah." Ethan huffed. "That pack was so isolated. Never went to council meetings. Rarely traded—and we can't feed our pack without our trading partners, people had been starving over there."

"Why did no one do anything? I mean Levi or your father?"

Ethan shook his head like he was still asking the question himself. "I don't know . . . I know they never had hard proof, and Levi was wary about stirring up hostilities after everything that happened with Aunt Eve."

Jesus Christ, Levi was going to have so many questions from me. Ethan paused a beat then finally said, "Jackson told me he was going to do it. Kill his father."

I could feel my beast's jaw go slack in the back of my mind.

"If it went bad, we had a plan to get Jane out. That's why he came to Eli and me—he didn't want the other pack leads knowing and potentially intervening. Eli and I agreed with him, and we worked on Jane's escape plan for weeks."

"Why didn't he take her and run?"

"He wouldn't leave all those people. He and his pack council now, well, back then, were finally old enough and big enough in size and numbers to be a real threat to his father and his father's followers. They weren't going to leave defenseless people to fend for themselves," he explained. "When the rogue attack happened, Jackson later told me he thought it was some divine intervention. He and Caden knew it was the perfect setup for them. They didn't get hit as hard as our pack did, but the rogues did attack. And it was enough chaos that his father was distracted.

"He ended his father himself, then he and his group killed everyone who was loyal to his father," he explained. "The Regional Council was always suspicious because of how late they sent aid to us, but we couldn't link that day, so he couldn't have heard anyone from our pack calling for help anyway. On the official record, his father was killed by rogues."

"Holy shit." I opened my mouth and closed it a few times before saying, "Surely if people knew the truth—I mean, his father was a maniac."

"In our world, people respect tradition and order. We need it. Without it we're a bunch of animals." He rubbed his jaw, which was sprinkled with stubble. "His father deserved to die, but a lot of packs did not like how the handover went. A lot were suspicious—many said if Jackson wanted the pack he should have challenged his father with evidence and had a vote, as we all have to do. This upcoming council meeting will be Jackson's first, because he wasn't invited last time. He wasn't recognized as a pack lead before."

"That changed?" I asked.

"The council voted on it last time—Lander and Talia voted for him. Wolves on the other side of the mountain did too. Lander spoke highly of Jackson, which was a kind thing he didn't have to do."

"Yeah, well, Lander is a saint."

Ethan breathed a laugh. "He is." He set his glass on the counter and leaned back on his elbows. "Jackson is in a precarious position, it's important you understand that."

"Explain."

"His pack is smaller than ours, growing, but they don't have the numbers or political capital to take hits like Thunderhead or to isolate themselves from trading partners again. People thought a lot of things about him back then—a lot of rumors swirled around about 'Jackson Bones,'" he said with air quotes. "He doesn't want to feed into that rumor, put his pack at risk. He was one of the first people to point out to me that if our investigation turned into something that we had to take to the Regional Council, we would need more than Thunderhead and Switchback bringing it forward. Thunderhead has allies that will back Levi, but the Regional Council is sometimes . . . antiquated with their opinions. Politically, we have to be smart."

"Then it's a good thing he wants to talk to Lander," I pointed out. Ethan hummed in agreement. "Why didn't you tell me?"

"I should have," he admitted. "I should have sooner, but, well, it's dangerous. You know why now. I guess—" He paused and breathed a tired smile. "I was trying to protect you."

I should drop it. I needed to drop it. The fact that he had kept it so well hidden grated at me—at old anxieties and fears—but I was keeping secrets from him for the same reason. I had no one to blame but myself; and I had no more strength to try to untangle my inner conflict tonight. No desire to pick a fight in which I could be forced into a corner to share what sent my beast into a manic panic.

With a long sip of water, I attempted to distract myself from my chaotic endless inner dialogue. I didn't want to go home. I didn't want to lie in bed alone where my mind could spin around and around thinking about the sound of the screams from the stone.

"Shit, are you hungry? You said you weren't when we left—"

Something warmed through me when I met his gaze. Looking away, I felt a flush cover my cheeks. I cleared my throat. "I'm not..."

"You ran all that way and you're not hungry?" There was a tease in his voice. Something that made the pull hum with heat in a silent message of its own. Ethan walked to me with sure steps. His hands latched around my waist. I swallowed and my heart started to race as he stepped between my legs while his free hand slid up my thighs.

I licked my lips. "First you miss breakfasts and now our dinner date..."

"She says she's not hungry..." he said, with a sly smile that turned into something softer when his lips neared mine. "Do you want to stay?"

The words were accompanied with a tide of heat that raced across the pull like waves crashing on a beach. I felt my canines itch to come out as the scent of him wrapped around me and begged me to sink my teeth into his neck.

"What's wrong?" he asked. He tugged my ponytail loose and let my hair fall around my neck.

Forever was such a long time.

"I just—people keep asking and I, well, it's not like I haven't thought about it and it's a lot. You know? I mean, Christ, it's our souls. Like our souls, Ethan! And then you could feel my emotions, and I don't want you to think I don't want to, I just, I want to. It's just a lot and I'm scared, and I am going to shut up."

My chest was practically heaving while he blinked back at me with wide eyes. "Me too."

"What?"

"All of that. Me too."

"Really?"

He nodded with a breathy laugh. "Yeah."

"Okay... is that good?"

"It's ours," he told me. "That's what it is. We make our own decisions. That's what matters."

"Okay?"

"Okay." He nipped at my lips. Hands grasped my legs and pulled me closer to him. "Do you want to stay?"

"Yes," I breathed.

His lips were on mine and the pull crackled to life like fireworks exploding on a hot summer night. I let myself moan back into his mouth, because I wanted this. I wanted to forget this pull, forget expectations, and let only the feeling of him enrapture me.

It was like the moment I said yes, something snapped in him. Suddenly it felt like there was no time for slow, no time to savor. Something grew hungrier, our hands grew needier as we tugged and pulled at clothing.

He yanked my shifter top off and kneaded my breasts while I frantically pulled his shorts down his perfect ass. My legs pulled him closer as a fever spiked along the pull—a flow of want.

He picked me up off the counter and latched his lips onto my neck while he stumbled through the kitchen with me; I could barely keep track of where we were going as I lost myself in a daze to the feeling of his hot kisses making their way along my neck back to my lips. Turning, he tried to ascend the stairs, but halfway up, I felt us falter off balance. He tried to use his body to soften my fall, but we both ended up splayed out on the carpeted stairs.

My eyes opened as a hand latched around my calf. He crawled up the step between us, the fall forgotten as he ripped my shorts off. Before I could catch my breath, his mouth found my center; my head fell back against a stair while his tongue did that thing I loved, driving me up to the edge. But before I could reach the peak, he was gone.

A whimper rippled from my lips. Ethan grinned like he had won the lottery as his hands latched around me, quickly flipping us so I was on top. Our lips made quick work, melting into each other's while our hands worked together to tear off his shifter shorts. My slick body moved over his with the same tide of fever as the pull sweeping between us.

He groaned into my mouth when his thick length entered me, and I forgot how to say real words when he rocked me against him. Our bodies slid together in a hurried rush as sweat pooled on the back of my neck while the tightness in my core built. Something moved along the pull, something that felt like cool water breaking over my scalp after a scorching summer day. My head tipped back as the peaks of bliss overtook me. I heard him groan my name before he slid out of me and something hot landed on my thigh.

We fell back against the stairs, my chest on his as they lifted in unison as we slowly caught our breaths. His fingers combed through my hair that had grown damp at the base of my neck. I tilted to look at him; hair in a mess and face covered in a dreamy flush.

"Do you think we'll make it to the bedroom next time?" he asked with a winded smile.

Something curled in my core, something delicious that made my nipples tighten as his gaze turned heavy with heat.

"We can try," I answered before I lost myself in him again.

CHAPTER SIXTEEN

Waking up early was hard when I was so content to stay tucked against Ethan—where I had been practically all weekend. I woke early and left him to his soft snores while I ran back to my house to shower and grab a change of clothes so I could start my day.

Andrea wasn't anywhere to be found at our cabin, but she had left empty bottles on the counter. My beast pawed at the back of my mind, but I shook her off. Andrea was an adult and was probably already out with the other guards.

The pack house was busy when I jogged inside. The dozens of eyes that combed me over made me wonder if I should have showered again until I realized they were all checking my neck and my wrist, and any other visible skin. I felt twitchy with the need to run, and my beast paced with the urge to hunt. I schooled her as I stirred my coffee. We needed to shake off the rumors—Ethan was right, what we choose to do in our relationship was our decision. Our business.

"Hi, Charlotte." Evangeline was standing in front of me like she wasn't sure if I was going to spring into my fur or not.

"Good morning," I answered back with a hesitant smile.

"Um, can you let me get to the creamer?" she tepidly asked.

She pointed to the canisters behind me that I hadn't realized I was blocking. I slid over for her while she quickly filled her cup like she was late to rob a bank or something. Her fingers shook as they tried to press the lid down.

I lowered my voice to a whisper and asked, "Are you okay?"

She jolted then turned to me with a heavy gaze. "Fine," she said in a clipped voice.

My beast tilted her head. Carefully, I reached for Evangeline's mind and found a space to tap on. She bit her lip and pressed her palms against the counter. Not two seconds after she let my link in, she repeated, "*I am fine.*" She sucked in a breath. "*Thomas stopped by Ethan's. He was—I hate it when he's like this.*"

"*What do you mean he 'stopped by'? I was just there.*" I bit my lip when I realized what I had just admitted. My cheeks warmed as her eyes widened in shock. I shook off the embarrassment. "*Did something happen?*"

"*I brought him muffins—well, I made them—he doesn't have any decent food at his house. Jake said you were there last night and I . . . muffins are good for breakfast.*" It was her turn to hide her gaze while she tried to shake away the flush on her cheeks. "*Thomas—something happened with Jackson Bones from Switchback. He was pretty angry . . .*"

Cold dread slid up my spine. "*What do you mean? Did he do*

anything to you?" She and I may not be on the best terms, but the need to protect her shoved its way front and center.

"He doesn't have to," she muttered. *"He can be a lot when he's worked up."*

I stepped closer to her. *"Evangeline, where's Ethan?"*

"There you are!" Miranda fluttered into the kitchen like a fairy emerging from a flower on a new spring day.

Evangeline stood up straighter next to me. I found my own spine stiffening to match her posture as I forced a smile to Miranda. "Morning!" I chirped, a little too high-pitched.

She walked to the refrigerator and grabbed a bottle of cranberry juice. "Good weekend?"

"Very," I stated with an exaggerated nod. "We had a cozy weekend in."

Her hand flew to her chest. "Thomas and I used to do those. They're the best."

"Yeah, it was hard to get back to the routine today," I answered, pulling a world-class facade forward.

Evangeline's eyes were growing too wide watching me. My foot nudged hers. *"Just breathe, she already knows something is up."*

"How do you know?" Evangeline croaked.

With women like Miranda, I knew behind that plastered-on smile and airy disposition there was a conniving, calculated strategy being executed.

"A past life," I told her.

"I had to practically shove Thomas out of bed," she stated. "He and Ethan have a long run today it seems."

I could tell she was trying to set a trap and, unfortunately for me, I was flying blind.

THE PACK

"Ethan didn't say anything about a trip today," I added, with a sprinkle of airiness to my voice, setting a trap of my own.

"Oh?" Miranda tilted her head. "Well, they're running to the Thunderhead border for a meeting. I'm surprised he didn't take you to see Levi?"

Me fucking too, Miranda.

I could sense Evangeline shift her weight ever so slightly next to me. I waved my hand flippantly. "You know men—literally one-track minds."

Miranda's laughter felt as smooth as sandpaper on my skin. "Do you have routes this morning?"

"I don't," I told her.

"Fantastic, do you want to help me today? The work for this meeting seems like it will never end."

"Of course," I answered, like I would love nothing more.

"Bless you," she said with a wink before fixing an icy gaze on Evangeline. "Darling, I told you not to linger. You're going to be late for Billy."

"I thought I was with you today?" Evangeline asked carefully, as if she was tiptoeing through traps in the Trapper's Forest.

Miranda rolled her eyes. "I swear, you're just like your mother sometimes," she grumbled under her breath. "No, dear," she correctly sweetly. "We talked about this yesterday, remember?"

"I'll catch up with you," I assured her.

"Talk to Ethan . . . please." She forced a smile to Miranda. "I'm so silly—of course I got the days mixed up. See you later, Charlotte."

She took brisk steps out the door, leaving just Miranda and me in the kitchen. Miranda took a long sip of her juice then wiped her mouth. "Well, shall we?"

"Lead the way," I told her.

As I followed her through the pack house, I quickly shot a link to Ethan. *"Miranda said you're going to the border? What's happening?"*

A few moments passed before he answered back. *"Jackson called a meeting with Levi and Thomas. I didn't think he'd do it this way..."*

"Evangeline said Thomas was upset?"

"He's not thrilled," he answered. *"I'll fill you in later. Try to keep your head down today, please?"*

"All right," I agreed. *"Be careful,"* I added before the link went silent, and stayed silent throughout the rest of the day.

I tried to turn my frustration into something productive while Miranda and I worked through the seating chart for the council meeting, along with plans for lodging, on a large bulletin board where we could tack names. She and I had mostly organized the seating chart in a way that made sense, but lodging was turning out to be a nightmare. While Hemlock had space, it wasn't always as straightforward as we needed it to be.

Miranda and I worked through the afternoon until we were able to come up with a shell of a plan that pleased her enough.

"This is a good start," she mused while she bit the end of her pen. "We'll be able to tweak it once we have the final head count."

"I say we leave this as is until then. We don't need to create more headaches if we don't have to."

"I agree," she answered. "Thank the moon you're here. I can't imagine doing this without you."

Swallowing, I compelled myself to smile back. "Of course."

"And if you and Ethan are not busy tonight, well, I would love to have you over for dinner?"

I bit my bottom lip. "We'd love to." After I figured out what the hell happened today.

When I left the pack house I ran straight to Ethan's. His place was empty, and I lingered alone inside for what felt like hours until my anxiety couldn't take it. I stumbled outside and sat among the flowers on the edge of the hill while the sun teased the idea of setting in the sky.

The moment I could feel something flutter over the bond, I sprang to my feet. He slid the back door open and stood in the doorway. Exhaustion hovered around him like a waiting reaper. His chest rose with a sigh that escaped past a newly split lip.

The grass was soft under my feet as I went to him. I carefully traced the new shiner on his cheek. His eyes fluttered closed.

"What happened?"

His hands slid down my shoulders. "Levi wants you to come home."

My beast snapped her jaws at the notion. "Levi can tell me himself."

His eyes snapped opened. "And what would you say?"

I almost scoffed at the question until I could see the genuine concern behind his dual-colored eyes. "This is my choice. He knows that."

Ethan's shoulders relaxed, but only barely. "Lander said the same thing."

"And?"

"We had a scuffle." He paused then conceded. "I may have told Levi he was, among other things, a bastard." I hissed a wince. He nodded slowly. "Then he proceeded to fuck up my pretty face."

I cupped his cheek and turned him to face me directly. "What happened? Your sister said Thomas was upset this morning, then the next thing I hear, it's from Miranda saying you're going to Thunderhead? That something happened with Jackson?"

Ethan looked over my shoulder then pulled me inside and slid the door closed. "We can't be too careful," he grumbled. "Jackson, in a very Jackson fashion, decided to tell both Levi and Thomas about the stone this morning. Levi immediately wanted a meeting, which Jackson quickly agreed to. Thomas was more or less forced to go or it would be bad optics for him, and he won't risk his reputation with the regional meeting coming up."

He walked back to the kitchen and poured himself a full glass of whiskey. I jumped up and slid back to sit on the counter next to him.

"Not an hour after you left, my sister shows up with muffins because I apparently don't know how to feed you—"

"Ethan . . ." I chastised him.

He closed his mouth then relented. "It was kind, but horrible timing because Thomas showed up in a roar. I told Lina to go upstairs but she's so headstrong, and Thomas wanted her to see him like that. Wanted me to see how scared she was." His eyes looked far off. "He asked if I'd been snooping around—if I'd been talking to Jackson. Naturally, I lied."

"What happened at the meeting?" I swallowed the thousand other questions I had.

He rubbed his face. "Jackson plays the game well. He brought the stone and played dumb, like he had no idea about what you guys had found until Lander spoke up. Then he suggested we work together, suggesting it couldn't hurt, especially with so many high-profile wolves coming in for this meeting." He paused and took a long sip of whiskey. "It was a heated conversation—Thomas isn't convinced any of this is connected and does not want to collaborate with the other packs. But to our great luck and misfortune, Jackson and Levi get along very well. Jackson agreed to let Bowie send Remi over to help his trackers out. He also has free entry to Thunderhead with his trackers."

"That's progress. And Thomas?"

"He doesn't want outsiders snooping around the pack, but he agreed to a search."

His sober expression squashed my excitement. "Isn't that what we wanted?"

He nodded slowly with a look in his eyes that said he regretted wanting it in the first place. "This will be a hunt in name only. Lip service to the other packs while keeping his thumb on me—on you. On this pack."

My beast was pacing in the back of my mind. Pawing at me to say what I had been itching to say for weeks.

"When are you going to tell me?"

"Tell you what?"

"What's really going on with Thomas and you and this pack?"

He was quiet a moment. His nostrils flared as his hand came to cup my cheek. "What happened to you when you touched the Bloodstone?"

My blood ran cold at his words, like ice water had been poured over me. "Ethan—"

"I could feel it," he stated with firm conviction. "At Jackson's—whatever it was, I could fucking feel it." His thumb rubbed my cheek as my vision started to blur. "I also felt it during the full moon run. You weren't lost in the woods, were you?"

I didn't want to have secrets with him. I didn't want him to have secrets from me. But I didn't know how to break down the dams we had built—especially when I was terrified of what mine could mean for both of us.

He blew out a breath then pressed his lips to mine. "When you're ready, I'm ready," he told me, before he walked to the stairs.

I swiped away the wetness pooling in my eyes. I had done this to myself. I knew that.

"We're supposed to have dinner with them tonight."

"I know," he called back, leaving me to the memory of the whispers, of the screams from the stone that wailed through the quiet of the kitchen.

Ethan and I walked hand in hand toward a two-story cottage stacked between the trees. Moonflowers grew in wild vines along the iron fence that guarded the house. I smoothed out my cotton dress and tried to hide the tremble of my fingers; eventually, I shoved them into my pockets.

"You look beautiful," he murmured to me.

We hadn't said much to each other since our conversation in the kitchen, and the bond was heavy with a tension I wished I could shake off. Still, the feel of him next to me was enough to ease the rigidness in my back.

"You do too," I answered. He smirked and pulled me closer, pressing his mouth to my forehead.

Thomas opened the door before we could knock. "Welcome, you two," his said, his voice gravelly.

He opened his arms in a hug that I felt like I couldn't refuse. It felt like hugging that one uncle in your family you always thought watched you too long when you wore a bikini.

I had to fight the urge to shiver when he released me. Thankfully, Miranda floated over with a glass of wine in her hand. "Before I even step in the house." I laughed away my nerves and took the glass from her.

She quickly hugged me then gestured us inside. I followed her into a bright kitchen decorated with rooster-themed ceramics. Bowls of sides were scattered along the island while a grill outside smoked steadily into the blooming dusk sky.

Ethan took a beer from Thomas then found his way back to me; his arm wrapped around me as Miranda tied her apron on. "Ethan, she's been so great. Honestly, the moon blessed us so much. I could not be doing all this council business without her."

"You don't need to brag to me," he easily replied.

She clicked her tongue and approached him. Her thumb reached for the shiner on his cheek. "Oh, Ethan, darling, do you want some ice?"

Thomas slapped his shoulder. "He's fine, aren't you, son?"

Ethan laughed into his beer. "Fantastic."

Thomas winked at me. "You know, Ethan, all she needs is a nice mark and we can make her pack."

Ethan forced a chuckle. "You're the pack lead, you can always bend the rules."

Thomas winked at me. "Already getting him to break some laws for you. Well played."

Miranda swatted him with a towel. "Go make yourself useful and check the steaks."

Thomas pecked her on the cheek and padded outside. "Come on, Ethan, let's let the girls yap."

I watched him all the way to the back door then took a long sip of wine. "Can I help with anything?"

"Thank you for offering," Miranda answered with a gracious smile, "but, no, you just stand there and keep me company."

Footsteps padded to us, but it was a sweet, flowery perfume that greeted us first. Amber's makeup was painted on like she was ready to take the stage at a pageant. She flipped her perfectly curled hair over her shoulder and padded to the corner of the kitchen island opposite me.

"Ah, you're awake, dear. How was your nap?"

"Fine," she answered with a forced airiness in her.

I felt my beast cock her head. Amber drummed her dainty fingers against the marbled top. Miranda ignored her and started to toss a salad. "So, Charlotte, what did you do back in California?"

"I worked as an admin at a law firm," I answered. "But I studied journalism in school. I wanted to work at a magazine."

"Do you miss the California sun?" Miranda asked.

I snorted a laugh. "No."

Amber's firm mouth cracked a rare smile before she laughed under her breath. Then she paused, as if realizing she had made some kind of mistake. The smile faded and her poise returned.

"Do you mind if I use the bathroom?" I asked.

"Of course not," Miranda answered. "The guest one is broken, so use ours. Main hall, second door on your left."

Without pausing I strode through their room and into the bathroom, where I locked the door and splashed water on my face. The wolf in me was pacing. My eyes glowed back at me in the mirror. I splashed more water onto my face then emerged from the bathroom.

The beast in the back of my mind had started to calm, but then barely a whisper of a scent caught my attention. It was slight, but I thought I could smell stale burning sugar and hear a strange hum, like someone murmuring something to a baby.

There was a vanity in the corner of the bedroom with an oval mirror on top. Makeup was neatly stacked alongside jewelry laid out in long, rectangular velvet boxes. My head cocked while I crept toward the source of the sound.

Miranda knocked on the bedroom door and stepped inside with a breezy smile. "We're ready to eat. Are you well?"

"Oh, of course." *I was just working on the perfect bullshit excuse, but don't mind me.* "I was—I just saw your jewelry." I groaned inwardly at what was probably the worst stretch of an answer I could have come up with. "I couldn't help but look."

Miranda beamed. She took my hand and pulled me to the vanity. "Thomas did so well. I was going to wear this necklace tonight"—she held up a delicate gold chain strung with three pearly stones that matched her earrings. The stones seemed alive as they dangled in the air, and for a second I thought I could hear something babble quietly from them—"but I didn't want to get it dirty in the kitchen."

"It's beautiful," I forced myself to say.

She held the clasp open for me. "Come, try it on."

"Oh, I couldn't—"

"I insist, playing dress-up with friends is one of my favorite things," she countered.

"All right," I said on an uneasy breath.

Turning, I let her lower the chain over my head and latch it around my neck. When the cool surface of the stone hit my skin, the wailing started.

My hand flew to the stones as my teeth sunk into my lip, biting back a whimper. Cold sweat beaded along my lower back as cries of agony that could only be from torture blasted in my ears. My beast was howling in the back of my mind, begging me to rip it off, but I knew we couldn't react. All we could do was suffer silently until it was over.

Amber jogged into the room. Her steps faltered as she locked eyes with me.

"Dinner's ready," she announced.

"Doesn't this look so good on her?" Miranda gushed. "I think I'm going to have to get Thomas to put a bug in Ethan's ear."

Amber stood still and tried to pull her composure from earlier, but I didn't miss the tremble in her fingers. "I'm sure Ethan will get you one," I heard her monotone voice say.

I reached to unfasten the necklace. Amber watched me with dread until I successfully felt the clasp unhook. I didn't know what the hell those stones were, but I knew I didn't want them near my skin ever again.

I forced a smile at Miranda as I held the necklace by the smallest bit of chain possible and handed it back to her. "Thank you."

"Oh, Charlotte," she cooed. "You look so pale! Are you all right?"

"Just famished," I answered with a light laugh. "I better eat before I turn into a proper monster."

She laughed and waved me off. "Let's eat, then. We're sitting in the garden."

I followed Amber out of the room and to the kitchen, where I downed my glass of wine before Miranda could see.

Amber wordlessly poured me another glass, as if we were in whatever this thing was together. But the minute we were outside, her mask was up and her tits were pushed out as if she was trying to make a shelf with them.

THE PACK

At the table, Ethan's hand latched around my leg like it was a life raft. I kept watching Amber, patiently waiting for another crack to show. I picked at my plate. I wanted to hate the steak, but Thomas did know how to grill, which made my loss of appetite that much more annoying.

"Are you okay?" Ethan asked.

No, because I'm hearing fucking voices at your boss's house.

"So, what will this council meeting be like?" I asked the group in an attempt to distract myself.

Thomas wiped his mouth with a napkin. "Chaos. It's rare for our kind to gather like this, but I'm sure it's like a human event. There's always someone who gets pissed off at someone else's pack for something petty, people who want to party like degenerates, and of course, people who find their mates or a body to fu—"

"Thomas!" Miranda scolded.

He shrugged. "Like I said, I'm sure it's similar to humans."

Ethan reached for his beer. "Leo confirmed that he volunteered Derek, so we don't have to fly a vampire in."

Thomas grunted in approval. "Good, is he bringing that redhead?"

"You mean his mate?" Ethan corrected. "I'm sure he'll come. They're supposed to send two."

Miranda smiled at me. "I was thinking they could stay with you? Since you lived with them before?"

"Oh, I—"

"They're staying with me," Ethan announced. Amber blinked twice while Thomas cut his eyes to him. "Charlotte only has two bedrooms. We'd put Andrea out."

"Would hate to do that," Thomas drawled.

I tipped my glass back and prayed that the red wine gods would save me. Amber cocked her head at me. "Hitting it hard?"

"Keep up."

Her lips twitched. A smile was fighting through but quickly lost to her mask. Still, I took it as a small victory for myself.

"Ethan." Thomas's voice was low, almost a warning. Amber's smile fell as her eyes went distant. "Let's get the search team moving soon. Charlotte should be included. We need good trackers."

My gaze shifted to Ethan, who had somehow kept a relaxed posture in his seat. He took another bite of his steak and chewed then swallowed it before answering. "I can get a few people assembled. We'll keep it small, like we discussed."

Thomas casually waved him off, as if this was only a flippant chore. "I already notified a few wolves. No need to vet anyone. I agree with Levi, we should move fast and nip this in the bud before the council meeting."

My lips were parted, a question on my tongue, when Amber caught my gaze; she shook her head in the tiniest form of no. I kept my mouth shut and followed her lead.

She looked at her hands, almost like she was mustering some courage, then rested an elbow on the table. "Dad? Do I get to go?"

She cut her eyes expectantly to me, like a pitcher throwing a softball to a child in little league.

"Go where?" I asked slowly. "What are we looking for?"

Thomas snorted in disbelief. "Ethan hasn't told you?"

I licked my teeth. "Told me what?"

Ethan watched Thomas a moment then leaned into me. "Jackson found an alleged Bloodstone on his pack land."

"That's the Switchback pack lead, right?" I asked, with an added daintiness to my voice that I hadn't used in years.

"That's right," Ethan confirmed, as if we hadn't spent a whole night over at Jackson's over the weekend. "We're going to look here. Just in case."

I paused a beat then asked, "We'll be combing the Trapper's Forest, I assume? It's forbidden..."

"Not for the search team," Thomas avowed.

"I'll get us organized," Ethan assured him.

"Fantastic," Thomas said, tone clipped. He took a careful sip of beer that did little to stop a few beads of amber from escaping through the holes on the left side of his mouth.

Miranda slid forward in her seat. "Ethan, you're still planning to go into town to deliver the invitation to the witches?"

"I am," he answered. "And I was going to make it a long weekend. Charlotte's never been to Anchorage."

"Really?" Amber gawked at me.

"You know, I actually haven't."

Amber arched a brow. "That can't be right?"

"I drove through before I was bitten. I only stopped at a diner, but it was well outside of Anchorage. I've been to Talia's pack lands, but nothing farther south."

"Why didn't you stop?" Amber pressed.

I finished my wine. "I was running from someone, and I was not about to stop and give him the chance to catch me." Her mask started to break as her cold blue eyes flashed with something that looked familiar. "I would have run all the way to the end of the earth to keep him from putting his hands on me again."

Amber's lips thinned, but I didn't miss the quiver she was trying to hide.

Miranda's hand flew to her chest. "And we're so glad you're safe."

Thomas took a bite of his steak. "He'll get his."

"They all do, eventually," I countered, my gaze holding his for a beat before he jabbed his knife into his steak.

"Thank the moon for that," Thomas added.

My eyes lifted to see the crescent above us. She was thin and sharp and nothing as warm as the full. Cold emanated from her as her shallow light coated us.

The moon's glow danced off Miranda's earrings as she waved goodbye when we finally left. Neither Ethan nor I wanted to linger after the meal. We used our "early morning" as an excuse to escape, then made quick work to disappear into the trees. He followed me back to my place, which was still empty of Andrea.

Wordlessly he rummaged through the cabinets before pulling out a glass and a bottle of whiskey. The helping he poured was generous. He downed it in one throw.

I stepped up to the table as my beast pushed closer to me. "Can we talk about that?"

Ethan poured another glass. I snatched it from him. Taking a sip of my own, I didn't break from his tense stare.

"I need to talk about that," I pressed.

"Which part?" He laughed wryly. "The part where you flipped out over something in the house? Or the part where we get to figure out how to handle Thomas's handpicked lackeys while searching in the forest?"

"There's something wrong with that house," I insisted.

"I know." He took his glass back and took a long sip. "What happened inside?"

God, I wanted to tell him, bare every ugly inch of my soul to him, but it was so dangerous. And a part of me, a very tiny part of me, was worried what he would do when he knew.

Would he run? I couldn't blame him if he did, but the thought of losing him terrified me. I couldn't put him in danger. Put us and Andrea in danger.

"I don't—" I paused and shook my head. "I'm scared. I'm really scared. I don't know how to tell you—"

He cupped my cheeks like I was the egg he was keeping from cracking. "What are you afraid of?"

"Hurting you," I found myself confessing, before adding, "Losing you. It's not safe." An excuse I hoped he, out of all people, would understand.

He watched me a moment. "We have to take chances on each other."

"Then tell me about Thomas."

"I told you, when you're ready, I'm ready."

"Ethan—"

"I'm ready," he interjected before leaning back and waiting, hope heavy in his eyes.

Frustration and anger at myself boiled through me—why did it feel like I was ruining a good thing? Why did it feel like no matter what I did, my own bag of bones would forever litter the ground around us?

But what if I was broken? What if these voices were proof of that?

"It's not that simple," I found myself saying—a weak excuse my beast snapped her teeth at.

He rubbed the back of his neck and headed for the door. "I need to talk to Evan. You should talk to Levi."

"Ethan," I called after him, but all I heard was the door shut in return.

But I didn't talk to Levi. I needed to figure my shit out before

I opened the can of worms that was Levi. Instead, I sat on the back porch and drank my whiskey until I heard Andrea stumble in. I set my glass down and padded inside to see her at the kitchen table, digging feverishly in a box of cookies. She arched a delicate brow at me. Her eyes darted to the open back door where the bottle of whiskey was.

My eyes watered. Andrea pulled a chair out for me then offered me the box. Smiling, I dug out a handful and tossed a few into my mouth. "How was your day?" she asked.

My throat clenched. Painfully swallowing, I proceeded to tell her about the day—what had happened with Jackson, and dinner, and the impasse Ethan and I had had earlier.

Andrea picked at the edges of a cookie. "I'm sorry."

We fell into a peaceful quiet as we shared the box of cookies. Eventually Andrea leaned forward to ask, "You haven't told anyone else about the voices?"

I shook my head. "No."

She leaned her elbow on the table and rested her head in her palm. I bit my lip as my eyes teared up again. "I'm scared. It's dangerous, and what if there's something really wrong with me?"

She blew out a slow breath. "Have you heard them more?"

I bit my bottom lip as a tear rolled down my cheek. Carefully, I told her about what happened when I touched the stone—told her about the voices I heard when I was with Keeley, and about what happened when I put Miranda's necklace on.

After I was done Andrea rubbed her face then laced her fingers together. "Fuck, Char . . ."

"I know," I whimpered.

"I think you should tell him . . ."

"What?!" I gawked. "You said I shouldn't?"

"I was wrong," she answered with a shrug. "And to be fair, I didn't think it would get worse."

"But what if he thinks I'm nuts? What if there's something legitimately wrong with me and ... I feel like I'm holding my soul bare on a platter, and I'm afraid he's going to shatter it. I can't go through that again."

Andrea sighed and laid her hand palm up on the table. I slapped mine into it. She slid forward in her seat as her molten golden eyes held mine in careful regard. "You know what's scarier? Holding your bare soul on that platter with all the ugly parts of it showing, and the person you're baring your soul to loving you still. I think you and I both know that's much, much scarier." She paused then squeezed my hand gently in hers, as if she was holding a baby bird in her palm.

"I'm so fucked up, Andrea." I sniffled and wiped my eyes with my sleeve.

"Hey." She dipped her head to look at me. "We're all fucked up. You, me, Ethan. All of us. And you know what? The Charlotte I know doesn't care she's fucked up. She doesn't care how much it scares her—she's okay with being scared, because you know what? She knows that won't stop her."

I wiped my eyes with the sleeve of my shirt. Andrea squeezed my hand. "Charlotte, he's falling for you too. You can see it when he looks at you."

I leaned back in my seat. Shaking my head, I asked, "When do you decide to do forever?"

Andrea's eyes turned soft. She leaned closer. "Charlotte, at some point, you're going to have to make a choice. People are complicated. It doesn't matter if you're werewolf, human, or whatever—there's so many things that make up a person. So many details. So much history, how could anyone get to know every little beautiful thing about someone in a lifetime? It's impossible.

"What matters more, is knowing enough to make a choice. A choice that says, every day, 'I will choose you.' Because that's what real love is. It's choosing that person every day, even on bad days and really god-awful days, you say yes." She gently smiled, almost wistful with a memory of her own. "You're never going to know everything about a person. Neither of you are perfect. You never will be. The question for you is, what else do you need to know so you can make that choice?"

The questions that had been consuming me faded away as I realized how insignificant they were. What had been uncertainty turned into something else. Something peaceful that I didn't expect.

"I think you know," she whispered.

I ripped my hand from hers with a laugh. "You're an idiot."

"No, you are," she quipped. She thrust her hand back into the box of cookies. "But you're in love. We're all idiots when we're in love."

I couldn't stop the smile that found its way to my lips. "What if he does run?"

She shrugged. "Then you're stuck with me."

"I'm already stuck with you."

She grinned. "Forever and ever."

CHAPTER SEVENTEEN

Dirt slid down the thin crevices of a trap door in front of us. I nudged a corner of the wooden structure hidden by brush with my toes. Clods of dirt slipped through one of the cracks and pinged off something on the bottom.

Jake knelt down to listen. He was still for a moment before confirming my suspicions. "Silver."

I tugged my ponytail and scanned the area in front of us. The odds of this being the only trap here were unlikely.

"Hey! What, are you two trying to leave us in the forest?"

My head tipped back as our new babysitters, Orville and Jericho, finally caught up with us. While Thomas had agreed to let Ethan commission a small group to comb through the forest, he had arranged for wolves loyal to him to most certainly be a part of the search team. The only person who lucked out of having one in their group was Evangeline. She was paired off with Trey; more or less, they were having a picnic every day on the mountain side of the pack line where it was safe. Ethan absolutely did not want his sister trekking through the forest.

Orville stumbled forward. Sweat was beading on top of his shaved head. "Could have slowed down."

"Could have kept up," Jake said, words clipped.

"Maybe let someone else besides her set the pace?" Jericho sneered. The bear tattoo on his calf trembled on his spasming muscle. He stomped forward and ran a hand through his long, sandy locks. "We haven't found anything for three days—this isn't a search and rescue."

He went to take another step when I pressed him back by his shoulder. I nodded to the ground. "Trap door."

Jericho hissed under his breath. "Should we open it?"

I shook my head. "No, it could set off more traps."

"We shouldn't be out here," Orville stammered. His willowy frame trembled. "We shouldn't disturb this place."

"You're welcome to go home," Jake told them, and for a moment, both of them looked like they may take him up on his offer. Jake had told me to set the pace to wear them out in hopes that they would tap out and leave us on our own. To our disappointment, they clung to us like warts.

I was brushing my hands on my shifters when a cool breeze shook through the trees. My beast cocked her head as something hummed through my veins. With careful steps, I helped the group traverse the area as a silence seeped in like an oozing infection. Our footsteps grew muted—the trees stood still, practically petrified to their roots.

THE PACK

A hand grabbed my arm. Jericho was shaking. Desperation glowed in his eyes like they were trying to fight through the darkness. "I can't hear."

I could barely make out what he said. I tapped my head at him and Orville.

"It's a silent spot. It's blood magic—old blood magic. You're fine. Follow me."

Orville shook his head as heavy pants rolled out of his mouth. *"This is bad."*

"It is," I agreed, stepping farther into the silence.

It was like walking underwater down to the deepest end of a pool. My beast was snapping in the back of my mind while my moon blood sizzled through my veins. A murmur cut through the void, tempting me to follow it.

I stalled, scanning the area. Tiny tendrils of fresh blood magic hit my nose.

"Jake?" I said over my shoulder.

Both guards stilled in place. Jake had tilted his nose in the air, focused, when a loud crack broke the suffocating silence as it pounded across the ground.

Jericho's claws descended from his fingernails. "What the fuck was—"

Another series of pops sounded, like someone was throwing fireworks right next to our feet. I tried to stay still, tried to focus so I could place where the sound originated.

Orville shook his head. "We should go."

"So go," I snarled, frustration burning inside me.

Jake held up a hand, silencing the group, and lifted his glowing gaze to mine. "Your call."

I walked past him and let the beast come forward as the

smell of blood magic permeated the air. A snarl vibrated off me as the darkness murmured whispers. My beast snapped her teeth. I didn't try to calm her because like her, I was growing very tired of these damn voices in the forest.

Brush scraped against my arms as I trudged through the thick of it—following the heavy stench of blood magic until I could see sunlight streaking to a blanket of fresh grass ahead. I darted forward, running to the middle of the small clearing, but there was nothing there. I scanned the area—even though it looked as if the others already had. There had to be a Bloodstone nearby...

"Charlotte?" Jake knelt next to a stepping stone laid flat on the ground. He pointed across the clearing. "They line this place."

I followed his finger as it drew a line to each stone that circled the area. My breath caught. I tugged my ponytail tighter. "What are they?"

He rubbed his hand across his mouth. "No idea. It reeks of blood magic, though."

Both guards stood wordlessly at the edge of the clearing. Orville was staring off with distant eyes as his fingers trembled. "We weren't supposed to find anything," he mumbled. "He said there was nothing out here."

Jake's jaw ticked. He rose slowly and prowled toward him. "What did he tell you was out here?"

Orville clenched his mouth shut.

Jake cracked his neck. "Don't make me ask you again."

"He said there was nothing out here!" Orville pleaded, like he was trying to convince himself that we weren't standing in a cloud of fresh blood magic.

Jake jerked his chin at Jericho. "Did you know this was here?"

"What?" Jericho sneered like he had been burned. "Are you kidding me?!"

I started to walk the circumference of the clearing. "How about you tell us, or I let you find your way home on your own. I've made it through this forest before. Jake has too. We have no problem making our way alone."

"Our pack lead wants us together," Jericho ground out.

"He's not my pack lead," I growled back. I steeled myself. I clenched my eyes shut and forced my heart to stop racing. "Blood magic doesn't just show up. Things don't just appear—this may be a magical world, but even still, all magic has to have an explanation." Pausing, I stepped closer to them and held my hands up like a white flag. "We're standing in fresh blood magic. We heard that cracking noise and now we find whatever this is. Ethan loves this pack—why would he send you on a wild-goose chase? He wants to be done with the past, like you all do—and if he's wrong, he doesn't have a problem *admitting* it."

Jericho held my gaze while Orville shook his head. "Thomas said all the blood magic was old. Said Levi was seeing what he wanted to see," Orville stammered.

Jericho clenched his fists. He looked at the circle then regarded me like he was perturbed he had to play nice, even for a moment. "He's worried about a panic starting—about being undermined." He blew out a breath and tossed his hands to his sides. "He doesn't want you snitching to other packs."

Jake sneered. "If you used your fucking heads every once in a while, you'd see the kind of pawns you've turned into."

Jericho said nothing. He dipped his head and inhaled again. Fangs descended from his gums. "But we don't smell rogues?"

Leaves crunched under my feet as we walked back to the darkness of the forest. The other two spots had had a rogue camp near them. My beast snapped her jaws in the air; she felt like there was one nearby—I did too. I shut my eyes. My mind quieted and focused on the forest around us. Cold slithered over the ground to my toes and licked at them like a cat lapping up fresh milk.

When I opened my eyes to the void of darkness in front of me, it was in the cold that slid between the trees that I caught a tendril of a scent.

Electricity pulsed through me. "This way!" I yelled over my shoulder before shifting into my fur.

I let my beast charge ahead after the faint trail that we desperately latched onto. It was like chasing the whisper of a ghost, but soon that ghost turned into a full confluence of stench—of decay, of sickness, of something completely rotten—when I shifted to my feet and marched to an area where the grass was crushed as if someone had curled up in it to take a nap.

"Fuck me," I uttered into the air that was thick with the scent of rogues.

Quickly, I walked the perimeter, stepping in and out of the area. It was clear that the scent was contained except for the trail that I had found.

Jake shifted and darted forward to the grassy bed I had found. The two guards slid to a stop. Jake's eyes went furiously wide before a cold snarl tore out of his mouth.

"One of them had to have walked down that trail we just ran," I thought out loud. "The scent's boxed in. Just like the other spots."

Orville stepped into the clearing then fell to his hands and knees, panting as if he would pass out.

Jericho's eyes started to tear. He stepped farther into the grass and knelt down. His hands shook as they combed over the turf before he yanked them back to his chest like he had been burned. "They killed my bondmate. Her name was Carina." He clenched his clawed fists, drawing blood from his skin. "Stabbed her in the neck. I couldn't save her. She drowned in her own blood. My sister saved me and dragged me into our cellar. I had to sit there for hours, staring at her body through the cracks between the planks."

"I'm so sorry," I mumbled, in a sad attempt to console him.

Jericho shook his head. "I wanted to think it was just a nightmare we would all forget."

He stood then helped Orville up, but Orville was weak in the knees. He fell back against a tree with a whimper while Jericho walked in steady steps to me. He paused and looked me over, like he was seeing me for the very first time.

"Tell Ethan my beast is his." The words were uttered quietly, but in the still of the forest they bounced off the trees.

Jake handed him a stake. "Let's mark it and get the fuck out of here. I already called it in. Billy is going to come out here with Thomas."

Jericho jerked his chin in a nod and started to stake the perimeter. I walked to Orville and handed him a stake. He rubbed his face like he was hoping he'd see another scene when he opened his eyes. "Thomas will fix this." His words to himself were a weak promise that seemed to slowly break with each stake he drove into the ground.

"*We found something,*" I linked Ethan. "*We found a rogue patch and a strange clearing. No Bloodstone.*"

"*Billy told me,*" he answered. "*You're sure there wasn't a stone?*"

"Positive," I replied. *"Where are you?"*

"Still in the forest."

The darkness around me seemed to cackle at his response. My beast pawed at the back of my mind. Our welcome in this foul place was starting to wear out.

"Be careful," I murmured before telling the group out loud, "Let's get the other site marked up and go—I want to get out of here before nightfall."

We made quick work of staking both areas as well as the trail between the two. Jericho said nothing the whole run home. The darkness felt like it was tipping its head back in deep laughter as we ran through it. Like it had a joke that we would soon find out. My beast and I tried to shake off the building tension, but with each stride we took back to the pack the more my anxiety gnawed at my nerves. I thought I would feel better when I saw the lit lanterns swinging in the summer breeze like old friends welcoming us home, but instead dread swam through me.

People with flashlights were sprinting toward the barn, where a crowd had gathered outside. Their conversations were crawling into the sky, growing in a horrifying crescendo that made my heart hammer in my chest.

I shifted to my skin and was immediately covered in a cold sweat. Jake shifted next to me. "Something's wrong."

Pain seized my chest and screamed along the pull. My breath caught while my beast howled as the pull coiled like a snake ready to strike.

"Ethan?!" Only silence answered me. I tugged at my ponytail. *"Ethan, where are you?"*

But there was no answer.

"No, no, no, no, no," I whimpered. *"Ethan!"* I cried across the link, where the sound of my own voice echoed along the walls until it settled into a terrifying quiet.

I could hear Thomas arguing with someone and feet stomping as wolves rushed past me, but the sound of my beast crying in the back of my mind drowned the noise out.

A pair of hands yanked me around. Andrea's golden eyes greeted me like headlights.

"Ethan's in the forest," I choked out.

"I know," she said. "They should have been back—Evangeline said she and Trey heard something. They ran, but she got separated from Trey. Ethan went after them. He and Trey haven't come back. Dad has already taken a team out to look for him."

I shoved around her and fought upstream through the outgoing procession of wolves to the front of the crowd, where Thomas was in a heated argument with Evan.

"You're staying put! We do not need anyone else going missing!" Thomas bellowed.

"How long has he been missing?" My voice was tight with terror.

Thomas whipped around to face me, his expression softening slightly. "I'm not sure."

"My sister has been back for three fucking hours!" Evan snarled.

Evangeline whimpered from her place at the edge of the barn next to Amber. Her hair was a mess of leaves, and her chin was starting to show a nasty bruise along with cuts all over her arms.

"Where were you?" I asked her.

Her eyes were wet, a plea in them. "We were on the east side of the mountain line. It's outside of the forest. Ethan said we'd be safe—"

"Where?!" I couldn't stop the desperation from barking out of me.

Evangeline jumped back but Amber steadied her. Evangeline wiped her eyes then fixed her gaze on me. "Near a rock formation straight north. Eli used to take us to these rocks all the time when we were little—we called them the finger rocks because they stick out of the ground like fingers," she whimpered. "That's where we were before . . . then there was popping everywhere and I followed Trey to look for it—I should have made him stay back!"

"I know where it is," Evan confirmed behind me.

"You're not going." I heard Thomas, but I ignored him.

Evangeline went on. "Trey told me to run so I did. I thought he was behind me but suddenly he was gone—and I was lost. Ethan found me, he took me back to the border then went after Trey. He was fine when I saw him!" she sobbed.

There was tapping on my brain. Amber's icy eyes held me in their frozen grip as something cold shot through my mind. *"It's a long run, but there's a shortcut through the forest. You'll get there in half the time. Go northeast until you see a tree split in half—it was struck by lightning. There's an old, hidden footrail. You won't miss it."*

Amber dipped her head at me, urging me with a determination in her glacial eyes. My beast pawed at the corners of my mind—ready to run.

I turned on my heel and marched back to Jake, who nodded to me in a silent confirmation that I would not have to make this search alone.

"Charlotte!" Thomas's voice shook through the night like a fist.

My beast shook out her fur. I turned to face him as the moon blood sizzled through my veins.

His steps were slow and deliberate as they closed the space between us. "We already have a team out. You're staying put."

"No, I'm not," I countered.

He put his hands on his hips, addressing me like I was a child. "I won't have you put yourself or anyone else at risk!"

I scoffed. "He's my fucking mate and I'll be damned if you think I'm going to sit here and do nothing!"

The moon blood fizzled and snapped until it flowed like a steady hum pouring off me. From my peripheral, I could see Evan walking around Thomas. His turquoise eyes were like two fiery stars burning hot as a hum started to roll off him.

Thomas's jaw ticked, and the darkness of the night created ghoulish shadows along his face against the waning light from the lanterns.

"Are you going to ignore the command of a pack lead?"

"I'm sure if we asked Levi, he would say that I have all the permission I need," I bit back. "Ethan's your fucking second—he would go after you, and you know it."

He lowered his head until we were eye level. My beast was snarling in the back of my mind, itching for a fight. Thomas may be a pack lead, but I didn't care who I had to plow through to find Ethan.

"It's for your own good," he whispered roughly, pleading. "I'm trying to protect you. Can't you see that?"

My beast flashed her teeth, and I didn't miss the way his skin twitched in response. "I'm going after him. If you want to stop me, you'll have to catch me."

Thomas straightened and looked over my shoulder at the

people that I knew were waiting on me. "If you go, there will be consequences."

I turned my back to him and marched ahead. Jake pulled Evan along with him while Andrea fanned around to walk on my right. Jake tapped his head then pulled me into a group link.

"We're going northeast," I told them.

Jake nudged my shoulder. *"Set the pace."*

The blood in my veins pulsed while my beast howled in anticipation. I let the shift overtake me and sprinted back to the Trapper's Forest.

CHAPTER EIGHTEEN

The air grew thin as we ascended toward the mountains. Evan's copper paws hammered the ground next to me. *"Has he linked you back?"*

"*No.*" And it wasn't for a lack of trying. The pull was twisted with pain, but that pain became my saving grace—because it meant he was alive.

The footpath Amber tipped me off on had been easy enough to find, but soon we cut away from it and headed farther east toward the formation Evangeline had noted. We shifted to our skin once we heard silver, like a swarm of mosquitos in the air. Jake had noted earlier that the area we were headed into had been nicknamed the Silver Mines by Hemlock trackers.

I held my hand up and stopped Andrea, then pointed up;

above us, wooden balls edged with metal spikes swayed in the trees as if they were nothing but acorns.

Jake cracked his neck. "You lead us through here," he told me.

Blowing out a breath, I stepped into the darkness, where the glimmer of silver lines laced in the trees like tinsel, and the teeth of traps laid patiently waiting in the cover of brush for their next meal.

We kept going until we punched through the brush, out of the forest, to find the boulder formation jutting from the ground like a hand reaching to the stars for help.

I took off in a sprint, shifting to my fur and letting my beast run a full circle around it before we intersected with the group. I could smell Evangeline and another wolf that had to be Trey.

I shifted to my skin and peered back into the darkness of the trees.

Jake pointed down the tree line. "That's the trail they took to get here. Goes around the forest."

Evan waved us back into the forest. "They went this way," he called before disappearing back into the trees.

Soon we were sprinting in our skin after him, cold blowing past us as if it was challenging us to a race. The sounds of our feet on the ground grew muffled. Jake halted the group. He tipped his nose to the air, and I caught it too—blood magic. It was old, but the fading noise around me let us know that it was still powerful.

"We're in a silent spot."

Evan closed his eyes. "Evangeline said it wasn't that far past the rocks—Ethan should be somewhere around here—how the fuck is his scent gone?!"

Jake looked over his shoulder. "I don't smell Trey either—where the fuck are they?"

"Maybe they went another way? We should backtrack," Andrea suggested.

"Dammit!" I hissed as the bond singed like it had been set on fire.

Stepping away from the group, I closed my eyes and willed myself to focus.

"Charlotte..." a whisper called from the darkness.

My feet carried me forward as the sounds of the others faded.

"Charlotte," it murmured again, sweet, like a lullaby.

An idea bloomed. My beast hated it, but with the sharp pangs zapping across the pull, she relented. Together, we walked farther into the darkness, away from the group. Cold slithered up my legs as hushed voices surrounded me. It was a bad idea, but when it came to Ethan, I didn't care if it was the worst idea.

The quiet fell still around me, as if it was waiting patiently for me to speak.

"Where is he?" I asked.

A breeze rushed around my legs then rustled the leaves in front of me and cut through the trees. A branch in front of me waved like an old friend, fanning a scent into the air that had originated from the tiny drops of blood on its leaves.

I recognized it the second it hit me, and when I held the leaf to my nose, hope rose in my chest. Ethan.

"This way!" I cried over my shoulder.

I didn't wait for them to catch up. I shifted to my fur and sprinted along the path the darkness had cut for me through the forest—a path that had droplets of blood adorning it like rose petals. My beast snapped her teeth as whispers echoed in front of me, leading me farther and farther into the Trapper's Forest, where the air grew stale and hung like a carcass rotting in the sun.

I could hear the others behind me. Andrea curled around to run next to me. *"Where are we going?!"*

I had no idea. I kept charging ahead until I picked another scent. Quickly, I shifted to my skin and jogged ahead on the dry ground. Old blood magic mixed with the faint scent of coppery blood perfumed the air, but it smelled muted—like something was trying to suppress it.

Evan shifted to his skin. His eyes pulsed an anxious glow. "Where are we? What is it?" he asked.

I held a hand up, signaling them to stay put, and walked ahead. Dry leaves and dirt crunched under my feet, until they turned to mush; and with the cold and the wet came the smell.

The horrid scent of old blood magic mixed with the vile, vibrant perfume of new blood magic. Through it, I could smell him. I could smell Ethan as clear as day. His scent was littered all over the ground in front of me, which reeked of metallic iron.

But the scent of blood magic wasn't what sent my beast into a panicked spiral. It was the putrid, decaying scent of rogues.

"What is it?" Andrea called.

My beast was crying in the back of my mind. The ground was practically a crimson carpet ahead of me. I blew out a breath and tried to steel my nerves—tried to hide the shake of my hands, but it felt like something was breaking—splintering like ice.

Feet crunched behind me before I could hear steps sink with a squish in the gory ground. Jake was the first to reach me. "Fuck me," he seethed.

Evan gaped. "Rogues."

Andrea frantically looked around. "Do you think they're here? Rogues?"

"I don't care," I snarled. My beast came forward; together we scanned the area until we saw something hanging from a tree in the distance. Cocking my head, I focused to see Ethan hanging by his leg in a silver snare that was slowly eating through his skin. Between us and him, the forest floor was crisscrossed with trap lines. Horror soaked into all of my pores.

Evan tossed a pack over his shoulder, furious determination filling his posture. He flicked his gaze to me. "Lead us through."

Something snapped in me. My feet started to move as Jake fanned around my side. He found a rare spot of dry dirt and picked it up then flung it over the path ahead, illuminating the trap lines for me.

"Go," he said.

I could hear him behind me as I sailed over the lines like lightning streaming across the sky. Together, we led the others to where Ethan was suspended in the air. Blood trickled down his body into a puddle on the ground that I dared not step in.

"Ethan?!" I cried.

No answer.

The rope that was holding him up was coiled around a tree. Evan ran to the tree and inspected the rope while Jake jerked on a pair of magicked gloves.

"Get the tarp!" Evan barked.

Andrea and I yanked a tarp out of a bag and laid it out on the ground under Ethan. Jake took hold of the silver-laced rope while Evan cut it free from the tree. Carefully, Jake lowered Ethan, who groaned in pain, to the tarp.

Andrea and I sprang into action. She pulled medical supplies out of the bag while I surveyed his vitals. Ethan's eyes cracked open and blinked lethargically at me before closing again.

I put my fingers on his neck. His pulse was faint but it was steady.

"Oh, god, okay," I sobbed. "You're okay. You're going to be okay."

Jake started to untangle the snare from his leg. "Lucky this fucker didn't rip his leg off."

"We need help!" Andrea wiped her forehead with a shudder. "My dad's on his way. I've been updating him."

"We need to get out of here. It's not safe," Jake stated quietly, before he shifted his eyes to the trees. "We need to call Sam—he needs a doctor. Fuck, where is Trey?!"

Evan clicked a flashlight on and shone it over Ethan's body. My mouth went slack when I saw bite marks, claw marks, and a deep gash on his shoulder. Evan leaned closer. "Someone fucking stabbed him."

He was covered in blood, but the smell of it sent my beast into a frenzy. Because he wasn't just covered in his own blood. "He reeks of rogues," I panted. The smell of it was enough to almost draw vomit from me.

Evan ran the flashlight beam over the ground. "Where are the fucking bodies? There's blood all over this place..."

"Do you think they're still here?" Andrea asked, lowering her voice.

"Doesn't matter, get him ready to go. We need to find Trey then get the fuck out of here," Evan directed.

Andrea blew out a frenetic breath and continued to help me wrap Ethan's wounds. Evan kept searching the area. His flashlight swung like an anxious pendulum in front of his feet. He walked a good twenty feet away before he froze in place at the edge of the dark mouth of a pit.

"Shit! Get over here!"

"Evan—"

"No, right fucking now!" Evan snapped.

Jake sprinted to the pit. "Oh, fuck me. Trey!" He dropped to his knees next to Evan. "Trey! Can you hear me? We're gonna get you out!"

"Go!" I urged Andrea.

She bolted to them then knelt with Jake by the edge. "Lower me!"

Jake took her arms and delicately dropped her. I could hear groaning and Andrea's distraught voice bouncing off the dirt walls inside the pit. My hands uncontrollably shook as I taped more gauze over Ethan.

He blinked his eyes open again to look at me dazedly.

"I'm getting you home. Stay awake for me," I pleaded.

His hand struggled to squeeze mine. Wiping the tears from my eyes I tilted my head to Jake and Andrea. "What is it? What happened?!"

Jake and Evan pulled a body up by its arms, leaving a thick streak of blood on the ground. Jake immediately rolled away then reached down and yanked Andrea out of the pit. Her face was white as she scrambled across the ground, wildly shoving herself away from the edge.

Jake slapped Trey's cheek. "Come on, man! Wake up!"

"Trey!" Andrea shrieked. She pressed her ear to his chest. "He's alive!"

I could see Trey roll his head to the side. He coughed so hard I thought a lung would come up, before he very clearly wheezed, "They're here."

"Trey, what do you mean? What did you see?" Andrea shrieked.

Trey only moaned incoherent words back.

Jake scrambled up with the flashlight in hand. He swept the light around us, but only sickly trees and mangy animals landed in the light.

Evan stood and wiped his bloody hands on his shifters as a new determination took hold of him. "We need to get out of here. Now. Can he stand?"

Jake scanned Trey over. "No. I'll carry him on my back."

Andrea gawked at them. "We should wait for help! We don't know what's out there and we'll need backup!"

Evan snarled at her. "The Reaper is knocking at my brother's door and these woods aren't safe. Jake, get Trey on your back. We're leaving."

Andrea's golden eyes pulsed a sunbeam. "Evan!"

Evan growled as the moon blood in his veins snapped like teeth in the air. "We're sitting ducks if we stay. Our chances are better if we move. We're going. Now."

Andrea snapped her mouth shut and helped us tie the tarp corners to fallen limbs to create a makeshift stretcher for Ethan. Evan helped Trey onto Jake's back then tied an extra tarp around them to secure Trey.

Evan cupped Trey's face. "Hey, you gotta hold on, man. Sam is gonna beat your ass if you think about walking to the moon without her."

Trey blinked a few times and then, ever so faintly, nodded. Evan walked around and picked up the front of Ethan's improvised basket stretcher while Andrea and I supported the back. We set off in a hot march, our pace increasing with every step.

"This place needs to be combed down. Tonight, before everyone and their mother pollutes the scent," Evan told Jake.

It seemed the weight on Jake's back didn't bother him at all. He trudged forward like the forest needed to get out of his way. "Billy said he'll handle it—he said to get them the hell out of here."

We did not stop the whole way back to Ethan's home. A woman with a dark pixie cut was pacing in front of the front door, next to Keeley and Evangeline, when we arrived. With a scream, she dropped the large leather bag she'd been holding and sprinted to Jake. Her hands swooped over Trey as tears burst from her eyes.

"Sam, we need to get them inside," Evan told her before he nodded to Evangeline, who could only stare at us in horror. "Lina, get the door."

Tears streaked down Evangeline's cheeks. "They smell like rogues, Evan..."

"The door!" Evan barked.

Keeley jumped and shoved Evangeline out of the way. She pushed the door open and waved us in. "Kitchen," she stated.

A plastic folding table was set up next to the kitchen table. Medical supplies were already spread out all over the counters. We laid both men on the tables, where the sheets that had been laid out quickly started to absorb blood.

Sam's shoulders were shaking as she murmured to Trey. I stood paralyzed next to Ethan, waiting for the pack doctor's instruction.

"Sam," Keeley pressed.

No reply. The woman held her mate's face in her hands, imploring.

"Why do they smell like rogues?" Sam whispered, voice like a hollow cold wind.

"We don't know," Jake answered.

Sam covered her mouth as her shoulders shook. She stood stunned, almost petrified, with glassy eyes that were glued to Trey.

Keeley hissed under her breath and reached for a pair of scissors. She stomped around to her cousin and pushed her back then shoved the scissors into her hand. "He needs your help. They both do."

Sam wiped her eyes with a large inhale then started to cut away the bottom of Trey's shifter shorts until they exposed a deep gash. She started to scan over Trey, systematically assessing the damage.

"What do I do?" I asked.

Sam lifted her pained eyes to me. "Get the gauze off Ethan so I can see the damage."

I felt Keeley press some scissors into my shaking hand. Swallowing, I cut away the bloody bandages and peeled them back. When I got to Ethan's shoulder, my fingers stilled. Evan wasn't wrong. Someone had stabbed him. The wound was too clean—too precise to be from claws or teeth.

Sam sucked in a breath. She began to look over Ethan, jotting down quick notes as she examined him.

"Will he be okay?" I couldn't stop my voice from stammering.

She jerked a nod. "They're both in bad shape," she admitted. "They've lost a lot of blood, but the injuries don't appear to be life-threatening. No sign of poison or silver in the system either." Her fingers carefully tested the open laceration on his shoulder. Hissing under her breath, she lifted her grim eyes to me.

Trembling, she said, "We need to clean everything off as

much as we can. Start with the open wounds. I'll mend them up as we go. You'll want some gloves for this. It will get messy."

I could only nod back. Keeley handed me a pair of latex gloves that I quickly pulled on. Evan brought over a bowl of hot water and gauze. He grabbed a piece of gauze with tongs, then pressed the tongs into my unsteady hands. Tears rolled down my cheeks while I dabbed at Ethan's mangled skin.

Sam cursed under her breath. "Someone better start fucking talking. Why the fuck do they smell like rogues?"

Andrea handed a bowl of hot water and gauze to Keeley, who started to clean off Trey. "There was a brawl. Something happened. But all we found was them."

"It was like the other times," I muttered. "Boxed in . . ."

Sam shook her head in disbelief. "But how the hell did they get in?"

"Probably because someone let them in," Evan answered, tone curt. He brought a fresh bowl of gauze to Evangeline, who started to help me clean Ethan.

Andrea shook her head in desperate disbelief. "Evan—"

"He's not wrong, Andrea," Jake countered tightly. "You saw the area—smelled it. Look at them," he snarled. "We would have smelled a trail of rogues if they'd came in from one of the borders. There's no trace of them—only in that area. Rogues are not enough in their right mind to pull something like that off."

Sam's eyes caught mine and mirrored my inner terror that was growing into something else. My chest was burning as something scalded through my veins. Anger licked its lips in delight. My beast wanted blood for her mate, and I did too.

"You think someone from the pack planned this?" Sam gaped at Evan in horror.

Evan ran his hands through his coppery locks. "If they didn't, then why box the fucking scent in?"

Keeley shifted her weight next to Jake. "We should sound the alarm, lock down the pack."

"I know, but that's not our call." Jake rubbed his face and shoved away from the table. "Billy's looking for them in the forest. We never found bodies, but Ev is right, and I'll fucking say it—someone wanted them dead." The air was sucked out of the room. Jake turned to Evan. "We need to lock this house down. Make sure we're not being watched."

Andrea watched him for a moment, pleading, before she relented. "I'll go with you."

When the door closed behind them, Sam threw her scissors down. Her chest heaved. Tears leaked from her eyes. "What the fuck is happening to this pack? What the fuck, Ev?!"

Evan turned the coffeepot on. It gurgled to life, filling the stifling silence of the room. "Evangeline, did you see anything else out there?"

The young woman's shoulders shook as she turned to face her brother. "Just what I told you," she swallowed. "There was popping in the forest, then we smelled them—the rogues. I should have never gone in with Trey. I should have made him stay on the pack line with me! It's my fault, I'm so sorry."

"No it's not," I assured her. "This isn't on you."

Sam blew out a tired breath. "I want some answers, Evan."

"Yeah, well, me too, Sam," he shot back.

"Let's focus on getting them patched up," Keeley offered. "I'll go with Jake when he gets back and look at the area where you found them. See if I can't find more answers."

"Thomas won't like that," Evan warned her.

THE PACK

"Thomas doesn't have to know," Keeley scoffed in return.

Together, our group polished off two pots of coffee while the sounds of gauze tearing and stitches being tied filled the room. I didn't like how quiet Ethan was during the whole process. How out of it he was. At least Trey could utter a few words here or there. But Ethan was barely with us except for the faint beat of his heart. Evan told me he had seen worse, but even though we were werewolves, we weren't invincible.

When Jake returned he confirmed we weren't being watched—we were safe, for now; he and Keeley set out to meet up with Billy and comb down the area, but Andrea stayed behind. She took charge of patrolling the house with Evan, each of them taking turns every hour. Still, even locked in the house, it felt anything but secure.

My nerves were frayed by the time we finished up, and none of us were going to attempt carrying the deadweights up the stairs. We managed to move Trey to a couch and Ethan to another opposite him. Andrea brought me extra clothes from our house; I ended up giving them to Sam. She disappeared into the bathroom while Evan and I cleaned up the kitchen.

He had his hair tied back with one of my ties. Copper locks had fallen around his face.

"How did you know? That something was wrong?"

"I felt it," I answered with a shiver from the memory.

Evan stilled before he slowly lifted his turquoise eyes to me. "He's lucky he has you . . . I was wrong. My feelings about Levi, I shouldn't have projected that on you."

"Thank you," I returned, with a tired smile. "Do you need anything?"

He shook his head. "Get some rest. I'll finish up here."

I squeezed his shoulder then jogged up the stairs to change into one of Ethan's shirts and a pair of sweats. Sam was passed out in a chair when I came back into the living room. I grabbed a blanket and curled up on the floor next to Ethan.

I took his hand and pressed it to my mouth. "I think I may love you," I whispered to him before I laid my head against the couch and fell asleep.

I peeled my eyes open and stretched my stiff back. Ethan was still sleeping behind me and Evan was snoring next to me. He had a pillow clutched to his chest and his head rested back against the arm of the couch. In the kitchen, Evangeline was furiously whipping something in a bowl while Sam nursed a cup of coffee.

I draped my blanket over Evan then tiptoed to the kitchen.

Sam had dark circles under her eyes, and I was confident I had a set to match. We had barely slept all night. We'd taken shifts watching over Ethan and Trey, in case their condition worsened overnight.

Evangeline stopped her task. She blew a red curl that had fallen from her bun out of her face. "I'm making coffee cake—I made some granola, too, and cookie bars . . ."

I looked over my shoulder at Evan. She offered me a meek smile. "He can sleep through anything."

I felt my brows lift. "You did all that?"

She shyly shrugged. "I couldn't sleep, and I like to bake."

"Thank you," I returned, which earned me a small smile from her.

"There's coffee," Sam told me.

I sank into a chair across from her. The clock on the wall read eight in the morning. "Where's Andrea?"

"She went out to run another route around the house," she answered, before pushing herself to stand. "Mind if I use the shower upstairs?"

"Help yourself."

She breathed a tired smile. "Thank you."

"Do you think they'll wake up today?" I asked.

"Maybe? But I wouldn't be surprised if they slept all day."

I watched her trot up the stairs.

A mug was placed in front of me. Evangeline hesitated by the table, then finally said, "Thank you."

Her eyes filled with tears. Mine began to water too. Exhaustion had eaten away at my resolve. I blinked and Evangeline threw herself into my arms. Her sobs were muffled against my shoulder; I helplessly tried to swallow mine.

"I'm scared," she whispered.

"Me too," I quietly admitted. "I'm sorry about snapping at you yesterday."

She wiped her eyes with a sniffle. "It's fine. You were scared—I was too."

I wiped my eyes on my sleeves. "Do you want help?"

She bit her lip. "Andrea said you're terrible at baking."

"Yeah." I breathed a laugh.

She waved me to the counter and handed me a bowl. "Stir."

I arched a playful brow.

She shrugged. "It's hard to screw up stirring."

We worked quietly together while watching a boring sitcom on the television. I helped her spoon the cake into two bread pans that she then pushed into the warm oven. After, I found myself staring at a photo on the wall that I hadn't noticed before. It was of their entire family in the fall. The trees were red and orange behind them as they all beamed at the camera.

Ethan's father, Chris, had bright-red hair and green eyes that looked like emeralds. His smile was warm, the kind that could brighten anyone's day. He was holding Evangeline in his arms; she couldn't have been more than six or seven. Her red curls were wild around her head as she screamed in laughter.

Evan was latched around his mother's waist. She had long black hair and kind hazel eyes with specks of blue and gold in them. She was gorgeous, with high cheekbones and a dainty frame that made her seem ethereal. But what struck me was how similar Ethan looked to his older brother.

Ethan was riding piggyback on Eli, who looked like he was about to nosedive them into a pile of leaves. He and Eli could have been twins except for the eyes; Eli had green eyes like Evangeline. Eli and Ethan looked like their mother. Both built with her cheekbones and her full mouth.

"They always said I was my father's daughter."

I tilted my head. "You look like her too."

"No one says that."

"You have her nose and her eye shape," I replied. "She was beautiful."

"Katerina," Evangeline murmured. "I always loved her name. It's my middle name."

"It's lovely," I told her. I licked my lips before pointing at Ethan and Eli. "They look like twins."

Evangeline snorted. "For years I would get them confused," she admitted with a little laugh. "They were always together. Best friends."

"I should have tried harder with you and Evan," I admitted quietly, my own voice slightly cracking.

"Oh my god," she breathed, as her head fell into her hands. She started to cry again. "I shouldn't have been such a brat—he cares about you so much. I just, I didn't want to lose him again. I guess Ev and I are as protective of him as he is of us. I mean, after hearing that Levi was raising some rogue-bitten girl, we half thought you were feral."

"I am at times," I replied, with a small smile.

She rubbed her face as the stairs creaked.

Sam walked back into the kitchen, finger-combing her wet hair. She glanced back at the men in the living room. "The moon was looking out for them. No major injuries—should make a full recovery in a few days." She placed her hands on her hips and shook her head in disbelief. "What the hell happened out there?"

"Jake hasn't said anything yet. He and Keeley were out there with Billy the rest of the night," Evangeline told us. "I've asked. A lot."

Sam picked her coffee up then took a long sip. "You know, when I thought we should do a girls' day to get to know each other, this is not what I meant," she told me.

"I figured—" There was a knock at the door. My skin twitched as my beast shook out her fur.

Evan roused from the floor. I strode through the living room to the front door where Thomas, Miranda, and Amber were waiting. Miranda pulled me into a hug the second I opened the door. I thanked her for the basket of muffins that Amber awkwardly shoved into my hands.

Sam moved to stand next to me.

Thomas put a hand on each of our shoulders. "How are they?"

"Stable," Sam answered for us.

Thomas blew out a breath of relief. "How are you girls holding up?"

I forced a smile. "We've been better."

"You poor things," Miranda cooed. "That forest—it's not safe, Thomas."

"I know," he breathed raggedly.

"Have they found anything?" I asked.

"We're still combing it," Thomas assured me, with a sentiment that I was sure was meant to provide relief, but it only made my skin crawl. "You worry about getting him on his feet again."

"They were drenched in rogue blood—the area was soaked with it," I stressed. "The scent was boxed in, like the area we found earlier—like what we saw at Thunderhead."

Thomas took a step closer. "Charlotte," he gently said. "You almost lost your mate last night. Let me worry about keeping this pack safe, keeping all of you safe."

"Thomas, if there are rogues in the forest—"

"You let me handle them," he finished, a dark promise in his voice.

Something hot burned through me. Before I could say something I might regret, I caught Amber's subtle head shake. My beast snarled in the back of my mind. I forced her to calm down before I returned a short nod to Thomas.

He fixed a tight smile on his mouth. "Have either of them said what happened?"

All I could think about was the stab wound and the defensive injuries Ethan had while the word *rogue* bellowed through my mind. Sam's eyes shifted to me.

I swallowed and shook my head. "No."

Thomas nodded like that was the answer he'd expected. "We're lucky to have you, Sammy."

Sam's smile was thin. "Thomas . . . what if they're here? Like before?"

"That won't happen again," he answered calmly. But by the look in his eyes, he looked as annoyed as someone running late for their tee time. "Billy is tearing through the forest. If there are rogues, he will find them."

Sam raised her hands up, pleading. "Thomas, they were covered in rogue blood. Trey almost died! There has got to be—"

"Sammy," he calmly interrupted. "I understand, all right? I almost lost two of our best last night. We're doing everything we can. I promise."

He paused and exhaled a deep breath, like he had been the one up all night praying to the moon that their mate didn't die.

"And girls?" He lowered his voice. "I don't want to cause a panic. We don't need people tearing through that place and getting hurt on a fear-driven witch hunt. I would appreciate it if we kept things quiet—between us, for now, until we know more."

Go on, show your hand, then, Thomas.

Sam's eyes began to water. "They almost died, Thomas."

His smile was almost as thin as his patience, which seemed to be gone. "I know, Sammy. I know."

"We understand," I told him with a feigned plea in my voice that seemed to sate his appetite for control. "We just want the pack to be safe."

He smiled, relieved. "I knew you would."

Miranda hugged Sam and I again before they left. We stood rooted in the doorway until they disappeared into the tree line. After, Evan yanked us inside and slammed the door closed. His footsteps echoed on the walls as he marched into the kitchen, where Evangeline was hovering by the kitchen table, biting her nails.

Sam stormed after him. "What the fuck is going on? Evan! What the fuck?"

Evan tipped the basket of Miranda's muffins into the trash. He pressed his palms on the counter as his turquoise gaze pulsed a glow.

"Ev?" I stepped closer to him. I didn't want to beg, but, shit, I was about to.

His jaw clenched. "I need to find Jake. Stay here. Do not leave this house."

"Evan!" Sam shrieked at his back as he marched for the front door.

"He's onto us," he bit out. "Whatever happened out there last night, we weren't supposed to see it. Any of us."

"But that means . . . working with rogues?" Sam shook her head in horror.

"They never got here on their own. Not back then, not now." Evan yanked the door open. "Stay here," he ordered before the door slammed shut.

"Screw this," Evangeline grumbled. "I'll try to talk to him."

She ran out the door, leaving Sam and me alone in the kitchen. Sam crossed her arms over her chest. She nibbled at the corner of her thumb then lifted her gaze to me.

"Say it. What you're thinking."

"I think . . . Evan's right."

She nodded slowly then dropped her arms. "Me too."

CHAPTER NINETEEN

I found Ethan sitting in the sunlight that was gently flooding the tiny balcony outside his bedroom.

With sure steps I carried myself outside. With even surer movements, I took his hand in mine. "You're awake."

"Yeah," he rasped. "How long was I out?"

"Two days." It had felt like an eternity. His form grew blurry, like watercolors in front of me.

His bandaged hand moved to cup my cheek. "Baby, don't cry."

"I was so scared." I choked the whispered words through dry sobs.

"Me too," he quietly admitted.

He nudged his nose with mine. It felt like we both knew the

dams we had built to hold back what we had been hiding were about to break. "Ask."

"What happened in the forest?" I murmured against his lips.

Without missing a beat, he answered, "Thomas tried to have me killed. He's been trying to kill me. For years."

"Oh," I mumbled back, blinking.

"It's not a great working relationship," he added with a smirk. Leveling his gaze with mine, he asked, "How did you find me?"

I squeezed my eyes shut as the memories of the whispers cackled in the back of my mind. My beast snapped at them and chased them away as something fluttered along the pull, something that gave me the courage to finally say what I should have said a long time ago.

"I hear voices in the forest. Whispers. It's how I found you."

"Voices in the forest?" he queried, eyes wide.

I nodded slowly. "Yes . . . Andrea told me what it could mean—about witches and blood magic." I blew out a breath. "It's hard to explain, but they call me. By name sometimes."

"How long has this been happening?" he asked.

"Since last year. I heard them before the Hunt. I—well, they weren't a problem, and now I don't know . . ." I licked my lips then told him about each time I had heard them. From finding the first Bloodstone to when he was missing, ending with the screams I heard from the stone itself. That set his jaw tight. The hair on his neck rose.

"Ethan, I was a human before. I've never done blood magic. I wouldn't even know where to start if I wanted to."

"I believe you," he assured me.

"Do you think there's something wrong with me?" I asked in a voice that was smaller than I would have liked.

"No," he answered quickly. "No," he said again, as if he was helping me convince myself. "You're not crazy. I believe you. Who else knows besides Andrea?"

"No one," I told him. "I know it's dangerous."

"Levi doesn't know?"

I shook my head. "I should have told him, but I didn't want to stress him out. I'm sorry I didn't tell you. I was scared. I didn't want people to think the worst about me—or you."

"I understand." He rubbed his jaw and stared off in thought before saying, "I've never heard of anything like it. Aside from what you've heard about the blood-magic curse. We can talk to one of my contacts when we go to Anchorage. He's a witch. Discreet. He may know how to help."

His thumb rubbed the back of my hand. He was quiet in a heavy, contemplative moment. "Andrea was not wrong to advise you to keep quiet. People . . . well, they are not always rational. This needs to stay between us until we know more. Andrea won't say anything?"

"No," I insisted. "She would never."

"Good." He blew out a breath, then said, "I need to show you something."

Under the staircase, there was a closet with a long row of coats that Ethan shoved aside to reveal a hidden door. Behind the door, was only darkness until he clicked on a light to reveal an unfinished wooden staircase spiraling down.

"This was originally Eli's house. We helped him build it— Dad, me, Uncle Levi, and Lucas. Eli thought it would be funny to hide the basement door."

With careful steps we descended into the under layer of the house, where the floor was covered with rough carpet. Ethan flicked a light switch on. The basement was half a living room and half a storage area. Boxes occupied one corner while a sectional and a makeshift coffee table made of cinder blocks and plywood occupied the other. A dinky refrigerator with lonely flower magnets stuck all over its front hummed next to the boxes.

Ethan released my hand and walked to the bookshelf that took up the entire back wall. "Lander is right, you have a good nose. I should have told you so much so long ago. I was stupid to think you wouldn't start figuring things out." He smiled to himself. "I didn't want you to get caught up in my own personal hell. I was trying to protect you, but I see now that I can't protect you if I keep you in the dark."

The bookshelf, I realized, was not one big built-in, but was divided into three sections. He paused in front of a baseball resting on the middle shelf in the center section. He tapped on it twice. "Eli loved baseball. The ball on the shelf is what opens it."

Ethan pulled the ball toward him with a click. The shelf lifted an inch to reveal wheels on the bottom, allowing it to swing open and reveal another room half the size of the one we were in.

Whiteboards had been nailed onto the entire back wall in the hidden room. They were covered with hundreds of photos, handwritten notes, newspaper clippings, random objects like a piece of cloth and hooks, and other scribblings in dry-erase marker. A table in the middle had coffee stains all over the dirty plastic top. A map of the three packs was laid out on the center of the table: Hemlock, Switchback, and Thunderhead. Dozens of sticky notes were placed on them.

"Okay," I breathed, taking it all in.

"I should have made you breakfast."

I smirked. "No manners at all."

Ethan ran his hand through his thick hair, which looked auburn in the poor yellow lighting coming from the two bulbs hanging in the secret room. He turned and leaned against a safe in the corner that stood guard in a row with filing cabinets kitty-corner to the whiteboard wall.

"There were so many things that did not add up after the attack, and there were so many people here aiding in the investigation. It was chaos. Eventually, it became so damn political and ran mindlessly into dead end after dead end. I got tired of it all and deviated, charted my own course.

"It never made sense to me why Thomas did not die with my father," he stated. He turned to open the safe behind him. "It's Evangeline's birthday." He told me the combo before he unlocked it. He swung the heavy door open, revealing shelves that were bloated with papers and boxes. Ethan dug through a few stacks of notepads before he pulled a manila folder out. He laid it on the table and flipped it open to reveal dozens of lined yellow note pages with rough sketches covering the face of the paper.

Ethan flipped through a few then pulled one to the top. There was a hand-drawn tree with five *X*s in bold marker in front of it. Four more bold *X*s sat together in a row on the outside of the initial cluster. Outside of that were dozens of *X*s in a thinner pen.

"This is an original sketch of where they died—Dad, Mom, Eli, Eve, and Lucas," he explained while his pointer finger rounded the bold *X*s in front of the tree. "The other darker *X*s are the other members of my father's pack council: Cash, our Head Tracker, and Falcon, our Head of Security, along with his mate, Jake's parents." Ethan tapped the letters in thinner ink. "These were all guards or trackers who were executed with them, but they were some of our most seasoned—the best of the best."

"Where was Thomas?" I asked.

Ethan pointed to the fourth X in the row of the late pack council. "They found him here. He said he was tortured and doesn't remember by who, but the witches confirmed he was either magicked or a powerful vampire wiped his mind. The thing is, there's only one vampire who can do that—compel creatures other than humans—and he was spotted in New York during the time of the attack," he explained.

It looked like an execution—like someone was trying to wipe the slate clean and start over. I tugged my ponytail and opened my mouth before closing it.

"Say it," he carefully urged.

I swallowed. "No coup with half a brain would have left the number two alive—they would expose themselves to easy retaliation. Either something went wrong, and by some wild miracle, Thomas did make it, or—it has to be intentional. But if they wanted to take over . . ." I bit my lip. "Something like this is too big to be an inside job. There had to be outside help. But it doesn't make sense. I mean, Thomas is the pack lead, but it's not like any outsiders are on the council."

"It's nice to hear someone else say it so I don't feel insane," he acknowledged, relieved. "Cash told me once that everything leaves a trail. I have found so much that is circumstantial around Thomas since the attack: blood magic around his house, money moved in odd ways to new accounts, documents shredded—things of my father's missing. I was given one bullshit explanation after another. I tried to save as much as I could of my dad's when I started to suspect something was off.

"But fuck me if you point a finger at Thomas. It's sacrilegious. Witches worked overtime to make sure he could walk again. Everyone thinks it's a fucking miracle he survived, bought easily into his bullshit story. He starts to rebuild the pack and looks like a goddamned hero, but if you want to question him, his loyalists point the finger and say that your grief is getting the best of you." A bitter smile jerked at his lips. "I heard that a lot. He said half of why he made me his second was so I could put my anger to work—help him build something my father would have been proud of."

I shook my head. I turned and lifted myself up to sit on the table, next to the folder. "But if this was about Thomas taking the pack for himself, then why not take out only your father? Why have this huge invasion and kill so many people?"

Ethan nodded in agreement, then said, "Did you know Levi was supposed to be there? But—"

"He was running late and sent Eve and Lucas ahead of him." I finished, before swallowing. "It couldn't have just been about your dad. But—why murder two pack leads and their families?" My beast flashed her teeth at the thought of it. Anger burned inside me but I pushed it away and focused. "Thomas can't be the only player in all this. There has to be more."

"I know," he answered with a tired smile. "I thought when I took the post as his second I could keep an eye on him—see if he showed his hand. But he's not that stupid. He's been keeping an eye on me too—keeping me in line. I've had to fly under the radar, it's when I try to push the limit or get too close to something that he retaliates. I found that out the first time he tried to kill me."

"What?" I gawked at him.

He rubbed the back of his neck. "There are spells that can be used to trace a murder weapon to the assailant. But they never found the knife that slit my family's throats. The weapons they did trace only pointed to rogues. I took a different approach. I did some searching and found a witch who told me the reverse could be done—blood could point you to the weapon that spilled it.

"It's much harder to do. You need a clean sample to have a chance. I couldn't use their clothes because they were soaked in rogue blood—they had been fighting for their lives. Going back to the crime scene was a long shot. Too much time had passed; anything that may have been there, had probably been washed away by the rains, but I didn't have any other options.

"I went back and searched for hours and hours until I was standing in front of the tree—that fucking tree," he cursed under his breath. "Those handprints never wash off. Never fade. Even with the storms. When we were kids, we asked why, and Dad always said the moon protected that place," he scoffed before he quieted.

"When I was standing in front of that tree, I remembered that they found a pool of Eli's blood at the base of it, among the roots. It didn't take me long to find his handprint on the bark. Preserved, just like all the pack leads that had sworn their loyalty to the fucking moon." Shrugging, he said, "I cut off a piece of his print. I didn't care if I was desecrating the fucking thing. I thought this was our chance; and at the time, I trusted Thomas, so I told him. Then the next thing you know, I'm sent to check out some traps that had apparently been firing on their own, and almost lost my actual head. When I recovered, I was told the sample I cut was contaminated with rogue blood and had been destroyed. I also got a long lecture about debasing the tree. And that was that."

"What the fuck, Ethan?" I hissed.

THE PACK

Ethan shrugged like he was talking about a routine chore he performed every Sunday. "I told you, I'm hard to kill. I've been poisoned by wolfsbane, sent into mountain lion territory—I genuinely think he prays to the moon for the forest to take me every time I step into it. Unfortunately, being his second, I can't always say no to his requests. He's very good with politics. Clever," he added with a bite in his voice.

"How has no one caught on?"

"I think some have," he admitted. "A lot of people keep quiet because they're afraid. But for some, he's a savior. The moon's 'miracle' who pieced this pack back together. Worst of it is that the people who support him truly believe that."

I turned to look at the drawing and the map. "So who the hell was he working with then?"

"I don't know," he answered with a tick of his jaw. "I never could gain traction on that front. The only explanation I could think of is the rebels—the Pure Seven. A lot of people thought they were quashed when they got the treaty signed. There's been whispers of small groups, but nothing serious. But, based on their history, they seem like the only group that would be wild enough for something like this, but there's nothing to tie him to them. He had a loose association with the Pure Seven through Jeremiah Bones and my grandfather, but nothing direct."

"Let's say the Pure Seven are in on this with him—what was the point?" I asked. "What's in it for them? Taking out that many high-profile wolves sends a message, but a message about what?"

He knocked on the table. "This has been my literal hamster wheel for years. For ages I searched for ways to tie all the loose ends together. My best friend was a bottle or a cup of coffee—I never slept. Evan eventually straightened me out. I was the only adult left, all he and Evangeline had. They needed me. I needed to protect them.

"So, I got my shit together. I always felt like whoever was behind what happened would eventually show their hand. And I can wait," he promised with a dark threat in his voice. "I put this room away and only obliged myself on a rainy day or when something new happened. And nothing new happened for a long time. A really fucking long time—but then a human girl was bitten by rogues..."

The glow of my eyes was reflected in his gaze. He went on, "Then rogues start to pop up in numbers and in ways that are incredibly unusual for a group of wolves who are supposed to be completely insane. Then there's scents of fresh blood magic in the forest... I started keeping track of things. Coming back here more to see if anything connects."

My throat constricted while my beast prodded closer. "What happened in the forest?"

He rested his palms on top of my thighs. "Evangeline and Trey heard the popping, then they smelled rogues. Trey told her to run for help. He linked me and immediately I went after them. Thomas—he and Miranda think Evangeline doesn't know anything. Ev and I have tried to keep her out of it, but she's clever. Still, they've never put her in danger. I thought she would be safe.

"I found her in the forest then took her back to the line and told her to run back. It took me hours to find Trey. He was conscious but in a bad way—his ankle was stuck in a silver-laced snare. He said a rogue had chased him into a trap. I could smell them close by. I got him out of the trap and onto his feet, but..." He shook his head almost as if he didn't believe it himself. "For a second, I thought I was fucking hallucinating..."

A chill ran over my skin. "There were four of them. One me.

One barely functioning Trey." His jaw tightened as a hum rolled off him. "They had come with weapons. Silver laced. I killed one and injured the others, but I had no idea if more were coming. I picked Trey up and started to run but the three caught up to us. I didn't realize where we were. I was too busy trying to fight them off. The last thing I remember was seeing one waving at me while I hung upside down in that trap."

"You killed one?" I asked.

"Yes," he answered. "Trey actually shoved one into a trap."

"But there were no bodies?"

"Billy didn't find them." His words set off a sickening fuse of dread in me. "And I don't think we're going to find them. Billy said the scent was already fading fast."

"But it's bodies," I snapped. "I don't care that it's magic. Bodies don't just vanish."

"But you've seen scent vanish before," he pointed out.

"This is different."

He hummed in agreement. "Thomas has to be helping them get into the pack. He has to be tied to the activity that's been occurring in the region. And we must be getting close to the truth, because this was actually one of his better murder attempts." He sounded almost impressed.

"The rogue camp Jake and I found earlier?" I muttered as horror wrapped its sickly fingers around my chest. "Do you think he attacked you because of that?"

"Thomas is right to be suspicious of you. He did not love that Levi's claimed pup, a fucking amazing tracker, was coming here and asking all the right questions that people were too afraid to ask. With me dead, he would have sent you back to Levi and wiped his hands of both of us."

My heart raced while my wolf pawed at the back of my mind. "I need to sit."

He smirked. "You are."

"Who else knows about all of this?" I asked. "Obviously Ev, but Billy? Jackson?"

"Yes," he confirmed. "That's it, though."

"What about Jake? And Keeley?"

"Jake doesn't have all the history. But he's probably pieced together enough—same with Keeley," he explained.

"The council meeting . . ." I thought out loud.

He nodded slowly. "He's planning something, I have no doubt. And he'll have friends coming, other pack leads stuck in the old ways."

"We have friends too," I countered, leaning closer. "People like Thomas get ahead because they're very good at leveraging their pawns and keeping the others isolated so they can't organize. We need to beat him at his own game. I mean, you're going to have to explain to Sam what the hell happened, she's not stupid, and deserves to know. She and Trey both do."

"I know," he agreed. "Thomas won't try anything again until the council meeting. Attempting anything that drastic so close to the event poses a high chance of exposure—too risky. Buys us a little time. Evan may have bought us more too."

I cocked my head. "What do you mean?"

Ethan smirked. "You know, Ev can be a real chatterbox . . ." I gawked back at him. Evan shrugged easily. "I talked to him when I woke up this morning. He said that Thomas stopped by when I was out—asked you all to keep quiet. Evan thought people should know if we have a threat, *and* he thought that Thomas would have a hard time maneuvering if he had a panicked, anxious pack ready to combust if so much as a leaf moved wrong."

"He told the pack?" I uttered, impressed.

"He may have let it slip to a few wolves who have a tendency to talk." He rubbed the bandaged area of his shoulder where he had been stabbed. "The look on Thomas's face during the full is going to be priceless."

"Ethan—" I quickly shook my head. "The full run is a bad idea."

"I won't let him think he's won," he replied before scoffing a laugh. "Besides, he's going to let the pack run. Otherwise, he's admitting that there's an issue here, and he will eat his own hide before he does that."

I suppressed a frustrated groan. "I don't like it."

"I know," he replied, then pressed his lips to mine. "For now, we need to figure out how he's getting rogues in, or we're all fucked."

I pointed to the drawing on the table. "I think it's tied to the clearings. It's the most consistent variable."

"Go on," he urged.

"Each time we've found a rogue camp, it's near a clearing. The first time with you, we found the camp first, but not far away was the clearing with the Bloodstone. Same case with Jackson. Same case with what Jake and I found the other day, except we only found the clearing—no Bloodstone." I bit the bottom of my lip. "But I feel like the Bloodstones go with the clearings somehow. Part of me wonders if we had looked around more when we were out there if we would have found it? Maybe an animal or something moved it?"

"Wouldn't you have heard it?" he prompted.

I tilted my head back and forth. "Fair. Regardless, these clearings are open to the sky. Always on the borders or close to them. Always soaked with blood magic. I don't know how, but I would put my money on those as being connected to how they're getting here."

"Hopefully my cloister contacts can help us piece it together. You're right, it's a pattern."

"If you tie him to what happened back then, and now the rogues today . . . he'll be removed as pack lead. There's no way even the people who support him could stomach the sight of him," I observed carefully, before asking, "Would you take over? The pack?"

"I don't know," he admitted. "Eli wanted this. It was all he wanted, to be just like Dad."

"And you?"

"I wanted to go to school. Get out of here for a while. See the world, tan my cheeks on a beach in Florida. I wanted to travel and see everything," he answered wistfully. "I told Eli when I was tired of the sun I'd come back to help him."

My lips curled into a smile and I laughed quietly with him. Ethan took my hand in his. "Regardless, I owe it to him, to them, to set things right. To make this right."

"You need to tell them—Keeley, Jake, Sam—they need to know. After what happened, they deserve to," I pressed. "So does Levi. We need him."

"I know," he breathed. He cupped my cheek. "I want you to promise me you'll tell me when you hear voices again."

"I promise," I agreed.

"Tonight, then," he decided. "We need to organize tonight."

CHAPTER TWENTY

There was a Bloodstone sitting in the middle of the plastic table in Ethan's basement next to a map he had laid out of the Hemlock Pack lands. My blood had run cold when the Bloodstone hit the table. The scene was too familiar—the sound of the murmurs like acid corroding my skin.

I could feel Andrea shift uncomfortably next to me. She took a long drink of the vodka that she had been nursing in a red Solo cup, then offered it to me. I took a long sip and handed it back to her.

Sam opened her mouth to say something but sank back to sit on the arm of the chair Trey had melted into. She continued to bite her nails, while Evan nervously bounced his leg on the other side of me.

My eyes lifted to meet Ethan's, heavy with a question in them. *"I can hear it,"* I told him.

I had heard it even before Billy pulled it out of his satchel and set it on the table. It was the only thing I could hear in the silent room cramped with over a dozen wolves Ethan trusted and had personally invited; but he kept the bookshelf closed. Some cards you didn't just play close to the chest; you carved open your chest and buried them there.

Evangeline was the first to break the silence. She set the tray of cookies she had been holding down then carefully walked to the table. For a long moment she watched the stone then lifted her big green eyes to her brother. "Ethan?"

"It's called a Bloodstone. Keeley found it with Billy and Andrea this morning in the forest."

All the eyes in the room shifted. Keeley was pale. Hair was falling out of her space buns. Her eyes were heavy with exhaustion.

Jake squeezed her shoulder. She stepped forward to address the room. "Where they found Ethan and Trey is a dense part of the forest. There's so much brush back there you can hardly see three feet in front of you. I'm not surprised it took us so long to find it. So much silver back there—" She shuddered then walked to the table. Her finger traced west on the map from a red circle then tapped. "There was a clearing about half a furlong away from where Ethan and Trey were found. In the center of it was this stone."

I clenched my eyes shut then opened them as Andrea released a shaky breath. She had been white as a sheet when she followed her father down the stairs. The golden in her eyes dimmed. "It smelled like fresh blood magic—reeked of it."

Ethan moved to stand at the head of the table, facing the room. "Trey and I were attacked by rogues. The area where we were found was covered in their blood, but the scent was boxed in. There are other instances like this, and there are other instances of clearings being found with Bloodstones in them."

"We think that the clearings could be how the rogues got in here, and now—" He turned to Billy. "With what you all found, you can't tell me that it wasn't staged."

Billy ran a hand over his face. His bright gold eyes were grimly dim. "I know," he reluctantly agreed.

"Ethan." One of the guards trod forward. "Shit, man—" He shoved his hands into his pant pockets and seemed to chew on his words for a moment before he held his palms up in defeat. "Fuck it, I'm going to say it. Look, we've danced around this in our conversations, but are you saying *he* set up a hit with rogues?"

"Yeah, I am," Ethan confessed. "Before we get further, you all know the consequences of this kind of talk. If you don't want any part of it, then leave. I don't blame you and no one will think less of you," he told everyone, like he genuinely wished he could choose that option.

Trey stood up slowly with a hiss of pain. He licked his fangs, which were already poking through his gums. "We almost died because of that bastard," he seethed. "I'm not afraid to say it— Thomas can kiss my ass. I'm done hiding and keeping my head low." The other wolves hummed in agreement. "We're with you," he said, eyes holding Ethan's. "All of us."

Ethan rested his hands on the table. "I need to catch you up, then."

Without hesitation he explained to them what we had found. He told them about how he had suspected Thomas, laid out everything he knew in concise detail, and then described each time Thomas had tried to have him killed. Including the last time. Trey shifted in his seat as the muscles in his back grew rigid, while Jake and the guards around him looked like they were about to burst out their skin.

When Ethan was done, he pointed to the map that we had marked up earlier in the day. "Each one of these places is where we have found something: a clearing, a clearing and a Bloodstone, or a rogue camp. All on the borders of the three mountain packs—Switchback, Hemlock, and Thunderhead," he explained.

Keeley walked up the table and scanned the map. Her eyes teared before she turned to look at the trackers in the corner of the room. One jerked a firm nod to her. She turned back with a fire in her eyes. "I believe you." Her tone was unwavering. Firm. "I've, well, I've been doing some stalking on my own—we have," she added before jerking her thumb behind her to the other trackers. "Thomas doesn't do his own dirty work—we've followed some of the trackers he uses. I followed one once who went to an open area of the woods like you described. He stood there in the middle like he was waiting for something, but nothing happened. Then he left."

Another tracker lifted his hand. "I saw the same thing. Weirdest shit. Guy just stood there, waited for like an hour, then nothing."

"Maybe they're scouting spots for whatever this is," Keeley thought out loud. "They went to the Thunderhead border a lot."

One of the guards raised a hand. "And you're saying that Jackson motherfucking Bones found a stone, too, and is on our side? I mean, if what you're saying is true, how did the region not go after his father?"

"No idea," Ethan answered.

The guard nodded back, amused. "Met him once on patrol. Yapped my fucking ear off." Ethan snickered under his breath. "Fuck, the rebels are a stretch. My old man said they were basically antiques, but anyone with a brain knew that the attack was the workings of something bigger. What's happening today feels like that—bigger. That and, well, another invasion is ballsy, but the guy hates vampires like the night is dark. After what he tried to do to you and now Trey, too, I don't put it past him." The guard rubbed his jaw.

"What's the point, though?" Evan asked, meeting his brother's eyes. "What the hell do they want with us? Why our pack?"

Sam's legs trembled like a filly's when she stood. She reached for the arm of the chair and steadied herself. "Whatever the reason, the point is Thomas is planning something. He's always planning something," she explained with a wry laugh. "He scares people so they don't talk. Don't collaborate. They just do as they're told, like good little ants. I'm tired of it. My uncle Cash died, Keeley's dad died—we all lost so much. We need to act."

Jake held his hands up. "Agreed, but we need to be smart. We need to block and tackle right now—we don't have the luxury of time to figure out why he's into the fucked-up shit he's into. We need to find these clearings and put eyes on them and figure out how they work so we can stop them, or we're fucked."

"Fucked right now? Or fucked in another month?" a guard asked. "The full moon is the day after tomorrow. The whole pack will be out."

Jake approached the table. He picked up a pen and tapped it on the table. "He won't try anything again so soon—at least, if I was him, I wouldn't. I think we have some time, but not a shit ton."

"What are you thinking?" Ethan asked him.

"Whatever his main target is, he's going to prioritize that over everything else. Thomas is smart. He knows that people are worked up, anxious and watching thanks to a little bird called Evan," he added with a snicker. "It's going to be harder to cover up a hit so close to the council meeting."

Billy rubbed his jaw. "You think the council meeting is the 'when' in all this?" he asked Jake.

Jake nodded. "Taking Ethan out wasn't the goal, it was a stop along the way. Because you can't tell me with all these clearings and Bloodstones that we found that he would have stopped after Ethan was dead? No way. Ethan is right—he got too close."

"So, what's your rec?" Evan spoke up. "We don't have a lot of time."

"He's right." Jake turned to Ethan. "The best offense is a solid defense."

Ethan lifted his gaze to Billy. "He doesn't know we know about the stone yet?"

"No," Billy confirmed. "What do you want to do?"

"Keep it standard. Bring it to him with your report but only tell him that you and the people you brought out to the woods know about it. Let him think it's a secret—that he got away with it," Ethan urged, then looked at Keeley. "We need our own map. We need to find these clearings. See if more Bloodstones are out there."

"He's going to have eyes watching that forest," Jake pointed out.

Keeley propped her hand on her hip. "Did you listen at all to the part when I told you I've already been stalking Thomas?" The trackers behind her snickered, devious smiles on their faces.

"We'll be careful and we can work together. Create distractions if needed."

One of the guards lifted a brow. "Shit, it would make patrols more interesting. I'm down."

"I'll go with you," I told Keeley.

Her lips curled into a smile, but the look on Ethan's face was anything but amused.

"It's what I do best. I hunt," I stated into our link.

His nostrils flared before he nodded in concession. "We'll keep the map here and you can start plotting," he informed her. "We need eyes on Thomas and the family too. See if any of them slip and spill their plan."

Evangeline kicked off the wall from her place next to Jake. "I can do it." Evan opened his mouth, but I put a hand on his shoulder. He quieted as Evangeline stood taller. "They think I am naive and clueless. They'll have no idea."

"It's not a bad idea," I offered in support.

Evangeline's eyes grew a hair wider before she bit back a smile.

Ethan crossed his arms over his chest. "Lina—"

"I can do this." She pushed back. "They won't suspect a thing."

"She's right," Sam chimed in, "and I'll help. I already have to interact with them a lot too."

Ethan looked at the floor then jerked his chin in a nod to Evangeline. "Fine."

Evan was stiff next to me. I squeezed his shoulder, but it was like squeezing concrete.

"You have to trust her. She's smart. She can do this," I told him.

Evan's jaw ticked. *"She's still the same baby sister Eli made me promise to keep safe."*

I looked away because I had nothing to say to that.

Billy stood straight and crossed his arms over his chest. "When are you meeting with the witches?" Billy asked Ethan. "We need to know how those clearings and the stones work. In the meantime, Jake and I can rethink our security for the council meeting."

"After the full," Ethan told Billy, before he looked to the guards in the corner. "There're other people for you to watch. His spies."

Each of them curled their lips in wicked smiles. Sam clapped her hands. "This feels good, Ethan—it feels right."

"It does," a guard echoed.

"Finally," a tracker chimed in.

"It feels like hope," Sam uttered, a thought that hit me square in the chest and sat with me even after everyone filed out. Because up until now, hope had felt like someone we kept chasing but couldn't quite catch.

Evangeline lingered after the meeting until she decided she was sleeping on the couch. Jake watched her with weary eyes and told me he would put her in the guest room and take the couch for himself.

I walked outside to find Ethan sitting on the edge of the hill. Morning would come soon; dawn would be breaking over the mountains.

He reached for my hand. "If I asked you to run, would you?"

"No." I snorted.

"Charlotte..."

I wasn't answering the question because I was done running from monsters. "Don't ask me again," I persisted, the sharpness in my voice holding no room for negotiation.

Ethan blew out a breath. I felt him kiss my cheek, letting go of the conversation. He rested his elbows on his legs and turned to me.

"I think you should move in."

I lifted a brow. "When?"

"Yesterday?"

Both of us laughed quietly before he asked, "Can you ever hear what the voices in the Bloodstone are saying?"

I lay back in the grass and stared up at the dwindling night sky losing its fight to the rays of sunbeams. "No."

CHAPTER TWENTY-ONE

"Are you sure the full moon run tonight is a good idea?" I asked.

Ethan's eyes pulsed a glow. "Very much so."

Jake cracked his neck. "All about the optics."

I rubbed my temples. Ethan and I had argued about it earlier in the day. I didn't want him to risk anything, but he didn't want Thomas to think he'd gotten the better of him. And from the looks of it, plenty of people seemed relieved to see us when we arrived.

Dozens of wolves were gathered in the yard of the pack house, where grills and tables were set up for the potluck. A bonfire burned in front of the structure, bright flames rolling high to the sky, as if it was challenging the sun.

Evangeline waved at Keeley and Sam, who were seated at a small picnic table with Andrea.

THE PACK

Ethan squeezed my waist. "I'm going to find Evan and make the rounds."

Jake snatched a cupcake from Evangeline's basket with a sly grin, then took off after Ethan. Evangeline and I set our baskets on a plastic table and quickly unloaded the contents. She wiped her hands on her shifters then took my hand and pulled me over to Keeley's table.

Sam patted the seat next to her for me. "Hey, you two."

I slid onto the bench then nudged Andrea's foot with mine under the table. Her golden eyes frantically locked onto my neck, then my wrist. "So are you officially moving in with him or what?"

She took a long pull from a lukewarm beer, which I could smell in the muggy air along with the scent of whiskey clinging to her shifter top. I licked my lips. "Did he tell you?"

Her lips parted in surprise and I realized my error. Inwardly, I cursed myself as my beast started to pace.

"So you *are* moving in with him?"

"We haven't really had time to talk about logistics," I offered, in hopes of calming her down.

She lifted her chin in a pensive nod and stood. "I'm getting another drink." She stomped off.

Keeley's space buns bounced as she whipped her head around to face me. "Something is up with her—I don't care if she can hear."

"I don't know what's going on." I took a red Solo cup of wine from Evangeline. "I should talk to her." Keeley tapped her head. Sam and I both slid forward in our seats. I closed my eyes as a link shot through like a hummingbird buzzing among fresh spring flowers.

"*Do it fast—there's too much at stake,*" Keeley said.

"*I can talk to her,*" Sam offered. "*Maybe it's easier with a neutral party?*"

I took a sip of wine. "*Maybe.*"

"*Should be fine,*" Keeley assured us. "*Jake has our guards squared off and I have trackers on point at the forest edges. We'll just take a moonlight prance through the wildflowers.*"

"*Flowers sound good,*" I answered, with a slight sigh of relief.

"Okay, enough of that talk," Keeley teased as she twisted a bun back into place. "Charlotte, was there anyone cute at Thunderhead? I'm in a dry spell and there's nothing here that's doing it for me."

"Keeley!" Sam groaned.

Evangeline's cheeks flushed before giggles bubbled out of her mouth. Keeley waved Sam off. "Look, I have needs!"

I swirled my drink around. "Well, maybe some will come for the council meeting and I can introduce you."

Keeley tossed her hands up in praise. "Thank the moon. What about you, Evangeline—anyone you have your eye on these days?"

Evangeline sank in her seat with a blush while Keeley prattled on. I got up to refresh our drinks. I was making my way to a set of coolers when Jake almost collided into me.

"You need to come now—I can't get her to calm down."

"What are you talking about?"

His eyes pulsed a wild glow. "Andrea. She's at the pits. It's not good."

I didn't wait for Jake. I shifted to my fur and tore off down the path, past the full moon potluck, and down the switchbacks to the place behind the barn that Billy called his "playground."

THE PACK

Next to a metal jungle gym dome were three round dirt circles under the full view of the moon.

A crowd was centered around one, their cheers dancing into the incoming moonlight. I shifted to my skin and shoved through to the front with Jake. Andrea was standing in the center of the fighting ring with blood running from her mouth onto her gray shifter sports bra. She was grinning viciously while Amber and Piper circled her. She cracked her knuckles, which were red and missing skin, and shook out her legs that sported fresh cuts and claw marks down them.

The other girls were both covered with their own fair share of wear and tear, but based on the alcohol-induced haze in Andrea's eyes, I wasn't sure that she would know how to stop fighting now, to back down for her own good. The fist Piper sent straight to Andrea's stomach told me as much.

"They came at her," Jake explained without taking his eyes away from her. "Wanted a two-against-one. She's—fuck, she's really drunk. I tried to get her to stop. She won't listen to me. She'll listen to you."

My eyes met Amber's. Her icy gaze widened in shock. *"What are you doing?"* I pleaded with her, but her stance became frigid. The mask was up.

I bit my lip. "Shit."

Andrea took another fist to the stomach, and without hesitating I ran into the ring.

The shouting inflamed like fuel on a fire, but I ignored it, because all I could hear was the sound of my best friend wheezing as I jerked her away. Flames of fury ignited in Piper's wide eyes. I held one hand up in front of me while the other shoved Andrea behind me. "She's done!"

Amber was pacing behind Piper. Her blond locks had stains of red on them. Her brows furrowed as she watched me.

Whipping around to face Andrea, I shoved her toward Jake. "You're done. We're leaving."

She shoved me back. The crowd roared. "Then help me end it," she bit out.

"I am," I jabbed back. *"Andrea . . . what are you doing?"* I asked across our link.

Her lips quivered and her eyes grew glassy. As I wiped the blood from her face, I thought she was going to take the hand that Jake was holding out for her, but she darted around me and plowed straight for Piper.

The younger woman grinned when she saw Andrea storming for her. Her steps became struts as a coy smile curled on her thin lips.

I noticed it before Andrea did. The song of the silver humming into the air—a buzzing noise that even through the roar of the crowd I could easily catch. Without hesitation I lunged forward, colliding with Andrea before the brass knuckles, layered with silver on the top, could meet her cheek.

When we hit the ground, I rolled Andrea under me then jumped up as silver hissed through the air.

Leaning out of the way, I turned to see that the unsuccessful punch had been thrown by Amber. She and Piper each had a set of the silver knuckles. "I don't want to do this with you," I implored Amber.

Andrea was struggling to lift herself up. Jake scrambled to reach her.

"She's done." My beast snapped her jaw as I stood square in front of the two women. "We're done."

Piper snarled. "I don't think so."

Her silver knuckles screamed through the air as she attempted to wheel around me in search of Andrea, but I caught her wrist and yanked her back then sent a fist of my own into her ribs. She hunched over with a wheeze and stared up at me in shock.

My eyes darted to Amber. She bounced her gaze from her friend then back to me, torn between what to do.

"Please stop," I pleaded with her. I didn't want to hurt her—there was no way this was her idea.

But she didn't listen. She bounced on her heels then sailed for me. Guilt created a pit in my stomach as I leaned around her. She moved too fast and without control; using her own momentum against her made it easy to catch her free hand and pin it behind her. I yanked her to my front as her silver-knuckled fist flew backward toward my head. My free hand caught her wrist midair and twisted it aside with a sharp snap.

Her legs gave out as a scream ripped through her. I held her up and yanked her back so my face was next to her ear. "Let them go. Now."

Her fingers wiggled like wet noodles until the foul weapon slid onto the dirt. I shoved her to the sidelines and kicked the knuckles to Jake, who was holding Andrea back. Her eyes were glassy, close to leaking tears. "I'm sorry," she mouthed.

Piper spat blood in the dirt next to her and cracked her neck.

"Where did you get those?" I asked her.

She shrugged playfully. "I know a guy."

My beast snapped. "These aren't fucking drugs. Where did you get them?"

Her jaw ticked. My feet moved on their own as I walked the

perimeter of the circle. I could feel something crackle in me, something pulse to life as my beast paced in the back of my mind.

"Ah, so we're going to play the silent game." I licked my lips. My patience was wearing thin. My beast snapped her teeth.

I knew we needed to lie low, but I was sick and tired of this girl and her petty schemes. They had gone too far—I had let them go too far.

"I would prefer that we end this, this is your chance to be done," I told her.

She cackled. "Right, and you're going to teach me a lesson?"

"You're so past that." Pausing in front of her, I nodded to the silver on her hand. "Does it feel good using that on your own pack? Something that has tortured so many wolves—killed so many wolves?" The crowd quieted around us. Piper's dark eyes narrowed as her lips thinned. "We're done here."

She barked a laugh. "No, I don't think we are."

A wicked smile pulled at my lips as my blood hummed and sang a song of electricity through my veins. "Part of me was hoping you'd say something like that."

She charged me with a wild cry. With sure steps I advanced, and with focused movements dodged out of the way of the silver. Her free hand hit my gut, but I had been ready for it—hoping she would take that exact shot. Because it made it easier to use her own weight against her when I seized her wrist and yanked her to the side. My elbow crunched into her nose while my hand quickly snapped her wrist—the silver knuckles fell to the ground at the same time that I kicked her legs from under her. She hit the dirt with an airless thud.

I shoved the silver knuckles back to her with my foot. "Pick them up."

The fingers on her good hand slithered back through the knuckles. She pushed herself up and readied herself in front of me, holding her broken wrist against her chest, her other hand up and ready.

My beast was close now; she snapped her teeth as my pulse pounded harder. I could feel my blood crackling in my veins before it snapped around me like teeth.

Piper's eyes widened a hair, showing a rare moment of hesitation, but her rage took over and drove her forward.

She kicked dirt into my face, but even without seeing it, I could still hear the silver. I tracked the song of it as it flew closer and ducked under her swing. My clawed thumb then caught her side, dug into the tender flesh of her rib cage, which Elliot had taught me would cause quite a cry.

She screamed and the silver slipped off her fingers again. Shoving her into the dirt, I nudged my chin toward her silver knuckles. "Pick them up."

Her fingers reached for them before curling away. I arched a brow. "You wanted your toys, now pick them up," I snarled.

Her nostrils flared as her eyes pulsed a glow. I took a step back and readied myself for her next move. Something shifted along the pull. I could feel him watching behind me—his scent easily finding me through that of all the others around.

But I couldn't look back. Not quite yet.

Piper lunged toward me as brindled fur covered her skin. I let my beast tear forward as we sprang to meet her in the air. We plowed into her shoulder, our teeth finding flesh as they sawed down. By the time we hit the ground, our teeth had found bone.

My wolf released her and stalked around her. She snapped

her jaws in the air as Piper's blood tricked down our lips. Piper jumped up with a stumble on her front paw. Her hand would give her hell for days, and I didn't feel bad about it.

I didn't feel bad when she lunged for me again, and in turn, my beast slid around her to latch onto her foot. I didn't feel bad when we clamped down until something crunched under our sawing jaw. And I did not feel bad when we kept grinding our teeth until we knew those delicate bones were good and broken.

My wolf released her then leaped away; we shifted back until I was standing in my skin. Piper's screams ripped through the air as her skin rippled over her. She clutched her mangled foot with her good hand and tried to squirm away across the dirt. Thomas and Billy broke through the crowd.

Thomas scanned the area with wide eyes before he dipped his head to see the silver knuckles at his feet. "What the fuck is this?!" he roared.

I nodded my head to Piper. "Tell him," I demanded.

She sobbed and rolled back and forth, her fingers slipping on her mangled flesh as she darted her eyes to Amber in a plea for help.

I tilted my head as something vibrated off me. "You were so happy to use them earlier. Tell him what you did."

"Charlotte." I heard Billy's calm voice cut through the chaos.

Turning to face him, I willed my beast to settle. "They brought out silver knuckles. I was trying to get Andrea away. She had taken them two on one. They came at her while we were leaving."

Jake tossed another pair of silver knuckles at Thomas's feet. Thomas turned his disgusted gaze to his daughter. "We almost buried two wolves because of silver and now this?!" A snarl vibrated off him. "Get out of my sight."

Amber stilled for a moment then tore off into the trees. Thomas turned his sights on Piper. "You should be ashamed of yourself," he spat. "Someone get her out of here."

"I'll call Sam," Jake told him.

"No," he hissed. "Let her sit with that for a while and think about what she's done," he added a little louder.

I tried to hide the shock on my face. Thomas looked down and let out a deep breath then turned to the crowd. "Out of here. All of you," he said, too calmly. The sound of his voice felt cold, like a damp winter wind working its way under my skin.

"Are you all right?" he asked me.

My beast cocked her head. "I'm fine," I answered with a voice that I forced to stay even.

He released his breath and rubbed his jaw. "We can't catch a fucking break, can we?"

"I'm sorry," I told him. I wasn't, but I was playing a game that I intended to win.

Thomas grasped my shoulder. "Nothing to be sorry for. You were taking up for your friend. An honorable thing to do." He squeezed my shoulder. "I'll see you up top," he replied, then stormed away from the dissipating crowd.

I looked around. Ethan was walking toward me, but I stepped around him and charged after the long legs and chestnut hair starting to run away. "Hey!"

She picked up speed. I ground my teeth and started to sprint. Andrea was too late to increase her gait; I curled around her and tackled her to the ground.

She shoved me off. "What the hell?!"

I jumped up and tossed leaves at her. "Are you kidding me?!" I spat. "Andrea! What the fuck was that?"

"Nothing," she said. "Bad fight."

"Bad fight?" I scoffed. "You almost got your skin torn off!" I closed my mouth and willed myself to calm down. *"Andrea, please talk to me?"*

Tears leaked down her cheeks. She looked at the crowd behind us then sucked in a breath. Slowly she stood up with a bitter smile.

"My best friend is fucking falling in love and I'm not handling it well, okay? I'm losing you."

"You are not," I countered. *"You know that's not true."*

Her lips lifted in a glum smile.

"Andrea, you're not losing me."

She wiped her eyes. *"Everything is so fucked up."*

I cocked my head. *"What? What do you mean? Did something happen?"*

"It's nothing," I heard her whisper through her silent sobs.

"Andrea, please . . ."

Footsteps approached us. Billy put a hand on my shoulder. "Let's get you home," he told Andrea.

Her eyes grew teary as she watched him. He reached for her, but she turned and sprinted into the forest. Billy released a long sigh. "I got it from here. Go run. Be careful."

"Are you sure?"

"More than sure," he answered.

I looked ahead to where she had run off before I relented. "I'm sorry, Billy."

"Me too," he added before he ran after her.

CHAPTER TWENTY-TWO

Ethan was a warm, solid presence next to me. "Are you okay?"

"No." Andrea was my best friend—I didn't know to fix it.

"Whatever it is, she probably needs to work it out on her own," he suggested.

"Maybe," I grumbled, as we walked back up the trail.

Keeley fell in step with us. "Regardless, that was pretty badass, Char."

I was about to reply when I saw Evan barreling for us.

"What is it?" Ethan called to him.

He skidded to a stop and pointed to the valley. "Evangeline, she went after Amber!"

Ethan snarled. "What?! You were supposed to stay with her tonight!"

Evan panted, catching his breath. "She linked me and said

something about Amber heading to the mountains—she was afraid she'd cut through the forest. She gave me the fucking slip, all right?"

Dread sank in my gut as guilt filled me. I'd never wanted to hurt Amber.

Keeley shoved past them. "Enough. Let's find her. She's not safe alone. Neither of them are." She grabbed my hand. We sprinted up the trail, halfway up the switchbacks until we had a bird's-eye view of the valley where the pack was supposed to be running tonight.

My beast came closer. Together we studied every tree, every rock, every little curve of land until we saw something blond dart between trees.

Keeley's finger snapped through the air with a point. "There!" A flash of red was hurtling after the tan wolf Keeley had spotted.

The two of them were like flames rushing between trees. They ran along the edge then dipped into evergreen, into the darkness of the trees.

"Shit," I heard Ethan curse behind me.

"I'm linking Jake," Evan said.

Keeley smacked my shoulder. "Let's go."

We took off along the trail. I let my beast tear forward as we skidded around the curves of the switchbacks until our four paws hit the flat land. Ethan was running in stride next to me. Our paws pounded the ground like thunder as we roared across the valley, past the barn and up the tree line where green flags waved to us in a silent greeting.

Keeley and I pushed harder to get ahead of the boys. We dipped our noses, together quickly finding the scent of Evangeline through the grass.

THE PACK

Ethan nudged his chin forward. *"Find her."*

Keeley and I tore off, leaving Ethan and Evan to cover our flanks. We wound around trees and made our way up the incline of hills, steep slabs of stone, and boulders. The trees around us grew closer together. Their skinny bases twisted and turned in ways that made my body hurt from looking at them. Keeley's hackles rose. We were near the border of the Trapper's Forest.

Ethan surged to catch up with me. His shoulder brushed against mine as Evan covered Keeley's other side. Ethan's eyes scanned the area in front of us in a frenzy as stress twisted the pull between us.

"Has she answered her links?" I asked the group.

Evan snarled into the darkness. *"No."*

My beast hissed. Cold fingers slithered through my fur. I felt it growing thicker around us; suddenly the sound of our paws grew muted, as if they were farther away. I stopped moving. Closing my eyes, I sat back to let my beast take in the scents around us. We were in a cloud of old blood magic. A silent spot.

"Charlotte." A whisper cut through the fog.

My beast snapped her teeth as Ethan cut his eyes to me. *"We're in a silent spot, we need to punch out of it."*

If Keeley was scared, she did a good job of hiding it. Her beast clamped her jaw shut and led the group through the billow of quiet that made it feel as if I couldn't even hear myself breathe.

"Charlotte," I heard again.

Shit.

"Ethan, I hear them."

His eyes pulsed a glow as dread filled them. *"We need to get you out of here—"*

"We're close," I countered, and we were. Evangeline's scent

had grown stronger—we had to be only a few minutes behind her at this point. *"Let's find her and leave."*

Keeley led us up a hill. When we reached the top, the sound of the forest rang clear to us again. She yipped into the darkness as we left the silent spot behind.

"We're close!" she called over the link.

Their scents were fresh. At the pace we were running, we would probably run right into both Evangeline and Amber. My beast and I homed in on the vibrant trail that cut through the darkness. We were sliding around a bend, pushing farther into the darkness, when cracking noises popped through the forest.

Keeley started to slow but I snapped at her. *"Keep moving!"*

"What is that?"

"Just keep running, Keeley!" Ethan called to her as more cracking echoed around us.

My beast hurtled through some bushes as hushed voices danced around us. She snapped her teeth at them as something shone ahead. Blinking, we realized it was moonlight shining over an open space through the trees where Evangeline stood.

Red runes glowed on smooth stones circling the ground. The glow cascaded off Evangeline's red hair and made her loose curls look like tendrils of fire falling down her back. Blood magic swirled to the sky almost as if it was praising the moon for the new blood that had easily walked into its circle.

Evangeline stumbled backward as cracks sounded from inside the circle. Turning to us with wild eyes, she pointed at something red and glowing at the center of the clearing—a Bloodstone.

I shifted to my skin and sprinted ahead. "Evangeline! Get away from there!"

THE PACK

Ethan shifted to his skin and charged ahead of me. He snatched Evangeline back to the safety of the trees as more popping sounded in the circle.

"What the fuck is that?" Keeley cried.

Evan turned Evangeline to face him. "What the hell, Lina?!"

Her eyes were wet as her lips trembled. "She wouldn't stop! Something happened and she kept running! I tried to stop her but I lost her—" Her words were replaced with a scream as more cracking came from the circle. The Bloodstone glowed a pulse then started to mist. Red vapor spored through the air.

"Run!" I screamed.

My feet moved on their own. Whispers called me as the red mist trailed us, but I kept pumping my arms as my legs pounded through the darkness to safety.

Evan ran with Evangeline in hand. He yanked her too hard across a smooth stone slab; she tripped on a jagged edge and lost her footing, taking him down with her, tumbling to the bottom of the steep decline. The two of them hit the ground with a thud before the sound of their groans signaled that they were at least all right.

I skidded to a stop next to Ethan. Keeley darted past us. "I'll go help them! We'll meet you in the valley!" she called before she shifted back to her fur and made her way down to them.

Ethan's hand yanked mine forward. "Let's go!"

We charged together through the darkness. I had no idea in which direction to go other than away from the sound of cracking.

"Charlotte," I heard murmured through the darkness.

My beast snapped her teeth in the back of my mind as I pumped my arms and legs harder, but the hushed voices felt like they were forming a tunnel around me. Wetness blurred my eyesight as they called me, over and over and over, with a desperate plea.

Cracking sounded in front of us. I turned on my heel and chased the safety of the quiet until the grass under my feet felt familiar. The quiet around me thickened. Dread pooled in my gut as my anxiety roared over the pull.

My eyes lifted to the white oathing tree with blood from crimson handprints oozing down its pristine bark as its branches swayed in the moonlight, as if it was waving us home.

Ethan's mouth parted. "We're getting out of here."

Cracking echoed nearby.

My feet became clumsy as fear engulfed me. The leaves on the tree trembled as we neared it, but there was no wind moving through the forest to cause such a shudder.

"We shouldn't be here," Ethan stated.

He reached for my hand and tried to pull me in another direction, but my toe caught something on the ground. I lost my balance and fell down the small slope of soft grass and into the open moonlight that shone over the tree.

"Charlotte," a whisper called.

Standing, I didn't dare look at that tree. I kept my eyes forward and started to run to Ethan, who was sprinting for me.

"Charlotte!" another whisper cried, but this time it felt like it was right behind me, breathing down the back of my neck.

Stumbling forward, I felt myself fall, heading for the hard roots of the tree instead of the soft grass. My eyes closed as my body braced for the impact. When my knees hit the ground, they landed with a wet splat.

I opened my eyes to look at frantic green ones staring back at me.

THE PACK

There was a woman with red hair that flowed in long curls like Evangeline's. She had porcelain skin and the most perfect set of full, rose-colored lips that were parted as short pants fell through them. A silver knife hovered over the thin skin of her delicate neck.

My eyes flickered down to the pool of blood that carpeted the ground between us.

"Charlotte."

Her voice was like velvet as it cut through the silence. I realized that I had seen her before. I was staring at Eve.

"What—" I gasped and whipped my head to the side. Lucas was lying lifeless, face down next to me.

"Do you see now, Charlotte?" Her voice was calm, almost serene, but the question felt like ice being poured on top of a fire.

I whipped my head back to face her. "What's happening?"

The knife pressed tighter against her neck. She sucked in a wince as it singed her skin.

"Please see," her strained voice begged me. Her eyes pooled with terror as she tried to lean away from the knife.

"No! Eve!" I reached for her but my knees were stuck in place and my arms weren't long enough to grab her. "Please, no!"

"Run!" she screamed.

"Eve!" I howled. "Eve, no!"

"Levi!" she cried, as the knife sliced into her skin.

Her blood peppered my face as the knife zipped across her neck. I closed my eyes as her gurgled wail tore through the darkness.

I could still hear her wailing when my eyes opened.

Ethan was staring at me in horror. My legs were sandwiched between tree roots that squeezed my calves to keep me in their hold. I opened my mouth to say something just as a scream ripped through the air.

My body jerked in place as another howl rang like a siren behind me. Another scream raged from my side followed by a wail that felt like it was howling right next to my ear. I hunched over as another pierced the sky in a cry that I knew would haunt my dreams. Torment and agony were the notes that the cries carried in vicious circles around me, like vultures gnawing at pieces of my sanity with every shrieking wail.

Ethan yanked my upper body up as the screaming swirled around me. Tears pooled in my eyes. I could see his lips moving, but the sound of the crying cyclone around me was all I could hear. My hands flew to my ears as yet another shriek tore through the space between us. My ears rang. I felt my own voice build before my mouth opened with a howl of my own.

Soon my screams added to the symphony around me. Ethan held me in his arms while I cried out into the night with the screams. I felt something wet run down the sides of my cheeks from my ears. My head grew dizzy as the sounds twisted around me in a suffocating hug—my lungs burned, begging for relief.

Then, abruptly, it fell silent. I felt the roots release my legs.

One last scream echoed around us. It wasn't until I felt the rush of oxygen sucked back into my lungs that I realized it was mine.

Ringing pounded in my ears. Ethan held me silently for the longest time before I felt his arms push me back slightly so he could look at me.

"Baby?"

Hot tears rolled down my cheeks. "I think there's something wrong with me."

His finger swiped the skin under my ears. "Shit," he hissed at the blood coating his index finger. "We need to get you out of here. You need Sam."

When I opened my mouth, nothing came out. My beast was curled in a ball in the back of my mind. I could hear her agonizing whimpers as she lay stupefied with me.

Ethan pulled me to stand then dipped to scoop up my feet so he could carry me. Evangeline jogged to us. I felt her cold hand on my arm.

"You need to go." Evan's voice sounded garbled as it came out of his mouth. "There's no way people didn't hear that. We'll work on a diversion. What the hell happened?"

"I don't know," Ethan answered back.

"Char?" Keeley's tiny voice called through the ringing in my ears, but I couldn't do anything but bury my face against Ethan's chest.

"I'll do it," I heard Evangeline say. Something about her voice was calming, like cool water pouring over me. "I got lost in the forest and ran into something bad and got scared. Keeley and Evan can walk me out like they found me."

"What about Amber?" Keeley asked.

"Fuck her," Evan snarled.

"No," I heard myself whimper. I didn't want the forest to have her too.

"Send trackers out," Ethan countered. He pulled me tighter to him. "Go now," he told them before he started to move.

He was silent the entire way home.

Sam was waiting for us. She put drops in my ears then gave me a sleeping pill. When she left, Ethan slid in next to me and curled his body around mine. I felt him press his lips to my shoulder while his arms locked around me, almost as tightly as they had in front of the tree.

"Try to sleep," he urged me.

I closed my eyes and let myself drift. When I finally found sleep, I regretted it immediately. Because once I was asleep, I could hear the screaming again.

CHAPTER TWENTY-THREE

A giant plate of gooey cheese fries topped with crispy bacon, chives, and sour cream floated past us as we sank down in a booth. My mouth instantly watered.

Ethan grinned. "I told you this place is good."

"Thank god, I'm starving."

I hadn't eaten since we'd left the pack lands. It was afternoon when I finally woke, and Ethan was waiting with a cup of coffee in hand. When I finally could form sentences, I told him what I had seen, what I had heard—Eve, the blood, and all those horrible screams. In response, he told me we were getting out of the pack for the weekend. We were going to hand deliver the witches their letter in Anchorage.

He looked up from his menu and scanned my face. "How are your ears?"

They still had a dull throb. Sam told me they would for a day or two. I had eardrops in my purse, which she'd prescribed once every two hours for the first twenty-four hours.

"They'll be fine."

"We can always get this to go and go back to the condo?" Ethan and Evan's private escape when they needed to get away and apparently my abode for the weekend.

"No." I shook my head and took in my surroundings. The Bootlegger looked like what happened when a bunch of drunk pirates decided to build a burger joint that even the devil himself could appreciate. "I want to stay."

He reached across the table and took my hand. I bit my lip then finally asked, "Has Ev asked any more about what happened?"

The wolves that had run close to the forest had heard screaming, but thanks to Evangeline, they bought her story—that she'd gotten lost and been frightened by the red-eyed creatures. Amber claimed Evangeline got lost on her own; as frustrating as that was, it did help our cover.

But I was more afraid of the whispers being exposed—of putting us in danger, especially with everything going on.

"No," Ethan assured me. He told our group that we had run into blood magic, that it had sent a ringing through my ears that almost burst my eardrums—which wasn't totally untrue.

"That cover is safe too," he assured me, but the anxiety bubbling in my gut made it hard to believe him.

"Have you talked to Jackson?"

"Sunshine." His rich voice cut through the air. "Tonight, we're not talking about the pack, or the forest, or the rogues, and especially not fucking Jackson. We're eating, then we're having drinks downstairs."

Something warm melted along the pull. "Are we now?" I teased back.

"That's the plan," he answered slyly.

"And after that?"

He dipped his eyes to study his menu again. "Behave and you'll find out."

I raised my menu to cover my quiet laughter.

I was so stuffed after we ate that I opted to pass on dessert, much to Ethan's disappointment.

We left and walked down the grimy alley next to the building. My beast cocked her head as we stepped over trash that had fallen out of a dumpster. "Where are we?"

The corner of his mouth lifted in a sly smile. A single light hung over a green-painted basement door at the bottom of three concrete steps. He jogged down the stairs. Looking over his shoulder, he studied my face with his dual-colored eyes. "You feel all right still?"

I nodded. "I haven't been through a green door before."

He knocked on the door three times. A small window slid open. "Yeah?" A whiny voice leaked out.

"We need two boxes from the cellar," Ethan told him.

The window snapped shut and the door unlocked with a groan. A small, round, balding man held the door open. We stepped through and went down more stairs that were dimly lit by flickering light bulbs hanging from the ceiling. At the bottom of the long staircase was another green door.

Ethan knocked three times. Another window slid open. "Hemlock," Ethan said.

The man on the other side lifted his chin in amusement. "It's been a minute, Ethan. Come on in."

The door opened to a small, sleepy dive bar. Inside, the space was covered with vintage posters and postcards from all over the world. Lava lamps glowed blue and purple around the room, giving it a strange celestial hue. A sleepy jukebox rested in the corner close to the very real burning fireplace that was crafted entirely out of empty beer cans and some kind of foam.

"How is that not burning?"

Ethan smiled. "Magic."

"I love this place," I answered in awe as Ethan led me to the bar.

The old wooden bar top was canopied with plants I had never seen before in my life. They glowed and bloomed in colors I didn't think existed outside of rainforests and smelled absolutely divine. A giant wooden shelf stood proud against the back wall. It was filled with many bottles of liquids, dried fruits, flowers, grains, and other mysterious things.

A man with a pink-and-blue paint-splattered ball cap stepped from the door behind the bar. His round face broke into a dopey grin when he saw Ethan.

"My man!"

Ethan smiled and slapped his palm in the man's. "Finn. This is Charlotte."

Finn turned his boyish smile to me. "Dude, I heard, congrats. And welcome, my lady," he told me with a small bow. "I am your boy's favorite warlock, well, bartender. Honestly, I'm really only good at getting people drunk."

"Me, too, although no one has ever called me a wizard," I quipped.

"Ethan," he said as he pointed his finger at me. "This girl. I like her. All right." He rubbed his hands together. "What can I get you? On the house—don't bitch at me, man, we're celebrating. Now, Charlotte, pick your poison. Green fairy?"

THE PACK

"No," Ethan quickly answered for me.

I tilted my head to look at him. "What's wrong with the fairy?"

"You will be seeing them for three days straight," Ethan told me seriously. "They are not green."

Finn waved him off. "Semantics. Turquoise, blue, green, who cares?"

I bit my lip. "I think maybe no fairies. Maybe something tame?"

"You like brambleberries?"

I tilted my head. "What's a brambleberry?"

"Right." Ethan stepped in for me. "Finn, Charlotte's never been to a bar like this before."

Finn squinted like he thought Ethan would grow two heads.

"What he means is I, um, well this is my first nonhuman bar. I was a human before."

"Oh, fuck me," Finn gasped. "You've—oh, hell, yeah! I've never met a first-timer."

Ethan waved his hand at him. "Finn, you cannot get her fucked up. She had a rough night last night—Sam should have called about eardrops for her?"

Finn feigned a hurt expression. "Wounding me, man. You think I'm going to let her have a bad first time at my bar?"

Ethan rolled his eyes then said, "Oh, forgot to ask you, did Bernard check in with you?"

Finn shook his head. "No, but you know how he is. Last minute to everything. You're delivering the invitation to him?"

"Current plan," Ethan noted.

"Sick. I got that popcorn you like in, too, by the way."

Ethan's eyes lit up. "That's the best news I've heard all day."

He leaned closer and murmured, "I also need a consult . . . from you."

Finn considered him for a long moment then said, "Consult on what?" Ethan cut his eyes to me then back to Finn, who nodded slowly in understanding. He pushed open the saloon door behind the bar and waved us back.

Ethan's hand pressed on the small of my back and guided me down a hall into a small back room. Finn had a desk shoved against a wall in a corner where an underground greenhouse ruled the vast space around us. My jaw dropped.

"We got anything you want down here," Finn told me with pride. "A-plus weed, and other things . . ." He pulled a chair out for me. "Take a seat."

I sank into the chair. Finn took a seat on a rolling stool. "It was her ears?" he asked Ethan.

Ethan jerked a nod. Finn reached for a magnifying glass that glittered in the light. "Mind if I look at your ears, doll?"

"No," I answered easily.

He turned my chin then peered down my ear with a long, low whistle. "Man, fucked up them eardrums. What did you do?"

My eyes lifted to Ethan. He blew out a breath then said, "Finn, discreet. How much?"

Finn jerked back like he had been burned. "Bro, we're friends. I'll oath it with you—I know how your kind get about their mates."

Ethan dipped his head to level his gaze with Finn's. "You told me once I got a favor from you?"

Finn cocked his head. He peered at me then slowly looked back to Ethan. Wordlessly, he walked over to the door and closed it, then returned.

THE PACK

"It's soundproof—magicked," he assured me, before he turned to Ethan. The playfulness in his eyes was gone. "Save that favor for when you really need it. We're friends. We help each other."

Ethan pulled a stool forward and sat next to me. His hand took mine. "Tell him. It's safe."

My beast was pacing in the back of my mind. Finn waited patiently before laughing lightly. "Maybe I should get you a hit of something good?"

"No," I insisted. "It's just—I heard voices, in the Trapper's Forest."

Finn cocked his head. "Voices almost blew out your eardrums?"

"No." I shook my head. "Well, yes." I paused and calmed my beast enough so I could focus. "I've heard voices in the forest, whispers. They call to me, by name," I explained.

He leaned forward on his forearms and nodded to me to go on.

"I don't know what Ethan has told you about the forest..."

"I'm read in," Finn informed me. "Some wild shit happening over there."

I blew out a breath and told him about the whispers, about the murmurs from Bloodstones and what happened last night—the tree, Eve, and the screaming.

Finn had laced his fingers together when I finished, his eyes cast down like he was having a hard time processing it; I knew I still was.

He lifted his head to us. "I'm sorry you had to experience that."

"Thanks," I muttered.

He rubbed his face. "Bloodstones are bad business, Ethan. People think they're a myth. If you really have them over there—I dunno, man. It's bad magic to make them, and bad magic is used with them."

"What about the voices?" I asked. "I heard that only witches, that there's—"

"A blood curse?" Finn finished.

I nodded.

He shrugged. "It's a misconception. I've known witches who have done blood magic. They never heard anything. It's an old, superstitious belief, if you ask me, but some of you wolves like to hold on to your old wives' tales."

I sucked in a breath. "Well, what is it, then?"

Finn clicked his tongue. "I don't know. You were totally a human before?"

"Totally," I affirmed.

He rubbed the back of his neck. "Hearing voices is never good, that much I know, unless you are a medium—but that talent runs in families, which in your case isn't possible." He thought for a minute then said, "I'll look into it myself. Things like this, considering how it's happened for you—well, you're right to keep quiet."

"What should we do, then?" Ethan asked him.

"You need to start keeping a diary of any time you hear them." He issued an instruction to me. "All the details you can think of. The more detail you have, the more it can help. We need to identify what's triggering them. And I am gonna have to advise you to not follow the voices. Not until we know what they are. It's dangerous."

"All right," I agreed.

"Now." He slapped the tops of his thighs. "Let's get you some more meds for those ears."

He stood and walked to a cabinet containing dozens of vials. He thumbed through them then pulled out two and handed them to me. "On the house."

"You don't have to," I said.

He waved me off. "I want to. Now, can I get you two drunk or what?"

Ethan and I laughed with him and made our way to a round booth upholstered in red velvet that had gold stitching in the shapes of tiny flowers. Ethan tossed an arm over my shoulders while I continued to stare around the bar like I was a kid at the zoo for the first time.

"That was really generous of him. How long have you known him?" I asked.

"A long time," he answered. "He's a good guy. Has the laziest teacup pig as a familiar, but he can make the best drinks, and obviously he's great with potions. Makes a lot of medicine that we buy. He also has a business partner that he distills liquor with for both the magical community and humans. Evan and I invested in it actually."

"And?"

"It was a really good investment," he answered simply. "Evan, it's his thing. He loves numbers. Took over our family finances when he was like seventeen. He's been printing money ever since."

I tried not to gape at him.

Ethan shrugged. "I know." He brushed my hair behind my ears and studied both of them. "You good?"

"Yeah, I just wish Finn would have had more answers."

"I know," he said sympathetically. "He'll find out something. If Finn is anything, it's resourceful."

Finn rounded the corner and set a tall glass that was colored like a sunset in front of me. Flowers hung over the side, and tiny blue butterflies rested on the glass. Ethan took a drink from him in a short glass—a black liquid that swirled around two large square ice cubes.

I took a sip from the purple curly straw. The butterflies took flight and burst into a blue mist that smelled like the ocean. The drink tasted like mango but it wasn't sweet and, surprisingly, it wasn't creamy. It was almost citrusy, with a cool refreshing aftertaste that made me feel like I was about to lie back under the sun on the beach.

"Thoughts?" Finn asked as he placed a giant bucket of popcorn in front of Ethan.

"It's delicious," I answered. My lips pulled into a brighter smile. "So, so good—were the butterflies real?"

"For you, it's all real, doll," he replied with a wink. "I'll come back to check on you."

He left for the bar while Ethan shoved a handful of popcorn into his mouth. I reached for some but he lifted it away from me. "No, not for you."

"Seriously?!"

He tossed another handful in his mouth then grabbed a kernel and tossed it toward me. Jumping in my seat, I caught it in mouth. Parmesan and at least five other savory cheese flavors burst to life in my mouth. My eyes went wide. Ethan tipped his head back and laughed before he tossed another at me.

My cheeks flushed after I caught it again. My beast yipped

in the back of my mind, both of us wishing we could pause this moment and stay in it forever.

"It's so amazing, he won't tell me what's in it," he explained. He dug his hand into the bucket and shoved more in his mouth.

"This is nice," I admitted.

"Just nice? Baby, this is the finest dining."

I snorted a laugh. "How did you find this place?"

"The magical community is small. You hear enough eventually, but this place? Eli brought me here." He snickered under his breath. "I was underage. He paid the old bartender off."

"Wait, what?" I laughed with him. "Seriously?"

He nodded with an easy smile. "Had my first proper mixed drink here. I was so hungover the next day. Dad was fuming mad." He snorted.

"What was he like? Eli? Evangeline said you guys were like twins?"

"Yeah," he breathed. "We could have been. We weren't that far apart in age, and I guess we looked similar, but we were night and day. He was—" He paused while he thought, as if he was being careful of what to say, before he tossed back a long sip of his drink. "Well, he took up the whole room. He was a people person, you know? He was good with everyone. It made it easy when we were kids."

"You didn't like people?" I teased.

He shrugged with a sly smile. "They're okay?"

I rolled my eyes.

He swirled his drink around. "He loved our pack. Since he was a kid, that was what he wanted to do. He wanted to be just like Dad, and Dad fucking loved that. Eli and Lucas were best friends—like best fucking friends. And I don't know, I think Dad loved seeing the two of them grow up knowing they'd run things like he and Levi did." He shook his head and took another sip of his drink. "It's really all Eli ever wanted."

I playfully poked his chest. "And you, Florida man?"

"That is so unfair . . ."

"Just saying," I answered with in a singsong voice.

He laughed under his breath before he quieted, growing a hair more serious. "We were really different. He was my best friend, but we wanted different things."

I finished my drink right as Finn arrived with two new ones. He took my old glass and replaced it with one that swirled with different shades of blue, as if it was a night sky. Little golden specks of light shone through the inky liquid. Finn tapped the glass twice and uttered something under his breath. The gold lights lifted out of the liquid, becoming little fireflies that floated around my glass.

Ethan shook his head at Finn with a pointed expression. "You're really pulling out all the stops."

Finn replaced Ethan's empty glass with a fresh one. "Gotta shoot my shot, man."

Ethan rolled his eyes as Finn padded away from us. I leaned forward and took a long sip. Blackberries and mint. Delicious chills swept over my arms as I swallowed the liquid that reminded me of a cool night breeze in the hot summer.

"So, what about now?" I asked him.

"What do you mean?"

"I mean we have a lot going on, but things will pass." I licked my lips and let my words flow without fear. "What then? What do you want?"

He put his glass down as he watched me with the same

expression that he'd had when I first saw him after he chased me up a tree. It was like he was watching a sunrise for the first time and realizing that the next morning, he'd see it again. The glow of the fireflies reflected off us as they ventured a little farther from my drink.

"Do you remember when I took you to see the borders reset?"

"Our unofficial first date?"

"Yeah," he breathed with a light laugh. "I remember looking at you seeing magic for the first time and thinking that I really didn't care what happened next as long as you were in it."

Something warm flooded the pull. It felt as comforting as a hug yet full of energy like electricity sizzling to life. The hair on my arms rose as my pulse quickened.

There were so many things I wanted to say. So many things I needed to say. But they all felt stuck on the roof of my mouth.

Someone clicked the jukebox on. The record skipped a few times before the melody of "Hey Jude" softly played from the speakers.

At some point, I would have to make a choice. At some point, I had to say what I wanted and commit to it every day. Because I was never going to know everything about him, and he was never going to know everything about me. But I knew enough to know that while forever may be a long time, I didn't want to do it without him.

"I love you." It came out faster than I planned, but the words were clear as I spoke them. "So much."

His hands cupped my face as he leaned into me. "Finally, you caught up." He laughed lightly as my mouth slightly dropped. "I told you, I'm a patient man."

His lips melted against mine as the pull crackled to life

between us. I felt his fingers run through my hair as heat swirled over me.

"Get a room!" Finn called from across the bar.

Ethan laughed against my lips. "Do you want to get out of here?"

"Yes," I answered quickly.

"Yes?"

"Yes, please."

His eyes pulsed with something heavy, something needy that made the tips of my nipples tighten. Ethan slapped cash on the table and had me out of the bar before I could even say goodbye to Finn. We were barely able to wait until we reached our building, and the moment the elevator doors closed, we lunged for each other.

I didn't even hear the ding as we passed each floor because his mouth was on my neck and his hands were yanking my shirt off. My legs wrapped around his waist as he lifted me against the wall. A moan escaped my mouth as he squeezed my ass before he yanked my bra off; suddenly I became desperate to feel his skin against mine. My hands became frantic as they ripped off his shirt, the pull between us fueling the needy fire that drove my fingers to work on his belt.

The elevator doors opened directly into the condo. Ethan stumbled into the entry, where cold air kissed my back as he carried me with sure steps to the bedroom. Fire licked down the pull and across my skin down to my center, which I knew was drenched with need. He kicked off his pants as he laid me on the bed then playfully bit my hip as he tugged off mine.

His lips trailed over my skin as he crawled over me. He hovered a moment, watching me with a question in his eyes that I quickly answered.

"Yes," I panted.

His hand slid over my stomach as something vibrated over him.

"Where?"

My nose scrunched because this was the part I hadn't really thought about, so I answered with my gut instinct. I looked at his neck. I could hear his pulse pumping through his veins.

"If we're going to do this, then we should do this."

His lips curled into a pleased smile. "Good," he answered before his mouth covered mine.

Something crackled through me when I felt my panties torn off. The tips of my breasts pressed against his chest and my back arched as a delicious tightness built in me while his fingers found the rhythm that I had grown to crave. I bit his bottom lip, and he playfully smacked my ass while I rode his hand to the edge before he yanked his fingers from me, replacing them with his thick length.

The pull drummed between us and set the beat that we rocked against. Heat flooded the bond and poured through me—a new, manic need created as a tightness rebuilt in me. His fingers dug into my hips as my canines itched at my gums. My eyes snapped open and latched onto a space on his neck, the curve that fell to his broad shoulders.

Something moved again along the bond between us, something that stole my breath while he murmured my name against my neck. The feeling in my core pulled taught, like it was dancing on a tightrope that was ready to snap. When he pressed his lips against mine again, it was like I was floating as the early peak of the euphoric rush broken over my skin.

His hand gripped my hair and yanked my head to the side

to expose my neck. I didn't even see his fangs descend to my skin because mine were lifting to his neck—piercing my desired target. Blood coated my mouth as an orgasmic high ripped through my body. My eyes shut as the dam cracked, the pull breaking as something else replaced it.

A new sensation raced through my mind like a comet and coated me with so much love that I could have cried. Tendrils of pleasure coursed through me as this new thing twined itself around my heart and fused itself a permanent home. A new bond kick-drummed to life. A bond that felt solid, safe, and ever alive as it sparked raw electricity through my veins.

I released his neck with a gasp as my vision swirled. Exhaustion slammed into me and my languid body begged for sleep. Ethan released my neck with a gasp of his own. He rolled off me and pulled me to his side. Blinking my eyes closed, I curled into him as I let sleep take me away.

When I woke, it was to the feeling of someone kissing my neck. Teeth playfully nipped at the flesh before they were replaced with a long lick that made my toes curl with need.

I rubbed my eyes. "Did we die?"

His hand snaked up my hip while the other covered a breast. "Afterlife's not so bad if we did," he mumbled against my skin.

A drowsy arousal flooded the bond between us. "I feel a lot."

"Mmm," he hummed alongside my jaw. His lips brushed against mine before they quirked into something sly.

An image of me riding him in this bedroom flooded my mind. In the image a dewy sheen of sweat covered my skin as my breasts bounced with each thrust. My mouth parted as I gaped up at him.

"Calm down," he chuckled. "Just focus. Like you would if you were linking me but instead think of the images."

My nose scrunched while I focused on the bond. The image I chose was the one of him hovering above me; for the sake of learning, I figured the simpler the better.

Ethan smiled down at me. "That's my girl."

"I did it?"

"You did it." He laughed.

Something buzzed on the nightstand. Ethan ignored it to press hot kisses to my neck. It buzzed again.

"Maybe you should answer it?"

"I'm going to flush it down the toilet."

"What if it's your sister?"

"She's fine."

His phone continued to buzz. I snatched it and unlocked it for him. "It's Jackson."

"Even better," he grumbled against my breasts. "Well, what the hell does he want?"

I turned the phone so he could read it. Jackson had sent him a picture of a map and asked if Ethan had seen anything like it. The top of it read SWITCHBACK. Ethan clicked on the photo Jackson had sent and zoomed in on the old text, written on paper so thin it almost looked like silk.

"Apparently there were a few wedged between books in the back of the library. Caden's kid found it while playing hide-and-seek—was running around with it. We always suspected Jeremiah Bones had a lot of information about the rebels, but Jackson always thought he'd burned a lot of it before he died."

He zoomed in on another photo of the map and my breath caught. Ethan tilted his head toward me. "What is it?"

"I have a map just like that."

"What?" He laughed incredulously.

My beast started to pace. I took the phone and zoomed in more—the delicate text and drawings of trees and mountains were an identical style to one I was intimately familiar with.

"When we did the Hunt, Jake had a map just like this, but it was of Thunderhead. He got it from Billy. It's the same style and everything."

Ethan furrowed his brows and stared back at the photo. "There's no way."

"Ethan, I studied that thing for days—weeks," I breathed before pointing to the strange drawing of cats in the corner where it noted mountain lion territory. "I always thought those looked like cows. Jake's map has them too."

He looked back at the phone. "Do you have a picture?"

"No, it's in my—wait." I bit my lip then thought back to the memory of Levi looking over the map at his kitchen table. I was standing next to him while he added another note to it.

Tapping the link, I let the memory slide down it to Ethan, as if I was sending water down a pipe.

His eyes went distant for a moment before they grew wide. "Nice work," he noted with a cheeky grin before he rubbed his jaw in thought. "Billy also took a lot of Dad's things from the pack house to keep anyone from taking them—it has to be from that . . . he's such a pack rat."

I tried not to let the ill feeling spread through me. I took the phone and tossed it into a drawer of the nightstand. "We won't solve anything tonight."

"What did you have in mind?"

An image flooded through the link of me bent over the bed. Ethan's lips twisted in a devious smile. "I have some ideas," I answered.

His mouth nipped at mine. "You have good ideas," he murmured back, before we found ourselves lost in each other once again.

CHAPTER TWENTY-FOUR

Cruise ship passengers scattered like ants along the dock. Ethan led me past the tourists and away from the main area of the marina to a set of abandoned buildings facing the water.

One of them read WEIGH STATION. It smelled like the sea and old fish inside. He guided us through a dark hall until we stopped at a door painted green, a shuttered window next to it; the salt in the air had chipped away the paint on the old, swollen wood.

Ethan knocked twice on the window. After a pause, it cracked open. "Two for the scale," he said.

"Port?"

"Hemlock."

The lock clicked. Ethan pushed the door open and led me

into an elegant emerald hall with gold-framed mirrors and expensive planters adorning the walls. The hall spilled into a large room that overlooked the ocean through tall double French doors lining the back wall. Sunlight and sea breeze poured through the room, dancing around the wind chimes and chandeliers hanging from the ceiling and rustling the bottoms of crisp white linens neatly laid over tables scattered throughout the restaurant.

We sat in a far corner at a booth with an unobstructed view of the water. The waiter who greeted us sported a buttoned shirt just as clean pressed as the tablecloths. He took our drink order then made himself scarce.

I looked around the bougie setting. "This is where the warlock wants to meet?"

Ethan dropped his head into his palm. "It is when I'm paying."

I slid my hand over his knee. The crescent moon-shaped bite on his neck peeked from his collar. Both of our marks had already started to heal. They were slightly pink and forming a scar, which at this rate would show by sundown. A blush bloomed over my cheeks as memories of the night fluttered into my mind. Slowly, his lips melted into a soft smile.

The waiter set a glass of wine in front of me and a beer in front of Ethan. When he left, a dainty woman with long, wavy cotton candy–pink hair stood in his place. She held a large black tote in hand.

She lifted her round, pitch-black sunglasses and scanned us with pink eyes that matched the shade of her hair. "Ethan Everette? Hemlock second?"

Ethan lifted a brow. "We were expecting—"

"Bernard," she answered with an eye-roll. She stepped

forward with a tan suede-gloved handed extended. "He is occupied. I'm Stella."

Ethan shook her hand. "Occupied?"

She shrugged off her well-tailored cream blazer and hung it on the back of the chair. "He'll kill me for saying this, but I don't care. It's his fault," she grumbled. "He got caught purchasing some illegal plants and is now having to fly back to our cloister's headquarters to answer to daddy for his mess." Sitting with an exasperated breath, she crossed her legs. "He's filled me in. Now, you have an invitation for me?"

"You're part of his cloister?" Ethan inquired.

"Yes." With a groan, she picked up the tote and slugged it on the table. Sand spilled from a few seams while she dug around inside. She finally whipped out a wallet. Flipping it open, she pulled out a silver coin and handed it to Ethan. It was stamped with a bird's nest around the outside and an Eagle soaring in the middle. "The Nest is happy to partner with you."

Ethan handed her the coin back then offered her the invitation that was folded in a simple envelope. She carefully tore it open and eyed the contents.

"Perfect. Obviously, we'll be there. However, the elders are married to their formalities," she rambled. "Bernard said you have questions—" Before she continued, she turned to me with a warm smile. "I am so rude. I'm Stella."

With a smile in return, I replied, "Charlotte. It's nice to meet you."

Her cheeks were rosy and her smile grew before her lips parted in a gasp when her pink eyes floated from my neck to Ethan's. "And newly mated?" I nodded in confirmation. "Congratulations, you two! You must let me get the first round."

THE PACK

Ethan continued to study her.

"We won't say no to that," I answered for him.

Stella waved our waiter back and ordered a cocktail. She also insisted that we order at least dessert to celebrate. Ethan didn't seem thrilled, but the witch seemed agreeable enough. After the waiter brought the drinks over, Ethan got up to use the bathroom, leaving me alone with her.

Stella watched me for a moment then said, "It's always lovely to see two people so happy."

It was my turn to blush. "Thank you."

Her bag shook on the table. Yellow eyes in a light-pink scaled head looked back at me. A tongue flicked in the air, and the horned snake rose an inch from her bag. My veins turned to ice while my beast howled in the back of my mind.

"What's—oh! Kevin!" She wiggled her finger at the snake. "I told you to stay in the bag! You're scaring her." She watched him a moment then rolled her eyes. "You ate already. You don't need a snack—no, you cannot have fries, they make you constipated for days!"

"Are you talking to the snake in your purse?" I gaped.

"Well, yes, he's my familiar. Kevin," she added with a laugh. "Honestly, he's very sweet, and for a desert viper, he's really quite calm."

"You have a desert viper in your bag," I repeated, while my beast continued to howl for me to run.

"Well, he's my familiar," she said, like that explained it. She narrowed her gaze at me. "Really, he looks scarier than he is."

I took a long sip of wine and tried to force myself to not look at the snake watching me. "You said you can talk to him? Sorry, I just—I was a human, this is all really new to me."

She beamed. "Oh! You should have started with that! Well, yes, all witches and warlocks can talk with their familiars. Usually, we can hear them when we start to inherit our magic. Mine came in around thirteen. Kevin found me before then. Thank the sweet suffering goddess that my mother had an inkling of what he was. She set up a terrarium for him and then not long after my magic came, I could hear him. We've been inseparable ever since."

"And you named him Kevin?"

She shrugged. "He told me his name was Kevin. Believe me, nothing sounds more nonthreatening than fucking 'Kevin.'"

A laugh tumbled out of my lips and then we were laughing together. She waved the waiter down and gestured to her bag. "Sorry, can I get a cup of water for him and an order of fries?"

The waiter nodded and walked away, and Kevin settled back in her purse. Sand tumbled across the white tablecloth. She swept it away with dainty hands adorned with soft pink fingernails.

"Poor thing, he really needs a dry climate. We lived in New Mexico before, so he was in his element. Now I only have a few sandboxes for him. I've had to make do. The cold, wet weather really doesn't suit him."

"You transferred?"

She nodded. "I was on assignment for a few years down there. The Nest is my home cloister. Our head, Caleb, called me back to help here. So, you said you were human? When did you shift? Humans rarely make it. It's so great to see someone doing so well."

"Around two years ago. On the blood moon in October—I won't ever forget that."

Her eyes went wide. "Is that right? She does favor you, then. Congratulations. That's truly incredible."

"Thank you," I replied.

Kevin slithered slightly out of his bag. She gave him a long look. "Charlotte doesn't want to cuddle with you. Get in the bag. We talked about this." She turned to me with an apology in her eyes. "Sorry, he—well, he's a lover. Especially when he likes you. I think he likes you."

"Right..."

Something cold shot across the bond. I could feel a hum from Ethan only a few feet away. He looked at me, the snake, and Stella. "What the hell is this?"

"He's Kevin," I answered, as if the snake and I were now best friends. "Her familiar. We got him fries."

"You got fries for a fucking snake?"

I patted the seat next to me. Ethan stalked carefully back around the table and sat pressed against me. His body was angled toward the snake, slightly blocking me from Kevin's view.

Stella didn't seem bothered at all. She leaned her forearms on the table. "Now, Bernard said you wanted a consult?"

"What's the price?" Ethan asked.

She cocked her head. "Cash is always preferred. I'll charge the same hourly rate Bernard does, seeing as you were expecting him. It's only fair."

"Cash it is," Ethan agreed. "Bernard is very good at—"

"Discretion?" she finished with a grin. "Nothing to worry about here, Her Second."

"Really?" I pressed.

"Like the attorney client thing humans have," she explained. Her finger traced the rim of her champagne coupe. "I have questions, too, though. I was telling your mate that I was recently brought back up here from my assignment in New Mexico.

I'll be straight with you—I'm here for the rogues. Our cloister head is concerned, he wants to see movement, so to speak." She drummed her fingers on the table. "I like to make things move."

"*What do you think?*" I asked.

"*She seems like a shark.*"

I tipped my head in the smallest of nods to Ethan in encouragement. "*Maybe that's what we need?*"

Ethan leaned back and crossed his arms over his chest. "Witches from your cloister are supposed to visit Thunderhead days before the council meeting for a . . . consult."

A coy smile teased her lips. "They are, Her Second."

Ethan's mouth pulled into a tight smile. "I don't want to wait."

"Clearly not, you're here asking for a consult." She paused and swirled her drink in her glass. "I have the sense you'd like to see movement too?"

"Something like that," he agreed.

She nodded with a teasing flicker of a smile. "I've been briefed by the witches in the area. Thunderhead's pack lead has sent notes on what is occurring. Interesting case. New blood magic, a 'domed-in' rogue scent, then of course the rogues of it all as well. But there's more you've found, isn't there?"

Ethan opened a photo of a Bloodstone on his phone then wordlessly slid it across the table to her. Kevin rose out of the bag and slithered over to look at the screen. Ethan stiffened in his seat. His hand reached for my knee under the table; in doing so, his arm created a block between me and the snake.

Stella zoomed in on the photo and studied it with a stunned expression. "Do you have more photos?"

"Swipe to the right," he told her.

She swiped to the next two then swiped back. Shaking her

head, she said, "This can't be possible." She paused and looked over her shoulder. "I apologize, but added discretion is needed for this conversation."

She lifted her palm next to her head and uttered words in what sounded like Latin under her breath. When she snapped her fingers, something that looked like plastic wrap shot up around us and to the ceiling before the blur it created faded, leaving only the smell of burning sugar behind.

"Don't worry, no one can see it," she assured us. "It keeps our conversation between us, which is good. Because if I am right, that's a photo of a Bloodstone—this is very bad."

"How are you sure?" I asked.

She leaned forward and laced her fingers together. "How's it smell?"

"Like blood magic," I said. "Fresh blood magic. It always smells—concentrated? I don't know if that makes sense."

She nodded slowly. "It does. Blood magic, like any magic, can be confined to a lot of things—objects both of the natural world, so like a stone or a log, or unnatural, like a piece of jewelry or a box. It likes to grab onto things, so it's fairly easy to fuse with something else. But Bloodstones are rare and probably one of the most illegal forms because they are one of the most powerful ways to wield blood magic. It's very condensed in that form. That's why it smells the way it does to you. But they take a lot of blood to make and are very tricky, very difficult magic to use. They haven't been known to have been made successfully for at least two to three hundred years—"

"On Hemlock alone, we've had three," Ethan told her.

Her fingers covered her lips as her eyes went wide.

"Switchback found one too," he elaborated.

"How long ago?"

"Over the past few months."

"Did you find only these?"

"No." Ethan hesitated then went on. "They were in a clearing under moonlight. The last one was circled by stones with runes on them."

"A full circle?" she queried.

He nodded. "Yes, a perfect circle."

She drummed her fingers on the table and looked at Kevin. "Yes, I think you're right," she told the snake. "Kevin thinks you may have found a circumpunct. They're used for advanced magic. They aren't illegal, we use them now. But usually, their purpose is to help pull off big spells. They are able to harness energy and focus it to the center for whatever purpose the spell dictates—you can use stones or crystals to create the circle, it doesn't matter. But whatever you use has to form a circle around the object for the object to be amplified. Runes are usually also a key part of making them work. Can you remember the runes you saw or do you have a photo?"

Ethan shook his head. "We had to get out of there, the Bloodstone started to spray a mist and we didn't want to stick around for that."

"I can imagine." She shuddered.

"It's been a nightmare to trace the origin of it. The scent dies off or is boxed in," I explained. "So on the ground, there's no trail. But that's illogical. Everything leaves a trace. You can't just make things disappear."

She smacked her lips. "No, you can't."

Unease stirred in me. I bounced my eyes to Ethan's. His gaze was steady but I could feel anxiety brewing over the bond.

THE PACK

The waiter rounded back with a cup of water and fries. Stella set them in front of Kevin, who quickly swallowed a few crispy pieces.

She slid the phone back to Ethan. "You think these are connected to the rogues? I read the case files from the attack. These elements you're discussing—the Bloodstones, circumpuncts—they were not noted before. Although to be fair, that doesn't mean that they weren't used. It just means no one found them."

"I saw one, a Bloodstone, two weeks before the attack," he stated evenly. "When I took my brother back to look at it, it was gone. Of course, I never thought it was connected until recently."

"And the rogue patches? Did you find those before?"

"No," Ethan told her. "But we have them now, and I had four rogues on my pack lands try to kill me a few days ago."

Stella gaped back at him. "I'd like to see the bodies."

"Gone," he said, tone clipped.

"Gone?" She gawked at him.

"No bodies were recovered," he answered. "We were hoping you could help us explain how, as well."

She blew out a long breath and rested her palms on the table. "I'll see if I can come early. It's best if my colleagues coming to the council meeting aren't privy to this—they, well, let's just say that I don't agree with their antiquated methods and bureaucratic nonsense," she drawled.

"Our pack lead won't have that, he's . . . not proactive. Averse to inquiries," Ethan said carefully.

Stella watched him a moment. She laced her fingers together. "Technically, I work for the cloister, who is contracted by the pack, not your pack lead. I will defer to you on how to proceed, but I will be able to make more headway with my feet on the ground."

"I don't see Thomas letting you come early—we may have to get creative while you're there." I rubbed my temples. "Could the circumpuncts be how the rogues are getting in?"

"Paired with a Bloodstone, a circumpunct could make a powerful transportation spell. But that is tricky magic. Have they always had runes around them?"

"No," I answered. "The case Ethan told you about was the first time we saw the runes. In the other cases, they were in a clearing with grass. Although I did find a clearing before he was attacked—stones lined the outside but they didn't have runes on them."

She hummed and drummed her fingers on the table. "It feels like someone is trying to work something out. Maybe this last time during this new rogue attack, they cracked the code," she mused.

"What do you mean?"

She rested her chin on her fist. "Magic is like cooking. There's a recipe that includes ingredients and an order of operations. Things won't work unless the recipe—or spell—is just right. It can take a while to get it right.

"What you're explaining feels like they're trying to come up with something new—they could be basing it off an old spell, combining spells—but if they are talented enough to make a Bloodstone, then they are not using an existing spell. Something existing is too obvious, and they would have most likely figured it out, but maybe they are trying to hide in the obvious. No one would think to look—"

She paused and looked to Kevin. Her eyes were focused while she drummed her fingers, like she was trying to piece a puzzle of all-black tiles together.

"I can look into transportation spells. There's more for this kind of thing than you think." She drummed her fingers again, nodding to herself. "The runes are going to be the key. They'll tell us what it's really being used for and include details about the spell required. If you're able to get pictures or remember anything, send it to me. I'll leave my contact information. Kevin is very good with runes."

"We have our trackers in search of more clearings—circumpuncts. We're trying to map them. We're still working through the plan for the council meeting—we're hoping information from this meeting may give us some direction," Ethan noted to her.

"And you don't know who is behind this?" Stella asked.

"No," Ethan lied.

She watched him a moment. "Find the clearings," she urged him. "I'll work on the spell side of this. If we can figure out what their 'recipe' is, so to speak, we can figure out how to stop it."

Ethan asked for the bill when the waiter went by. I bit my lip and took his phone then flipped to another photo Jackson had sent us—the one of his father's maps.

"Have you ever seen a map like this?" I asked Stella.

"That's easy. It's a star map."

Ethan and I leaned forward to listen.

"It's a map that shows its true contents in the starlight."

"What do you mean by 'true contents'?" Ethan asked.

"Well, there's a map here, obviously," she said as she pointed to the lines drawn on Jackson's map. "But in starlight, you can see the real image the mapmaker intended—like invisible ink. They were fairly popular back in the late eighteen hundreds and then came back to popularity in the seventies."

The blood in my veins turned cold. Ethan's hand was like iron around my knee. I covered his fingers with mine and squeezed in hopes that it would remind him to breathe next to me.

"Just starlight?" I asked quietly.

"Mm-hmm," she hummed. "Take it outside at night. Has to be a clear night."

Stella finished her drink and shortly after, I downed mine. "Anything else?"

"That's it," Ethan told her in a clipped tone. He was moving fast, almost jittery, as he slid out of the booth. "We need to get moving, it's getting late."

Ethan got the bill and threw a wad of cash down. He stood and helped me out of the booth. "How much do we owe you?"

She stood and turned to face us. "On the house. I have a feeling we're going to be helping each other quite a bit in the future."

CHAPTER TWENTY-FIVE

The truck flew down the highway while we sat in the silence of our thoughts. I'd been working through all the details Stella had given us, only ending at the same conclusion over and over.

Licking my lips, I broke the silence. "If we keep finding Bloodstones or these circles, maybe it's a good thing? Maybe it means they haven't figured it out and are still trying..."

"Or it means they have and they're setting the stage." He squeezed the steering wheel. "I don't know. Where is the map?"

"In the back of my underwear drawer."

"Of course it is," he grumbled. "Evan will bring it to Jackson's. Levi is meeting us there."

Ethan pressed down on the gas and broke at least three state laws to get us to Switchback as the night set in. Gravel and dirt flew up behind us as we rolled in. Jackson was already marching for the truck when we jumped out of the cab.

"What did you learn?" he asked, but I ran past him over to where Evan was standing with Jake and Caden. Evan started to say something to me when I yanked the bag from his hands and dug out the map. "What the hell?!"

I raced until I found a break in the trees where the night sky was all that was above us. Unfolding the map, I laid it on the ground. Silver lines started to glitter and etch across it, appearing in the starlight. In the corner was a symbol: a full moon with seven stars around it.

"Holy fucking shit," Jackson said from behind me. He knelt and tapped the image. "That's the rebel brand. The Pure Seven."

"Seven stars for the seven blessings of beasts the moon bestowed upon the men. A sacred gift to be unadulterated by our shortcomings and protected from all adversaries. Blessed is he who walks in her light." Caden's solemn voice quieted before he lifted his gaze to us. "Some of the older writings of our kind, they took as their own. Jeremiah had them drilled into pack education. We had to know so many of these on call as kids."

"Get the other maps." Jackson's jaw ticked before he swore under his breath. "My fucking bastard father . . ."

Caden was soon laying two additional maps next to mine. Silver lines came up across the old, delicate paper and created new maps on top of the old ink. In the corner of each, there was a glowing rebel brand.

Evan squatted next to the papers. He pointed to the top where the pack name was written. "There's a map for each of us— Hemlock, Switchback, and Thunderhead." He tugged his copper hair then rearranged the maps around each other. "Which means they should go together."

He leaned back once the markings lined up perfectly, creating a brand-new map of the three packs.

"It's our packs," Evan said. "It's all three packs—"

Jackson hissed under his breath. Ethan rubbed his jaw and tapped on the Hemlock map close to where runes and notes were scribbled. "Rogues came in here during the attack. This was one of the places they were seen."

"And here," Jackson added as he pointed to a spot on Switchback's map. "And here too."

I took out Ethan's phone to take photos of the runes. "For Stella," I told him.

Evan looked at the spot I was photographing, then the hair on the back of his neck rose. He pointed to a new spot close to the Hemlock Pack line before warily lifting his eyes to Ethan. "I remember seeing them here. Before Eli found us."

"What does all the text mean?" Jackson pointed to one of the words on the Hemlock map. "This word, *Miles*, is all over these maps. Distance, maybe?"

"It means soldier." Jake's voice was solemn as he stood over the Thunderhead map—the one he had received from Billy. "It's old Roman. My dad loved that shit. Watched all kinds of documentaries. The Roman soldiers would leave markers every thousand paces they went—a Roman mile." He pointed to a glowing dot on the Thunderhead-Hemlock border. "That's where my father was sent first when they heard of the rogues. Apparently, a muster of them was found here."

"It's from then—this is the attack back then." Evan leaned back in shock and looked to his brother, but Ethan only had unnerving silence to offer as he continued to stare at the map.

Jackson turned to Jake and asked, "Where did you say you got this?"

"Billy gave it to Jake," I explained when Jake remained silent, struck with a dumbfounded expression. "Before the Hunt, we used it to study the forest."

"Technically, he didn't give it to me ..."

My head whipped to face Jake. "What?"

He rubbed the back of his neck. His normally stoic demeanor quickly cracked. "He's a pack rat, we all know that," he said directly to Ethan. "I wasn't going into that forest unprepared. I had seen maps down there before. When I found it, it was sitting in a box collecting dust. I figured he wouldn't miss it."

Jackson pinched the bridge of his nose. "And you trust this guy?" He was looking directly at Ethan, eyes hard as he probed for answers.

Evan spoke up. "He's always looked out for us—he's always had your back when it came to Thomas. Got you out of some bad situations—got us both out of some bad spots. He's believed you from the start that things are fucked up."

"I didn't ask you." Jackson's cold voice sliced through the air. Gone was the carefree tease. The ruthless pack lead that the stories were created about was now very present.

Ethan lifted his gaze to Jackson. "Would you let a map like this leave your sight if it could implicate you?"

Jackson relented with a nod. "Definitely not."

"He saved a lot of things of my father's—we both did. So many things were taken during the investigation it's hard to know what we got back and what we'll never get back," Ethan explained.

Jackson furrowed his brows. "Do you think it was your dad's map?"

Ethan rubbed his face. "If Dad had this map and knew what it said, we would not be having this conversation."

Jake laced his hands behind his head. "If we think they used these star maps back then, what is to say they are not using them now?"

Jackson groused. "Where's Levi?"

Ethan rubbed his jaw. "Close."

I stood as soon as the skin on my back twitched. I looked back toward the road. A pair of silver eyes pulsed through the darkness; in the distance, I could see another silver pair, and some lavender ones bouncing like a bunny behind them.

Levi stepped into the moonlight and marched straight for the glowing paper on the ground. He stopped at the edge of the maps and stood wordlessly as his glowing eyes combed them over.

I went to his side without hesitation. He didn't react. I put a hand on his arm, which jerked his attention to me.

"Hi," I uttered quietly.

Before I could blink, he was hugging me to him. He held me tightly for several long seconds. Having him there made the situation feel like something we could handle.

"You can always come home," Levi said.

"I'm not," I replied before he released me.

Lander squeezed my shoulder with a tired smile as he came around to stand on Levi's right. Levi knelt as Jackson approached. His fingers traced over the rebel brand on one corner of a map. "And here we thought they were gone."

Jackson dropped to a squat and tapped the papers. "My old

man said they never would be. I always thought he was full of shit. Fucking jackass."

Levi's eyes pulsed a glow. "Your pop was a grade-A bastard, but you're not your father."

Levi's words seemed to take Jackson aback, but quickly, he recovered. "Well, not most days."

Levi's lips twitched in amusement.

Remi nudged his shoulder with mine and gave me a rueful smile. "Hey, buddy."

"Where's your mom?" I asked.

"Talia's," Lander answered for him. Then he nudged his chin at Ethan. "I think it's time you caught us up."

Ethan knelt to the map and explained what we had learned: the circumpuncts, Bloodstones, the attempt on Ethan's life, and the rogues. The whole time I found myself somehow making my way back to Ethan until I was standing next to him. Wordlessly, he put an arm around my shoulders and left it there, as if the feeling of me next to him was keeping him above water.

When Ethan finished, Levi yanked away from the group with a snarl.

Lander tilted his head. "She was helpful, this witch."

"She was," Ethan agreed.

"What will be helpful is to figure out their plan." Levi stepped back with a glow pulsing in his eyes.

"Things are ramping up," Lander added. "And the council meeting is coming up on the next full—time is not on our side."

"The full," I murmured.

Lander cocked his head at me while I chewed the inside of my cheek. "She said that magic is like a recipe. Takes time to get it perfect," I thought out loud. "When we told her about how each

Bloodstone was found—about the clearings, she said, 'It sounds like someone's trying to work something out.'"

I stood up as my beast started to pace. "If they're trying to make something work, there are going to be things they keep in the spell. Each time we have found something it's been the same with a slight difference. Whatever is being carried over must be what they think is working—the latest iteration has to incorporate things they think will make the spell work." My beast pawed at my mind. It felt like I was close to connecting all the edges of a puzzle together. "The last time was the other night—the full moon, the runes."

"We didn't smell rogues," Ethan pointed out.

"But we did the night you were attacked. Keeley confirmed the Bloodstone in the clearing." I bit my lip. "Either we missed the rogues, or something did not work."

"The full could be a consistent variable," Remi noted. "All the other cases have been around a full give or take a few days—but that doesn't mean they weren't set up during the full, we just didn't find them on the full moon."

Lander rubbed his face. "If what you're saying has legs, if they need a full moon to make these circumpuncts really work, this is a goddamn nightmare. There's going to be witch reps; pack leads and usually their families; Derek, and now Elliot, are the vampire representatives—and Derek, who, I should remind you all, is practically vampire royalty, besides being Leo's favorite."

Levi was quiet for a long time. Something hummed off him, something cold and sharp that cut through the group. Slowly, he turned his gaze to Ethan. "We're behind. Do you understand?"

Lander leaned forward. "Things are quickening, Ethan. You're the closest to Thomas. You need to get ahead—"

Something crackled through Ethan, something that spread through the bond and hit me in my chest. "You think I don't know that?" Ethan snarled.

Jackson stepped forward and held his hands up. "Look, if Charlotte is right—it only confirms what we suspected. That they're going to make a move during the meeting. We need to figure out who the target or targets are and how to stop the circumpuncts."

"Can you get that witch on pack grounds before the meeting?" Lander asked Ethan.

He shook his head. "Odds are no, and besides, she said the runes are one of the most important pieces and we can't show her them, because they're gone."

Lander furrowed his brows. Evan leaned forward and confirmed what Ethan had said. "I went back myself. The stones lining the clearing are there but no runes."

Levi rubbed his jaw. "Jackson is right, we need to figure out the target. There could be hundreds of these clearings. Even with all our resources, we don't have the people to cover that."

Lander set his hands on his hips. "Charlotte, has everyone confirmed attendance at the meeting?"

I nodded. "Ninety-five percent. There are a few packs that can't for personal matters that check out—I'm waiting on them to confirm who they are sending as their substitutes."

Lander clapped his hands. "I'll call Talia. We need to start organizing our allies. Get a motion moving to have an official investigation opened. We need the resources."

Levi hummed as he thought. "Thomas put in a request to have extra security on the borders during the meeting."

"I got that too. Yesterday," Jackson added.

THE PACK

Levi nodded. "Thunderhead can do it, and I'm assuming Switchback can?"

Jackson jerked a nod in confirmation. "But that means that we'll be spread thin. We have to watch our packs too."

Jake walked over and looked at the maps. Shaking his head, he said, "Jackson's right. It's going to be too much territory to cover. Even if we pool our resources together."

"For now, Ethan, we need to prioritize creating that map of the open areas where circumpuncts could show up, if we really think those are what're bringing the rogues in. You got a head start—but we need to do this for our own packs too. We can look at the maps we put together and plan how to allocate our people," Levi told him.

Lander tapped on the map again. "Jake, this was your map? Where did you get this again?"

"I had it," I injected. Lander furrowed his brows while Levi stood up slowly. "After the Hunt, Jake left it, and then, well, it was at the bottom of my bag when I arrived at Hemlock. I thought you put it there?" I directed at Levi.

"That was not me," Levi uttered, words like concrete that hit me like cold bricks.

"Derek?" I wondered aloud. "Elliot?"

His silence was the answer I didn't want to hear. He turned to Remi, who quickly shook his head. Levi's eyes pulsed a glow as something crackled off him. "Tell Bowie we may have a rat," he ordered Lander.

Cold dread poured over me. "Levi?"

His jaw ticked as he turned to face Ethan again. "You need to check for them in your pack, too, son."

"You think I don't fucking know that?" Ethan bit out.

Levi studied him. "Then fucking handle it."

"Any more orders, Her First?" Ethan asked, words clipped.

Levi narrowed his gaze. "If you find something, it impacts your whole pack and ours too. The moves you make affect everyone—"

"Don't you lecture me about giving a shit," Ethan bit out with a growl that shook the map on the ground. His beast was close to his skin, his eyes closer to animal than human.

Lander put a hand on Levi's shoulder. "We have some calls to make." He turned to Ethan with an empathetic expression. "I don't envy you."

Jackson turned his gaze to Ethan in a silent conversation, before the two of them walked off together.

Levi tilted his head to me. "Come with me."

I followed. We walked toward the Thunderhead border until it was only us, the trees, and the sound of crickets chirping into the night. Levi looked at the stars and watched them, like he was waiting for them to speak.

He turned to face me. "Do you remember where that path is?"

"Levi . . ."

"Do you remember?" His hushed voice had a way of thundering through the quiet between us.

"Yes," I answered.

"I want you to show Evangeline and Andrea."

"Levi." I kicked the dirt in front of me. "I won't leave him."

He snorted. "Well, not now that he marked you." I opened my mouth and closed it when he raised a hand. "I have fucking eyes."

"I won't leave him," I asserted. "I love him. Don't ask me to."

He hissed under his breath. "He can come too."

"Levi."

He ignored my tone and leveled his gaze with mine. "Keep an eye on him. He needs you, probably more than he wants to admit."

"Why do you say that?"

He smiled softy. "Past experience."

I looked down at my toes—I had nothing else to add.

In the distance, we could hear Remi laughing. Levi shook his head with an annoyed expression. "Fucking kid walks into the house all the time and drinks my beer like he lives there."

I couldn't stop the laughter from bubbling out of my mouth. "I told you he was a pest."

"He misses you."

"I miss you all," I admitted as my heart panged in my chest. "But I'm not coming back."

Levi relented and walked me back to the group. He squeezed my shoulder. "You know the way back," he told me before he whistled in the air. "Remi! Let's move!"

He shifted and started running without waiting for the others.

Lander gave my shoulder a pat and followed. Remi sprinted past, his lavender eyes tracking us with mischievous delight before they disappeared into the darkness.

Ethan turned to me. "How do you feel about moving in tomorrow?"

A laugh bubbled out of my lips. "You really are the most romantic person."

His shoulders relaxed as his lips quirked into a smirk. "The full package."

I rolled my eyes. "You're serious?"

"Yeah," he breathed. "Ev and I will help you."

"I should talk to Andrea."

"Who's Andrea?" Jackson prowled forward. "Hot friend?"

I grimaced. "You cannot hit on my friends. You know what? This is a rule."

"What—no, that's not how this works," he taunted back. "Come on, is she hot?"

"Oh, she's a ten." Jake snickered. "Who will kick your ass six ways to next Sunday."

Jackson rocked back on his heels while his eyes glowered in devious delight. "Nothing about this sounds bad to me."

Ethan's phone vibrated. He swiped it open and scanned the screen. Then he shoved the phone into Jackson's hands like he had been burned before storming away from us.

"Ethan?" Evan called after him, but he didn't answer.

Jackson's eyes lowered to the screen. "Fuck... Stella said one of those runes means *Berserkr*, or Berserker."

Evan clenched his eyes shut while Jackson released a ragged breath. "There's no denying it now."

"What does it mean?" I asked Evan.

"In the old days, they called rogues Berserker because of how wild they would become—uncontrollable." Evan swallowed as his turquoise eyes pulsed a glow. "We learned about it as kids:

"Best beware of the *Berserkr*, for he leaves a bloody wake of disorder,

"Through his pain he cannot see, if it is you, I, friend, or tree,

"Flee you must from his sight, or he shall doom you to his plight."

CHAPTER TWENTY-SIX

Jake nursed a cup of coffee next to me while we watched Keeley put another pin in our map, marking where she and her small group of trackers had found another clearing in the grim hours of the night—one of the few windows when we could sneak into the forest unnoticed. A few clearings were found in the interior of the pack lands, but the majority of the pins were surrounding the Hemlock Pack lands and extended partially up the borders of Switchback and Thunderhead like a virus.

Keeley pressed her palm against the map. "It's too much territory to cover."

"Keels." Jake's tired voice was gentle. "We'll figure it out."

She sucked in a breath. "It's been so quiet, Jake."

Last night in my group, Trey thought he heard popping, but

like all the other nights, it was just another silver-laced trap set off by one of the beady-red-eyed vermin of the forest.

Day after day, the forest had remained the same. Time trickled away like grains of sand in an hourglass. We didn't smell rogues. We didn't hear popping. We didn't even smell fresh blood magic. We spent too many hours burning our very short supply of midnight oil only to be sucked back into pre–council meeting preparations when the sun came up.

"Why has it been so quiet?" Keeley stammered.

"Because they're ready. The wolves are sleeping." Andrea's somber voice scraped its way from the corner of the room where she stood. "Resting before they need to show their teeth."

Her golden eyes pulsed a glow when they caught mine. *"Have you heard anything in the forest?"*

"Yes." My beast snapped her teeth.

The voices were the only thing I kept hearing. It didn't matter where I was; the night before I'd shattered a glass I was cleaning in the kitchen when I heard a whisper. The sound of it had been so clear, so near it'd felt like it was running up the side of my arm. The anger brewing in me wanted me to follow it, but Ethan reminded me of Finn's advice.

Jake finished his coffee. "Be nice if they slipped for once."

Evangeline had nothing to report. Thomas and the wolves loyal to him were being extra careful with their words. Evan wanted to search their homes and offices—break in. But our scent would cover the area, easily giving us away. The last thing we needed.

"What do you want to do?" Keeley asked.

"I'll talk to Ethan and Billy. You should get some rest," Jake told her. "Sun's coming up soon."

Keeley cast the map a withering parting glance. "It's a trap—it's a trap, and we're letting people walk into it."

"No one is walking into anything," Jake countered. He dipped his head and caught her tired eyes, holding them a moment before he wrapped an arm around her shoulders. "Come on."

I followed them out of the basement into the kitchen. Keeley took herself upstairs to the guest room to shower while Jake took a seat on a moving box of mine in the kitchen that I had been procrastinating on unpacking. Wordlessly, I moved for the coffeepot as Andrea blew past us.

"Want to stay?" Jake asked.

"No, I need to go to Dad's," she tossed over her shoulder. "That basement isn't going to search itself."

She had taken it upon herself to look through the boxes in Billy's basement once they learned about the map. I barely saw her, but it felt like that was intentional, because when I did see her, our conversations were always short—curt. They had been like that since she'd spotted the mark on my neck after Ethan and I returned from Anchorage.

"Need help?" Jake offered.

"No." The front door slammed shut behind her.

I refilled Jake's mug. "She's going through it," he told me. "She'll come around."

She was my best friend—a piece of me I didn't want to lose. But it felt like she was purposefully tearing the threads between us apart.

I was pouring myself a cup of coffee when the skin on my arms prickled; I poured another mug for Ethan right as he pushed open the front door. He rounded the counter and pressed a quick kiss to my lips then took the coffee from me.

"Thanks," he murmured before taking a long sip. "Lander confirmed the witches are coming a day before to Thunderhead."

"Good." Jake rested his head back against the cabinets. "We need to look at the security plans again. Keeley found more clearings."

Ethan rubbed his face. We needed to sleep, although when we did try to squeeze in a few hours, it never lasted long—more times than not I found myself lying wide awake while my mind spun around and around.

"You want to look now?" Ethan asked.

Jake pushed off the cabinets. "Why not?"

Ethan took his coffee and led Jake back down to the basement, leaving me a few moments of peace before I found myself sucked into pre-event preparations that had turned to borderline chaos as the days bled by.

It wasn't until the early, golden hour of dawn that I found myself watching a great white tent being pulled upright in front of the pack house.

"It looks good," Miranda noted, while men and women in the pack nailed stakes into the ground to keep the tent held up.

The side flaps of the tent had not been tied up. They waved and rippled in the wind, like loose, mangled flesh.

Miranda squeezed my arm. "It's coming together." She beamed me a smile. "I couldn't have done this without you. Evangeline and Amber—" She exhaled a long breath. "Thank goodness the moon sent you to us."

"Of course," was all my weary mind could answer back.

She looked over her clipboard. "Back into the frying pan, then?"

Together we worked under the smoldering summer sun

to ensure everything was set up and staged: from the meeting tent to the concession tent to the meeting materials—everything was staged down to the last paperclip. Once dusk set in I could feel my energy slipping into an exhausted quicksand. I finished up what I could with Miranda then excused myself for the evening.

When I was only a few yards away from the house, Ethan opened the door for me.

I shifted to my skin and jogged through. Wordlessly, he took my hand and led me to the kitchen table where Evan was seated. A handful of porous black rocks were scattered across the grainy wood in front of him.

He picked one up and handed it to me. "Smell it."

I held it to my nose and inhaled. "It doesn't smell like anything?"

"Absolutely fucking nothing," Evan groused.

I cut my gaze to him then slowly met Ethan's glowing eyes. "What's going on?"

"Levi took the witches to the place where you and Remi smelled those rogues and where we found the Bloodstone. Remi said that they were taking samples when Stella's snake spat one of these into her palm. She took it to Bowie's and immediately tested it, then asked if we could see if we had them too. Jackson found them at the clearing on his pack lands and I found these at two that Keeley marked," Ethan explained.

"They suck up scent," Evan expounded. "They smell like nothing because they suck up what's around them and turn it to nothing—" He paused to look at me. "I haven't gone back there, but I am willing to bet it's why we couldn't smell Ethan the night he was attacked." He crushed the stone in his hand. Black sand slipped through his fingers and scattered across the table. "It's how they're covering the scent—trapping it in."

I blinked as my tired mind tried to wrap around the new information. "Did Stella say anything else?"

"She told us stones like this date back to the old wars—back when vampires and wolves fought. There were a lot of casualties and they needed a way to keep the smell under control until they could burn the bodies. So, they came up with these to buy a little time while they built pyres," Ethan shared. "Caden and his mate searched Jackson's library. They found some old texts that confirm what she's said."

Fingers of dread wrapped around my stomach. I felt nausea bubbling in my gut.

"And we can't tie it to anyone, not yet, at least," Evan clipped before he released a tense breath, slowly simmering down.

We were out of time and losing cards to play—the truth grated against me and drew my beast to snap her teeth.

"There has to be something," I muttered. "There's always a trail."

Ethan rested his palms on the table. "How the fuck are we here? Packs are coming in tomorrow."

Evan crushed another stone in his palm. Sand danced as it fell along the surface of the table. "I need to go find Lina. She doesn't need to be running around tonight."

Ethan was silent as Evan left. I rounded the table to him. His hand reached to cup my cheek. "I love you . . . so much."

I covered my lips with his. "We'll be all right." He hummed in shallow agreement, a sentiment that sank like a rock in my gut.

The rest of the evening we worked through contingency plan after contingency plan until we agreed to try to squeeze in a few hours of sleep, although the few hours we had felt like nothing

THE PACK

when we woke to meet up with Miranda, Thomas, and Amber—Amber and I were on duty passing out welcome bags and checking packs in while Thomas, Miranda, and Ethan greeted the incoming guests, as was custom, according to Miranda.

Sweat was beading on the back of my neck while Amber fanned herself with a wooden, custom-made HEMLOCK fan that she'd convinced us all to order. A shrill buzzing whirled around us, then a fly landed on our small table. Amber snarled, whacked the fly with her fan, then swiped away its carcass with it.

I picked a fan up. "These were a good idea," I told her.

"It's not even eight in the morning," she seethed, as she lifted a box of welcome bags onto the table.

I pulled at the collar of my T-shirt dress. The hot, sticky air made the cotton feel like it was clinging to me. It didn't bode well for the rest of the day.

"At least we have this tent," I offered.

It wasn't much, but the small tent that Ethan had set up for us did its job of blocking the sun.

"Thank the moon for that," Amber agreed.

Up at the top of the valley I could see silver waving like a flag in the wind. Talia strode forward with sure steps, Ajax next to her and her guards around her. Passing in front of us, she greeted Thomas and Miranda with what seemed like polite enough pleasantries before rounding to me.

Her hand cupped my cheek. "It's good to see you."

I pulled her into a hug. "I miss the water."

"It misses you." She laughed. "You'll need to visit—bring your other half," she added as she tilted her head at Ethan, who was talking to Ajax, her mate.

"We will," I promised. I handed her a bag and watched her

retreat before I caught Miranda's curious gaze. "Sometimes it's nice to tan your cheeks."

The firm line on Amber's mouth twitched as if it was about to crack into a smile. Miranda waved me off with light laugher of her own that didn't reach her eyes. As she passed by, her earrings glimmered in the light, and the sound of voices hummed faintly from them.

"You all right?" Amber asked.

I jumped, startled. "Yeah, sorry—it's been a week."

"Yeah, well heads-up, Cache Pack is here." She paused and tossed her long blond hair over her shoulder. "Darlene's an acquired taste."

A woman with a short brown bob, a heavy set of hips, and a button nose walked up. She cocked her hips to the side and gave Ethan a slow once-over. "You're looking well, Ethan."

Thomas stepped forward, extending a hand. "It's good to see you, Darlene."

She snorted then walked around him and over to me, where I had a bag extended for her. "Hate these things. Waste of my time." She paused as her eyes locked in on the mark on my neck. Looking back over her shoulder at Ethan, she lifted her brows in amusement. "Well, good for you two. Tell me you have us lodged somewhere with a tub?"

She took the bag from my hands. I pointed to the folder inside. "There's a map of the grounds, your room assignment, and your binder for the meeting. I don't know about the tub. Sorry."

"You're not." She laughed. My mouth dropped a hair. She snickered under her breath. "Tell Levi to find me when he gets here—you still smell like him, in case you're wondering."

"Thanks?"

She stomped off, leaving Amber and me speechless. I turned to her with wide eyes. Amber's icy eyes slightly melted. "Told you."

"Uncouth," Miranda snipped.

"Speaking of," Amber grumbled under her breath, "this should be fun."

Jackson was strutting in like this was his homecoming. Caden followed him with an annoyed look on his face. Ethan stood in place while Thomas stepped out to meet Jackson.

Jackson grinned with all his teeth showing. "Thomas."

I could see the hair on the back of Thomas's neck rise. "It's good Switchback is represented."

Jackson barked a laugh and walked around him. "Your small talk has not improved from what I can see."

"Fast talking only gets you so far, Jackie," Thomas sneered, with a pompous smirk of his own.

But Jackson wasn't bothered. He dipped his head to Ethan. "Her Second."

"Her First," Ethan replied politely.

Jackson walked over and paused, eying Amber and me up and down like we were new snacks. He leaned back and cocked a smile at Thomas. "The welcoming committee is very appreciated, Her First."

Miranda snarled under her breath. Jackson waved her off. "Easy, mother wolf," he chastised her, before tossing a wink to Amber. A rare blush bloomed on her cheeks.

Jackson lifted a brow to me before clicking his tongue. "He's a lucky bastard who snatched you up."

I shoved a bag into his hands, struggling to keep my eyes from rolling.

"Housing arrangements are in the bag?" Jackson asked.

"They are, her First," I answered back. *"You know we have to deal with them once you saunter off?"* I chastised him across a link.

"Good think you are well equipped," he quipped in reply.

"Fantastic," he said out loud before adding, "Caden, let's find the bar."

Caden dipped his head in a brief hello to us before following Jackson out of the tent. Miranda fluttered over to us. She examined Amber as if just being near Jackson was enough to have defiled her.

Amber swatted her hand away. "I'm fine." Miranda continued to fuss with Amber's hair. Amber snarled lowly. "Stop touching me."

Miranda retracted her hand with a bemused smile. "I'm your mother. I fuss. It's what I do."

Amber looked away, ignoring her. Miranda took it as her cue to skirt back over to Thomas. I shifted my weight on my feet and turned to Amber, tapping my temple.

She cast a quick glance at her parents, who were busy welcoming a new pack before nodding to me.

"If you want to take a break—"

"I'm fine."

The word hit me in the gut because it sounded like a voice I had heard so many years ago. A voice that had once belonged to me. Evangeline was right; Amber wasn't like her parents. I recognized someone trying to stay above water—I had treaded it myself for far too long.

"You're not," I replied, certain.

She didn't flinch. She moved away from me and started to retrieve the bags for the wolves still chatting with Miranda.

"*Saying it out loud helps,*" I added.

She scoffed. "*Yeah? I'm sure it saved you too.*"

"*No,*" I gently corrected her. "*Running did.*"

The ice melted. Her fingers slipped and she dropped a bag.

Derek was furiously texting while he nursed a glass of wine mixed with coppery blood. I sank down next to him on the couch in the basement. "Are you okay?"

He hissed under his breath. "Fucking Dominic is going to be the death of me."

"Who?"

"Problematic vampire," Elliot answered for him. He slid to sit on the arm of the couch. "Who is not Derek's problem," he added pointedly.

"He is when he won't check in with Leo," Derek said, tone curt.

Elliot rolled his eyes. "He's on bloody holiday and you know it."

"I'm going to feed." Derek rose from his seat.

Lander cocked his head at him from his seat in a plastic chair next to Derek. "We're about to start?"

"Elliot can fill me in," he clipped before zipping up the stairs in a blur.

"Leave it." Levi's cold voice cut through the room. He was peering over the map with Billy, both of them carefully making notations. "Charlotte, where is your mate?"

"I'm not his keeper."

Something cold hummed off Levi and snapped through the

air. Part of me was starting to regret keeping Levi, Lander, and the vampires under the same roof as us.

"If people spot us lingering together—gathering—there will be questions," Levi tersely stated. "We need to get this pre-whatever the hell it is council meeting moving."

A hand came to rest on my shoulder. Evan's grip was teetering on uncomfortable while he held a rag to his bloody nose.

"Are you okay?" I asked, quickly inspecting his nose.

He yanked his hot gaze away from Levi to look at me. "You think it's going to mess my face up?" he asked, with a sparkle of mischief that was starting to show up more in our conversations.

"I don't think even the Jackknife guards could make your mug any better, mate," Elliot teased as Evan took Derek's seat next to me.

"They always want a fight," Levi griped. "Bastards don't think you can have a good time without one."

Elliot clicked his tongue. "A good brawl is a fine way to start a gatherin', Levi."

The basement door suddenly sprang open. A stampede of footsteps echoed as Ethan led Jackson into the basement. Jackson jogged down the last step, walked directly to Levi, and shook his hand.

Ethan paused at the edge of the table. "Sorry we're late, Jackson made friends."

"Darlene has a crush on me." Jackson grinned.

Levi snorted. "I bet she does. What did she want?"

"She sensed something was off," Ethan told him.

"Yeah, figured she would catch on. She's no dummy," Levi stated.

"No, she's not," Ethan agreed. "I decided to read her in. Dad always spoke highly of her—she was always loyal to him. She's called extra guards in from the other side of the mountain. She said she would vote with us as well—I told her to talk to you about that, Lander."

"I'll handle it," Lander confirmed; his mouth cracked in a small, pleased smile.

Levi cut his eyes to Ethan. "The vote is inconsequential if we get invaded. Do we have any intel on their plan?"

"I reached out to a few of my contacts in packs where we know Thomas is friendly with their pack leads," Billy remarked. "But I got nothing useful."

"But we know they are most likely using those circumpuncts to get in," I offered.

"Where's the witch?" Levi asked.

"Jake took her to the clearing where we saw the runes," Ethan informed him. "She's trying to find a common denominator."

"We only have so many resources between our packs," Lander reminded the room.

"We don't know the target or targets," Ethan admitted. "But we can assume any of the guests for the meeting are fair game." Ethan leaned over the table and pointed to one of the pins in the interior of the pack lands that notated a clearing. "Our best strategy is to station people around these clearings closest to the pack. If something happens, they can react quickly and dispatch accordingly."

"We should have people ready at the border," Jackson offered. "They can come in to support or help pack members if things go to the shitter and we need to evacuate people."

"Agreed." Levi's eyes pulsed a glow as they moved to Ethan. "David and Bowie already have Thunderhead wolves on standby, positioned close to the border."

"My wolves are ready too," Jackson said. "They're keeping a

healthy distance for now. We don't want to raise an alarm. What about Talia?"

Lander spoke up. "She has extra people coming this evening. We'll park them at Thunderhead. We can allocate some of Talia's people to your pack if you feel the need?"

"I would appreciate that," Jackson answered him.

Ethan hummed and pointed back to the map. "If your wolves can help with our borders, then we can move our better guards and trackers to the interior clearings."

"What about the ones loyal to Thomas?" Lander asked.

"Jake has restationed them," Ethan explained. "He put them on easier posts on the border, which none of them seemed to think much of. A few will be watching the meeting, but we have a backup plan in case we need a distraction."

"Distraction?" Levi repeated blandly.

"Mountain lions are bad business, and it's such a pain when they crawl close to a heard," Ethan explained, a dark promise in his voice.

Billy snickered. "Andrea knows where a few dens are. I'll almost be sad if she doesn't get to have some fun."

"Where is she now?" I asked. I didn't care if she was avoiding me; she was my best friend and I couldn't not worry about her.

"She's keeping an eye out while we're in here," Billy replied.

"What about the Hunt tomorrow night?" Levi asked.

"It's laid out down the valley away from the forest. Guests go first, as they always do. It will be a short, easy jog, maybe not a whole lot of deer," Billy added ruefully.

"And who is watching Thomas?" Levi asked.

"Keeley," Ethan answered. "She's been keeping watch all month. Trey has eyes on Miranda, and Evangeline has been keeping tabs on Amber. Keeley also has wolves designated to watch key pack leads we know Thomas is chummy with."

"You put your fucking sister on Amber?" Levi hissed, eyes wide.

Lander calmly held his gaze as his eyes pulsed silver. Levi broke their staring contest with a huff and took a long drink; Lander shook his head at the ground.

"She's more than capable," Ethan countered tightly.

Lander leaned his arms on his legs. "All right, let's talk about the meeting tomorrow," he announced in a tone that held no room for diversion from either Levi or Ethan. "We have enough evidence to warrant an official investigation, but we need the resources from packs outside our own, which an investigation would grant us." The room hummed back in agreement. "Talia has agreed to present the case and call for the inquiry. She's well liked by the region, almost as good as a neutral party."

"She's a good choice," Jackson chimed in. "Whose idea?"

Lander's silver eyes glittered as he smiled. "Mine."

"How do we think the other pack leads will vote?" Billy asked.

"We know we have Cache with Darlene," Lander pointed out. "And most likely the neighboring packs, since they have had sightings and tend to follow Darlene's lead. Obviously our packs. Talia and I will be working our networks as well—our case is strong and there are enough open ears that will vote our way. Ethan, if you feel like you can maneuver under Thomas's eye, then I think we should leverage you. You are well received in the region."

"He's going have eyes all over you and you know it." The irritation in Levi's voice was not missed.

"He always has, and we've made it work," Ethan evenly rebutted.

Levi snickered. "Really? Is that what you call being almost murdered?" Levi tossed his glass back. "All of this is good and fine unless we're fucking attacked."

"Levi," Lander warned.

Levi hissed under his breath as he stormed out of the basement. Ethan quickly followed, the muscles in his back twitching as waves rolled off him. Lander shook his head and jogged after his brother before Evan tossed down the rag he had been holding to his bloody nose and followed their trail.

"Shit," I hissed under my breath.

"I'm going to turn in," Jackson told me. "You have your hands full here."

Elliot caught my eye and linked me. *"Let's check on all the lads, shall we?"* I followed him to the backyard where shouting was echoing around the trees. Lander was warily standing with a hand on Evan's shoulder, which Evan didn't shrug away. It was as though they were in solidarity as they watched the storm in front of them.

"You don't think I don't understand what we're up against?" Ethan bellowed.

"Do you?" Levi shouted back as something cold whipped off him into the air. "Do you fucking understand?"

"You think I'm not doing everything I can to keep her safe?!" Ethan hollered back.

Levi's face was practically red. "You have no idea what you're keeping her safe from!"

"And you do?!"

I started to move forward but Elliot stopped me. "Just wait," he murmured.

A cold pulse hummed off Levi. His fangs showed when he

spoke again, low and calm, like the steady hum of an engine. "I'm not talking about just her! I'm taking about you and your brother and your sister! I'm here now. Do you understand? I am here now." He was quiet again. Wind swept across the backyard, rustling through the grass. Finally, Levi spoke again. "I promised Eve. I am here."

Ethan tipped his head down. His chest shook with a wry laugh. "What would you have me do? What else do you want me to fucking do?!"

"Levi." Elliot gestured to the woods down the hill. "There's wolves close by. Inside, the lot of you. I need to bring Derek back."

Levi jerked a nod to him. "I'm finishing my drink."

Lander squeezed Evan's shoulder. "Come on. Inside."

Evan wordlessly followed, while Elliot took off into the woods. Ethan watched me a moment.

"I'll stay with him," I said.

Ethan nodded and followed Evan into the house, leaving me with the quiet and the smell of whiskey. I rubbed my face while Levi swirled the liquid in his cup.

"They're only upset because they love you and they're scared."

He tossed the drink back then looked at me. "Do you remember the way home?"

My arms dropped to my sides. "I do."

"Good." Cursing under his breath, he shoved the drink into my hands. "You need this more than me."

I blew out a breath. "We know more this time. That has to count for something."

He was quiet a while then said, "Knowing makes it worse."

CHAPTER TWENTY-SEVEN

People were swarming to the great tent like flies, buzzing around in a strange reunion of friendly greetings, quiet gossip, and curious stares. I kept smoothing my shorter locks, which luckily Derek had trimmed for me this morning.

He reached for my hand. "Stop it, it looks fine."

Elliot straightened Derek's chic tie, which matched his fine, tailored suit. "All will be well."

Derek's face remained stoic. He pulled me along with him through the main tent where Miranda was ushering everyone in. Her long blond hair was pulled back into a slick ponytail, earrings on full display, singing an eerie hum for only me to hear.

She did a poor job of hiding the stunned expression on her

face when her eyes lasered in on where Derek's hand held mine. Forcing a smile, she said, "You look so lovely, Charlotte."

Derek's grip stiffened. "Derek trimmed me up," I replied and forced a polite smile.

Miranda laced her fingers together. "We're pleased you're both here."

Elliot stepped around him, Derek's binder tucked under his arm. He tipped his chin to Miranda then buried a hand in his front pant pocket. "Miranda, it's been some time. Seems you've warmed up, but only slightly, love."

She waved him off with a feigned laugh. "Charlotte, why don't you help them to their seats?"

By her tone, I could tell it wasn't a request, and I wasn't about to argue. My beast prowled forward, pacing, as anxiety ate at my nerves. I pulled Derek forward to the center of the tent.

Long tables were set up to form a circle where the thirty-three packs representing our region would be seated to conduct the meeting. Two packs would share a table, and four chairs waited for two of each attending pack's ambassadors—typically that included the pack lead and their second. If they could not come, alternates were sent in their place. The witch and vampire representatives shared a table within the circle as well. Behind the circle of tables were two rows of chairs for approved attendees for the meeting—typically additional guests from the incoming parties.

At the head of the circle facing north was one table on a platform raised a few inches above the ground. One seat was behind it. It was for the commissioner, whose sole job was to run the meeting. Levi said they had a very complex way of picking the individual to do it—drawing a name out of a hat. On the table was an ornate cardstock nameplate embossed with pine trees at the edges that read JACKKNIFE FIRST.

Lander lifted a hand to us; his other was clutching a Styrofoam cup of coffee. He had arrived here over an hour early to secure their seats and have a hand in where the others sat. He had cleverly positioned Thunderhead at the same table as Hemlock; the table next to them hosted the vampires, where Elliot was settling down into a seat next to Derek. Timber was seated next to Hemlock, at the same table as Switchback.

"We all good?" I asked in the group link Ethan had set up this morning.

"Ready," Jake answered.

"We are as well," Keeley said.

"Heading for you," Evangeline noted.

"Already have eyes on you," Evan added.

I pinched my brow and tried to focus on the chatter when a hand grasped my arm. Stella smiled at me, but it didn't reach her pink eyes.

"Charlotte, let me introduce you to my fellow cloister representative."

Behind her was a tall wiry woman with ocean-blue hair, blue nails, and blue lips held in a thin line. A pretentious blue jay sat on her shoulder. She dragged her left foot behind her, then sank into a deep, traditional curtsy.

"Ragna," the blue witch said, as if I should already know.

Stella kept a hold of my arm. "I would love some coffee. Charlotte, would you show me?"

"We should use the bathroom first, we won't have as many breaks as you think," I carefully offered instead.

She watched a moment then clapped her hands. "Wonderful."

Quickly, I led her inside the pack house to a single bathroom, where I was quick to lock the door. She stood in front of it and uttered a few words under her breath then snapped her fingers. A familiar watery shield fell from the ceiling before turning into a mist, leaving only the smell of burning sugar behind.

She turned to face me. "I'm sorry I didn't find you sooner—I needed to have my feet on the ground before I made any assumptions." She twisted her wrist and looked at her watch. "We don't have much time, so I'll be forward—high-profile people are here, it's a full moon, which means it's a good night for powerful magic, and based on what you tasked me to research, there may be an attack."

"Stella—"

She held up her hands, pleading. "I am here to help. Let me."

I bit my lip and tapped into my link with Ethan. Quickly, I let the scene unfold. Without hesitation, he said, *"I trust your judgment."*

"We don't know the target," I admitted. "We're focused on monitoring the clearings we've mapped out—the areas where there could be circumpuncts."

"That's good—what I was going to recommend." She exhaled. "Since we've last met, I've been working on researching a way to deactivate these things. After looking at that clearing last night, I was able to narrow my focus."

She quickly pulled a folder out of her tote and set it on the sink. Flipping through a few pages, she landed on an old page protected by a clear plastic sleeve. It was wrinkled, torn down the side like it had been ripped out of a book. On its face were dozens of runes, drawings, and words that were written in what appeared to be Latin. "Based on what I saw in the clearing last night, I think they're using this transportation spell. It's used to handle delicate material, which would make the bones of it good to use for moving organic material—bodies, which is very hard to pull off."

She paused and looked at her watch again then hissed under her breath. "We don't have time to go into all the mechanics—the main thing is, for this to work there is a sender and a receiver. The sender has to create a tether between themselves and the receiver, which allows the transport. They do this, more or less, by using a power source and runes to send a signal to the receiver's source. Power will recognize power and create a connection between the two sources."

"What about the runes?"

"When the tether is established, the runes that the sender is using in their circumpunct transfer first to the recipient's circumpunct. That's how the sender knows that the tether is secure, and ready for transport," she replied quickly. She licked her fingers and flipped through a few pages to a yellow legal page with tons of new notes and scribbles in fresh blue ink. She tapped on a diagram of the circle with a diamond in the middle. "In the old spell, it calls for a few types of crystals to be the source, but for you—"

"Bloodstones." I paused and let the previous scenes flood to Ethan.

She looked at her watch again. Quickly, she closed the folder and shoved it into her bag next to Kevin. "Yes," she uttered quietly. "But this makes things simple for us—no power source, no dice. The sender has to have a source or it won't work."

"If the sender . . . Someone has to set it up."

"Yes," she confirmed. "Keep your resources on those clearings.

If for some reason someone sets up a circumpunct, they literally need to take the stone out of the circle. It will stop the transfer."

"What about the meeting—are you going to share this with them?" I pressed.

She shook her head. "Our advantage now is they don't know that we know how to disarm these things. If they find out, they could change course, and in that case we'd be in a very undesirable position. If I'm asked, I'll keep it vague."

I nodded and continued to push her words to Ethan over the link. I felt him shift across the pull. *"She's right—I'm sharing this with Keeley and the others. This is good. We can work with this."*

"Our trackers are being updated," I informed her.

"Good, now come on, we'll be late, and we don't need our absence to cause talk."

Picking up her bag, she took my hand and led me out of the bathroom. Once outside, she looked around before leaning closer to me. "You have no leads on who could be setting up the ... ?"

I shook my head as cold fingers of fear seized my torso—we had a rat that was about to set this pack ablaze.

Discreetly, Stella took Kevin out of her bag and placed him on the ground. She ushered him across the grass, where his scales changed from bands of pink and tan to green, blending him in perfectly with his surroundings.

She blew out a breath. "He has many talents, my familiar. He'll see what he can dig up."

"Thank you," I breathed.

She squeezed my arm. "Don't thank me yet," she answered, as the slam of a gavel rang out. "You know how to find me," Stella whispered, then strode quickly back to the main tent.

I picked up my long blue summer dress and briskly walked to my own seat. Evangeline was waiting for me. She patted the chair next to her. I sat alongside Miranda and Amber. Across from us were Ethan and Thomas.

Ethan's eyes quickly found mine. *"Keeley is sending more people out around the clearings—she's giving everyone instructions on how to disarm them."* A small smile tugged on his lips. *"This is good—all you."*

It was hard to celebrate a small victory when it felt like we still had legions to fight. *"We need that map."*

"We need to find out who has a fucking stack of Bloodstones." And I wanted to hunt for them. My beast licked her teeth before snapping them, but we couldn't leave. Not without drawing Miranda's unwanted attention.

A man stood behind the commissioner's table. He was broad, built like a bear, with a thick scar down his cheek. The ends of his white moustache were braided, and his left hand was missing two fingers.

He slammed the gavel on the table again, completely silencing the circle.

Evangeline's hand reached for mine. *"I couldn't sleep all night."*

My eyes caught Levi's across the room. His silver eyes pulsed a glow as they darted to Evangeline then to me.

"There's a pond on the east side of the pack. Right now, it's surrounded by wild daisies. Has a stream that runs from the mountains. Do you know it?" I asked Evangeline in a link with just the two of us.

"Yes?" Evangeline answered.

The commissioner held his hands out to welcome everyone,

THE PACK

but the dark glint in his eyes offered a different type of greeting. "Welcome, all! Today, we, the thirty-three packs that make up the Alaskan region of wolves, will commence our annual Regional Council meeting! Thank you all for coming, and thank you to Hemlock for hosting. We know you were thrilled..."

Snickers and sardonic laughter filled the room. I squeezed Evangeline's hand. *"There's a foot trail behind it. That trail leads to a creek. That creek leads to Thunderhead. The route total is around two to three hours from the pond to Levi's door."*

"I am honored to serve as your commissioner this year—"

"Sure you are, Tyrell!" someone in a corner razzed.

Tyrell smirked then scanned the sheet in front of him—instructions that I had seen Miranda carefully put together. "As it has always been, we discuss old business today and new business tomorrow. We have seven topics to review today. I will call on you when it is your turn to speak on items you submitted. At the end of each section we will vote on new topics and initiatives to be deliberated tomorrow."

Evangeline's hand trembled in mine. *"Why are you telling me this?"*

I swallowed and kept my eyes forward. *"In case you need to run."*

She stiffened in her seat as her lips started to quiver. *"I won't leave my brothers."*

"You may not have a choice," I told her honestly.

"Now!" Tyrell announced. "Roll call. We'll go region by region, and save our guests for last."

"Aw, come on!" someone groaned, followed by a "Seriously?" from across the circle.

He twisted the end of his moustache. "I don't make the rules, just oversee them. Let's move clockwise and get this done."

One by one, each of the packs quickly noted their attendance until only the vampires and witches were left. After Ragna had introduced herself to the group, Derek stood cool and expressionless as he turned to face the room.

"Diederik Festus Damocles Cleopas of the coven Cleopas, first son of Leo, the ancient, who sends his regards."

Jesus, Levi was right, Derek really was vampire royalty.

The room was silent except for the sound of bristling among wolves. Thomas shifted in his seat, watching Derek with intrigue, like he was wondering how Derek would look as taxidermy in the pack house.

Elliot stood slowly and lifted a hand to the group. "Elliot O'Brien. Also coven Cleopas." He leaned past Derek to look directly at Thomas. "Echoin' our commissioner, our thanks for hosting Tommy boy. Glad you acquired proper beer this time," he added with a foxlike grin as he sat back down, drawing a few chuckles from the audience.

Tyrell beat the gavel on the table, gathering everyone's attention. "The sections for discussion are as follows: trade and economics, agriculture, technological and magical advances, human affairs, defense and security, and to conclude, international interspecies relations, in which we'll have each of our guests speak for their communities." Tyrell sat down. "Let's begin."

The sun was high in the afternoon sky as the meeting drawled on for what seemed to be an eternity. At one point Evangeline left with Amber for the pack house. I wished I could have left with them, or gone into the forest with Keeley. Part of me wondered if I could slip away for a few hours; but knowing Miranda, my absence would not go unnoticed.

THE PACK

The sound of the gavel slamming against the table echoed through the room. I jumped slightly in my seat as I was shook from my thoughts. "We move now to defense and security," Tyrell announced. "Timber Pack, I believe the floor is yours."

"Thank you, Commissioner." Talia offered him a respectful dip of her head before standing. The room watched with curious eyes as she opened her binder to a notepad. Running her elegant fingers over the pages, she addressed the room with cool confidence.

"First, I would like to thank Hemlock for hosting this event. I have hosted myself, we did not do so as elegantly as you all have."

Miranda preened with satisfaction next to me.

Talia went on smoothly. "Today, I would like to discuss the topic that seems to have been haunting us for some time now—rogues."

I expected there to be an outburst, but Lander had been right about letting Talia present this. The pack leads in the room all watched with reverence as they waited to see what she had to say next.

"We're here to discuss the facts as we know them, so tomorrow, on the day of the new moon, we can forge a solution. I've taken the liberty of compiling a brief on the topic, which includes additional information related to key points. I have copies for everyone, Commissioner, if it's permitted to pass them around?"

Tyrell waved her on. "Please."

Ajax stood and passed out packets of paper stapled together to the room. A few extras were passed back. Miranda was quick to snatch one.

Talia surveyed the room as whispers swarmed in the air. "Within the packets before you, you will find a review of the facts as we know them. We have had multiple instances of rogues being seen or scented in our region.

"In the case of sightings, they have unfortunately been mostly in areas with humans. You will find instances confirmed by Cache Pack and Thunderhead Pack, where rogues were found close to a human hiking trail and at a grocer along the highway.

"Cases of rogues being scented on pack land have also been reported and recorded in the brief by multiple packs, including Thunderhead, Hemlock, and Switchback. It should be noted that two abnormalities are found within these cases: The first is that all packs have reported that the scent was confined to an area—trapped. A witch has confirmed that a particular kind of stone is used to do this. Secondly, nearby most of these areas, in almost all the reports, it appears a Bloodstone was found."

Ragna hissed under her breath. "Impossible!"

Talia turned to face the blue witch with a polite smile. "I will ask you to save your comments until I conclude, if that works for you?" Her tone was low, in warning. Ragna closed her mouth and leaned back against her seat.

Talia turned back to the room of wolves held in astonished silence before looking at Tyrell. "For the record, note that all the packs mentioned in my brief and by name here, today, have all signed individually next to their reports—validating their testimony—and can do so here today if called upon."

I cut my eyes to the packet in Miranda's hands. She flipped a page and found a bullet with a brief description of my attack—back when I was bitten. Levi's signature was next to it.

Miranda's finger trailed to a few bullets below and froze on one—it had a brief description of the rogue attack on Ethan. The night he almost died. I lifted my gaze to his. I felt something shudder over the bond.

"It will be all right," he assured me, with a faint pulse in his eyes.

Tyrell leaned back in his seat. "State your request, Her First."

"That we, the thirty-three packs of the Alaskan region of wolves, open a formal investigation into the instances of rogues and lend any necessary resources needed to aid in doing so," Talia answered.

Murmurs and whispers picked up like a racing heartbeat. Tyrell stood from his seat and slammed the gavel on the table. "Quiet!" he barked, then slammed the gavel again.

The room quieted. Tyrell nodded to Talia. "Thank you, Her First. We'll move into discussion before we vote. Anyone with additional information to help guide us to the right conclusion is welcome to have the floor."

Darlene stood. "I would like to add some context, Commissioner."

"Granted," Tyrell answered.

"I know." Darlene snorted before straightening her spine. "When my guards found the rogues on the hiking trail, they were able to capture two of them and bring them in for questioning. They are not like what we are used to," she explained to the room, as her voice dropped an eerie octave. "They are of sound mind—one spoke coherently to me, mostly using profanities I will not repeat sober. Whatever they are, this is new territory for all of us that direly warrants looking into."

A man stood from a table. The nameplate in front of him read HOWLER PACK. He flipped the pages in his packet then looked at Talia. He ran a hand through his short black buzz cut. "This reads that a human was attacked—bitten. That the Hemlock second was attacked? Is this true? Sorry, Her First."

Talia offered him a soft smile. "It's all right, Johnny."

Miranda sucked in a breath next to me. Levi stood and rested his hands on the table. He dipped his chin Johnny's way. "It is, Her Second. Around two years ago they followed a human from a diner to the border of our land. Attacked her. She survived the attack and the turn.

"The diner was the one off Highway Three—open to humans and our kind. I can confirm what Darlene stated, they were not like the rogues we're used to; these were calculating and organized."

Whispers swirled the room. Levi leaned forward on the table as something crackled through him, and the murmurs promptly died as eyes turned to him. "In the case of the scent, Talia is right. The scent is domed in. We've found black stones—gravel—around the areas that the witches here confirmed are the cause. I should add"—Levi's silver eyes cut directly to Thomas—"the case we've had of rogue trails are solely on the Hemlock border."

Thomas didn't move. He didn't flinch even as all the eyes from the Hemlock Pack wolves turned to him. His gaze faded into what I assumed was an unspoken conversation. After a few tense seconds, Ethan stood.

"Her First." Ethan spoke to Talia. "If I may?"

Her green eyes pulsed a glow, as if she was about to lock in on her kill. "Of course, Her Second."

"I can attest to the accounts provided in your brief related to the Hemlock Pack," Ethan stated. "I'd like to provide color to a few things for the council."

I saw Evan lean over and pass Ethan a few papers from his

seat behind him, which he laid out in front of him, along with a small burlap bag.

"I can confirm what Levi has stated. We have found rogue scents on the border between Hemlock and Thunderhead. I can also confirm that we have also found multiple rogue patches on our land, Bloodstones, and I can verify that both myself and another Hemlock Pack member were attacked on our territory."

A man jumped from his seat, red in the face. "This reads that there are no bodies? How the hell does that happen?! Thomas, can you confirm this?"

"No bodies were recovered," Thomas stated carefully.

"But their blood stained our grass," Ethan noted evenly.

If Thomas could have struck Ethan with a lightning bolt of silver, the gaze he offered him said he would do it in a heartbeat.

A man next to Johnny stood up. He grunted a few words to Johnny, while he twisted one of the braids in his long beard around his stubby fingers, then turned to the room. "How is this possible? Did anyone else see this?"

"The guard with me did, Her First," Ethan answered. "Our Head of Security and the wolves who recovered me can also attest to the evident scent of rogues that they found in the area."

"Sounds like it's been a minute since you've seen a rogue," someone spat.

An electric pulse whipped off Ethan and snapped in the air. I felt it surge through the bond like steam screaming out of a kettle. His eyes darkened, turning more animal than human before a dry, dark laugh vibrated from his chest and reverberated through the still room.

"My family was slaughtered by rogues. I was the first one to find them. Why the hell would I make this up? I want to be done with this business—anyone who survived what happened here years ago wants to move on."

Miranda hissed under her breath, "This is ridiculous."

I felt my own blood sizzle until it lashed out. A hum drummed off me. Her eyes grew wide in shock. "My mate almost being murdered is not ridiculous."

Standing abruptly, she smoothed out her dress. "I'm going to the ladies' room."

"Grand," I drawled.

A pack lead across from Talia raised his hand. The nameplate in front of him read SNAGGLE TOOTH PACK. He crossed an arm over his chest. "So, the Hemlock Pack second gets attacked but we have no bodies. I'm also failing to see how this is connected to the Bloodstones?" A murmur of agreements sounded around the circle. "I'm not saying that we don't have a problem, but I'm failing to see how these things are related."

"Because, Her First, the rogues are showing up as if they're appearing out of nowhere," Ethan answered. "The explanation has to be a magical one, Carey. With all the fresh blood magic and Bloodstones, it would lead one to believe that dark magic is being used to usher the rogues in."

Someone scoffed before Stella stood with her hand raised like a student in their favorite class. "Moving multiple people from one place to another would take a great amount of power. It's not inconceivable that a Bloodstone could be used," she explained evenly.

Carey took Stella in before turning to Ethan, imploring, "But do we know these are real Bloodstones? My pa's mentioned them—they sound like a myth."

Jackson stood, tall and proud—completely unbothered by

the flashes of disgust on the faces around him. "Her First," he said to Carey. "I can help us with this."

Caden handed Jackson a small leather bag. In that bag was a swirling crimson Bloodstone that Jackson set on the table in front of him.

The murmurs from it hummed like gnats buzzing around my ears. I weaved my fingers together while my beast paced back and forth and tried to ignore it.

Something pulsed across the bond. I lifted my eyes to see Ethan's dual-colored ones watching me with worry.

"I'm fine," I said, an assurance that sounded weak and felt weaker as the murmurs continued to whisper from the stone.

"This was found on my pack land," Jackson told the room. "It's identical to what Hemlock found."

"Is this true?" a pack lead asked Thomas.

Thomas laced his fingers together on the table. "They're locked up. Witches have yet to confirm their true nature."

Jackson smiled, like a cat about to swallow a mouse whole. "It's good the witches are here." He turned to Stella with an award-winning smile. "And since we have our witches here, why not let them test one of the stones for all of us to see?"

Tyrell stood and waved the witches forward. "Might as well, since you're here."

Ragna and Stella stood together, then in sync rounded their table and strode to where Jackson stood. Ragna's blue jay bristled on her shoulders.

"This will be easy. We need to release the magic," Stella explained.

"Release the magic?" Lander echoed back slowly.

She nodded to him. "The stone is the container for the

magic—like a genie in a lamp. If it's a Bloodstone, then under the surface must be blood magic. We have to open the lamp, so to speak." Stella stepped aside. "Ragna? Do us the honors."

Ragna watched Stella for a heavy moment before turning on her heel. Her skirts flew behind her, the blue gem on her necklace lit up, and a beam of cobalt magic streamed from her finger toward the Bloodstone.

I clenched my eyes shut, but I knew when it shattered—when it broke open, not only could I smell it in the air, but I could hear the wailing screams ascend into the sky. In the link with Ethan, I let the agonizing cries pour through.

"Charlotte?" I heard him say.

"It's almost over. I'm okay," I gritted out.

Darlene was pale. She lifted her eyes to the fading sun then turned to Thomas. "I would suggest you let the witches review your stones, as small as they may be," she griped before she turned to Talia. "You said there's something covering the scent up?"

Ethan grabbed the bag in front of him and reached for a handful of porous black rocks then dumped them on the table. He picked up a handful then crushed them in his hand and let the sand fall.

Stella picked one up and tossed it onto the ground. With a snap of her fingers, a pink fire shot out and engulfed the rock, leaving only the smell of burning sugar. After, she wiped her hands. "It's a simple sandstone that's been used in a binding spell. It takes in the scent around it. Sand is a ripe conduit for any magic."

Darlene gritted her teeth. She marched to Ethan's table and looked at the sand in front of him. "Sorry, Levi," she grumbled as she snatched Levi's coffee, placing it in the middle of the sand.

THE PACK

A few moments passed before she turned with a snarl. "You can't smell it."

The room erupted with people rising and jogging over to the table to see for themselves.

Tyrell slammed the gavel on the table again. "Order! Enough! To your seats!"

Wolves shuffled back and sat down slowly, staring in horror at the small black-sand beach in front of Ethan.

Talia looked at Derek. "Have the vampires seen anything in your territories?"

Derek stood. "No, Her First. However, Leo is concerned. He and our coven are supportive of whatever direction you choose. He's willing to lend aid."

"Our business is not the business of vampires!" someone hissed from the circle of pack leads.

Derek smiled coldly and straightened his crisp black jacket. "If it threatens the secrecy and safety of both of worlds, then it is. And mind you, these rogues were seen in places with humans."

"Like your kind ever gave a shit!" someone spat.

Derek's fangs descended. "I would recommend that you remember that the freedoms you enjoy and that have enabled you to sit at your table are here because my coven and I worked with your forefathers to make it so."

"Freedom," Thomas scoffed. "I think our definitions are quite different," he sneered at Derek.

"Enough." Talia's calm voice easily cut through the noise. Elliot pulled Derek back down to sit. Talia turned to face Tyrell. "I would like to put this to a vote, Commissioner."

"We vote, then," Tyrell agreed, then stood. "All against the request to start an official investigation, raise your hand."

It was no surprise to me that Thomas raised his hand along with almost half the room. I bit my lip as I tried to count quickly before Tyrell ushered the hands down.

"All those in favor?"

Ethan raised his hand along with more hands than I expected. Darlene leaned back with a smug smile as her hand lifted into the air at the same time as Levi's and Lander's.

The commissioner counted then picked up his gavel. "The yeses have it. Tomorrow, we discuss an official inquiry." The gavel slammed on the table, ending the discussion. "To conclude, we'll hear updates from both the witches and our vampire representative."

I blew out a shaky breath and caught Ethan's gaze in mine. *"I'm proud of you."*

He rubbed his chin. *"I just put a giant fucking target on all our backs."*

"We already had one," I grimly reminded him.

The witches started to talk. I was about to excuse myself when Evangeline put a hand on my arm, discreetly grabbing my attention. Her eyes cut to Amber, who had found her seat in Miranda's old one. Amber folded her hands in her lap, her face impassive as she watched the circle in front of us with a distant look.

"You made it," Evangeline told her with teary eyes.

Amber clenched her eyes shut. They were damp when she opened them. Evangeline rubbed her palms on her thighs then focused ahead of her. I felt a link bloom between the three of us.

It was quiet for a moment; it reminded me of listening to static on an old television.

"You can trust her, Ambs," Evangeline urged.

THE PACK

A few more moments of silence passed before I heard, *"I want out."* Amber's voice was as clear as day in my mind. *"I want a new start. I want out of their house and out of this pack."*

I tried to keep my body from reacting. Licking my lips, I pushed the conversation to Ethan, praying I could somehow transmit it to him in real time.

"What happened?" I asked.

Amber looked like she wasn't breathing. Everything about her was impeccably in place, from her perfectly pleated coral dress to the smooth golden locks rolling in waves down her back.

"They are monsters. I have information. I don't want people to get hurt. I tried to do the right thing. I just want out."

"What do you mean by 'tried'?"

"Evangeline," she replied. Her lips almost cracked into the tiniest of smiles, but held steady in their thin line. *"They think she's daft. I did that. I kept her off their list. I couldn't with the boys."*

"Why would you do that?"

"Because her mother was the only real mother I ever knew," Amber admitted. *"And I miss them."*

"What do you want?" I asked.

"I want a new start," she told me. *"Cash to get out of here and start over. Evangeline said you would help me?"*

Without missing a beat, Ethan's voice sounded through the link I shared with only him. *"Do it."*

"All right," I promised her.

She let out a breath through her nose as Ragna continued answering questions. My beast prodded forward to listen.

"I remember hearing the screaming," she told me. *"My mother put me in the basement. I was so scared. I wanted her to stay with*

me. I wanted someone to stay with me down there in the dark. I knew they had been up to something, but I was a dumb teenage girl caught up in all the things that at the time seemed so much more important than what my parents were doing.

"I asked what was happening before Mom left. She said we would be okay. She said after it was over, that Dad would have made us all proud. Made history. When she came back without him, she was so upset. I asked where he was, although at the time, I had prayed that the rogues had taken him from us.

"Mom said it would be hard but it would be worth it. She told me Dad would be our new pack lead and over time everything would fall into place."

"What would fall into place?" I asked.

"I don't know," she answered, her voice breaking. "They don't tell me everything. Bits and pieces they think are inconsequential.

"I remember always thinking maybe Mom wasn't as bad as Dad. Maybe if he was gone, I'd be safe. But after she told me that, the smile on her face was so evil, so sick—I felt trapped. I've I felt that way for a long time. I don't want to be trapped anymore."

My breath caught. "Amber, what did they do to you?"

"I was just a pawn for them. He used to only take his anger out on Mom, then he took it out on me. I thought she would be on my side, but it's like she thinks if we're perfect enough it will make him happy and we'll be happy. I'm not a strong person, Charlotte. I don't know if I know how to be. I need to get away from them, because I know they know that."

Sucking in a breath, I asked, "What are they planning?"

"There's going to be a meeting at our house before the pre-Hunt party tonight. I don't know why, I don't think they trust me as much as they used to. I know there will be a blood oath involved and I know the end result is I will be engaged to one of the pack leads whether I want it or not. I overheard Dad saying to one of the pack leads that it would begin tonight."

My beast snarled in the back of my mind as the hair on my arms rose. "What will begin?"

"I don't exactly know, but I know the vampires are the target. He let it slip when he was drunk the other night," she said. "He wants them to die in there. Said it won't be hard to hunt them. I think he wants you all to die in there. Don't go in there tonight. Keep the vampires somewhere safe," she added.

I covered my mouth to hide my heavy, stressed panting.

"What do I do?" Amber asked in a small, frail voice.

I had to keep her safe. I had to keep Derek and Elliot safe. I had to get them all out of this pack.

"Why the vampires?"

"He hates them," she offered weakly.

"Please, Amber. There has to be a reason other than that. Please, try to think," I pleaded.

She chewed on her bottom lip and shook her head then finally said, "I overheard him talking to Mom about Leo. There was something about forcing his hand..."

It wasn't making sense. I rubbed my temples and tried to move the puzzle pieces around, but it felt like all I had were corner pieces. "What about the rogues?"

"All I know is it's in the forest—he wants you to run into it tonight."

"You said 'us,'" I clarified. She nodded. "What about the rest of the pack?"

"I don't know, but I think he's going to delay the run for them somehow." She nibbled her lip. "They're supposed to go after the pack leads—all week Mom has told me that I need to be dressed and ready for the party no later than seven. But just earlier, she 'reminded' me that the time was nine. She doesn't make mistakes like that."

"*She doesn't,*" I agreed. Miranda didn't make last-minute changes like that.

"*I can't stay here,*" she pleaded as Ragna sat down, concluding her statement to the council.

"*I know,*" I agreed as the gavel slammed on the table and Tyrell's booming voice announced, "Dismissed!" to the group.

CHAPTER TWENTY-EIGHT

Arguments, laughter, shouting, and petty whispers swirled around me like an oozing potion in a cauldron.

"*I'm coming to you,*" Ethan said.

The bond sizzled as he thundered toward me. Evan flanked him, checking over his shoulder. Evan put an arm around Amber's shoulders and walked her away from the group and around the corner of the concessions tent while Ethan, Evangeline, and I jogged after them.

"You have clearance to go to Thunderhead," Ethan told her.

Amber's breath hitched. "What—how? When?"

"Right fucking now," Evan told her.

I squeezed her hand. "Levi won't let anything happen to you."

Ethan peered back into the tent where Thomas was in a heated argument with Darlene and Levi. He turned to Amber.

"She's right. Levi has already alerted his trackers and guards. They are expecting you."

Amber looked panicky. "I've never run that—I don't—"

"I'll go with you," Evangeline stated. Her green eyes slid to meet mine. "I know a way. It's safe. Levi and Aunt Eve made it. No one will know." Evangeline stepped closer to her brother. "I'm getting her out of here."

Ethan held Evangeline's gaze a moment then relented with a nod. "Don't veer off the course."

Evangeline threw her arms around his neck. "Watch your hide, idiot."

I leveled my gaze with Amber's. "No turning back. Run hard."

Evangeline stepped away from Ethan and extended her palm to Amber.

Amber regarded the outstretched hand a moment, then grasped it firmly in her own. She took a step forward but paused and turned over her shoulder to me. "May the moon's favor be with you."

I swallowed back tears. "Go."

We watched them jog into the trees. Ethan took my hand.

I linked Ethan and Evan together. *"We need to get the vampires somewhere safe—now."*

"Derek is vampire royalty," Ethan snarled. *"The residual fallout would be catastrophic, even for packs that weren't involved."*

"How did Thomas convince some rogue wolves to do his dirty work?" Evan commented.

Ethan pulled me with him back into the main tent and though the crowd, where in the corner of the room Levi had stepped into a heated, silent argument with Elliot and Derek, while Lander looked as if he was going to tear his hair out. Elliot

THE PACK

snarled under his breath when Levi stepped closer to him. "Elliot, we have to play smart."

Elliot cut his eyes to us then clenched his mouth shut. I felt a new group link prickle in my mind; a few links shot through. *"I'll be damned if I hide from the wanks,"* he hissed into a link with only the group standing with him.

"Your ass is going to fucking hide," Levi snarled. *"I ought to send your hides back to Leo."*

Derek's fangs glimmered in the fading sunlight. "Wolves came to our aid when we needed it. We won't leave you—it's our fight too. We see this through."

Jackson curled around Lander with his hands up, almost pleading. "Look, as much as I want to side with you, we cannot risk you. Levi is right." He turned to Levi. "They can't go back to Thunderhead. That's the first place they'll expect them to go. The run is too far to Switchback this late in the day. The best bet is to hide them here," he explained before looking back at the vampires. "We need to lock in on what Thomas is planning, and we can't do that if we're chasing after you two all night."

"Jackson's right," Ethan pressed. "We are losing time."

"Lander and I will take care of Derek and Elliot," Levi said in our group link. *"Ethan, after your performance, your place is the least safe place in the world. Your parents had a cellar under your old house. It may be burned to the ground but the cellar should be okay. We stow the vampires there."*

Ethan shrugged off his jacket while Levi laid his on a table. Evan scanned the room then slipped out of his shoes. "Based on what Amber said, if the vampires are the target—"

"And us," Ethan said, tone short, before unbuttoning his sleeves.

"And us," Evan echoed. "I don't think he's going to go after the *pack. I think based on what Amber said, he's going to deter them somehow so he can do his fucked-up shit."*

"*So we let them,*" I thought out loud.

Levi's steely silver gaze sliced to me. "*What was that?*"

My beast stepped forward and shook her fur out. "*Amber said they're meeting at his house—taking oaths. Look, we know he's a part of something bigger. We let the meeting happen, then let him show his hand with whatever he directs the pack to do. We can have people in place to stop them if for any reason the direction given puts the pack in danger.*"

I turned to face Ethan, imploring. "*We don't have anything to tie to him other than Amber's word, and people like Thomas are going to find an easy excuse to discredit her—we can't raise the alarm. But we can follow him and we can keep this pack safe.*"

Something crackled over the bond. Something warm and so full of tenderness I could have cried.

Ethan's hand cupped my cheek. "*Go,*" I urged him. "*Follow Thomas. Help Keeley.*"

Jackson clapped Ethan on the shoulder. "*I'm with you. Let's nail the son of a bitch.*"

Levi cracked his neck. "*Char—*"

"Charlotte!" a voice cried, hoarse and ragged like a worn piece of leather.

A streak of chestnut blurred across my vision. Crying golden eyes ran toward me. I ran out from under the tent and across the soft grass. My arms reached to catch Andrea as she fell to the ground in a sob.

"I need to talk to you. I'm so sorry," she choked.

I lifted her and caught one of her wrists. They had red marks around them—they looked like rope burns. Panic erupted in me. "Andrea, who did this to you? What happened?"

"Please," she pleaded as tears streamed down her face. "Please don't hate me, I'm so sorry."

"Tell me what it is," I begged. "Andrea, please talk to me!"

She shook her head as she started to pant. It looked as if she should be sprinting, but instead she was sobbing on her knees in the grass. I bent down to help her up as she gulped heavy breaths of air like a fish suffocating on the ground.

"Andrea?!"

The hair on her arms rose as her eyes glowed. She closed her mouth and inhaled through her nose then shook her head back and forth like she was being attacked by bees.

"Andrea! Please, talk to me!"

Something vibrated over the grass to us. Andrea whimpered and stumbled up as I slowly turned to see Jackson staring at her. His eyes pulsed a heavy glow as molten heat flooded in them. A smile slowly pulled on his lips like he had just won the lottery as the wind swirled around us.

I knew that look. I had seen that look.

Andrea choked another sob. "Are you fucking kidding me? This can't be happening."

Jackson's grin deepened as his eyes pulsed a glow in delight. "Sweet thing, this is one hundred percent happening."

Andrea cringed away from him. "What the—no, I can't do this right now!" she shouted, as she pushed herself to her feet and took off running into the forest.

"Wait! Andrea!" I cried.

Jackson sprinted after her. Caden jerked away from the snack tent with wide eyes, muttering a quick "Fuck," before he bolted after Jackson.

Ethan started to run after them, but Levi curled around him and pushed him back. From the other end of the tent, Thomas was walking into the woods, hand in hand with Miranda while Piper trailed them. Tyrell and a few wolves from the north followed behind.

"You have a duty to your pack, go," Levi said lowly.

"*Shit*," Ethan hissed before he pressed his lips to mine. "*I'll find you*," he promised before he darted for the trees. Evan squeezed my shoulder and charged off in another direction.

A cool breeze curled around my ankles, skittering some papers on a table.

"Charlotte," something whispered.

I cocked my head and peered into the woods, where the whisper had come from.

"Charlotte," it murmured again.

"Charlotte!" Levi barked out loud. He turned me by the shoulders to face him. His silver eyes were level with mine and his beast close to jumping out of his skin.

"Sorry." I shook my head and tried to calm my beast, who was pawing at the back of my mind.

"*We need something to tie him to the Bloodstones—to the rogues, any of it, do you understand?*"

Another chilly breeze tickled my ankles. Hushed voices danced on its wings. I wondered if a Bloodstone was nearby.

"Did you hear me?" Levi snapped.

"I heard—" I paused as a light bulb went off. "I did." But I didn't hear him. I could hear the whispers—including the whispers from the stones. Which meant that if they were being hidden, I may be able to find them.

I had started to backpedal away when I heard, "Charlie."

Freezing, I turned back to face Levi. Derek and Elliot stood behind him. Levi watched me for a moment, like he was making sure to burn the image in his brain. "Watch your hide," he told me, before he yanked both vampires into the woods after him.

I pulled off my dress and let my beast come forward. Of all the places to search, I knew that now of all times, I had to risk it.

I snatched the small bag of black rocks still sitting on Ethan's table, then sprinted for the pack house. Inside there was a flurry of wolves moving about and prepping the food for tonight, making it easy for me to sneak upstairs unnoticed to Thomas's office. I paused at the door and tested the knob. Locked.

My beast snapped her teeth. "Fuck it."

Taking a few steps back, I hurtled forward and rammed myself into it, breaking the lock and opening the door.

Dropping the rocks on his desk, I blew out a breath and closed my eyes. My beast pressed forward so we could listen.

But after a few moments, we heard nothing. I snapped my eyes open and marched to his desk and pressed my ears against the top, praying I would hear something through the old, stained wood surface. After more silence, all inclination I had to be careful was thrown out the window. As day faded to dusk outside, I tore through his office and shoved my ears into every corner, desperate to hear anything.

I took in the destroyed room. A snarl vibrated off me. My fingers snaked through my hair. The last hours of daylight had faded and the moon was starting to pulse in the sky. The evening would come like a fast woman in this part of the world.

"Charlotte?"

My heart skipped a beat. I turned slowly to see Stella gaping at me from the doorway.

Her lips parted as she scanned the office. "Right." She stepped inside and closed the door behind her then stomped over to me. "Charlotte, what the hell are you doing?"

"Why are you here?" I pressed her.

"I was looking for you and one of the wolves downstairs said they saw you run up here." She paused and shifted her tote on her shoulder.

"I thought I could hear ... we need something to tie him to things. Have you found anything?"

She shook her head. "No," she confessed. "I've been prodding Ragna—Kevin picked up bits and pieces of conversation but nothing useful."

Something cold ran up my spine. "Charlotte," I heard whispered outside the window.

The wind began to howl.

I clenched my eyes shut as she continued to prattle on. I didn't know what to say. I didn't know how much to say—screaming for help is hard when all the words you want to say are crowding the space in your throat.

She pressed her dainty hand to my arm. My eyes snapped open.

"Charlotte?"

I felt my eyes tear. I knew I shouldn't tell her. I knew I should keep it a secret. But to play the game, you had to play your cards—and in this game, we had to win.

"I can hear voices—whispers in the forest, calling me by name. I can hear them from the Bloodstones too. It's why I came here. I thought I could hear one."

She blinked. "Say all that again?"

The word vomit came out of me before I could stop myself. I told her about what Amber had disclosed to me—about the vampires, the gathering at Thomas's, the pack. I told her about the forest whispers and the Bloodstone, and how I could hear it screaming when I touched it. Sweat was beading on the back of my neck when I finished.

"Has anything else done this or something like the Bloodstone when you touched it?"

I tossed my arms to my sides because at this point, what did I have to lose?

"The tree," I uttered. "When I touched the roots of the tree, it was like I was sucked into a dream. A really horrible dream. The things I saw . . . the last time, after I came out of it, I heard screaming so bad it almost burst my eardrums."

She blinked a few times then pulled her gloves off. "It's a statement to kill Leo's favored one. He himself would bring the whole coven here to declare war, but maybe that's the point?"

Ambers words echoed in my brain. "Forcing his hand," I murmured under my breath. "Drawing Leo here. But that's . . . I mean that's an absurd idea."

"Arrogance breeds absurd ideas," Stella coolly replied. "I mean, how else to reignite a rebellion than with a bang?"

My fingers combed through my hair. "Fuck—we have to prove it. I need to prove it. It's the only way to stop all this."

She bit her lip. "It's a mad idea." She tapped her shoe then nodded to Kevin in her bag. "You said you it was like a dream when you touched that tree?"

"That's right?"

"And they all died there?" she asked. "The old pack lead and his family?"

"Yes, Ethan and Levi's family died around that tree."

"Memories can be stored in blood. There was a lot of blood

spilled that day on that ground, which means the roots soaked it up. Accessing them isn't an exact science. But the dead, well, sometimes they have something to say. Which means—"

"The tree . . ." I breathed as realization poured over me.

"If the dead want to speak to you, perhaps you should listen?"

My breath caught. "It was bad last time. I don't know . . ."

"But you were forced," she pointed out. "You didn't go willingly. Intention matters with these kinds of things. You need to ask them to show you what they want you to see. And besides, if what they have to show you is key to putting the last nail in Thomas's coffin, it's going to be worth the pain."

My beast paced in the back of my mind, both of us at a loss on what to do. "What if I'm incapacitated like last time?"

She smirked. "I'm a witch, Charlotte. You're in good hands."

"Fuck it," I agreed. "Let's go."

She turned and kept pace with me to the woods. We had stepped onto the path when I felt something fizzle in my link with Ethan.

"The pack has been told the run is delayed by an hour. Thomas didn't announce it in our pack link—had his cronies pass the word around."

"What are you going to do?"

"Blowback be damned, we're going to keep them safe. I have Jake using our people to spread a message to the pack—they're to stay indoors." He paused.

Stella struggled to keep up with me. "What's wrong?"

"The pack has been told the run is delayed an hour."

She started to swing her arms faster to keep up with her legs. "Let him show his hand. Foolish, foolish little lamb."

I could feel the bond as easily as I could feel the air

rushing past my cheeks. I tapped it, then asked, *"Have you found anything?"*

"We're still here," he replied. *"No one has left."*

I sucked in a breath. *"I need to show you something. I know you're not going to be happy, and I know this is a dumb idea, but please trust me."*

He didn't say anything as I let the conversation with Stella flood through the bond. All I could hear was the sound of the leaves on the ground crunching under our feet.

"Charlotte—baby, no. You can't—"

"I'm going," I interjected. *"I'm going to get you what you need."*

"Charlotte—he wants us to walk into those woods tonight! How do you know you can trust her?!" His anger wasn't lost on me, and I didn't blame him for it. In his shoes, I would be raging mad, but I also knew that I would do anything to keep him safe.

"We're out of good ideas right now."

"I don't want to argue, I'm coming after you," he promised.

I didn't answer back because I knew now I had even less time for what could possibly be a fucking disastrous idea.

I turned to Stella. "I'm going to shift. You're going to get on my back and hold on. We don't have time to go on foot."

My bones made quick work of shifting into place and she made even faster work of crawling onto my back. We tore off into the forest as night blanketed the trees around us, and found our way to the Trapper's Forest like we were finding our way home. Quiet slowly settled in around us. I kept my mind on the task at hand as my paws pounded the ground, even after the cold fingers of an icy wind swept across my legs, carrying a whisper with them.

"Charlotte," it called.

My beast pushed hard, even after another "Charlotte" sounded next to us, like the voice was running alongside me.

Soon, our paws hit soft grass. My beast was careful to avoid the slick rocks this time as we approached the decline. The white tree stood proud in the middle of a clearing, bleeding down its bark as if it was weeping tears of crimson.

My beast stopped at the edge of the stones that surrounded the tree. We knelt and let Stella slide off our back, then I shifted to my skin.

Tree branches swayed in the wind that caressed my cheeks.

Stella sucked in a breath. "Has it done that before?"

The tree continued to weep red. "Yes."

"Charlotte," a whisper called.

Clenching my eyes shut, I released a shaky breath when another voice called, "Charlotte," from across the grass.

"Can you hear them now?" Stella stepped around to face me.

"Yes," I uttered.

She squeezed my arm while my beast paced back and forth and back and forth. She picked Kevin up from her tote and let him curl around her neck. Cracking her knuckles, she flexed her fingers.

"I am here and I will not let anything happen to you," she said. "Remember, go willingly. Ask them to show you what they want you to see. They were people once. Talk to them."

I opened and closed my fists a few times. "Ethan will be here soon. Tell him I'm sorry."

Her smile was soft. "Tell him yourself."

I lifted my foot and crossed the line the stones made around the tree, carrying myself inside the perimeter of the circle. The blood on the tree swirled as I neared it, as if it was ready to talk, and dammit these whispers had followed me long enough.

Maybe it was time I listened.

I felt my beast press against my skin, as if she was letting me know that she was with me.

"It's okay," I told her, even as my heart pounded in my chest. But I didn't stop. Not even when the blood swirled again. Not even when I heard the faint sound of screaming.

I stopped a few inches from the bloody trunk. Stella said to state my intention, but finding the right words felt impossible.

"I think you've been calling for me for a while," I told the tree. "I was scared. I'm still scared. I don't know what's going to happen—" I paused as a breeze swirled around me. The branches waved in a wind that did not extend to the trees outside of the circle.

I blew out a shaky breath. "I think you have something you want me to see. I have something I want to know—I want to help them. Levi and Ethan and the others—they're in danger." Pausing, I laughed wryly. "We all are, and I think, well, maybe you can help us?"

The blood spiraled like hurricane clouds in front of me—the bands almost like dainty fingers beckoning me forward.

"I'm ready to listen," I said again. "Show me."

Closing my eyes, I pressed my hand against the bark, and was yanked into a sea of darkness.

CHAPTER TWENTY-NINE

The mountains were on fire. Flames blazed over the forest, carrying echoes of wails and screams into the night. The full moon sat high in the sky, watching rogues pour out of the trees. There were wolves, warriors, fighting in the valley. Women were running with screaming children in their arms, while the men ran out to protect them. Blood streamed across the grass, creating pools that trickled off the ledge behind the pack house.

My vision blurred, and I was pulled.

A rush of darkness whooshed past me until my feet hit the firm ground.

The trees shook as Lucas and Eli ran between them. I sprang into a run to catch up with them. Lucas slowed his pace when he saw three people hurtling in their direction. Ethan was carrying

THE PACK

Evangeline while Evan ran next to him. Ethan was thinner than he was now, lanky, with longer hair that curled at the ends.

He set his sister down and jogged to Eli. "We need to go. They're in the valley."

Eli didn't say anything. He waited until Ethan turned to Evan then marched forward, his fist clenched so tight it looked like it would shatter.

Ethan didn't see the punch coming—and when it came, it knocked him straight out.

"Eli!" Evan cried. The teenage boy with copper hair and teary turquoise eyes gaped at his unconscious brother.

Eli fireman carried Ethan over his shoulder. "Come on, Evan, we need to go," he ordered, doing a poor job of hiding the shake in his voice.

Lucas bent and picked up Evangeline. The little girl was sobbing quietly. Lucas muttered to her, "Shhh, he'll be fine. He's just going to wake up with a bad headache."

She wiped her eyes as they walked through the forest. "Where are we going, Eli?"

"Somewhere safe, Lina," Eli promised her.

Darkness pulled me again. Nothingness zipped past me and then I tumbled onto the steps in front of the pack house with a groan. Standing, I jumped to the side to avoid Lucas and Eli racing up the steps.

They flung the pack house doors open in time to see a large man with red hair marching for them. The man had a build just like Ethan's, but Evangeline was right, she was her father's daughter.

"Uncle Chris, we can't link," Lucas quickly said. "I can't get my dad or anyone outside the pack."

Chris put his hands on each of their shoulders. "You two need to leave. Now."

"No," Eli snarled. "I'm not leaving you."

"We need to stall until my dad comes," Lucas insisted.

Chris's expression fell as he turned to Lucas. "I don't think we're going to have time to wait, son, you need to get cousins and go," he implored Lucas.

"Fuck that." Lucas jerked away from him. "My dad will be here. You know he will."

"Lucas . . ." Chris clenched his eyes shut and turned to Eli. "They may not have come in down by the east. Go get your siblings and take them to the footpath."

"Sir." A guard jogged over. "Sorry, sir, but they have come in through the east. Cash is ordering everyone there to fall back from the forest."

Chris's jaw clenched. Eli looked at the ground, then with determination faced his father. "Ethan and the others are safe. We hid them away. They won't be found. Lucas and I will find Mom and Aunt Eve."

"Son," Chris pleaded. "I can't have you here."

Eli grinned, but it didn't reach his eyes. "It's our pack, Dad. They don't get to take it from us without a fight."

Lucas cracked his neck. "I've been itching for a good one for days, anyway." He backpedaled with a dark smile. "We can help stall until my dad gets here. Come on, Eli, let's find our moms."

I was pulled again. Dark swirled past me like water, almost careful when it dropped me onto familiar soft grass.

Looking up, all I could see was the darkness of the forest in front of me. The ghoulish trees looked on like they were spectators about to watch the latest victim enter the arena.

My hands shook when I glanced to my side. I was on my

THE PACK

knees, at the end of a row of people. I picked out Chris and Eli. Lucas was near me. They all looked like they had been to battle—and lost badly. There were people pacing behind us, but they were blurry—their images foggy.

Cracking echoed around us through the forest.

Chris clenched his eyes shut. "More are coming."

Eli jerked forward and tried to escape. Like all the others, his hands were tied behind his back with rope laced with silver that sang clearly with a hiss as it ate at the skin of his wrists.

Someone sent a punch to Eli's face, breaking his jaw so it hung lopsided on his chin.

"Leave him alone!" Chris howled next to me.

He was missing an eye and three fingers. There was a deep cut across his chest and two silver bullets lodged in his thigh. His blood streaked the grass. Someone slapped him across the face and sneered, "Quiet."

Next to Eli was his mother, Katerina. I recognized her from the picture Evangeline had shown me. She was even more beautiful in person, with eyes like a mesmerizing pair of gemstones. She bit back a sob and dipped her head, revealing an empty space where her ear had been cut off.

Farther down the row, Eve and Lucas were next to each other. Lucas didn't look scared. He watched the darkness like he was hopeful someone would come. He sniffled and tried to clear his broken nose, while shifting his weight to take pressure off his ankle, which was bent in a sickening direction.

I could barely look at Eve.

Her breath was heavy as she tried to keep it even. They hadn't harmed her like they had the others. Horror rolled over me at the thought of what they had planned for her.

Her green eyes cut to mine. "Watch."

I blinked as Chris struggled to get away from the guard holding him. There were murmurs of voices behind us, close to the tree, but they were garbled, as if they were underwater and their figures covered in a haze.

Chris was able to bend forward. He looked over at a body lying in a pool of blood nearby. "Thomas!" he shouted.

Someone yanked Chris back as another guard started to cut the other ear off his mate. "See what happens when you misbehave?" a cold voice taunted as Katerina screamed into the darkness. The sound of her voice sucked the air out of my lungs as my heart continued to break.

I caught a flash of blond. Blond hair with icy eyes that darted through the trees. The group of people next to me perked up as Miranda dashed forward, as if she was going to help them. She slid down next to the prone body and helped it out of the bloody puddle. Thomas groaned as she stood him up. He stumbled backward then steadied himself with a breezy smile.

He still had all his dark hair and the skin on his face was smooth. There were no holes in his skin, no horrible scars to look at, just a dimpled smile and bright eyes.

"Thomas?" Chris called.

Thomas wiped his face and trudged over to the group. His lips lifted in a disparaging smile as he wound his arm back; silver sang through the air as his fist flew at Chris's face. The silver knuckles tore off a chunk of skin from his cheek.

Thomas yanked Chris up by his chin. "This was too easy," he sneered.

Standing, he planted a wet kiss on Miranda's lips. She walked over to Eve and leaned next to her. Eve kept her eyes forward, refusing to acknowledge the grinning woman.

"You're lucky we're letting you live to see this," Miranda snarled.

Eve spat next to her. "Fuck you!"

Miranda's hand was fast. It hit Eve square in the jaw, knocking her to the ground.

Darkness took me again.

I was on the other side of Eli when I woke. The group of people were now lying flat on the ground. I crawled to Eve, who darted her eyes to me. She nudged her chin over her shoulder. "Watch."

I turned; the images of the aggressors were still blurry. "Eve, I can't see—it's a cloud."

"You can't see if you're scared." Her voice cut through to me as my heart pounded faster.

I closed my eyes as my beast came forward. Together we worked to keep our racing nerves in check, to focus on the words the voices were making until I could hear them.

"It isn't working!" a woman cried.

I couldn't make out who they were; their figures were still murky. But I could hear them clearly, which was enough for now.

"Hayden, let go, this isn't working!"

"No!" a man roared. "We need more blood! It's me! You know it's me!" A cold growl cut through the forest. "Bring me one of them!"

Hands grabbed Eli and yanked him backward toward the tree. His body faded into a blur as his mother cried out for him. Chris struggled to get to his son, while Lucas rolled onto his back. A gun clicked as it was pointed at Eve. Lucas froze in place at the same time Eli howled into the night alongside his mother's screams.

There was a thud as Katerina continued to wail against the ground. A man dragged Eli's body back and tossed it next to her. His neck was gashed so deeply that his head was barely attached.

My hand flew to my mouth as I fell to my knees. My beast howled in the back of my mind as Eli's blood flowed to my toes. I jumped away; touching it seemed like a foul thing to do.

"Hayden! Enough!"

"No!" someone cried.

I focused myself back on the voices. I had to know what had happened. They hadn't died for me to lose track of why I was here.

There were more people shouting. The sounds of a skirmish. I could make out bodies slumping to the ground as more blood pooled around us.

"We need to abort," someone said—a voice I knew.

I heard the sound of grappling and snarling before there was a snap. The firm thud of a body falling to the ground.

"Billy, what have you done?" someone gasped.

"You need to go," Thomas said. "You are now our Head of the Stars. It should have always been you. You have to go—"

"But Hayden—" a woman's voice choked out.

"Today may have failed, that doesn't mean the mission has," Thomas urged. "But it will if you die. You have to go."

"He's right," the voice I knew to be Billy's stated. "Aid will be here soon. When it gets here, it will be too late. Go now."

A woman whimpered. "But this place . . ."

"We'll fix it," Thomas promised. "We'll cover it up. The witches here can help clean up."

"But we need to get them out—"

"No." Billy's voice cut in. "They are not getting out. This is too important."

"Go," Thomas said again. "The circle is ready."

The woman sobbed quietly before footsteps faded away. It was quiet, and then a crack sounded nearby, as if someone had lit a firework not far from the tree.

"You need to go back to Timber," Thomas said. "Your cover is solid."

"Let's finish here," Billy answered. "I can spare the time."

I blinked and was yanked into darkness. It curled around me like a storm, carrying the sounds of wailing with it. I fell through a pit of nothing until I landed on my knees in the wet grass.

I was facing Eve. She had a knife to her neck. I had seen this scene before.

"No," I stuttered, as tears rolled down my cheeks.

I scrambled to my feet to see that they had the group facing each other in a circle. My heart twisted in my chest as more tears streamed down my face.

"Charlotte."

I turned to see Lucas watching me with a plea in his eyes.

"Look."

I stumbled backward until I realized that the trees now had guards hanging from them like ornaments. Their fangs were missing, their fingernails were ripped off, and someone had stripped the skin off their backs.

My hands flew to my mouth as Billy pulled a man into a tree. He was oozing blood but still, with the little life he had left he was kicking and fighting the silver-laced rope around his neck to be free.

Billy tied the rope off then walked back to the group. He paused in front of Thomas.

Thomas released a long breath as he nodded at Billy. "I know what I have to do."

"No," Miranda pleaded.

"Yes," Thomas implored her. "This is the price we pay. We knew the risks and they will be well worth it. A new era is worth it."

"He's right," Billy agreed, before he jerked his chin to the group on their knees. "What about them?"

Thomas pulled out a knife. "We get rid of them," he said simply.

He tossed the knife to Miranda. She caught it by the handle then in two steps was behind Ethan's mother. Miranda grimaced bitterly at Chris before the knife pressed through Katerina's neck from the back.

Chris roared into the night as his mate's body fell forward.

Eve looked at the moon, her eyes pleading.

Thomas sneered at her. "She won't help you."

She shook her head at him as he knelt in front of her. "All of this and you're still such a pussy, Thomas."

He snatched her jaw. "I was going to save you for something special," he hissed with a dark look in his eyes. "Lucky for you, our plans changed."

Miranda drove the knife into Eve's thigh as Thomas forced her mouth open. Eve's cries rang through my head as he ripped out her fangs. She curled forward and spat blood on the ground as Thomas stalked to Miranda.

Smiling widely, he held the teeth up to Miranda's ears. "These will shine well on you, my love."

Miranda took the teeth from him with a pleased smile. She tossed the knife to Billy. He curled around and stopped in front of Lucas.

Lucas looked at him like this whole thing was a joke before he barked a laugh, then spat a bloody chunk a few feet in front of him.

Billy cocked his head. "I don't like being mocked, little Thorne."

"I'm not mocking you, Billy," Lucas croaked.

"Then what brings you joy at this grim hour?"

Lucas's eyes pulsed a glow. "Only thoughts of my father's revenge. We both know he'll savor that day."

Billy wasn't fazed. He yanked Lucas's head back by his hair then stabbed the knife through the side of his neck and yanked it out. Lucas fell forward, choking on his own blood.

Tears streamed down my cheeks and my heart felt like it was ripping in two. I couldn't move. I could barely stand at the sound of Eve crying out for Lucas.

Thomas grabbed Eve by the hair, and it was the same scene I had seen before. I dropped to my knees in front of her. She smiled to me as tears ran down her cheeks. "Watch," she told me again.

I shook my head at her as a sob ripped from me. "No, please, no," I pleaded. "Please, Eve."

Thomas slid a knife across Eve's delicate neck. The minute the silver broke her skin, her lips opened wide and screamed, "Levi!" into the night.

My eyes lifted to Chris, who looked at the circle around him in shock. I closed my eyes when a knife slid across his neck; hot blood hit my skin.

I was pulled again.

The darkness was almost gentle as it whirled me around, as if it knew how fraught I'd been made by what I had seen. When I woke, I was lying next to Lucas in a pool of blood.

He was shaking as he dipped in and out of consciousness. Blood oozed from the hole in his neck. Billy had done a vile thing by stabbing him instead of ending him quickly.

"Lucas..."

"Watch," he choked with a sad, fangless smile.

I pushed myself up and turned to where Lucas was looking. Thomas yanked out Chris's fangs. He tossed them into a small black bag then handed it to Billy.

"Keep these for us. We'll share them."

Billy put the bag into a leather satchel he had slung across his body. He pulled Thomas into a tight hug. "Are you ready?"

Thomas nodded at him. "Go, Miranda," he said over his shoulder.

"No," she pleaded.

"It will be okay, Miranda," Billy assured her. "Go home to Amber."

"Go," Thomas ordered, the softness from his voice gone as something icy took over.

She stumbled back a few steps then ran into the woods.

Billy carefully took a set of silver-plated brass knuckles out of his leather bag. He rubbed the back of his neck. "I'm sorry, Thomas."

Thomas grasped his shoulder. "We can't always win. It's the moon's will. You can handle the witches?"

"The one is useful and allied with us. She and I can handle this. I'll get rid of the rest before I go," Billy answered with a dark promise. He stepped away from Thomas and slipped the silver knuckles onto his hands. "Are you ready?"

Thomas jerked his chin to Billy. "I am."

"As you wish, Her First," Billy told him. Then he pulled back and punched him across the face, again, and again, ripping off the skin of his lips and cheek with the silver knuckles.

I stumbled backward as Thomas fell over. I tugged my hair as my chest tightened while my beast wailed in the back of my mind.

"Charlotte."

Eve watched me from her place in the blood-soaked grass, an expression of deep sadness on her too-pale face.

"Do you see? Do you see now, Charlie girl?"

CHAPTER THIRTY

Cold air splashed my face as I stumbled backward. A pair of arms caught me and eased my fall to the ground. I curled to my side and hurled the contents of my stomach onto the grass.

"I got you," Stella murmured. "Kevin! The water!"

She pulled my hair out of my face as another wave of nausea rolled over me. Vomit spilled from my mouth.

She wiped my mouth with a pink handkerchief then moved me to sit upright. She held the water to my mouth. "Drink, it will help."

"Stella," I croaked as tears streamed down my cheeks. "It's her earrings. Their jewelry. Their *teeth*."

The bottle pressed to my lips. "Drink first, you can't pass out on me."

I seized the bottle and gulped it down. She wiped the residual vomit off my cheek.

"That was fast," she said. "Wherever you went, it was only around maybe ten or twenty minutes?"

Cracks sounded through the forest around us. The pit of my stomach dropped as my eyes tipped to the sky. The moon was peeking above the trees. They would start the run soon. Pack leads would be ushered into the forest.

"We have to get back. Ethan, I need Ethan—"

"Come on." She stood with her bag and helped me to my feet then tossed my arm over her shoulder. Kevin slithered over the ground in front of us.

"I think it's happening," I told her as we stumbled across the grass.

"What? What do you mean?"

Before I could reply, I smelled it. The sickly scent of rogues.

A hiss froze us in place. Kevin was half raised, hissing at a man with hazy red eyes emerging from the brush. He stumbled in front of us, his legs disjointed like he was being controlled like a marionette.

"This way." Stella yanked me in another direction, but we were faced with two more rogues.

With a confident step in front of me, she spread her hands as the smell of burning sugar oozed off her. Whatever haze had been hovering over me was gone and my veins pulsed to life. Something crackled in me as my blood hummed under my skin. I pressed my back against Stella's and searched for a way out.

Billy stepped out from around a tree.

My eyes fuzzed over, seeing him.

"Billy." My voice unintentionally cracked. I could barely force out the question. "What have you done?"

Regret oozed from his eyes. "You have been so good to my Andrea. I don't want to do this, Charlotte. There's still time. I can spare you. Let me save you."

I could barely look at him because each time I did, I saw what he had done to Lucas over and over in my mind.

"I don't understand. Please, I don't understand." The hurt he could hear seemed to soften his stance. He thought he was swaying me. Stella was right—arrogance bred absurd ideas, blew hot air into an overinflated balloon of ego. "This can't all be about vampires."

He held his hands up in a plea. "Andrea's mother never left me," he admitted. He rubbed his jaw with a shake of his head. "Vampires murdered her. Raped her. She and a friend had gone into the city. From what I was told, she walked for blocks and blocks after the attack, desperate for help, until a human family found her. She died in their apartment."

"I'm so sorry." And I was, for Andrea.

"I wanted revenge, as anyone would. The coven didn't even execute the vampires responsible. I couldn't bear to tell Andrea what really happened." He shook his head. "I didn't want her to have the same hate in her heart that I did."

Stella cast a wary glance at me.

Billy continued, "Thomas brought me in early. Our world needs an adjustment, Charlotte. It's off balance. There's no justice anymore if you know the right people and can pay the price."

The three rogues circling us were licking their teeth. I felt Stella grab my hand and squeeze gently while my beast readied herself for our shift.

"But you love this pack," I stated, because I thought he did love the pack. "People that we both care about are going to get hurt."

"I know," he agreed. "But sometimes it's better to be on the side of the devil than in his path, Charlotte." He leveled his gaze at me. "I am not an altruistic man. I care about my daughter, and I want a world for her that is safe. This side is not perfect, but no side is. At least I'm choosing a path where our kind are truly protected." He stepped closer to me. "They will spare Andrea through all this. I can spare you too. I don't want to see you hurt in all this, kiddo. It's not even really your fight to partake in."

I shook my head slowly and released Stella's hand. "It is my fight, Billy. The minute those rogues bit me, it very much became my world." My beast shook her fur out and showed her teeth. "If I say no, will you stab me like you did Lucas? Will you let me slowly drown in my own blood?"

Billy's eyes went wide. "How could you—"

"Will you?" I asked. "Will you rip out my fangs then take the skin from my back?"

"Charlotte, don't make me do this," he pleaded.

"How could you do this? Ethan and Evan . . . they looked up to you! You played being their confidant this whole time! You helped Ethan! Helped us!" My throat clenched. "I trusted you."

The tattooed letters spelling *peacemaker* across his knuckles danced as he cracked each one. His bracelet with the pearl stone caught the moonlight; it emitted a strange whisper.

"Undercover work is no walk in the park," he answered tiredly.

"There was so little evidence left. How did you do it?" I breathed, as if I was impressed.

"It pays to have good blood magic in your pocket," he answered. "And decent witches. The portals helped too—I'm sure you put together what those are. You have a good nose, kiddo."

"The circumpuncts."

"I'm proud of you for getting as close as you did," he told me, like he was congratulating me on getting straight As in school.

"And the star map?"

"I thought we lost it," he admitted, genuine. "I destroyed a lot, but as you know, I hoard. I was as surprised as you when you found it." He held up his hands and took another step closer, the plea in his eyes so authentic it made me want to puke again. "Charlotte, please, don't do this."

My breath hitched as my heart twisted in my chest. I didn't know the man in front of me—the man who helped fix our house up—who always saw to repairs when he visited, who helped us can endless amounts of fish, and always gave us second helpings of dinner.

Everything we had been through, lived through with him, had been a fat, traitorous lie.

"Why don't you tell them?!" Andrea's voice boomed from between the trees.

A rogue fell to the ground, clutching his slit throat. Andrea stepped over his body and strode to my side.

But Andrea didn't look at me. She tossed a knife in her hand and pointed it at Billy. "Tell her how my own father! My own blood! Murdered so many in our pack! You told me that something was wrong and you started driving, but you already knew something was fucking wrong, didn't you?!"

"Andrea." Billy gaped, struck with fear at the sight of his daughter.

"No!" she shouted. "Tell Charlotte how you had me tied up and drugged in our fucking house for the last two days because I caught you dropping Bloodstones in the forest! You never had to find the Bloodstone that night Ethan was attacked—because you knew where it was this whole fucking time!"

My jaw dropped. Billy was the one setting up the circumpuncts.

Andrea's hands shook as tears rolled down her cheeks. "I was onto you, and I didn't want to believe it. I denied it for so long because you're my dad and you always protected this pack—fuck, you took Jake in. Told him his parents died bravely, you fucking murderer!" She snarled and stepped in front of us. "I always believed you back then—I always defended you!"

Kevin sat up from his coils as and flicked his tongue into the air. Venom burned on the ground as he hissed at a rogue who was creeping closer. There was motion in the trees as three more rogues lumbered into the clearing.

"You do want a war, don't you?" I breathed, realizing that Stella's idea was in fact right.

"Andrea, baby girl, you need to leave. Please go," Billy begged his daughter.

"Why are you like this?" she whispered in a hoarse voice that sounded close to shattering.

"Andrea..." I said.

She turned over her shoulder to me. *"I love you and I'm sorry I was a bitch."*

I clenched my fist and let the scene pour from my mind over the bond with Ethan. The bond twisted and jerked as if someone had poured acid over it.

I found Andrea's golden eyes and held my hand out palm up

to her. Tears rolled down her cheeks as she slapped her hand in mine.

"*Together?*"

She nodded. "*Together.*"

She turned and threw her knife. It found purchase in the skull of a rogue in front of her. Stella jumped in with her hands extended, whipping them around and tossing a glowing pink ball of magic into a rogue charging for her, sending them flying back into the forest.

Rolling around Andrea, I ducked out the way of a woman with a wild grin full of spit slashing a silver-bladed knife at me. My veins cracked to life, fire flowing through me as I spun. I seized her wrist and snapped it, then took the knife, which I quickly stabbed through the side of her skull.

Turning, I tossed the knife to Andrea, who threw it at another rogue. It landed dead in his heart and sent him to his knees.

Billy's face reddened. "Andrea!"

She pulled the knife out of the rogue's chest and flung it in his direction. "Fuck you!" The knife bounced harmlessly off a tree next to Billy.

I grabbed her hand. "*We cannot let anyone into this forest—the run's close to starting!*"

"*Jake knows!*" she answered.

Stella whirled her hands in a circle and created a pink whip that whistled in the air as it sliced the man who was charging at her in half.

Andrea grabbed Stella's free hand and jerked her forward. "Come on!"

Billy clicked his tongue. "I taught you better than to run," he told Andrea as his eyes pulsed a glow.

THE PACK

Stella swept up Kevin and ran with us for the woods, but we were met with a flood of incoming rogues that pushed us back toward the white oathing tree.

Stella jerked me away from the roots. "We can't risk you going in there again right now."

Billy's laughter echoed around us like a wind that caused the tree to sway. Andrea turned to look at it. "Does it always do that?"

The tree was still crying tears of blood, as if the scene before it was the cause. I swallowed and scanned around. Several more rogues with hungry red eyes and claws already covered in blood were edging toward us.

"We punch our way out," I said to Andrea. She nodded. "Stay close to me," I told Stella.

Andrea charged the wall of rogues. I was braced to lunge after her when a wild cry stopped me.

A woman raced at me from my right; in her hands was a long dagger that was already covered crimson, which matched the blood dripping from her teeth that had all been filed to points, to match her fangs.

The bond burst with a flood of icy rage. I felt my veins hum in return with a crackle like hot oil meeting water in a frying pan.

The woman was lifting the dagger to strike when a clawed hand shot through her throat. It seized her spine and ripped it out before she could even utter a sound.

Ethan tossed her vertebrae aside and caught her knife with his free hand. He stepped over her body, moving like a raging rapid as he sank the knife into an approaching rogue's throat.

He shoved the man away, then seized the strap of my shifter tank and yanked me to his chest, and pressed his lips to mine for the briefest of moments.

Wordlessly, I rolled around his side as something pulsed off him. He snapped a man's wrist and took his knife then tossed it to me. I caught it and shoved the knife into the man's gut, then tossed it back to Ethan.

Jackson pounded past us. He yanked a rogue away from Andrea and ripped its nose clean off its face, then shoved Andrea behind him.

"Been looking for you, sweet thing!"

Jackson started to storm toward Billy, who gave Andrea one last sorrowful look before bolting for the trees.

"Shit! No, we need him! His bracelet!" I shouted. "It's their jewelry! The evidence is their jewelry!"

Jackson sprinted ahead, immediately chasing after Billy. Andrea turned to me. "I'll bring him in," she promised, as she raced after her father.

Ethan grabbed my hand and started to pull me away. "We need to get out of here!"

"Wait! Ethan! I saw it!" He stopped in his tracks and gaped at me. I went on, "The tree, it showed me everything. I saw it. It's their jewelry. That's the evidence you need—it ties them to all of it."

"What do you mean you saw it?"

Stella scrambled over. "We have a window right now—we need to get out of here."

"No, listen to me!" I barked.

I grabbed his face and paused, because of the pain it would cause him to see everything—all of it. Instead, I flooded over the bond the scenes where their fangs were ripped out. Where Thomas held them up to Miranda's ears. I only showed him the parts that he needed to know for what had to be done, and saved the rest for when he asked for it.

When I was done, he yanked away from me with a guttural howl. Heavy breaths wheezed out of his mouth while he clutched his knees. Claws started to poke out from his fingernails.

"Ethan!" I grabbed his face and forced him to look at me. "Don't you see? It's their fangs. It's their fucking jewelry—they all have it. Her, Thomas, and Billy—" I paused and whipped around to face Stella. "There has to be something you can do? Like some magical fucking DNA test?"

"Get it in front of me and I can trace it," she confirmed.

"Ethan," I desperately implored him. "We can prove it. Now. We can do this right now."

"I'm going to fucking kill him," he snarled quietly, so only I could hear. His chest lifted as something vibrated off him. "Jake ordered the pack to stay in, but they're gathering around the tent demanding answers—they're growing frantic."

My blood pulsed again. "Stella, get on my back."

I shifted to my fur and knelt for Stella to climb on. Ethan ran a hand through the fur on my neck. "I'll go ahead of you."

He lunged into his shift. My beast pounced, running forward into the night. We followed him as the song of silver and the scent of rogues mixed with blood magic blossomed in the night air.

Stella fired pink orbs from her hands at a group of rogues charging at us in their fur, sending them flying backward into the dirt. Ethan took a more direct approach: he went straight for their necks, tearing them apart before they could even make it within a foot of me.

We hurtled toward the large tent in front of the pack house, where guests dressed in evening attire, long gowns and fancy suits, were gathered alongside panicked Hemlock Pack members.

They were all shouting and hurling questions at Thomas, who was in the center of the crowd.

The growl that rolled off Ethan rippled through the grass to the heels of the people standing at the edge of the tent. We both shifted and went forward in our skin. I grabbed Stella's hand and pulled her along with me as Ethan pushed through the crowd.

"You're out of line!" I heard Thomas boom over the crowd.

"There's fucking rogues in there!" Jake barked back as gasps sounded around us. "No one is going in there!"

"Do you smell any fucking rogues?!" Thomas roared back.

"I wonder why the hell that is?" Levi's cold voice cut through the room. "How many black rocks have you seeded throughout this pack?"

"Levi." Thomas laughed. "Your mind still isn't right."

A snarl ripped off Levi and cracked in the air like a whip as Ethan broke through the crowd. "There are rogues in the forest."

Thomas clenched his jaw shut while Miranda stared at me with wide eyes. Stella dipped her head in a firm nod to me. I let go of her hand and cut across to Ethan. Together, we stalked the edge of the circle.

"Well, go on, tell them. A plan like yours deserves some recognition," Ethan said, his voice dangerously controlled as he slid a bloody hand through his thick locks. "Tell our pack and all these guests how you brought in rogues to hunt the vampires to start a fucking war before they hunted us too!"

"Go on," I chimed. "You worked so very hard to make this happen. For years. Your perseverance is admirable, Her First," I spat.

Thomas's jaw clenched. "Levi, your pup is out of order."

THE PACK

Levi's silver eyes pulsed a glow. "I think you're the one out of line, Tommy."

Hushed voices bubbled up around the room. Ragna started to move away from the group but Talia put a hand on her shoulder. "It would be rude to leave a party so early," Talia told the witch.

Ethan glowered as he continued to stalk around the edge of the crowd. "Why don't you tell them how you used the circumpuncts to get the rogues in here, just like you used them to get all your friends out of here."

Ethan paused straight across from Thomas as more whispers filled the tent. "You'll notice that some of the packs from today are not here—and they won't be here, will they?" he sneered at Thomas. "They walked into your home, made a blood oath with you—you fucking Pure Seven loyalists—and then you shoved them through a circumpunct in your own backyard next to the petunias. Your own trackers and I saw it with our own eyes."

Gasps and snarls sounded around the room. Darlene shoved to the front and turned to Thomas with cold, glowing eyes.

Ethan continued to pace. "You let yourself be tortured—made yourself a fucking victim. Lied to this pack for years. Tried to kill me, over and over again, for years!"

A shriek tore through the room as people covered their mouths in shock.

Ethan stopped to stand with Evan.

I stopped in front of Levi and Lander as my beast shook out her fur. Facing Thomas and Miranda, I made sure to speak loudly and clearly. "Tell them what you did all those years ago. Tell them about the trophies you took from their pack lead and his family. About what you did with their teeth . . . with their fangs. The three of you wear them—you wear them daily in plain sight."

Jake whipped his head to look at me with wide eyes.

Thomas clenched his fists; his bracelet with pearly stones, just like Billy's, caught in the candlelight.

Outbursts and new muttering shot around the room as Andrea and Jackson dragged Billy forward through the gathered crowd. Andrea had her clawed fingers sunk into his shoulders like a fishhook while Jackson yanked him forward by the hair on his scalp. Sam and Trey pushed through the crowd behind them.

Together, they tossed him to the center of the room, where he stumbled on a leg that looked completely mangled, ready to give out.

"Andrea," he begged. "I'm your father."

She wiped his blood off her hand and onto Jackson's long shifter shorts. "No, you're not."

"Talk," Jackson demanded, with a violent growl that shook the tiles on the ground.

"Tell them!" Andrea barked as tears streamed down her cheeks. "All these years! Tell them how you lied!"

"Andrea, baby girl, please," Billy pleaded.

Stella strutted to Billy with sure steps. She snatched his wrist and looked at the bracelet with the pearly stone in the middle, then let his arm drop. Stepping away from him, she set Kevin on the ground.

The snake slithered around Billy with a sickening hiss. His long body coiled sideways, so he could wind around the former "peacemaker."

"Let me make this simple," she announced. "Rogues are in the forest because these three let them in, just like they did before—using circumpuncts to create a portal that is powered by the Bloodstones. Sounds correct, right, Ragna?"

Andrea stopped Jake from taking a step toward Billy. Stella looked Ragna up and down like she was debating how long it would take Kevin to swallow her. "But you knew that, didn't you, Ragna? Because you were one of the witches here on the scene back then." The heels of Stella's shoes echoed like raindrops through the tent as she strode over to the blue-haired witch. "I would advise honesty from here on out."

Ragna tried to backtrack out of the crowd, but Talia's hand on her shoulder cemented her in place. Talia's claws pierced the fabric of Ragna's blue dress, drawing a pained hiss from Ragna's blue-painted lips.

"You helped them cover it up, didn't you?" Stella quizzed with a sneer. "And you helped them make trophies. I should have spotted them earlier, but you are gifted with binding magical objects. It was probably very easy to craft Bloodstones for them too."

"You vile little twat!" Ragna spat.

Talia's fangs descended as she sniffed the delicate line of Ragna's throat. "Answer her," she ordered in a sonorous growl.

"Yes," Ragna whispered back. "Stella speaks no lies. Please, I don't want die."

"Tell them what the jewelry really is," Stella ordered.

Ragna's blue lips quivered. "It's an Anima."

"Well, don't be shy!" Stella urged with a cold laugh.

"It's blood magic that binds the soul to a stone. A soul stone."

I took a step closer to Levi, who was rigid in his boots. Lander had a hand on Levi's shoulder, his eyes wide in horror as realization sank in.

The traitors didn't just have their victims' fangs: they had pieces of their souls, which they carried with them—pieces that were kept here and not allowed to travel to the afterlife.

Miranda turned and tried to exit, but Darlene blocked her way with a snarl.

Thomas yanked Miranda back to him as Stella paused in the center of the room. Stella watched them a moment then propped her chin up in her fist. "Oh, you silly, traitorous little lambs. How far you have strayed from your flock."

"Do it," Ethan urged Stella.

Magic crackled in Stella's palm, the ring on her finger glowed fuchsia, and then an arc of pink light rushed forward and hit the bracelet on Thomas's arm. A cloud of red blood magic spewed from the shattered stone in the shape of a man—a man I had seen not long ago.

Chris reached his red, vaporous fingers toward the moon as he howled in agony. His cries only stopped when the mist dissipated.

Evan's eyes were wet and his mouth hung open in pure horror. His hands flew behind his head as he inhaled rapidly, but he didn't look away from the scene.

Ethan clenched his clawed hand. "Again."

Another bolt of light flew from Stella's hands. It hit the earrings on Miranda's ears. As they shattered, Eli and Katerina both came screaming out in the form of a crimson mist. My hand seized my chest; I staggered backward as sharp pain pulsed across the bond.

A tear jerked down Evan's cheek. Jackson pulled Andrea to his chest while she watched with teary eyes.

Levi shifted me to stand with Lander as he took a step closer to Stella. Lander quickly moved around me, inching closer to his brother, who stood with eerie, cool composure.

There was no mistaking the full, deep pain that laced Levi's voice when he told Stella, "Do it."

She shot pink lightning out of her hand. It sailed right for Billy's wrist, landing perfectly on the pearly stone. Red mist hurled out of it as it shattered—Lucas cried out into the night like the winds of a hurricane wailing before they broke land.

Levi's hand clenched his chest. My eyes locked on the necklace around Miranda's neck. The same one she'd had me try on at her home.

My hands flew to my mouth to stop the sob from coming out. Levi rubbed his hand over his heart as if he was trying to ease an achy muscle. He jerked his chin to Stella. "Again," he growled.

Her fingers quivered before they found their flow again. Pink lightning nailed the stone on Miranda's neck. Eve came screaming out as a whirlwind of red mist from the shattered stone. Her cries echoed around us as her mist brushed past Levi; his fingers lifted from his chest and let the red vapor fall onto them.

Thomas cut his furious gaze to Ethan. "I'm not afraid to die."

Miranda fell to her knees.

Ethan lifted a gaze that held a promise darker than the deepest midnight. "Good. Let's skip the formalities. I, Ethan Everette of the Hemlock Pack, do so hold you three guilty of murder, conspiracy, and treason, for which you all should be removed from your posts and punished accordingly."

Sam stepped forward, separating herself from the observing crowd. Her lips trembled. "Hemlock!" she called. "We need seven to support this motion before it moves to a vote." Sam stood tall but she could not help the sob that choked her at the end.

Jake sucked in a sharp breath. He made a noise like he was gagging as he stepped forward, blinking back the moisture in his eyes. "I second."

Evan was speaking almost before Jake finished. "Third."

Keeley stepped forward, with a few trackers behind her in solidarity. "Fourth."

Trey stepped into the circle. "Fifth."

Sam held up her hand. "Sixth."

The last person was Jericho. He pushed to the front and hissed under his breath, "Seven."

Soon members of the pack were pushing through the group to chime their consent.

Sam sucked in a shaky breath. "Hemlock Pack! All who vote guilty, raise your hand!"

Hands flew up. I didn't see a single person who belonged to Hemlock keep their hand down.

Sam wiped her eyes. "According to our pack laws, your crimes are punishable by death. We default to our pack second to decide how to proceed."

Ethan's steps were quiet as he padded forward. "You will all die. But how you die is up to you. How many rogues are in the forest?"

The three were silent. Miranda spat in Ethan's face. He wiped it off with a dark laugh. She started sobbing. Thomas held still next to her. He kept his eyes forward and shoulders stiff.

Billy looked at them, then at Ethan. "I know I'll die. I deserve to die." The room snickered and sneered at his words. Billy held his hands up. "I have requests."

Ethan lifted a brow. Andrea tried to go forward but Jackson pulled her back to his side and whispered into her ear.

Jake paced forward with heavy steps; he kicked Billy's knees out from under him with a snarl that vibrated the wooden tiles that had made up the center dance floor. "You have some fucking audacity."

"My daughter doesn't see me die." Billy spoke directly to Ethan. "Save her from that."

Jake's clawed hand reached for Billy's chin and yanked it forward until their faces were inches apart. "How. Many. Rogues."

"Around forty," he answered. He jerked his chin away from Jake.

"Where?" Ethan demanded.

"Circumpuncts stationed around the tree. There're three left. A mile from each other."

"We cleared that area." Keeley shoved to the front with furious, glowing eyes.

Billy offered her a grim smile. "Which is why you weren't paying attention to it."

Jake's jaw ticked. "Any more?"

"Not yet," Billy answered. "There's a map in the barn, behind the large one of the pack land. You'll find what you need there."

Jack snarled under his breath. Wordlessly, he nodded to a few trackers at the edge of the circle, who took off into the night.

"Ethan." Billy's voice was heavy with a warning in it. "You don't understand. You may have won today, but you're outnumbered in the long run. They will win. They have been prepping for years."

"Have you no self-respect?" Thomas roared at Billy. Jake's fist whistled through the air and nailed Thomas in the jaw.

Billy released a sharp breath. "You won't survive what's coming."

"Says the man on his knees," Ethan seethed.

Billy sighed, shoulders deflating. "The road from where I used to stand to where I am now, I have learned, is a short one."

I felt my toes curl. There was a truth to what he spoke, along with a foreboding that crawled under my skin.

Ethan leaned forward. "Your daughter will be advised to not watch you die, that's something no one should have to see, but her choices are her own." He stood slowly. Vibrations that shook the tiles all the way to my toes reverberated off Ethan's chest. "There's not a slow enough way to kill you but, dammit, we'll try our best. You tried to burn this pack down, so into the fire you will all go."

Dark snarls and cackles of delight filled the room. Ethan turned over his shoulder to Lander. "Bring any available guards that you can."

"We have no threats on our pack. Let us handle the rogues," Lander replied. Darlene rolled up her sleeves while the other pack leads in the room chimed in with their support.

Sam cracked her neck. "It's our pack. They don't get to take it again."

Hemlock Pack members stripped down to their shifters; one woman with a small child handed her baby to an elderly man then tied her hair up.

Ethan leveled his gaze with Keeley's. "Take the trackers and find the additional circumpuncts. I want the forest combed over again tonight."

Keeley bounced on her toes. "Done."

"Bring some in for questioning," he told Lander.

Lander was already wheeling out of the tent. He shouted to the assembled troop, "David's five minutes away—Bowie is three. With me!" He tore off for the forest, leading a horde of wolves behind him.

THE PACK

Evan marched forward with a vicious growl; claws descended from his fingers and his fangs protruded from his gums. He was reaching for Miranda when Levi grabbed his arm then carefully shoved him backward. "No."

Evan wheezed, like he had been punched in the gut. His eyes grew misty. Ethan took a step toward him and Levi shook his head. "Not this way."

"It hurts," Evan tearfully panted. "It should hurt."

Levi cupped his cheek and pushed his hair back. "Do you remember the stories we told you and your brothers when you were kids? About what happened to wolves who wronged others once they walked to the other side of the moon?"

I could hear the exhale of Ethan's breath while the onlookers under the tent waited in the terrible tension for Levi to continue.

Evan said nothing. Tears rolled down his cheeks. Levi wiped them away then turned to the foul beings still on their knees. "I remember when my son first asked me, 'Daddy, what happens to us when we die?' I told him if he was good, he would walk to the other side of the moon and find his mother and me waiting for him. When he got older, I explained to him that wolves who commit foul acts have to walk to the dark side of the moon."

Levi prowled forward as a cold hum poured off him, vibrating in warning like the tail of a rattlesnake. "It wasn't until he was much older that he asked me about the dark side of the moon—about what happens to traitors, to murderers, to rapists, and those who commit the worst of the crimes," he hissed. "It gives me some relief to know that when my son died, he had the peace of knowing what was in store for you all."

He knelt and rested his arms on his leg. "They say that for murderers, you are given the chance to try to escape the dark side of the moon—walk to the light where the just souls rest. But what awaits you on that dark side is a cold, doomed labyrinth with hungry creatures so horrifying that the poets of old didn't even give them a name.

"For murderers, it's written that if the creatures catch you, you have to suffer the murder that you committed while your victims have the pleasure of watching. And after you take your final breath, you will wake up to find yourself in the dark again—running from true monsters again, only to suffer that agonizing doom over and over and over. A perpetual race with only torture as the promised destination."

He breathed a laugh that turned into a calm, cold smile. "My only regret is that I will not be there with my mate and son to watch with them. But then again, death is promised to all of us. I am sure they'll have a seat ready when it's my time."

Levi stood tall then turned back to Ethan and Evan. "Let's end this."

Ethan held Levi's gaze for a moment then jerked a nod at him. "Build some fucking pyres," he called to the room.

Andrea's sobs wound into the sky. Jackson yanked her away from the tent, where her cries joined the orchestra of howls filling the night.

Stella turned to face Ragna. "We should have a chat!"

Ragna tried to run but Kevin slid around to block her. He lifted himself to stand with a sharp hiss that flung acidic venom her way. Her blue jay, however, took off after one hiss from the snake.

Magic crackled in Stella's hands. With a snap of her fingers, a pink cord wrapped around Ragna's wrists.

Stella looked over her shoulder at me. "I'll keep her locked up until you're ready to talk with her."

All I could do was nod. I stumbled backward into a pair of arms. Talia pulled me to her side. We watched with heavy eyes while people quickly threw together piles of firewood.

The moon was still full when they tied Thomas, Miranda, and Billy each to a stake. A hand fell on my shoulder as the sight before me began to blur. I wiped my eyes on my sleeve then turned to see Elliot and Derek standing next to me. Elliot took my hand.

Evan dumped gasoline on the base of the logs.

Derek ripped away from us. "I don't think I can watch this," he stammered. "I'll be at the house." He zipped away.

I squeezed Elliot's hand. "You?"

Elliot's green eyes were glassy. "I knew Lucas since before he was a wain. They were tortured for hours. Died in a vile way, so they did. Watching this is nothin' compared to what they went through. If anything, I wish I could watch it again and again and again."

Lander, back from clearing the forest of rogues, lit three torches and handed one each to Evan, Ethan, and Levi. Evan looked at his, then handed it to Keeley. She took Jake's hand and walked with him to stand next to Ethan and Levi. Evan moved next to his brother.

Together, they faced the row of the pyres.

Keeley threw her torch into one then quickly turned into Jake's arms and sobbed as the flames licked Billy's toes. Ethan watched Miranda for a long time as she sobbed and pleaded, then finally tossed his torch on the pyre. Levi stood in front of Thomas's pyre, watching him writhe against his ties for a heavy moment before dropping the torch onto the kindling below.

Levi stopped in front of Evan and Ethan. He pulled Ethan

into his arms. The two of them held each other like the ground was about to collapse below them. Levi lifted an arm and pulled Evan to him as well.

My eyes lifted to the flames. Yellow and orange licked up the stakes and tried to touch the sky as howls of agony filled it.

Bowie broke through the tree line. She jogged over and paused in front of Elliot and me. "The rogues are eliminated." I didn't know what to say. My mouth opened and closed a few times before I snapped it shut. She cupped my cheek. "Right and wrong—none of it feels good."

"What's it supposed to feel like?" I asked.

Her purple eyes danced back to the fire as the flames reflected in them. "This."

CHAPTER THIRTY-ONE

There was ash still floating in the air in the early hours of dawn as we walked the path between the ghoulish trees. Ethan's hand was firm in mine. He hadn't said anything to me since the pyres.

Ash skirted alongside the path we walked. The forest seemed to ingest the stench of burnt flesh, rogues, and blood magic—but, at least for now, we were safe.

The tree came into view. My steps faltered when I saw it.

Ethan darted his eyes to me. *"Can you hear it?"* he asked.

And as sure as the day was new, I could hear a whisper rushing across the ground to me. Instead of answering him, I let the scene flow through the bond. His hand released mine and slipped around my waist.

"I thought—" I bit my lip before leaning my head against his

chest. *"I thought after they showed me . . . I thought it would stop."*

I was so wrong. Because the closer we got to the tree, the more I heard them. The calls of "Charlotte" across the soft grass were as clear as day.

Ethan bristled next to me. He pressed his lips to my crown. *"We'll figure it out,"* he promised.

I found myself asking, *"Are you okay?"*

He looked down as we padded across the grass together. *"I don't know,"* he answered honestly.

Immediately after Thomas, Miranda, and Billy finished burning at the stake, the pack gathered. The pack link had been destroyed—the pack lead was gone. The need for new leadership was immediate.

Jake was the first to say that the pack lead should be Ethan.

The rest of the pack quickly agreed. The wolves who'd once supported Thomas did not vote for Ethan, but they did not object. I think they were all still reeling from the truth; the shock of these past events wasn't something that would wear off soon, for any of us.

Part of me wondered if we should have just run to the beach, disappeared to an island somewhere and started over.

But Ethan agreed to become pack lead.

Not a minute after he did, we were being ushered back to the tree.

We stopped at the edge of the rocks that outlined the tree. The pack and guests lined the circle, all watching with glowing eyes. The moon above still glimmered in the last hours of the night.

Levi walked to Ethan with a knife in his hand. "Are you ready?"

THE PACK

Ethan nodded. Levi put a hand on Ethan's shoulder. "Let's get to it, then."

He followed Levi across the soft grass to the trunk of the tree. The branches swayed in the wind like they were singing praises of hallelujah to the moon fading in the coming daylight. I felt a breeze whip around me as whispers combed through the leaves.

"Ethan Everette, do you swear to the moon to protect this pack to the best of your abilities? To serve as a pack lead for the Moon until you are called home to her?" Levi asked.

"I do," Ethan answered.

Levi handed him the knife. Ethan took it and slid it across his palm. Blood quickly pooled—the scent of it barreled toward me and smacked me in the chest.

Ethan watched his palm for a second then pressed it to the tree. I sucked in a breath.

"Say it," Levi told him.

"I, Ethan Everette, swear to the moon to protect this pack to the best of my abilities, and will serve as a pack lead for the Moon until I am called home to her," he stated, but there was another voice on top of his that spoke directly into my ear.

I turned over my shoulder to see Lucas watching me. His silver eyes danced in delight as they studied my face. My mouth dropped as he smiled.

"What are you doing?" I whispered to him.

"Watching you," he answered, as if it was a joke.

"Lucas..."

I blinked and he was gone. Evan snatched my hand and squeezed, drawing my attention to his confused turquoise eyes. *What was that?*

Ethan had pulled his palm away from the tree. He looked at it then turned his gaze to me. People around us clapped. There were whistles and hollers of delight.

But I couldn't move.

My eyes latched onto his bloody palm, and all that overcame me was dread.

Ethan shook me awake as the day waned into the early afternoon. The pack leads remaining had agreed to a late start for the second half of the council meeting.

I clutched a cup of coffee and took a seat next to Keeley and Jake. Evan sat next to Ethan—Ethan had been quick to make his brother his second, while also appointing Keeley and Jake to Head Tracker and Head of Security respectively.

Lander and Levi took their seats next to Jackson. I checked the seat behind him, but Andrea was missing.

Jackson caught my eye. "She's safe," he said.

"Where is she?"

"*She stayed with Talia last night. I think she preferred not to be here today.*"

Fuck, I couldn't imagine what she was going through.

Darlene took up the commissioner seat. She banged the gavel on the table, silencing the crowd.

"All right, well, welcome to day two of the shit show." She took a long sip of coffee from a mug that looked stolen from the pack house. "Normally the commissioner doesn't get a vote, but considering the circumstances, I am voting. Any arguments?"

Hums of agreement sounded around us.

Darlene nodded, pleased. She rolled up the sleeves of her blue plaid long-sleeve cotton shirt. "I think we skip all this other bullshit that should have been an email and discuss what the hell happened yesterday. Any objections?" She looked around the room. "Fantastic, because you were about to be overruled."

Keeley turned to look at me. *"She's wild."*

"I think she's great." I found myself laughing.

Darlene flipped through a few pages then tapped her pen on them. "Well, if any of us were wondering if we have a rogue problem, I think we can all agree now that we do. I have the list of questions we all compiled this morning—questions we need answers to. Before we get to them, I think it's important we level out with key information. A lot of shit has happened and I want to make sure we're not missing anything."

She set her mug down then spread some pages out on the table. "Here's what we know: Rogues came in last night by the hand of the former pack lead of the Hemlock Pack and his Head of Security. They conspired with witches, one of whom we have in custody. The circumpuncts, more or less, made a portal to transport the rogues and were powered by the Bloodstones. We also have reason to believe that Thomas and his associates were involved with rebels from the Pure Seven, who aided Thomas and his crew in conspiring and executing the prior attack on this pack. Am I missing anything?"

Heads shook and mutters of "No" filled the air.

Darlene collapsed in her seat. "Let's start with this star map." She turned to face Ethan. Her hard demeanor faded as a smile of admiration glowed on her face. "Her First, you recovered one here? You were telling us about them this morning?"

Ethan stood and flipped open his binder. Evan pointed to a

page that Ethan quickly pulled out. "Her First," he answered. "We were able to recover the map and confirm its true nature."

"True nature?" Darlene cut in.

"Her—"

She waved her hand frantically in front of her. "You know what? Screw it, these formalities are exhausting and I'm tired— we're all tired."

A fatigue-filled smile tugged on Ethan's tired face. "Stella explained this to my mate. The map is like any map, but when under starlight, a new map is drawn over it. Think of it like invisible ink," he explained with sure words. "We discovered them because Jackson found a few old maps in his father's things—he sent pictures and my mate recognized them. His maps, with hers, made an old battle map of the last attack."

He held up a page with a photo example of the maps. "This is a photo of it from my phone—you'll note the rebel brand in the corner." He handed the page to Evan, who passed it to Levi, who was seated next to him.

Ethan picked up another page. "This is the map we recovered last night. The trackers found it hidden in the barn, where Billy said it would be. We've already confirmed the glowing circles here"—he tapped his finger on one dot—"are where they brought in the rogues last night. You'll also notice the rebel brand in the corner."

Evan took the page from Ethan and passed it to Levi as Talia hissed under her breath at the sight of it. She passed the pages to Ajax, who only shook his head in disgust. "You said that the three maps of the packs made up the old battle map?" Talia asked.

"That's right," Ethan agreed.

Talia shook her head. "So we're missing at least two maps,

THE PACK

and who knows how many others. We don't really know what their scheme is."

"Actually, I think we do," Lander interjected. "Well, we have an idea. You see, Thomas's daughter made a deal with Charlotte and Ethan last night for protection in exchange for information. Thunderhead offered that protection. My mate has spoken with her—she confirmed that the targets were the vampires. Specifically Derek.

"Billy also confirmed as much to Charlotte," Lander added. "It seems they wanted to force Leo to retaliate. Force him to come here so they could take him out—make a statement."

Darlene turned her head to look right at me. "When was this?"

Slowly standing, I answered. "I took Stella to look into one of the clearings," I lied, and prayed the story Ethan had come up with for us would work. "Billy cornered us—he more or less bragged about what they were doing. I think he had assumed that he was on the winning side."

Jake stiffened in his seat. His eyes were red this morning; I had seen him sobbing on the pack house steps not long after the pyres were lit.

Levi rubbed his jaw. He had not come back to the house after the pyres. Lander hadn't either. But this morning I'd found Levi sitting on the ledge of the hill in the backyard with a cup of coffee in hand. I'd sat quietly with him while we watched the rest of the night fade.

"Last time the rebels gained momentum, they tried to gain territory. Establish a home base that they could expand from. This feels like that again," Levi noted.

"Do you think we should contact the stateside packs?" Talia asked.

"It may not hurt to start feeling them out to see if they have news," Levi replied.

"Stella, what did you find out from Ragna?" Darlene asked.

Stella sighed tiredly. "She wants a deal. She cast a spell that actually sewed her own lips shut—only she can break it."

"Sweet suffering moon," Darlene spat in disgust. "What does she want?"

"Probably not to die like the others," Stella answered before taking a giant bite out of a glazed doughnut. "Our cloister head, Caleb, would like to discuss it with you. He'd like permission to enter pack lands."

"Which pack land?" Lander asked.

"Hemlock."

All eyes turned to Ethan. "Granted," he told Stella.

Stella sat down. "I'll see what I can get out of her while we wait."

"What about her familiar?" Talia asked.

"He won't be far away," Stella answered. "They stay close. Kevin is on the lookout for him."

Evan raised his hand. Darlene nodded to him.

"In theory, the circumpuncts should not be activated unless there's an anchor. As of now, we don't know of any more Bloodstones. But before yesterday, we didn't think Billy was a fucking traitor." He shifted his weight to the side. "We need to keep a lockdown on the borders—we have no idea who else was involved or if there are more stones within pack territory."

Darlene nodded slowly to him. "What do you suggest?"

"We are stronger working together. I recommend that neighbors coordinate and pool resources." He paused and turned to face Levi. "We don't have as many trackers as you, and

THE PACK

Bowie is a machine. We have a heavy force of guards, though, and Switchback has a respectable number of guards and trackers for their size," he added with a nod to Jackson. "If we all pool our resources, we have more to leverage to keep our people safe."

Levi crossed his arms over his chest then jerked his chin at Jackson. "What say you?"

"I don't mind my neighbors," Jackson answered tiredly.

"My brother is right. We need to think of the whole rather than ourselves—we'll have gains over our enemies that way," Ethan agreed.

Darlene hummed in agreement. "We should do something similar on our side of the mountain. We can't be too careful."

Jackson raised his hand. Darlene pointed to him. "Go on."

"Sorry, can we go back to the circumpuncts? They're traveling from one place to another, which means they're all together in some location to begin with, right?"

Darlene furrowed her brows. "Well, where the hell do you think they are?"

"No," he scoffed. "What I mean is somewhere out there, someone is holding a horde of rogues. They have to have them together. It would be insanity and too much work to have them spread out in little groups stowed away."

Talia's eyes went wide as Darlene's lips parted.

Lander leaned forward in his seat. "They saw them camping by ice caves, right, Casey?"

"We did," the Howler Pack lead confirmed. When he stood, all the little beads braided into his long, graying beard clinked together. "Not a big group, though."

"Do you think they could be in the caves?" Darlene asked.

Casey wiggled his bald head back and forth before turning

to his second, Johnny. Casey's second nodded with a grunt then lifted his amber eyes to Darlene. "Could be, but right now with the melt they're too unstable. We need it to cool down—need the ice to firm up a bit." Before he sat, he asked, "What about the other pack leads? The ones who swore a blood oath to Thomas? I got one as my damn neighbor."

Darlene groaned. "Yeah, we do too—fucking Vic. I always knew that son of a bitch was up to something."

"We don't know if they went back to their packs," Lander pointed out. "Technically, we don't know where they went."

"I can't trace it back without the runes, either, unfortunately," Stella added.

"I can't imagine they'd leave their packs unguarded," Darlene thought out loud.

"We can't just go in there searching for them either," Casey added. "They would see it as an invasion. We'd be more or less declaring war."

"Isn't that what happened already?" Talia offered. "Although, for now, I agree with you Casey, we can't invade their packs. It would take too many resources and we have no idea if they're even there."

Darlene sat back in her seat. "Levi, we're going to have to call the vampires."

"Derek already phoned Leo," he answered. "I don't know what he'll want to do."

Jackson tapped his pen on the table. "Caden's mate has a team of people tearing through my bastard father's old shit."

"We're going to start combing through Thomas's and Billy's," Ethan added, with a long sigh.

"We need to find where they are storing the rogues," Talia

urged. "Before they decide to attack another pack. We cannot let them establish a home base—gain territory."

"And we need to figure out the long game," Levi stated. "All we know is they wanted the war to start here, but then what?"

Darlene ran a hand through her hair. "We've got our work cut out for us. Let's break for now. We'll divide and conquer after lunch—I need a goddamn cocktail."

She slammed the gavel and released everyone.

Ethan turned and headed straight for me. He held out his hand and we walked together back to his house, where I snatched a bottle of whiskey and carried it to our balcony.

I sat and let the sunlight kiss my bare toes peeking through the railing. The whiskey burned as it slid down my throat, a welcome feeling that settled my nerves.

The glass door slid open. Ethan stepped out with a tired smile on his face. He sank down next to me with a groan. I handed him the bottle. He took a long swig then set it between us.

"We should have run to the beach while we had the chance," I said.

He breathed a laugh. "I can put sand in the backyard. You can wear that cute bikini and pretend you're there."

I felt a smile tug at my lips, but silence was all that filled the space between us.

He pushed some hair behind my ears.

"What is it?" I asked.

Pausing, he pushed me back a hair so his dual-colored eyes could study mine. "What else did you see when you touched the tree?"

My eyes teared. I blinked the mist away. "All of it. That day. I saw it all."

He was quiet. I could see the battle occurring behind his eyes—I could feel his conflicted emotions over the bond between us.

Taking his hands in mine, I said, "I didn't tell you because we had to do what we did, so I gave you only what you needed. But if you want to know, I'll show you. It's yours to know."

He pressed his lips to my palm. He rested a hand on my knee. "What would you think if I told you I didn't want to know, right now, at least?"

"I think it's going to be horrible to watch and if I had the choice, I would do it when I was ready."

He hummed in agreement before saying, "It's not your burden, you shouldn't have to carry it."

"No, but I can carry it for us until you're ready," I promised. "But I did see something else—when you touched the tree. When you made your oath."

He studied my face as I tapped the bond and let the memory of Lucas standing next to me float in. Ethan's eyes went wide and his hands stilled.

"It feels like there is something wrong with me, Ethan."

His hands wrapped around my waist and pulled me closer to him. His eyes pulsed a glow like stars in the night sky.

"That can't be true, because you're the most perfect fucking thing I've ever seen." He leaned his forehead against mine. "We'll figure it out. Together."

"Together," I agreed and turned to rest my head on his shoulder.

He was quiet for a while and steadily stroked my hair. Eventually, I turned to face him and crossed my legs. My beast was pacing back and forth in anticipation of what I knew that we had to do.

Ethan cocked his head. "What is it?"

I held out my hand. "I would never have sworn into this pack under him, but I will to you."

His hand reached to cup my cheek as something hummed off him. The space closed between us, and his lips covered mine as our fingers intertwined. "You're sure?"

"Positive."

He pulled away. "Repeat after me. I, Charlotte..."

My blood crackled in my veins. A hum rolled across the bond when I began to speak. "I, Charlotte..."

"Swear my loyalty and fealty to the Hemlock Pack, just as it swears its loyalty and fealty to me."

My beast nudged forward. A smile pulled at my mouth when I repeated, "I swear my loyalty and fealty to the Hemlock Pack, just as it swears its loyalty and fealty to me."

His smile was like watching a sunrise; warmth curled around me across the bond, while another voice burst through my mind. A link sizzled to life as a chorus of voices chimed in with celebratory shouts and greetings.

He cupped my face with steady hands. "Welcome to the pack."

ACKNOWLEDGMENTS

This book was hard to write. As Levi would say, "It was a pain in the ass." The first two books came easy. *The Bite* was something that flowed onto the page and *The Hunt* was a story that wrote itself—my job, really, was trying to keep up with Charlotte. But *The Pack*... Oh, *The Pack*...

It's amazing how fast you can stop dead in your tracks when you're posed with the question: What is love? When I wrote this book, I found myself deep in my head about so many things and stressed to get this right—to ensure Charlotte and Ethan's story was just right. So many nights I remember pacing my apartment and wondering if I was going absolutely mad, but eventually, the story did start to come together, and when that very real labor of love did, I can say I have never been more proud of anything than what was put together.

I am so grateful for my editor, Margot, who, from day one, has seen my vision and somehow found calm in my chaos. With her magic, she has been able to help me push the series and elevate it in ways I would never have imagined.

A huge thank-you to the people who, more or less, bore this labor of love with me and listened to me rant and ramble, and kept me sane during this journey. To Steph and her abundance of kindness and gentle temperament that continually softens my heart. To Bex and Christi for never letting me doubt myself and always ordering good wine. Alex, thank you for listening to me fall into black holes—and more importantly for pulling me out of them. To Ali and Kelly for always being cheerleaders and supporting me since day one. Lastly to Holly and Morgan for being there for all the ups and downs—hopefully more moments to celebrate in the near future.

Thank you to my family, who have been incredibly supportive throughout this entire journey. Also Mom and Dad—sorry for all the sex, try to skip over those parts.

A huge shoutout to W, who have been the best champions of this series. A big thank-you to Deanna, Fiona, Delaney, Rebecca, and the rest of the team—I am so incredibly grateful for each of you and your collaboration and belief in me to continue Charlotte's journey.

To all my readers—thank you! Honestly, the last few years with this series have been such a wild ride. I am so humbled and so thankful for your support and kindness. I would absolutely not continue doing this without the support of all of you—thank you all for sticking with me and believing in me. I can't wait to continue Charlotte's journey with you all and take you along with me into other projects that I hope we can all be incredibly proud of.

Andrea told Charlotte that love is a choice. That eventually, you have to learn how to start saying *yes*, and saying it every day regardless of good days, horrible days, or days where it feels like the world is against you.

Jer, saying yes to you has been the easiest thing I've ever done and saying *yes*, every day, is something I feel blessed to do. This book was very hard to write until I met you. Then it was easy.

ABOUT THE AUTHOR

Z.W. Taylor is a writer and Watty Award–winning author who cannot believe the stories that once lived only in her head, on sticky notes, or in random Word documents have become something she now gets to do professionally. Taylor is the author of the Moon Blood Saga. She lives in North Texas with her thirteen-pound cat, who does not need a diet contrary to what others may say, and works in digital marketing. When she's not writing, she can be found hanging out with her friends, trying to tackle her TBR list, being active outdoors, or doing the thing she cherishes most: spending time with her incredible family.

THE MOON BLOOD SAGA
BOOK ONE

SOME THINGS YOU CAN'T OUTRUN

THE BITE

Z.W. TAYLOR

THE MOON BLOOD SAGA
BOOK TWO